D1575810

PRAISE FOR THE HEARTWARMING NOVELS OF
LINDA LAEL MILLER

MY LADY WAYWARD

COURTING SUSANNAH

"Enjoyable. . . . Linda Lael Miller provides her audience with a wonderful look at an Americana romance."
—Harriet Klausner, *Midwest Book Review*

TWO BROTHERS

"A fun read, full of Ms. Miller's simmering sensuality and humor, plus two fabulous brothers who will steal your heart."
—*Romantic Times*

"Excellent, believable stories. . . . Miller has created two sensational heroes and their equally fascinating heroines."
—*Rendezvous*

"Great western romance. . . . *The Lawman* is a five-star tale. . . . *The Gunslinger* is an entertaining, fun-to-read story. . . . Both novels are excellent."

—*Affaire de Coeur*

ONE WISH

"[A] story rich in tenderness, romance, and love. . . . An excellent book from an author destined to lead the romance genre into the next century."

—*Rendezvous*

"An author who genuinely cares about her characters, Miller also expresses the exuberance of Western life in her fresh, human, and empathetic prose and lively plot."

—*Booklist*

"Another triumph. . . . *One Wish* shows why Linda Lael Miller has remained one of the giantesses of the industry for the past decade."

—Harriet Klausner, Barnesandnoble.com

PRAISE FOR THE NOVELS IN
LINDA LAEL MILLER'S MARVELOUS SERIES

THE WOMEN OF PRIMROSE CREEK

"[A] warm saga. . . . Anybody who enjoys reading about the pioneers who tamed the West will enjoy *Bridget*. . . . *Christy* is an enjoyable, lighthearted romp. . . . *Skye* is a delightful battle of the sexes. . . . *Megan* is a warm tale of redemption . . . the most sensitive and compassionate of the quartet."

—Harriet Klausner, Barnesandnoble.com

THE ACCLAIMED BESTSELLING SERIES

SPRINGWATER SEASONS

"A delightful and delicious miniseries. . . . *Rachel* will charm you, enchant you, delight you, and quite simply hook you. . . . *Miranda* is a sensual marriage-of-convenience tale guaranteed to warm your heart all the way down to your toes. . . . The warmth that spreads through *Jessica* is captivating. . . . The gentle beauty of the tales and the delightful, warmhearted characters bring a slice of Americana straight onto readers' 'keeper' shelves. Linda Lael Miller's miniseries is a gift to treasure."

—*Romantic Times*

"All the books in this collection have the Linda Lael Miller touch. . . ."

—*Affaire de Coeur*

SPRINGWATER WEDDING

"Fans will be thrilled to join the action, suspense, and romance portrayed in [Linda Lael Miller's contemporary fiction]."

—*Romantic Times*

"Miller is a master craftswoman at creating unusual story lines [and] charming characters. . . . Pure delight from the beginning to the satisfying ending."

—*Rendezvous*

"*Springwater Wedding* is the perfect recipe for love. . . . Miller writes with a warm and loving heart."

—*BookPage*

Books by Linda Lael Miller

Banner O'Brien
Corbin's Fancy
Memory's Embrace
My Darling Melissa
Angelfire
Desire and Destiny
Fletcher's Woman
Lauralee
Moonfire
Wanton Angel
Willow
Princess Annie
The Legacy
Taming Charlotte
Yankee Wife
Daniel's Bride
Lily and the Major
Emma and the Outlaw
Caroline and the Raider
Pirates

Knights
My Outlaw
The Vow
Two Brothers
Springwater
Springwater Seasons series:
   Rachel
   Savannah
   Miranda
   Jessica
A Springwater Christmas
One Wish
The Women of Primrose
Creek series:
   Bridget
   Christy
   Skye
   Megan
Courting Susannah
Springwater Wedding

Writing as Lael St. James
My Lady Wayward

LAEL ST.JAMES

MY LADY WAYWARD

SONNET BOOKS
New York London Toronto Sydney Tokyo Singapore

This book is a work of fiction. Names, characters, places and
incidents are products of the author's imagination or are used
fictitiously. Any resemblance to actual events or locales or persons, living or dead, is entirely coincidental.

An *Original* Publication of POCKET BOOKS

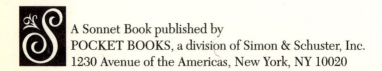 A Sonnet Book published by
POCKET BOOKS, a division of Simon & Schuster, Inc.
1230 Avenue of the Americas, New York, NY 10020

Copyright © 2001 by Linda Lael Miller

All rights reserved, including the right to reproduce
this book or portions thereof in any form whatsoever.
For information address Pocket Books, 1230 Avenue
of the Americas, New York, NY 10020

ISBN: 0-7394-2159-X

SONNET BOOKS and colophon are trademarks of
Simon & Schuster, Inc.

Cover art by Alan Ayers

Printed in the U.S.A.

For Terrie Lessor,
my assistant and housekeeper—
thank you.

My Lady Wayward

Prologue

❧

The boy opened his eyes, blinked, disbelieving. His flesh burned with fever, while his bones were chilled, brittle as ice on a puddle. He squinted. Yes, that was Sedgewick lying there, sprawled on his belly by the brook. The back of his head was matted with dried blood, and he was pale as tallow, and unmoving. It was the figure crouched beside the fallen man that made Blodwyn doubt the verity of his own senses, however, for it was as if Sedgewick had somehow risen out of himself, like a shade, so marked was the likeness of one man to the other.

Blodwyn shivered inside the bundle of blankets and hides he'd wrapped around himself, at the behest of the wily Dame Johanna, now nowhere to be seen, and slight as the motion was, it was enough to break the strange spell that had held him so utterly still. The second man rose from his haunches and turned to gaze in his direction. The specter was beautiful, like an archangel, and yet something in his regard made Blodwyn's simple soul quail within him. The man came toward him, one graceful hand resting on the hilt of the knife tucked into his belt.

Instinctively, Blodwyn pressed himself backward against the trunk of the tree that had sheltered him through at least one night, and mayhap several, but there was no escape. He was too weak to rise, barely able to speak. "Wh-who—?"

The man smiled, and Blodwyn realized that, although he resembled Sedgewick in face and form, the differences were as marked as the similarities. There was a look of cunning malice in the visitor's eyes, his flesh was faintly pockmarked, and his fine, aristocratic nose had been broken at least once. Sedgewick wore the finely made, if rugged, garb of a nobleman and a soldier, while his ghost was clothed in tatters of black and green velvet, all the shabbier for their lost grandeur.

"What happened here, lad?" asked the newcomer. "Were you robbed?"

Blodwyn swallowed hard and tried to recall. His throat ached, fair to shut off his breath, and the trees of the forest seemed to spin in a dizzy dance. His head lolled, and a memory—or was it a dream—flitted through his brain. He saw Dame Johanna step up behind Sedgewick, strike him with a stone, cross herself hastily, and scurry toward the stallion, Mithras. After that, he remembered naught.

Where was the horse? For that matter, where was his own mount, a slow-footed gelding called Chestnut?

"I don't—know," he managed to grind out at last. And it was the God's truth. Surely the good dame, a nun, a servant of the Holy Church, could not have done such things. "Who—who are you?"

A grin flashed in that face, so like Sedgewick's and, at the same time, so *unlike* it. He sketched a bow. "My name is not important. I am but a poor mummer, trying to make his way." He gestured toward the man lying so frighteningly still on the creek bank. "Is that your master, lad?"

"Aye," Blodwyn got out. "Sedgewick is—" *was?* "a soldier. A knight."

The mummer crouched, produced a flask from somewhere inside his coat, and extended it to Blodwyn. The boy did not hesitate, but accepted the offering, pulled the cork, and took a great draught of strong, sour wine. A violent but not unpleasant shudder moved through his slender frame.

"Gresham Sedgewick," the mummer mused, rubbing his chin while he waited for Blodwyn to return the flask. "I'd heard I had the look of him about me, but seeing it for myself gave me a turn."

"Is he—is he dead?" Blodwyn sat up, empowered by the wine. He felt bile surge into the back of his throat, and his head swam.

The player looked back at Sedgewick for a long time before replying with a shake of his head. "No," he said. "He's near it, though." With that, he got to his feet, stowing the flask again in the same motion, and walked back to the creek bank. While Blodwyn watched, confounded, he crouched again, went through Sedgewick's pockets, and relieved him of a small but weighty leather pouch, which he paused to admire for a moment, smiling, before pulling the signet ring from the other man's hand. This he pondered at some length and with a sober expression, before slipping it onto his own finger.

He'll kill me now, Blodwyn thought helplessly, watching as the stranger came toward him again. *Cut my throat and leave me to the worms.*

Indeed, the mummer stood over him for a long while, as if considering the question, before giving a low whistle through his front teeth. A slat-ribbed nag trotted out of the woods, reins dangling, and came nickering to the man's side.

"Where were you bound for, lad?"

Blodwyn interrupted a silent Hail Mary to reply. "St. Swithin's Abbey."

"I know the place," the mummer said with a nod, his expression still disturbingly reflective. Then, just when Blodwyn despaired of his life, he tossed him the flask again. "This will keep your blood running until I get back," he said. "In the meantime, the only Christian thing to do is see that poor Sedgewick there gets the tending he requires. I'll take him within crawling distance of the nuns—a day's journey at most—then return for you."

Blodwyn waited, more confounded than before. This man had robbed Sedgewick, and now he was laying plans to rescue him. It didn't tally.

"I have uses for a strapping, resilient lad like yourself," the mummer explained, unprompted. Then, with no more adieu, he turned, hoisted Sedgewick, a man of considerable size, belly down onto the horse's back. He mounted easily behind him, spared Blodwyn a brief and cheerful wave, and rode away into the forest.

Blodwyn lay for a long time, alternately thanking every saint he could think of that the mummer had left him in peace and at the same time wondering if he would, indeed, be back. When he'd gathered the strength to unstop the flask, he swallowed more wine, and then lay back on his cold bed of earth, feeling welcome warmth creep through his limbs.

The mummer was a thief, mayhap even a murderer, but, Blodwyn decided, he was also a man of his word. He would return, all right. And when he did, Gresham Sedgewick's squire meant to be far from that place.

1

They found him lying facedown amidst the hardened, frosty runnels of St. Swithin's squash patch, half frozen and out of his senses, with a crimson cap of blood crusted at the back of his head.

Elizabeth Redclift, the younger of the two sisters, hastily crossed herself and murmured a prayer, while Meg, the more direct of the pair, dropped to her knees beside the unfortunate fellow, turned him gently onto his back, and sought a pulse at the base of his throat.

Even in those straightened circumstances, it gave Meg something of a start, the look of him. He was fair, with features so finely chiseled they might have been shaped by an Italian sculptor instead of an often—in Meg's view, at least—careless deity. Just looking at him, she felt a strange shift, deep inside, a singular tension, as though she'd just stepped onto the crumbling edge of some precipice, either to fall or to soar like Icarus before his wings melted.

Even Elizabeth, who had sworn never to marry, preferring to take holy vows instead, drew in a breath and

spoke with awe. "Mercy," she said. "He looks like a favored angel, or a saint. Is he alive?"

Meg commenced wrapping the poor traveler in her
cloak, which was none too warm but better than his own
clothing, amounting to a torn, soiled shirt and once-fine
breeches in much the same state. "Aye, sweeting, he's
alive," she replied, "though truly it is a mystery why that
should be so. 'Tis plain he's been wandering a while—see
how dirty he is—and this wound is fair old."

"I'll fetch Mother Mary Benedict," Elizabeth said, and
started toward the postern gate gaping open behind
them, one of several like it, placed here and there in the
abbey's venerable walls. The good dame was abbess, and
therefore the ultimate authority.

Meg hastily grasped her sister's kirtle, which was hardly
in better condition than the stranger's garb, though cleaner
of course, and neatly mended, to stay her. The sheriff had
been at the front gates, just two days past, looking for a
man of similar countenance, and Meg both misliked and
mistrusted the king's man, for she'd seen him in the village
often enough, bullying peasants and even merchants.

"No, Elizabeth—we mustn't be too hasty. He may be
an outlaw, or a heretic, doomed to burn at the stake."

Elizabeth gasped again, spread one hand over her
bosom, swallowed and then crossed herself again. "Surely
there are reasons for the abbess's rules, Meg—the plague is
abroad, and there are knaves aplenty wandering the roads
in these hard times. We would be wise to be cautious."

Meg cherished her sister, would indeed have laid
down her very life for her, but in these moments she
sorely missed Gabriella, her twin, gone these several
months to Cornwall. Gabriella was bold and strong-
minded, and having her so far away, all the while knowing

little or naught of how she fared as the duly wedded wife of Lord Avendall, was akin to having a limb sundered. In all these months, there had been no word, and Dame Johanna, Gabriella's companion, had neither returned to the abbey, as expected, nor sent a message. Meg was secretly worried, though she put on a brave face for Elizabeth's sake.

"Never mind caution," she said, rather impatiently. "Go and fetch the pushcart from the potting shed—the big one we used to harvest pumpkins. It should support his weight, so that we can bring him in out of the cold. And mind you don't call attention to yourself while you're at it, Elizabeth Redclift. You'll give an accounting if you do."

Elizabeth looked pityingly at the wayfaring stranger, then turned, hoisting her kirtle and the skirts of the gown beneath, and dashed across the frost-scoured garden to disappear through the postern gate.

The god-man, barely alive by Meg's reckoning, murmured something and stirred, and Meg hastened to lend what comfort she could, gathering him up in her arms. "Here now," she said, "you've fallen amongst friends. We'll not turn you over for burning unless it comes out that you deserve it."

She thought just the faintest flicker of a smile touched the man's mouth at that moment, but of course she must have imagined it. He was surely too broken to feel mirth, and certainly too weak to show it if, for some unfathomable reason, he did.

"Come to that," Meg went on, holding him closer to lend what warmth she could, and rocking him back and forth as she'd oft done with Elizabeth, who had been sickly as a child, "it's hard to credit that anyone could warrant such a horror, isn't it? There's no need to be so cruel, it seems to me. If one merits condemning, then he should simply have his head chopped off, quick and clean. Or have an arrow put true through his heart . . ."

She was rambling a little, but there was nothing for it. Meg had ever tended to chatter when she was nervous.

The man's head had fallen back over Meg's supporting arm, revealing his throat and long, perfectly shaped, though unwashed, neck. Although his features would have been cherished by any woman, Meg noticed, with what was mayhap an unmaidenly degree of interest—for he could truly be called beautiful, in the way of saints and angels—there was nothing of the feminine in him. He was, for all his lithe build, his thick and lengthy lashes, his wondrously wrought face and limbs, completely, uncompromisingly, and inarguably male.

Pity, Meg thought, *that he's in such a sorry state, for we might have been wed, he and I, and traveled to Cornwall, to find Gabriella. He looks to be the adventuring sort—see his hand, calloused from the hilt of a sword, see the fine, sturdy form of his shoulders and forearms . . .*

"Have done, Margaret Redclift," Meg scolded herself, muttering. "You'll forfeit your immortal soul for such thoughts, if you haven't already."

A tendency toward unseemly reflections was, it seemed, her besetting sin. That she was wont to act upon her musings often made matters worse, of course.

A clatter at the postern gate revealed Elizabeth, hurrying with flushed cheeks over the hard, empty furrows of the field, pushing the garden cart before her. Her dark hair, truly her greatest glory, had escaped her wimple, tumbling tousled and gleaming over her slender shoulders and down her back.

Watching her, Meg thought with no little ruefulness

what an irony it was that Elizabeth, the most comely of all three Redcliff daughters, was the one who had no wish to marry. She'd be content, the little goose, to stay at St. Swithin's Abbey all her days, and never know the tender caresses of a man, the tug of an infant's mouth at her breast, the clash and clamor of everyday life out there in the wide, frightful, glorious world.

Meg, for her part, was certain that Gabriella's new husband would provide adequate dowries for his wife's sisters, if he had any honor at all. She wanted a certain sort of mate and, since her expectations were quite stringent, fully expected to purchase him, like a good horse at the summer fair. Elizabeth, on the other hand, wished to become a postulant and surrender the whole of her bride-price, should she ever actually have one, to the coffers of the Holy Church.

Mother Mary Benedict, the abbess, bless her soul forever and ever, had refused this offer, saying that Elizabeth must first live outside St. Swithin's for a year, mayhap with Gabriella in Cornwall, or even at court, attending some great lady of the king's household. Only when she'd experienced life beyond the convent walls, and found it truly wanting, would she be permitted to take her vows.

"What do you suppose he's called?" Elizabeth asked, her breathing belabored, as she and Meg hoisted the poor wounded sojourner into the pumpkin cart.

"It hardly matters just now, does it?" Meg countered, unreasonably and inexplicably nettled by her sister's question. "Come, we'll put him in the planting shed; it's warm enough, and no one ever goes there, now that the crops are in."

The journey back across the frozen runnels of dirt was trying indeed, for the stranger, though comely, was as ungainly to transport thus as Zacheus, one of the abbess's two white mules, would have been. Alas, both animals were gone, Zacheus, the elder, with Dame Johanna and Gabriella, on the journey to Cornwall, and Enoch, mysteriously vanished from a nearby pasture.

"It does matter," Elizabeth insisted, huffing, for she could be stubborn, despite all her saintly inclinations. "We can't refer to him as 'the stranger' forever, can we?"

"We shan't have cause to refer to him at all, I should think," Meg answered, nearly oversetting the cart in her efforts to traverse a particularly high furrow. It made her a little sad, to think of the man going away, whether under his own power or the sheriff's, as he inevitably would. "He looks hearty, for all his hurts, and he'll soon be gone from us."

Elizabeth persisted, and Meg reflected that there might be hope for her sister yet. If Elizabeth had a failing, it was that she was too docile in most matters, and she seemed to lack any inclination toward adventure. "He wants a name," she said, with resolution, gasping as she pushed mightily at the back of the cart.

"Zacheus, then," Meg teased, pausing to tuck a wisp of chestnut hair back into her own wimple. "For the mule."

Elizabeth looked sorrowful, and Meg was sorry she'd mentioned the creature. Zacheus, like Gabriella and Dame Johanna, was elsewhere, and Elizabeth had been almost as fond of him as she was of their sister.

"No," poor Elizabeth said, for though she was merry of spirit, she seldom knew a jest when she heard one, "that won't do. There is bound to be confusion, when Dame Johanna returns, as she left us, mounted upon Zacheus's back. She'll bear tidings of Gabriella, you may be certain."

Meg shook her head. She feared that Gabriella's party, for all the brawny and well-armed guards her husband-to-be had sent as an escort, might have been waylaid by bandits somewhere in the journey, and she was aware that the abbess shared her concern, though they said little about the matter. There should have been a letter by now, at the very least. And why had Dame Johanna, Gabriella's chaperon, failed to return, once her charge was safely married?

Presently, Meg and Elizabeth gained the planting shed, stumbling and struggling as they went, and made a bed for their fallen angel by pushing three long potting benches together in the center of the small, rickety structure. His mattress was of rough, empty seed bags—better than many in the abbey itself, for all that—and they laid him upon it with great care and industry, nearly exhausting themselves by that effort alone. Then, for good measure, they covered him in still more of the crude bags, that being all they had in the way of blankets.

"Mother would put him in the infirmary," Elizabeth said pointedly, surveying their wretched attempt at hospitaling.

"As will we," Meg replied briskly, "once we know he's in no danger of burning or hanging."

Elizabeth muttered something that might or might not have been a prayer for patience. "You'll kill the poor man, Meg Redclift, and all in the name of saving him from punishments that may exist only in your own fancy."

"I won't take the chance," Meg whispered, mayhap harshly, gripping Elizabeth's arm and dragging her aside. "I mean to ask him to take me to Gabriella, once he comes around. He's a fine specimen, isn't he—a soldier, I'll wager."

Elizabeth looked as horrified as Meg expected, and crossed herself, once more, this time violently. "Or an outlaw, certain to cut our throats the moment he awakes—Sister, I fear you are either a fool or a mad-woman, even to *think* of venturing—"

Meg glanced back at their captive and thought she saw his eyelashes flutter slightly. "He'll need water," she said brusquely. "And medicine. You go to the well, and I'll fetch the remedy box from the infirmary."

"You'll steal it, you mean," Elizabeth pressed. Now, of all times, she'd decided to be spirited. "Honestly, Meg, I despair of your soul sometimes."

"I depend wholly upon grace for my salvation," Meg said virtuously, batting her eyelashes. She was also lean-ing quite heavily on the hope that God had a better sense of humor than her sister did. "Now, do as I say, Elizabeth. Don't force water, mind you, unless he awakens—just put droplets on his tongue, or you'll choke the poor wretch."

Elizabeth's eyes went round, and she turned pale, though not, Meg suspected, at the prospect of choking the patient. It was the possibility of his waking up that frightened her.

"Donkey feathers," Meg snapped, impatient now, and not a little spent from the rescue effort. "What have you to fear if he does come round, he's that weak?"

"You mustn't curse," Elizabeth said, very righteously. Then, at the look on Meg's face, she turned and fled to fetch the required water.

Meg herself made quick work of stealing the medicine chest, and returned to find Elizabeth watering the stranger's tongue as carefully as if he were one of the spring seedlings she always nursed so tenderly. For all her timid ways, Elizabeth had a gift for looking after bro-ken and fragile things.

"He hasn't wakened, then?"

Elizabeth shook her head, flushed with noble works, hard exercise, and scandal. "He spoke once, though, and quite clearly, too. He cursed someone named Blodwyn to hell and perdition for stealing his purse. I always thought they were one and the same place—hell and perdition, I mean."

Meg set the remedy box down with a thump and raised its lid to peer none too knowledgeably at the contents. "Mayhap only the two names could suffice, so heartfelt was the curse," she said. "Do you suppose we should smear a paste on his chest?"

Elizabeth rolled her eyes; poultices and potions were her provence, for it was she who grew the herbs for them, and oversaw the crops and gardens that gave the inhabitants of St. Swithin's an unusually varied diet.

"You come and dribble the water, Meg," she said, with an authority she showed only when dealing with plants. "I shall mind the medicine box."

Meg smiled to herself and pretended to mild chagrin. "Aye, Sister," she said, and came to tend the stranger.

Before she'd had a chance to accustom herself to close proximity—there was something pleasantly disturbing about being so near this particular man—the splendid wretch opened his eyes and gazed up at Meg, perplexed.

She had never seen eyes so blue; the color of them fair stopped her heart and surely put an end to her breath.

"Who—?" he asked. "What—?"

Meg simply stared at him, and all but strangled before she remembered to breathe. "You've come to St. Swithin's Abbey," she managed, by a miracle no less impressive than the parting of the Red Sea or the multiplying of the loaves and fishes. "Devonshire."

The beautiful stranger frowned, as though he'd never heard of either place.

Elizabeth came promptly to stand just behind Meg. "What is your name, good sir?" she asked sweetly, showing no sign now that she feared him an outlaw or a heretic, as before. And where, pray, had her former shy and maidenly nature gone? "You are safe with us."

Meg gave her sister a baffled look, then turned her attention back to the man lying on the bed of planting benches. "You shan't be betrayed," she promised him, mayhap rashly, but in all sincerity nevertheless.

"I don't know," he said, at length. "What I'm called, I mean."

"Donkey feathers," Meg said again, vastly disappointed by this news.

"We shall just have to give you a name," Elizabeth announced brightly. "Raphael would suit you, for indeed you are quite lovely to look upon—"

The wretch curled his lip. No archangel he, it would seem. "No," he said, with conviction.

"Apollo, then," Meg blurted, not to be left out, and was instantly mortified.

He smiled, and showed that his teeth were as perfectly made as the rest of him. "My thanks to you, milady," he said slowly, and it was obvious that he was much spent, for all his magnificence. "But I hardly think it suits. A more practical name, pray—just until I've retrieved my own."

"George?" Meg said, thinking of the dragon-slaying saint, and never knowing where she got the courage to speak again, when she'd made such a fool of herself just moments before.

"Oh, no," Elizabeth protested, with enthusiasm. "Adam would suit ever so much better. You're certainly the first man—the first to live here at St. Swithin's, in any event—and, like the Adam of old, you have no memory."

"Adam, then," said Adam, and Meg was sore vexed that her sister had been the one to choose an acceptable name, when all the time *she'd* wanted to turn the poor fellow over to the sheriff, where he'd surely have met with heaven-knew-what sort of fate. Besides, she still thought "Apollo" fitted him better.

"Go and mix your medicines," Meg said to Elizabeth, and none too charitably, either.

Adam closed his eyes again, and slept.

"Turn him onto his stomach," Elizabeth said, undaunted, going back to the remedy chest and lifting out a tray in the top to reach for and extract a small mortar and pestle. "It's the wound on his head that wants care. After that, you can give him a bath, since you're so smitten as to compare him to a pagan god. Then he'd best have a little broth."

Even brazen Meg could not conceive of bathing the man, though she would be forced to confess, the very next time she visited the chapel, that she found the idea somewhat less repellent than might have been well. "And what do you propose to do with yourself, Saint Elizabeth, whilst I'm running a cloth over the flesh of a naked man and spooning soup into his mouth?"

Elizabeth had the good grace—and not a moment too soon—to blush. "You wouldn't want me to do it, would you?" she asked meekly.

"Of course not," Meg relented, glancing sidelong at Adam's long, loose-limbed body. Even in that state, he looked uncommon comfortable in his skin, as only a man who liked and trusted himself could do. "What do you suppose happened to him?"

"He was set upon by thieves and rogues, no doubt," Elizabeth whispered, wide-eyed. "You don't suppose he carries plague, do you?"

Now it was Meg who made the sign of the cross. They had been safe at the abbey, so far, but the pestilence raged all around them, and Mother Mary Benedict was careful whom she admitted within its walls for that reason. "He looks too—well, sturdy—for all his hurts," she said, after another close examination. "Do you really think we should bathe him?"

"That's what the dames do first, when one of the villagers comes to the infirmary," Elizabeth said. "Mayhap he has lice, or fleas."

Meg parted his blood-matted hair, much in need of washing, and squinted at his scalp. "No sign of lice, and it's too cold by half for fleas."

The visitor, so lucid only moments before, suddenly began to shiver. His teeth chattered, and both Meg and Elizabeth hastened to find more seed bags to put over him.

"We must tell," Elizabeth said solemnly. "He's very ill, Meg, and it's beyond our poor means to tend him proper."

"No," Meg replied, after a brief and agonizing tussle with her Christian conscience. "No, they'll send for the sheriff, just because he's a man, and a stranger. Come— I'll turn him over, and you take a look at the gash in his head, see if it wants stitching. While you're at it, I'll fetch water and some cloth."

"Meg—"

"Please, Elizabeth," Meg importuned, and was startled to realize that she'd taken Adam's hand in her own. "He's in danger, I know it—and we're his only friends just now."

"Fancies," Elizabeth scoffed, but she set herself to examining the wound, and Meg made haste to fetch a basin and cloth. Upon her return, she washed his hair and scalp thoroughly, but with care, so as not to aggravate the injury, and Elizabeth mixed a poultice and applied it. Then, using a strip of precious cloth, she made a bandage for his head.

Since Adam's clothes were mere rags anyway, it was no great revelation to strip away all but his trunks and, using rainwater and strong soap, scrub his flesh clean. That done, Meg hurried to cover him again.

They had not, so far, managed to purloin the broth they'd decided he needed. There had been risk enough in taking the medicine chest and the basins of water from the barrels outside the refectory door.

Meg had no small reputation for mischief, and therefore knew she must use great care not to draw notice from the nuns or the other residents of the convent.

"You'd best fetch the soup," Meg told Elizabeth, in a whisper. "Say it's for me, that I'm feeling poorly and cannot possibly come to vespers."

"I shall not lie on any account," Elizabeth said, with saintlike indignation. Then she swept out, in grand dudgeon, and left Meg alone with the man they had christened Adam.

He was resting more easily now, under the piles of rough sacks; it did seem that Elizabeth's poultice and the bath had soothed him a little.

Presently, Elizabeth returned, carrying a steaming wooden bowl in both hands, with a spoon protruding from the broth. Her expression was defiant; she had completed her mission without breaking any of the commandments.

Except perchance the one about stealing.

Meg wakened her patient to eat, supporting his head in the curve of her arm while spooning nourishing portions of broth into his mouth, and though he seemed disoriented, he took the food readily. There was no guessing how long it had been since the man had had so much as a morsel to eat, and he finished the soup with good appetite before lapsing back into a healing sleep.

Meg stayed with him until the vespers bell chimed, and would not have left him then, had Elizabeth not sternly reminded her that a few prayers, properly offered, would not go amiss—and could most particularly benefit the man they'd found in the squash patch. Dutifully, Meg attended vespers and, fervently, she prayed.

That night, alone in their cell, with Gabriella's empty cot as an ever-present reminder of their sister's absence, they made whispered plans. Elizabeth still refused to utter an untruth, no matter what happened, whereas Meg suffered no such scruples, but they were in agreement in one wise: it was their moral duty to save Adam's life, if they could.

For three days and nights, Meg and Elizabeth managed to keep their secret, sneaking back and forth, between prayers and the daily tasks that all were expected to perform, bringing food, changing bandages, smuggling blankets and even snitching trunk hose, soft leather boots, and a jerkin from the supply of old garments the nuns had gathered for the poor. During that time, he rallied occasionally, and if he made any attempts to leave under his own power, he did not succeed.

On the morning of the fourth day, Meg arrived, having slipped out of the refectory early, after breakfast, to find her charge on his feet, though unsteady, and wearing the ill-fitting but serviceable garments she and Elizabeth had provided.

He made, for all his grim efforts to hold himself up unsupported, a splendid and imposing figure, standing upright that way. Indeed, he *was* a soldier, sure as she breathed.

"You've recovered, then," she said, resigned.

"You sound disappointed," he remarked, reaching out to steady himself by grasping the edge of one of the high tables used for potting seeds in the early spring.

Meg swallowed, then summoned all her courage. "I shall give you my dowry if you'll take me to my sister," she said boldly. It was a rash bargain to propose, since she didn't actually *possess* a bride-price. "She is called Gabriella, and she went to Cornwall to be married, and we've heard naught of her since, nor have we seen Dame Johanna, her chaperon. Something may well be amiss."

Adam sat down heavily at this pronouncement, bemused. "Gabriella?" he said, frowning as he pondered. "I know that name. I have heard it oft, methinks, and it is not common."

Meg took a hopeful step toward him, then stopped. Mayhap he was a friend to Gabriella, but he might also have been the very one to do her harm. "Perhaps you have a sister by that name," she ventured, with growing excitement, "or a friend?"

"Aye, a friend," he agreed, with a sort of befogged certainty. "For I have no sisters, nor brothers either. I know that much of myself, at least."

"And what else?" Meg dared to ask. "What else do you remember, I mean?"

His blue eyes darkened, like water before a storm and, having shed his bandage long before, he thrust a hand through his hair. "I have scenes of battle in my head. Horrible visions of bloodshed and torment."

"Then you must indeed be a soldier," Meg said.

"Aye," he said again. He held out his hands, long and

elegant hands more fitted to plying the strings of a lute than wielding a sword, and examined them as though they belonged to someone else. "These callouses are those of a swordsman, not a farmer or a tradesman."

Meg shook her head. "No, I should not have taken you for a laborer. Your clothes, such as they were, were costly ones, finely made."

He jumped to his feet, swayed, and sat down again. "Where are they?" he asked, speaking moderately even though anxiety was plain in his eyes. "Was I wearing boots? Carrying anything?"

"No," Meg said, and produced the pitiful fragments of a shirt and breeches from the place where she had hidden them. "Someone had taken your boots and all else you had in the bargain. It is a wonder you did not die of cold, or suffer frostbite."

"Where did you find me? Show me, now."

"I can't," Meg replied, alarmed by the force of his insistence. She had been in the convent for some years, with her sisters, and was unused to the presence or habits of men. They were fascinating creatures, in her opinion, but they made a great deal of noise and took up considerable space. "It's still a secret that you're here. If we go out into the field, someone might see us."

He raised himself back to his feet, slowly and with some effort. "This is the end of your secret, I'm afraid," he said. "If you won't show me where you found me, straightaway, I'll go looking on my own. And I give you my warrant, milady, that I'll be noticed in the doing."

Meg flushed. "You are ungrateful, sir, if you will permit my saying it."

"It seems to me that you say whatever you wish," he retorted. "As to my ingratitude, there you are mistaken. I probably owe you my life, whatever it is." He swayed again, but this time he held his feet. The light of determination glowed fierce in his eyes. "God's teeth, demoiselle, you can't have expected to keep me here forever, like a pet mouse. I'm a man, and an unruly one—I've guessed that much of my nature, at least—and it does not suit, your being alone with me in such a wise!"

Meg bit her lower lip. Waited a moment or two, before returning to her truest concern. "Will you not take me to find Gabriella, then?"

"No," he said. "I will not." He frowned and went to the window, stooping a little to peer out, for he was tall as a giant. "What is this place?"

"St. Swithin's Abbey, Devonshire," Meg said. She'd told him that already, as it happened, given him her name, too, but he could not be blamed for forgetting, given the circumstances. Still, she wished he'd pay attention.

He turned, regarding her with surprise and no little censure. "Surely you're not a nun?"

Meg's temper, put aside heretofore, in the cause of mercy, flared slightly. "Do you think me unfit for the holy life?" she countered.

He smiled, and that left another sweet bruise on Meg's heart. "Peace, milady," he said. "I have no opinions about you at all, except that you're too beautiful for my liking, and too spirited, by half, for a proper maiden."

Meg simply stared at him, unable to discern whether she'd just been complimented, or insulted. She misliked his stated lack of opinions where she was concerned, misliked it indeed, for she wanted, she found, to fill his thoughts, to occupy his mind like an invading army. Still, he'd also said she was beautiful—no one had ever told her that before.

"You've been kind to me," he said at last, with a slight

and very courtly bow of his head. "I am ever in your debt."

"But not so much so that you will grant my boon and take me to see Gabriella?"

"Oh, more so, milady," he answered smoothly, and it came to Meg that he might have been a courtier as well as a soldier. He was certainly artful enough for it. "I would be no gentleman, if I took you from this place—nay, but the worst rascal ever God made. Surely you know it is a ruinous thing for a lass to travel with a man not of her family."

Meg hesitated, then burst out with the wildest portion of her scheme. "You could marry me."

He regarded her so long, and so thoughtfully, that Meg began to hope he meant to accept her proposal. "Nay, milady," he said at length, "though I find you charming, I must needs refuse. Has it not occurred to you that I might already have a wife?"

2

In her relative innocence, Meg had given only scant consideration to the possibility that her unlikely knight might have a wife awaiting him somewhere. It wasn't uncommon for men to woo and win a bride and promptly take to the roads, or even to the battlefields of France and the Levant, pledging their questionable loyalties to still other unsuspecting females they might encounter along the way. Often, like the dowries they'd garnered when the vows of holy matrimony were exchanged in some country kirk, these men vanished for good—oh, yes, she had heard just such appalling tales of perfidy and deception from gentlewomen exiled to St. Swithin's, and she was sure at least a few of them were quite credible.

"I suppose it *is* possible," Meg murmured, still woefully reluctant to concede the point that someone truly might have a valid claim upon this man's affections, and feeling as downcast as she ever had, but for the occasion of Gabriella's leave-taking several months before, of course, and the wretched day she and her sisters had come to reside at the abbey in the first place. "Surely, though, if you had a wife, or children, you would recall *something*—"

He shook his head, his expression distracted, even a little haunted. She knew from the ache pulsing in his eyes that he was telling the truth.

She swallowed hard. Her desire to leave the abbey and venture out into the great world beyond its borders burned within her, hot as embers of glowing coal in the bed of a winter fire, thrummed in the core of her being like some mystical, second heartbeat. There were times when she thought the restlessness alone would drag her in seven directions at once and be the finish of her.

Still, as passionately as she wanted to begin her true life as a woman, it would not be an easy matter to put the place behind her, because that would mean being parted from Elizabeth, mayhap for time and eternity. She had wept repeatedly over this quandary, unable to bear even the prospect of bidding her younger sister farewell, though she was always careful not to let anyone see or overhear. For all her sorrow, for all her love for her sister, it oft seemed to Meg that she would quite literally perish if she did not leave that place; she was drowning, a swimmer in over her head, and there were moments when she would have sworn that the venerable walls of the nunnery itself were closing in upon her, a fraction of an inch at a time, with each breath she drew. She heaved a great sigh, and let her shoulders go slack.

The knight took a few reluctant steps to stand before her, touched her unruly chestnut hair where it sprang from her wimple to tickle her cheek. "Is it so dull here, so miserable, that you would take to the road with a stranger?" he asked, in a voice gentle enough that it was nearly Meg's undoing, all on its own. She had known very little tenderness, but for the steady affection of her sisters, and coming from this man, the stuff had an odd and frightening magic, rousing dizzying sensations in her and causing her to wonder if she'd ever truly known herself at all.

Life at St. Swithin's was indeed dull, almost insufferably so, by Meg's lights at least. Still, it was not a cruel place; she had suffered no privations or abuse, and the company of Gabriella and Elizabeth had ever made a home of the place. Sometimes, though, just when the sun was setting, Meg yearned so for places she'd never been, sights she'd yet to see, that she thought sure she'd shatter into splinters from the sheer poignancy of her longings.

If only Elizabeth would agree to accompany her when she left, the problem would be solved, but alas, the youngest of the three Redclift sisters was, despite her retiring nature, every bit as stubborn as the white mule, Zacheus.

"I have not been ill used here," Meg admitted, to herself as well as to her companion, at some length. She wanted to describe what she felt, but could not find words that were big enough, wild enough. *Desperate* enough to encompass the magnitude of her truth. "It's just that—"

His blue eyes danced, though there was something bruised in them, something broken. "Just that what?" he prompted, obviously fighting a smile. What was it about her that amused him so, she wondered, not a little stung. She could think of several other reactions she would rather have inspired in him than mirth.

She spread her hands in frustration, let them fall disconsolately against her sides. "You simply cannot imagine what it's like, living here," she exclaimed. *"Nothing ever happens.* It's the same, day after day—prayers, and then breakfast, and more prayers. Morning tasks and lessons, then still other prayers. The midday meal, chores, and, once again, studies. Latin, stitchery. Things I'll never need to know. Supper, and then—"

"Prayers?" he teased.

She folded her arms and scowled up at him. "Yes," she said, a bit pettishly. "Merciful heaven, God Himself must weary of all that toadying, all those people nattering on and on about how wonderful and merciful He is—as if He didn't know what they *truly* think of Him, begging for this blessing and that—'help me find my lost pig' and the like—but never saying anything the least *bit* interesting—" She stopped and put her hands over her ears just to think of all that prattle, an incessant, babbling din surging heavenward from every corner of the earth.

The soldier chuckled softly, but stepped back, putting the slightest but most telling distance between them. The motion, though subtle as an indrawn breath, unsettled and confused Meg. She felt somehow abandoned, though she knew it was silly of her, because one cannot be deserted by someone who has neither a reason nor an obligation to stay.

"Mayhap even God grows lonely at times," he observed, "just as we poor mortals do." He paused, made an attempt at a smile. "I should think some of that 'toadying' is quite diverting."

"Well," Meg huffed, feeling unaccountably intractable, "it would all be ever so much more 'diverting,' wouldn't it, if God said something in *response,* every now and then. At least then one would know He was listening."

At this, the stranger laughed outright. "Ah, Meg, yours is an intrepid soul." He went still, studied her with shining eyes for a few moments, then went on. "Tell me, Lady Redclift, what do *you* ask for, when you pray?"

Meg bit her lower lip, reluctant to confide such precious secrets, for fear he would think her foolish. She liked the sound of his laughter, though, for it was merry and in no wise unkind, and so she answered his question. "I say all my beads first, of course," she told him earnestly, hoping to seem at least a little devout. "Then, when that's done, and any prayers of penance have been offered, I ask the Holy Virgin to send us word of Gabriella, and to keep my sisters safe and well." She drew a deep breath, let it out slowly. Her eyes stung with the intensity of missing her twin, and she looked away. "And I ask for—for a husband with a brave and faithful heart."

He traced the length of her nose with a forefinger, and the touch, so light as to seem imagined, unleashed a tumult within Meg, bestirring a tender ache in her woman parts and turning her blood to a spicy wine that tingled in her veins.

"I fear, sweet Meg," he said, in tones low and hoarse, "that I cannot be the fortunate man who takes you to wife." He fell silent, and his expression was thoughtful, even somber. "Surely I am no nobleman, for I find the most unseemly thoughts in my head, just now."

He searched her face, and drew nigh again, and might have kissed her then and there—or so Meg dared to speculate—for he inclined his magnificent head ever so slightly toward her, and closed his eyes, and she could almost feel the heat of his mouth upon hers. But, as ever it will, disaster struck at precisely that most inopportune of moments.

"And who is this, Margaret Redclift?" demanded the unmistakable voice of Mother Mary Benedict.

Meg whirled toward the shed's door to find the abbess

standing there, with Elizabeth hovering just behind her, looking woeful, resigned, and a little defiant, all of a piece.

"I didn't tell, I swear," the latter hastened to submit, when Meg flung her an accusing look.

"I believe I asked you a question, Margaret," said the abbess. "It would behoove you to answer it without delay."

"We found him in the squash patch," Meg burst out, in a hurry to set matters aright. Mother Mary Benedict was neither unkind nor unreasonable—that had proved a great blessing over the years—but St. Swithin's was her domain, nonetheless, and she took her responsibilities to heart, governing all within her charge, some of the inmates said, as forcibly as the archangel Michael must have dealt with the armies of heaven during the great and terrible rebellion.

The stranger, standing behind Meg, set her gently aside with his hands and respectfully inclined his head to the abbess. There was an easy grace in the motion; he might not have remembered his name or his past, but his manners had not deserted him, and they were those of someone born to the gentry.

Meg added this information to a gathering store of small details. He was of good family, her knight, educated and, soldier or none, polished.

"I am grateful to these mischievous Samaritans of yours, good Dame," he said, and at this Meg thought she saw a glimmer of good humor in the abbess's eyes, though of course that might have been more wishful thinking than reality. "They saved my life, it would seem."

"Aye, or risked it unnecessarily," replied the abbess briskly. "You should have been brought to the infirmary immediately, sir, just as I should certainly have been advised of your presence." Mother Mary Benedict glowered at Meg, then Elizabeth, who seemed to wilt under her visage, like a spring wildflower fallen upon a glowing hearth. "Margaret, Elizabeth, you will take yourselves to the chapel, there to pray and examine your souls, while I undertake to arrange proper lodgings for our guest. When I am ready to see you, I shall send someone to fetch you back."

Meg, all of nineteen and fearing that she would be kept unmarried in St. Swithin's Abbey until she shriveled, hurried to obey, as did Elizabeth, though for quite different reasons, of course. Elizabeth did not *want* to be free; she intended to be abbess herself someday, and she'd had the brass to say as much on several occasions.

"You told!" Meg snapped, in an agitated whisper, as she and Elizabeth fled along the stone path that led to the chapel, with its hard stone floors and simple altar. There were no statues at St. Swithin's, no gilt crucifixes. Mother believed that the sacred life should be a simple one, unadorned.

"By my own saint, I didn't!" Elizabeth retorted, her color high and her eyes glittering. "It was Dame Alice, I vow—she must have seen me taking porridge from the refectory this morning, that snoop, and followed—"

Meg sighed, regretting her snappish response. After all, this coil was her doing, not her sister's. Elizabeth had wanted to go to the abbess when they first found the poor wayfarer lying in the furrows. "Aye," she said, more gently. "Dame Alice has got her nose in everything, that one."

"Still, she is most dedicated to her tasks and observances," Elizabeth defended the absent offender, but without significant conviction.

They had reached the well-worn steps of the chapel,

and there their conversation ended. Meg entered first, genuflected and made the sign of the cross before approaching the altar, as did her sister after her.

The chapel, mercifully, was empty but for ancient Dame Claudia, who was nearly always there, face translucent with serenity, communing with the God she had served all her long life. Now that she was three score and ten, and every joint swollen with the common ills of such veneration, Mother Mary Benedict had forbidden the nun to pray upon her knees, so she sat on the first bench, head bowed, gnarled hands folded.

Dame Claudia did not look up when the Redclift sisters took their places before the altar, their own knees fitted into indentations made by generations of other penitents and petitioners. Though Elizabeth rarely required discipline—she was usually guilty only by association with one of her sisters—Meg was not unfamiliar with the posture she took now, nor had Gabriella been.

God bless Gabriella, wherever she was. After hastily and belatedly straightening her wimple, Meg clasped her hands together, lowered her head, and sought the forgiveness of sin.

Standing at the rear of the chapel, only minutes after concluding her interview with the secret guest, the man called "Adam," the abbess looked on, smiling to herself, as the young Redclift women continued to grapple, in prayer and penance, with the less worthy sides of their natures. She had been in long and close communion with her God, had Mother Mary Benedict, and her spirit was attuned to contentments the world could never offer, but she was not so old or so apart from the world as to forget the yearnings that stirred in young women's hearts. Nor had she failed to notice that the visitor they'd been hiding was comely to look upon.

Inwardly, the abbess sighed. Neither of these lasses were suited to convent life, any more than their sister Gabriella had been. They were meant to be given in marriage, these Redclift daughters, to bear children, to govern beside a worthy lord and manage his estates, all the while keeping his mind in thrall, as well as his body. But their household had fallen into poverty long ago, and they'd been sent to St. Swithin's when they reached the threshold of womanhood, at the behest of a man Mother Mary Benedict had promised never to name. Their feckless mother, the widow of a brave if somewhat unprincipled knight, had remarried, for love, rather than fortune. The erstwhile Lady Redclift, no doubt encouraged by her new husband, had, for all practical intents and purposes, relinquished all claim to her daughters. In time, their guardian, no doubt juggling many similar duties, had rewarded a certain baron, deserving or not, with the right to pick a wife from amongst them, like a pup from a litter. Gabriella had been the one to take his fancy.

The abbess moved soundlessly along the narrow aisle of the chapel, laid a gentle hand to the shoulder of Dame Claudia, and found her fragile as a hatchling. At a nod from Mother Mary Benedict, the elderly nun rose and shuffled out, taking her leave through a side door.

Elizabeth did not interrupt her prayers. Meg, on the other hand, glanced hopefully over one shoulder, and colored when she saw the abbess.

"Say your amens," Mother Mary Benedict instructed, in a tone deferential to her maker. "I would speak with you both in my quarters."

Hastily, and with no little theatrical skill, the prayers

were ended, and both Elizabeth and Meg gained their feet.

Elizabeth's eyes were round with contrition, Meg's bright with a passion more akin to rebellion than remorse.

In the privacy of her rooms, Mother Mary Benedict lectured her charges on the perils of taking in strangers in secret. There was the plague to be taken into account, widespread and wholly unpredictable. Outlaws of every stripe were abroad in the land, as well as mummers and magicians and simple scoundrels. Aye, these were dangerous, unruly times. Taxes were burdensome, and the king's war in France went on and on, putting a strain upon the purse and the temper of every citizen of the realm.

Listening, Elizabeth paled and, now and then, bit her lip. Meg looked ready to pack a bundle and scale one of the abbey walls, preferably before vespers. No doubt Meg had had enough of sacred prayer, for this day.

Mother Mary Benedict, weary of her own voice, but nevertheless committed to protecting and guiding those who came under her edict, made her pronouncement at last.

"You shall not attend the autumn fair," she said firmly.

Meg slipped to the edge of her chair, plainly prepared to protest and, if that failed, to beg, but Elizabeth, showing rare spirit, reached out and silenced her sister by grasping her arm.

"We will obey," she said and gave Meg a look that dared her to do otherwise.

Meg hesitated for several moments, her greater and lesser natures obviously engaged in bitter struggle, then rose to her feet. She spoke with surprising moderation.

"And the stranger?"

"He is no concern of yours, Meg," the abbess replied,

standing herself, though she would have preferred to sit awhile longer. The day was far from ended, and her duties, both private and public, would extend far into the night. "Dame Helena wants for help in the kitchen this morning. You will both go to her, please, and give me no more trouble."

Meg opened her mouth to offer said trouble, but Elizabeth interceded once more, caught her by the hand, and dragged her out before she could speak.

The abbess smiled again, but only after the sturdy door had closed behind them.

The knowledge came to him on a chilly breeze, after several days of recovery, while he was doing the only work he was then fitted for: feeding the abbey's multitude of chickens.

He was called Gresham.

He stopped where he was, grain dribbling through his fingers, hens squawking in complaint at his feet. Had his dam and sire proclaimed him thus upon his christening, or was it a surname? Mayhap it was even a territorial title, if he was a member of the gentry. He would ask for a map, first chance, and scour it for any reference.

He sighed and flung sprays of feed amongst the fretful birds. It was a place to start, at least, and mayhap other details would follow, now that he was sensible.

Finished with the chore the abbess had assigned him, more out of pity than to make him earn his keep, he suspected, Gresham turned and made his way back to the infirmary. He was to stay there, by Mother Mary Benedict's decree, until he was well enough to leave, or she had decided what to do with him, whichever came first.

Gresham smiled to himself, stooping to pass beneath

the low lintel of the infirmary door. He liked the abbess, he knew that much, if precious little else. She was a strong-minded woman, and fair. Those in her care could depend upon her to make the wisest, if not necessarily most popular, decisions.

His expression turned somber. Then there was the Lady Meg. An ache moved within him, deep and grinding, just to think of her. He liked—actually *liked*—listening to her, even when she prattled, and something about her invariably lifted his heart. Aye, she was a fetching creature, was Meg Redcliff, with her green eyes and clouds of chestnut hair, her slender but womanly figure, and that eager, ungovernable mind of hers. She was like an undiscovered country, and he wanted to explore her, mind, body and soul, though he knew better, even in his current ignorant state, than to trifle with the likes of Lady Redcliff.

He thrust a hand through his hair, frustrated and inherently restless, eager to get on with whatever he'd been doing before he found himself at St. Swithin's, and without the first idea of what that was.

The question of his past nagged at him incessantly. For all he could discern, he was pledged to someone else, or even long and purely wedded, with as many children as there were chickens in the abbey dooryard. While he would not have been above taking a mistress—it was an accepted and even lauded practice, after all—Meg was made for better things. Despite her poor clothes, he knew by the look in her eye and the set of her countenance that she came from gentlefolk. Thus, even if he'd been inclined toward despoiling guileless virgins, which he wasn't, bedding such a one would be folly indeed. For all her neglected state, she might well have a legion of brothers and uncles, sworn to draw and quarter any fool who got her on her back before churching.

The infirmary was empty and thus Gresham had the leisure to reflect, undisturbed. Enervated, though he would have denied it in the face of any penalty, he stretched out upon his allotted cot—certainly a welcome improvement over the benches shoved together in the potting shed—cupped his hands behind his head, and closed his eyes.

He had not planned or expected to sleep, but he did, and in his dreams he smelled the coppery scent of blood, saw the flash of steel and the sparks it threw, and heard the clash of sword against sword. The harrowing screams of those who fell to blade and arrow underlaid it all, coursing beneath his consciousness like a subterranean river.

The sheriff, word of a stranger recovering at the abbey having reached him at last, came at sunset on the seventh day, with half a dozen men. Her kitchen duties completed for the day, Meg contrived to be at the gate, partially concealed amid the hawthorne bushes, when Mother Mary Benedict came forth to greet him. Secure in the abbess's presence, Meg stepped forward and stood beside the older woman.

He was an ugly man, the sheriff, though Meg thought it was more a matter of his nature than his countenance, for his features, taken one by one, were unremarkable enough. She guessed he was near to one score and ten in age, and noted the way his hand hovered at the hilt of his sword, as if eager to draw and make use of it. There were four silent riders at his back, their expressions bland, their gazes fixed on the middle distance.

"Good even to you, Sheriff," the abbess said, and made no move to unlock the great metal gates and make him welcome, as she might have done with another traveler. Much depended, given the state of the realm, upon the specific situation.

The sheriff, who was called Prigg, and by no other name that Meg had ever heard, inclined his head in a manner that was more grudging than reverent. "There is talk in the village, good Dame, that you harbor a wayfarer here." He assessed the walls of the abbey, and visibly dismissed them, standing in his stirrups just briefly, as if to stretch his stocky limbs. "Such news always escapes, good Dame, no matter how you try to contain it."

The abbess stiffened slightly. Her hands were clasped loosely before her, and her chin was high. She misliked Prigg—everyone did, for he was known as a churl—but her sacred calling decreed that she must treat him with kindness and respect. "We have no secrets here," she said moderately.

Prigg curled his upper lip. "Of course not," he mocked.

Dame Alice, Meg thought, a little frantically. Ever the gossip, she must have told a passerby, a peddler, say, or a woodsman, about Adam's presence within the walls of the abbey. Clearly, she had described him as well. It amazed Meg, as well as frightened her, that such precise information had already found its way to the road and over the two miles of stubbly field that separated them from the village.

"Aye," replied Mother Mary Benedict, unintimidated. "We have a man among us. He was injured, and cannot tell us his name. We are looking after him."

"You will naturally want to rid yourselves of this unseemly burden," the sheriff said, cold-eyed. His hand tightened on the hilt of his sword when Meg fidgeted at the abbess's side. "You need only surrender him to us, and the problem will be solved."

"Why do you seek him?" the elderly nun asked.

Prigg delayed his answer as long as he could. He was a man accustomed to taking what he wanted, when he wanted it, according to the many tales told of his exploits, and he was obviously annoyed by the abbess's polite resistance. "There is a bandit on the loose, and I've been told this one bears a likeness to him."

"Our patient is but a poor traveler, and not an outlaw, I assure you," said the abbess.

Prigg's stubbled jaw tightened, relaxed forcibly. "Nonetheless, I bid you turn him over with no more ado, good Dame." He attempted a smile and failed, for this was not a habit he had cultivated, and he was awkward at it. "Surely he is but an inconvenience to you, as well as a possible danger to those who look to you for protection and spiritual guidance. This might be a criminal we are discussing, not some helpless peddler gone off his head, but a man who has robbed and killed and doubtless will not hesitate to do so again."

"I need not remind you, I am certain," the abbess replied, without a tremor of voice or limb, "that by law anyone may seek sanctuary within an abbey, a monastery, or a church for some forty days."

The sheriff flushed crimson, and his eyes narrowed, but he could not refute the abbess's claim.

"Our guest is wounded, and therefore of no threat to us in any case," the abbess went on. "Leave us, and return in forty days, when you may rightfully lay hands upon the man as a prisoner. In the meantime, there is no reason to believe he has done any wrong. Indeed, he seems the victim of unlawful practices, rather than one who commits them."

"Your logic is unsound," the sheriff insisted, grimly pleasant, though his thick neck still pulsed with color, "and quite deadly, given that yours is an establishment of women, unguarded and vulnerable."

"We are adequately looked after, I assure you," said Mother Mary Benedict. Then, with grave concern that might have contained the faintest hint of mockery, she added, "Pray you, Sheriff—make your way back to your rightful place, lest the darkness catch you abroad and open to attack. Failing that, you surely have other quarry to pursue than a single poor traveler, fallen upon hard times."

"Methinks," answered the sheriff, now purple at the neck and jowls, "you are too generous with your trust, good Dame."

The abbess smiled sweetly, and in a way that made Meg glad she was not the recipient of her present congeniality. "I am a servant of God, and an old woman. I confess I have no patience for such interviews as this one, and take no pleasure in them. I pray you—leave us to our supper and our simple devotions."

A muscle twitched in the sheriff's jaw, which was hard-clenched, then he reined his horse cruelly round, causing it to neigh pitifully at the bit, and thundered away into the twilight, his men pounding after him.

The abbess stood watching them, Meg uncharacteristically silent beside her, until they had vanished from sight.

"He will be back," Meg said, after a long time.

"Aye, child," Mother Mary Benedict replied, with a weary sigh, "that is true. Come—let us join the others at supper."

They walked together through the thickening gloom, their way lighted by lanterns that burned cheerily behind the leaded glass of the refectory windows. Inside were long tables, set with plain but nourishing food, lined with nuns and postulants and those women, young and old, who, like Meg and her sisters, were not wanted in their own homes. If they had homes, that is.

Some of the residents were elderly and sick, others were troublesome mothers, maiden aunts, sisters and daughters who were in some wise awkward to keep. Or simply marking time until a suitable marriage could be arranged for them. All, without exception, were from good families, though some of these, like Meg's own, were very poor, living in crumbling manor houses or drafty fortresses, void of the simplest comforts.

Although Meg wanted more than anything to leave St. Swithin's forever and begin her life, she was not unaware that she and her sisters had been fortunate in coming to the abbey. They had been educated, not only in spiritual matters, but in Latin and French as well. They could read, write and cipher, a rare thing even among the gentry, and although their clothes were mostly cast-offs from more prosperous members of that insular community, and thus threadbare, they had never gone hungry, or shivered with cold, as they might have done at home.

"Thank you," Meg said shyly, on the step outside the refectory door. Inside was happy chatter and light and warmth.

"For what, my child?" the abbess asked quietly, and with a touch of humor. "Defending your swordless knight?"

"That, too," Meg answered, pressing the nun's hand. "But mostly for taking us in—Gabriella and Elizabeth and me, I mean—and never making us feel like orphans."

The abbess smiled in the soft glow of a lantern on a table just beyond the window. "It has been a joy," she replied, with unusual openness, "though harrying at times. Do you think you and Gabriella are the only ones who love an adventure?"

Meg laughed. "We have been that, haven't we?"

"Aye," answered the abbess. "You most certainly have. Now, let us go inside and take our supper. I am certain you will have clearing and washing to do afterward, and you will need your nourishment."

The other nuns, abuzz over the sheriff's visit and the man who was the cause of it, fell silent the moment their mistress stepped over the refectory's threshold. Dame Alice kept her eyes downcast, a sure sign of guilt, and her cheeks were pink with defensive indignation.

Ignoring Dame Alice, Meg took her place beside Elizabeth, and murmured a quick prayer of thanks, even though the general company had, of course, already offered grace. Then, hungry from the events of the day, she reached eagerly for bread, and after that spooned a porridge made of dried peas into her bowl. All the while, through her lashes, she surveyed the large room, looking for the stranger.

"He isn't here," Elizabeth said, with some impatience. She could be annoyingly perceptive at times, and thick as a post at others. It was a matter of what happened to be most inconvenient for Meg at the time.

"No doubt he's hiding from the sheriff," Meg replied.

At this, there was a brief tension in the silence around them.

"You are insufferable," whispered Elizabeth. "Do you *like* being the subject of gossip?"

"Aye," said Meg merrily, for whatever the dangers, an adventure was an adventure, and they were rare enough at St. Swithin's. "I like it very much. But, alas, poor Elizabeth, I am your blood kin and you'll just have to put up with me."

Elizabeth's lips quivered in a smile, then promptly

straightened again. "I fear you're right," she said. "Will you wash, or dry?"

"I beg your pardon?"

"The bowls and trenchers and spoons," Elizabeth explained. "Have you forgotten the abbess's decree already? We must clear the tables after supper is through, and then scrub everything and set it out again, for breakfast. It is our punishment."

Ah, yes, Meg thought dismally, remembering. She despised such tasks. Furthermore, she misliked even the thought of breakfast—green porridge again, for a certainty, for there was more than plenty of the stuff, and Dame Helena, who did most of the cooking, was not one to waste the Lord's bounty. Washing and drying and laying of table, sweeping the floor and building up, then banking the fire. It was an endless cycle of sheer drudgery.

"I don't know how I shall manage to visit Adam," she fussed.

"I imagine that was the abbess's intent, at least in part," Elizabeth answered. "After all, she could not, being a sensible woman, have been hoping for repentance. Not from you, at least."

Meg gave her sister the benefit of an elbow. "You were in this, too, if you'll recall," she hissed. "You can stop trying to make it all my fault."

"But it *was* all your fault, wasn't it?" Elizabeth asked. "I wanted to tell Mother he was here in the first place, but you insisted on keeping him a secret—" Having emptied her bowl, she rose from the bench and began to go round the room, gathering up others like it, making a great awkward stack, like a mummer balancing plates at the fair.

The fair. Meg remembered then, and with crushing dejection, that she was forbidden to attend. She had looked forward to the event since mid-summer, the last time such a festivity had come to the village, and even saved a few coins, earned by reading aloud to one of the gentlewomen confined to the abbey, for a hair ribbon, or a piece of pretty paper.

Glumly, she finished her meal and looked around to see that most of the other diners had long since eaten and gone. She began gathering dirty dishes, keeping to one side of the room while Elizabeth studiously kept to the other.

They could not help meeting at the washtub in the kitchen, where they performed the labors to which they had been condemned.

Meg broke the silence first—'twas ever so, for she could not hold a grudge. The original grievance invariably slipped her mind, crowded out by plans, speculations, and private arguments.

"The sheriff wanted to take Adam away. Mother Mary Benedict refused."

"I know," Elizabeth said, scrubbing away at a kettle. She was always thorough in her work, where Meg liked to race through unpleasant tasks, finishing them as soon as possible. "Do you suppose he truly is a criminal?"

"Do you?" Meg countered, and gazed seriously at her sister.

Elizabeth considered the question for so long that Meg was tempted to duck her sister's head in the washtub before she finally made a reply. "No," she said. "There's kindness in him."

"They say there is kindness in the Black Prince, too," Meg reasoned, though she did not want to prove Elizabeth wrong. "And it doesn't stop him from swiping at Frenchmen's necks and bellies with his sword, does it?"

Elizabeth shivered. "That is different. It's war."

"Mayhap our stranger has been to war," Meg mused. "He says he remembers battles and blood."

Elizabeth made the sign of the cross with a skilled and soapy hand. "Heavens, Meg, do you think him good or not?"

"I'm merely trying to see both sides of the question," Meg answered. "Do you suppose he got enough to eat? He's a big man, and a body wants food to mend itself properly—"

"Don't you dare go near him, Meg Redclift," Elizabeth warned, flinging suds and water as she shook a finger in Meg's face. "We've got trouble enough because of you!"

Meg drew a deep breath and let it out slowly, to show that it wasn't only the saints who suffered. "I'm going to the fair," she said, in a confidential tone, making the decision only as she spoke the actual words. She was, as it happened, as horrified by the extent of her audacity as Elizabeth was, though she managed to hide the fact behind an air of defiance.

"You shall not!" Elizabeth breathed, standing stock-still, with a pot in one hand and a rag in the other.

"I shall," Meg corrected her. "I want to send a letter to Gabriella, and this may be the only chance I have before winter. There will be mummers there, and they move about, and will surely get to Cornwall."

"You are mad," Elizabeth hissed. "Suppose you are taken with plague, or carried off by men of dull conscience? Suppose—"

"Oh, be still," Meg interrupted. "None of those things will happen, and you know it. I shall send my letter by way of a mummer and come back to the abbey before anyone misses me."

Elizabeth was so vexed as to be speechless, though she glared at Meg.

"Mayhap I will bring you back a present," Meg said, in the vain hope of distracting her younger sister.

Alas, Elizabeth was no longer a child, and she was not swayed by temptation.

3

"You are called 'Gresham,' then?" Meg reflected, while her companion stood at the infirmary window, his back turned, gazing out upon the frosty, late-autumn night. Were it not for the abbey walls, she knew, with a certain sadness, the lights of Upper Gorse would be visible. Mayhap, even those of the village beyond. "The name suits you far better than Adam—I shall be glad to leave off calling you that."

He chuckled and turned to her. "You will surely be flogged, hanged, and burned if the abbess finds you here," he said. "Go—I would not have your disgrace and subsequent penance laid at my door."

Meg smiled. "I suppose I'm fortunate that Mother Mary Benedict does not employ harsh methods—were it so, I should have been long gone, with my twin, Gabriella."

At this reference he frowned darkly, and Meg feared, for the heartbeat of a hummingbird, that he might be one of those superstitious souls who believed that babes born together were a certain sign of perfidy on the wife's part. Meg herself had, as a small child, still living at Redclift Hall, been stigmatized by this fallacy, marked as illegitimate, for the late Sir Michael Redclift had been fair of coloring, as was his lady, and the firstborn of their twins, Gabriella. It was assumed, perforce, that Meg, with her chestnut hair and green eyes, must be the get of a second man.

The villagers had believed this, as had the servants, and, by her mother's own whispered admission, Sir Redclift himself. He had never forgiven his lady wife, who was surely as innocent as Meg herself had been, and after that had come home only to sire Elizabeth, probably in the midst of some black and lustful fury.

"What troubles you, milady?" Gresham asked, leaning back against the window frame now, his arms folded against his patched and poorly fitted jerkin. "You look as though you've just seen your own gravestone, and misliked what you read there."

Meg shook herself. Shook off the old and terrible feelings, the vague yet poignant memories of a handsome man, impossibly tall, cursing and raging, sodden with drink. Her father.

" 'Tis naught," she said, and went back to the subject of twins. She hoped he did not think she was illegitimate, by virtue of the double birth, though it galled her that she cared *that* for his opinion of her. "My sister was born first."

"What does she look like, this sister of yours?"

Meg felt a tightening in the pit of her stomach. *Dear God, Gabriella, send word! Tell me that you reached your new husband's side safely, and all is well with you.* "She is very beautiful—fair, with hazel eyes, and quite tall, for a woman."

Gresham appeared perplexed, to Meg's relief, rather than suspicious or condemning. "It snags in my mind, that name, that description. I see an image in my thoughts, a lady with her hair unbound, mounted upon a horse."

Meg took a step nearer the stranger without meaning to move at all. "Gabriella is renowned for refusing to wear a wimple or a veil," she said, and her pulse thrummed with excitement and frustration.

"Surely many women are reluctant to endure such constraint," Gresham reasoned, man-wise.

"Aye," Meg agreed, "but few enough dare to defy custom as Gabriella does." She clasped her hands together, and began to pace in her agitation. "Oh, I vow, if I do not find her soon, or at least learn that she is well, I shall go mad!"

"You love her so much as that?"

Meg stopped, amazed by the question. "Aye," she said again, softly. Wondrously. "They are flesh of my flesh and bone of my bone, my sisters. We've had no one but each other, all these years, and the bond between us is made of stuff stronger than steel. I will not—*cannot*—rest until I know that Gabriella is thriving."

"Suppose—" Gresham hesitated, took Meg's measure with his eyes, then went on. "Suppose your beloved sister is dead. What then?"

Meg swallowed, for the thought was so bitterly painful that it brought a swelling to her throat and a burning to her eyes. "Then we shall mourn her, Elizabeth and I. But we should know her fate, at least. God in heaven, we should *know.*"

He watched her in silence for a long while, her knight with no past and, if the sheriff had his way, no future, either. It almost seemed, in those few magical moments, that he had been conjured specifically to come to her aid. "At what cost will you make this search, Lady Meg?" he asked, his voice low and roughened by feelings she could not begin to discern. "Your virtue? For surely if you leave this place, as I suspect you are planning to do, you will not be taken back on the former terms. Mark me, milady—there are horrors beyond these walls that are quite beyond your innocent imaginings."

For all Gresham's sternness, it seemed to Meg that he was wavering, where his refusal to aid her in undertaking a search for Gabriella was concerned. She must be careful, she decided, not to upset the delicate balance. "I would gladly confront any hazard, my lord, if finding my sister were the result."

His eyes darkened in the dim light, and Meg was aware of him in other ways than as Gabriella's potential savior. Ways that quickened her breath and awakened places in her that had always slept, causing a pleasant hurt and a most enjoyable sense of desolation.

"Why do you call me 'my lord'?" he asked. "For all you know, I am a butcher or a dyer of cloth."

Meg sighed. "No, Gresham," she said. "You are the son of a noble house. Mayhap not the heir, but nonetheless, yours was a gentle birth. I see it in your eyes, and in your carriage."

He stood before her then, and she marveled, for she had not been aware that he'd moved at all. His hand, rough with the wielding of swords and other weapons, rose to curve lightly at her cheek.

"Oh, milady, I must be quit of this place, and soon. I am too happy here."

She stared up at him, shaken and far too confounded by the wonders his touch wrought in every part of her, temporal and physical, to speak or move away, as she should have done.

Gresham bent his head, and laid his mouth softly upon hers. Meg trembled violently, yet held her ground. By some unfamiliar and wholly delightful maneuvering, he shaped her lips with his own, and parted them, and then he was kissing her, and she raised her hands to his shoulders, gripping him there, lest she fall.

He slipped his arms around her waist, introduced his tongue. When Meg received it, moved by nature and a contentious will to spar with her own, he groaned and pulled her close against him.

Meg knew herself for a wanton and a harlot, by her own fevered response, and rejoiced even as another part of her mind cataloged the many and terrible consequences of discovery. After all, St. Swithin's was a convent.

It was Gresham who broke away, gasping once and looking as dazed as Meg felt. He spun away from her, muttering, thrusting a hand through his hair.

"Gresham Sedgewick," he growled, "you fool!"

They both stopped, stunned by what he'd said.

"Gresham *Sedgewick*," Meg repeated, as though reciting an unfamiliar spell, one that might bring down great good, or even greater wickedness, upon them both.

He turned back to face her, his eyes glittering. "I have that, if nothing else. A name. Leave me, milady, while I can still lay some faulty claim to honor."

"But—"

"Go. Now, or I fear I shall surely kiss you again."

Meg hurried away, overwhelmed by all he had introduced her to, within herself, jubilant and, at the same time, despondent, for Gresham's memory was plainly returning. While this was good news of the highest order, it also meant that he would soon be gone from this place.

Gone without Meg herself, if she wasn't very clever indeed.

She sat up late that night, a candle burning on the table beside her, working and reworking the proposed contents of Gabriella's letter in her head for a long time before setting words to the one precious scrap of parchment she possessed. Elizabeth had presented the paper to her at Christmastide, and the tiny vial of ink had been Gabriella's, as had the quill. That had come from the tail feathers of a crofter's goose, garnered at comical risk by Gabriella herself.

For a moment, Meg allowed herself to reflect upon certain memories, and the image of her twin sister, first chasing, and then being chased by that enormous and much offended bird, was bittersweet.

Presently, seeing that the tallow candle was burning low, and would soon gutter out, stranding her in the darkness, Meg dipped the carefully sharpened point of the quill and began to write.

Dearest and most cherished Sister. . . .

Two days later, on a crisp November morning, both Meg and Elizabeth watched from the abbey's crumbling bell tower as the fair assembled itself at the edge of Upper Gorse, like the brightly colored pieces of a church window, broken, then drawn together again, in merry, discordant order.

Meg did not realize the full extent of her consternation until she felt Elizabeth press her hand. Only then did she notice that there were tears standing in her eyes, so fierce was her longing to be away. The abbey walls, providing sanctuary to so many, including Sedgewick, were still as those of a prison to her.

Even if Gabriella had not been lost, she confessed to herself, 'twould yet be so, for she had a destiny far from where she stood, and was meant to become a person far greater than who she was. Only by venturing forth could she claim that portion due her.

"Please, Meg," Elizabeth pleaded, "do not defy the abbess's instructions. Stay here. There will be other fairs."

"Will there?" Meg asked, brushing one cheek with the back of her hand.

Elizabeth's smile was sad and soft. "I am your sister. Oft-times, methinks, I see the pattern of your schemes before you've finished weaving them. You aren't merely going to the fair, are you? You are leaving St. Swithin's, mayhap not tonight, or tomorrow, but very soon, and possibly forever."

Meg turned to face Elizabeth, gazing straight and deep into her eyes. "You cannot think I would go, for all time, and never lay eyes on you again? You, my wise and gentle and most beloved sister?"

"Gabriella has left us, and soon you will be away, too. What shall I do then? Oh, Meg, weren't you even going to bid me farewell?"

Meg touched her sister's hair. "Of course I was. Pray, goose, do not fret. We won't be parted long."

"I'll go with you," Elizabeth said quickly. "I know I've refused before, but—"

As much as Meg had wanted to hear those words, the many and varied threats of the outside world, so often heard and discarded as wild tales contrived to make women such as herself stay put, took on another hue entirely when Elizabeth was the one at risk. Certainly the child was safer at the abbey, tucked beneath the wing of the Church.

"No," Meg said, tenderly, but with firm conviction. "To see you taken with the plague, or lost to bandits upon the road—I could never bear it. For my own sake, as well as for yours, I cannot bring you." She considered, then brightened, and spoke with renewed enthusiasm. "But when I have found Gabriella, we shall send for you, and bring you to us. With a legion of soldiers to protect you along the road, and chaperons aplenty!"

Elizabeth's dark lashes were wet with tears. "You think me weak, a witless and timid child. Gabriella thought so, too. Well, I am six and ten—"

Meg embraced her sister, hastily and hard, for it would be easier to be parted from an arm or leg than from Elizabeth. And while it was true that she was the youngest and smallest, and Meg and Gabriella had ever been her self-appointed guardians, they knew that Elizabeth was the best of them all, in courage as well as in conscience.

"Timid and weak, is it?" Meg challenged, with a sniffly smile, holding her sister a little away to look at her. "Not you, Elizabeth Redclift. Never you."

"And yet you refuse to take me with you?"

"Not because you are in any way unsuited for the journey, but because you are infinitely precious. I should never forgive myself—and Gabriella would hate me, too—if ever I put you in the way of peril. The loss would be too great to bear, not only for us, but for many others."

Elizabeth snuffled. "You speak in riddles!" she accused, but she was no longer rigid, like a coil poised to spring. "Moreover, I have mind to tell Mother Mary Benedict what you're about, Margaret Redclift." At this, she looked fiery, full of tempest, her blue eyes storming.

"Come to the fair with me," Meg whispered, clasping her sister's hands. It was a reckless impulse, she knew, but suddenly she longed to share the experience with someone.

Elizabeth shook her head. "No," she said. "I mustn't."

"Why not?"

"Because I want to obey Mother Mary Benedict," Elizabeth answered, with prim resolve. "I might still tell, too. For your own good, of course."

Meg chuckled, tucked a dark curl back into Elizabeth's gray wimple, which, like her own, was a little askew. "You wouldn't betray me," she said. "You are too loyal by half."

"Would that I were not," Elizabeth murmured, drying her face. "Would that I were a traitor, with no scruples at all—"

Meg laughed and embraced her again and after that, no more was said of the forbidden fair or Meg's planned flight from St. Swithin's Abbey.

That same afternoon, while Mother Mary Benedict was taking her customary nap and Elizabeth was tending Dame Claudia, who had fallen ill after the midday meal, Meg let herself out of the abbey through a little-used postern gate, near the garden where she and Elizabeth had discovered Gresham Sedgewick. The letter for Gabriella, folded and stitched inside a pouch of cloth, was tucked into the pocket of her kirtle.

Having closed the gate behind her, Meg pulled the stifling wimple from her hair and hung it on the lantern hook, to be sure of finding it upon her return at eventide. She would set out upon her larger quest another, none-too-distant day; for the moment, she meant only to find a courier for her letter and take in the riotous sights, sounds and smells of the fair, to store up the images toward the dreary days of winter, soon upon them.

At suppertime, by her plan, Meg would have returned to St. Swithin's to take her place at the refectory table, face scrubbed, wimple in place. During vespers, she would be especially devout, and while she helped Elizabeth with their chores, she could share all that she had seen and heard in the village. Her sister could live the delights of the experience through her accounts.

For the moment, however, as she dashed across the frozen and well-gleaned fields of the abbey, hair trailing, Meg's mind was on mummers and trinkets and boys trying to win a prize by climbing a pole covered in swine grease.

Gresham had been poring over maps in the abbey's well-furnished library, hoping to come across a place he recognized, but the effort proved fruitless. Except for his name, a sense that he was very familiar with the city of London, and the fragmented memories of battle that had preyed on his mind from the first, he recollected nothing of any substance. His mind was full of ghosts, gray and vaporous, murmuring in voices he knew and yet could not assign to any single living person.

He was about to replace the tattered maps and go out to feed the chickens—about all he was good for, it seemed—when Elizabeth Redclift slipped shyly into the room, her wimple slipping to one side, her face alarmingly pale, her eyes enormous.

"I shouldn't have let her go!" she blurted.

Gresham felt his blood freeze in his veins. "What are you talking about?" he rasped, though he could have ventured a solid guess.

Elizabeth paced, growing more agitated with every step, and then sank onto one of the benches, her back to the long table where Gresham had been reading maps.

"Meg went to the fair," she confided. "The abbess specifically forbade—"

He took Elizabeth by her fragile shoulders and pulled her to her feet. "Meg left the abbey? *By herself?*"

Elizabeth bit down hard on her lower lip and nodded, her eyes filling with tears.

Gresham muttered a word unfitted to the presence of a lady and the interior of an abbey. "God's teeth," he ranted on. "She's really gone off on her own? She'd do better with a dragon than with most of the villains awaiting her out there!"

Elizabeth was by then so white that Gresham lowered her back onto the bench, fearing she would swoon. "If anything happens, it will be my fault," she murmured, in a voice so soft that he barely heard it. "Mine, and no one else's."

He had no time to comfort the child, though in his mind, the fault lay with Meg herself, whatever happened. After all, she hadn't been dragged or driven away, had she? She'd gone of her own foolish and reckless accord. "Elizabeth, is there a horse here, or a sword?" he asked.

She shook her head. "We had Zacheus, the white mule, but he went to Cornwall with Dame Johanna and Gabriella, at summer's end. And there is no sword at St. Swithin's because Dame Mary Benedict says truth and virtue are the only weapons we need." Elizabeth's lower lip wobbled, and a single tear slipped down her cheek. "I should gladly trade my expectation of heaven, just now, for a sharp-edged blade and a charger!"

Gresham forced a smile, bent and laid a brotherly kiss to the top of Elizabeth's head. If he was to walk to the village, unarmed, so be it. He would use whatever

came to hand for purposes of defense, and hope he
didn't encounter the sheriff or any of his men before he
found Meg.

"I'll bring her back," he vowed, and meant it. "And you
haven't told anyone else?"

Elizabeth shook her head. "No, my lord," she replied,
in a breathless rush. "What shall I do?"

"Just stay here, at the abbey. I require your sacred
promise on that, Elizabeth, for I shall have all I can do to
find one sister, let alone two."

"I promise," Elizabeth answered. "Please—hurry."

Leaving the abbey by the rear gate, mayhap a quarter
of an hour later, Gresham found a wimple hung carefully
from a lantern hook in the wall. Had the circumstances
been less urgent than they were, he might have been
amused that Meg had shed the veil the moment she set
foot outside the nunnery. He imagined that, had she her
druthers, she would have refused to wear it altogether, as
her missing sister had done.

Once again, amid all his tension, it niggled at Gresham,
a recollection just beyond his grasp. A woman's face and
form. *Gabriella.*

He crossed the field as quickly as he could, feeling as
exposed as a fat rabbit wandering onto an archery range.
He'd heard about the sheriff's recent visit to the abbey
from Meg, in exhaustive detail, and he needed no more
to convince him that the man was trouble, whether he,
Gresham, was guilty of a crime or not.

In the narrow wood beyond the rows of furrowed
ground, fortune turned, however fleetingly, in Gresham's
favor. He found a sturdy branch, hanging low from an oak
tree, and broke if off with a clean snap. It would serve as

a rod, as well as a staff, and was marginally better than nothing at all.

The sheriff's men, if they were abroad and looking for him, would naturally have blades, as well as bows. He hoped they were occupied elsewhere, but the grim likelihood was that at least some of them would be at the fair, either to keep the peace or to enjoy the attractions.

At the edge of the village, a woman tried to sell Gresham a chicken, squirming and squawking in her arms. With her was a gangling boy, no scholar he, wearing a ragged hood, which Gresham much coveted, for it would have made a semblance of a disguise. Alas, he had naught to trade and wasn't desperate enough to wrest it from the lad, even if he'd been foolhardy enough to incur the inevitable ruckus.

He shook off the pleas of the chicken woman and proceeded cautiously toward the noise and stink and spectacle of the fair itself, watching always for sheriff's men and for Meg.

Careful though he was, he was noticed, and remarked upon behind grubby hands. He was a stranger in and around the village and, by now, everyone must know that he'd been living at the abbey, and availing himself of the protection of the Church.

Meg's voice reached him from the other side of a cart, where a merchant's wife sold eel pies and other delicacies. Gresham's stomach rumbled with hunger, while every other part of him tensed with irritation and relief.

"I tell you, that is our mule," Meg piped, in plain and rising irritation. "His name is Enoch, and he is the brother of Zacheus. He wandered away from the abbey months ago. See how he eats from my hand—he remembers me!"

The reply was a defiant mutter; Gresham could not make out the words.

"Where did you get him?" Meg pressed. "Did you find him upon the road? Or mayhap you untied him from his stall in the first place?" She paused, waited. Her voice was a note higher in pitch when she went on. "Nothing to say, then? Well, we'll see if you won't speak more freely to the sheriff!"

At this threat, Gresham bolted around the pie cart and caught Meg by the arm to stay her from summoning the law.

She looked at him in surprise at first, and then in wary suspicion.

The boy holding the mule's halter gaped at Gresham, dropped the reins, and turned to make a high-stepping dash for the wood. Gresham, cursing at the attention drawn, sprinted after him, for while he did not remember the lad, it would have been obvious to an idiot that the lad remembered *him.*

He caught the bulky, spot-faced boy in a copse of birch trees, and slammed him to the ground with such force that the wrongful possessor of St. Swithin's erstwhile misplaced mule lost his wind, and could only gasp.

Gresham held his walking stick across the lad's throat, with just enough pressure to let his captive know he would not be gaining his feet anytime soon.

"Where did you get the mule?" Gresham demanded. He was aware that Meg had come after him, leading the great white beast, but blessedly the others seemed to have taken no further interest in the incident, being more interested in the fair.

The boy spat, and Gresham got him by the ties of his breeches, giving a powerful upward wrench.

"I found him," the lad said, after an involuntary whimper.

"And why did you run from me just now?"

"It weren't me what hit you. I swear it weren't me."

"But you know who did hit me, don't you?"

Silence.

Gresham rolled the walking stick the length of the boy's neck, from chin to collarbone. "Tell me."

The lad looked at Meg with bulging, beseeching eyes. " 'Twas the nun. She picked up a rock and struck you from behind and stole your horse. I had no part in it, I swear—"

Pictures flickered in Gresham's head—there *had* been a nun. And this boy. They'd been traveling together, the three of them, bound he knew not where, on business he could not recall. The frustration surged into his throat like bile.

"You had a horse," he said, rough-voiced, and to his credit the boy knew the tone for the warning it was.

"Aye, but he ran off, in the fracas. I never saw him again!"

"My sister," Meg said, kneeling in the frost-crackly leaves beside the captive. "You must know something of my sister. Gabriella." It was the mention of the stone-wielding nun, no doubt, that caused her to suspect.

The boy spat again, red in the face. "Chalstrey's whore, that's all she is, and I'll say no more. Take your bloody mule and leave me in peace, or I'll be the one to fetch the sheriff."

Gresham drew back, no longer interested in the whelp he'd pursued into the woods. He was looking at Meg, whose eyes were luminous with tears of outrage.

The rascal scrambled to his feet, but before he could get away, Meg had snatched the walking stick from Gresham's hands and leaped up, wielding it ably, fury made in the form of a woman.

"You lie," she cried, ready to strike. "You dare to speak so of my sister? My sister, worth a hundred such wretches as you?"

Gresham admired Meg for a while before stepping in and taking the stick gently from her hands. The boy fled, away from the fair rather than toward it, and Meg, fierce until that moment, suddenly began to sob. No superficial grief, this—her cries came from the secret regions of her soul, places unknown and unmapped.

He gathered her against him, broken by her breaking.

"Meg," Gresham murmured. "Meg, sweeting. Pray, do not weep so—I cannot endure it."

Nearby, the mule brayed and then raised his great ugly head to nibble at the few leaves still clinging to a tree branch.

Meg looked up at Gresham, awash in sorrow, and yet her immeasurable courage was visible still, like the flame of a candle burning behind a drapery of fine lace.

"Gabriella is no whore," she said.

Gresham smoothed Meg's wild, beautiful hair back from her face. Their breaths mingled between them, white and vaporous in the cold air. "Of course she isn't."

"This Chalstrey—who is he?"

An infinite sadness swept through Gresham, and he kissed Meg's forehead. "I know not," he answered. "But we'll find him, you and I, and we'll find your sister, if we have to ride this villainous mule from one end of England to the other in the doing."

She was very still for a long moment, gazing up at him, searching his face with those wondrous eyes. "You speak true?" she asked, presently, her voice gone soft with hope and the dread of disappointment. "A pox on you if you don't, for a false promise is the cruelest treachery of all—"

He could not help but touch her, look upon her, hold her. What spell had she worked, to make a lunatic's crusade sound plausible?

"My promise is true, my lady," he heard himself say. "Now, come—we'll make for the abbey—you, me and the mule—and mayhap amid the joys of reunion, no one will notice that we two were ever gone."

She smiled at last and, like a majestic sunrise, it was worth all Gresham had done and pledged to do to see it. "The dames of St. Swithin's will indeed be glad to see Enoch again," she said, glancing fondly at the beast. "Despite his heathen ways."

Gresham gathered the mule's trailing reins and swung easily onto its back. Then, reaching down, he brought Meg up before him, and felt only a little light-headed at the effort. With supper, a draught of the abbess's secret store of sherry, and a good night's sleep, he would be restored.

The morning was soon enough, surely, to lay plans for Meg's quest.

"We should begin our search in London-town, methinks," Meg said brightly, as he urged the none-too-malleable mule toward the abbey. In her quicksilver mind, the journey was already half made, the prize half won. "It is on the way to Cornwall and surely someone there will have heard of you, and of Gabriella—"

He smiled, content to listen to her chatter. "Aye," he said, to encourage her.

She turned a little, to look into his face. "I did manage to send my letter," she told him.

"Letter?"

"To Gabriella. I gave it to a mummer—he looked

rather like you, as it happens. That's what made me remember the letter. The resemblance, I mean."

Gresham frowned, intrigued and not a little alarmed.
"A man who looked like me?"

"Aye," Meg said, with a nod. "Blue eyes, straw-colored
hair. But he isn't half so handsome as you are."

He looked about them, profoundly uneasy. They were
well away from the village; he had recovered Meg and,
indirectly, the mule, which he had not known was missing. None of which meant they couldn't be set upon by
the sheriff's men at any moment. "Tell me more about
this man."

"There is naught to tell," Meg answered, giving a little
sigh and turning to face forward again. "I told him of
Gabriella's husband, in Cornwall, and he promised to de-
liver the letter if he could. They will journey there in the
spring, he and his troupe."

Gresham considered the sheriff's visit to the abbey a
few nights past, in search of a criminal. The connection
was wholly instinctive, but he made it anyway; if it proved
wrong, he could ascribe the misjudgment to the blow to
his head.

He wondered at the mummer's boldness, plying his
trade at a village fair, and concluded that the man was
safe, and knew it well. The sheriff believed his prey had
taken sanctuary within St. Swithin's Abbey, and that conviction had blinded him to other possibilities. From
there, his thoughts strayed to the quest he had promised
to undertake with Meg. It was an outlandish and inherently dangerous idea, traveling to Cornwall—he began to
cast about mentally for a way to get out of the proposition.

They were in the middle of the same field they had

both crossed earlier, though separately, when Gresham heard a horseman behind them, and looked back to see a rider coming up fast from the right.

Sweet *Jesu*—the man would be upon them in a matter of moments.

With a curse, Gresham spurred the mule to a braying, kicking run, and had barely gotten the animal and, thus, himself and Meg, through the abbey's rear gate and slammed it behind them in time to evade capture.

The sheriff's man shouted from without, and pounded hard at the thick wooden gate, probably with the hilt of a dagger.

Exhilarated by the narrow escape, Gresham smiled to himself. He felt stronger for having faced even a small challenge, and prevailing, and concluded that, whatever his identity, he was the sort who relished a skirmish. An alliance with Meg Redclift, he reflected wryly, was sure to stir his memory as well as his blood.

4

The return of Enoch the mule was the cause of great rejoicing within the ancient and august walls of St. Swithin's, and Gresham was right: his absence, not to mention Meg's forbidden sojourn to the fair, garnered little notice. Only Elizabeth offered an immediate comment, saying haughtily that she might not have been so upset by her sister's disappearance, if she'd known she was only going to fetch back a lost mule. As for Mother Mary Benedict, well, she did seem to watch Meg more carefully in subsequent days, each of which was more bitterly cold than the one before it, but she bided her time where a reprimand was concerned.

The abbess had greater concerns, as it happened, for Dame Claudia's ailment proved more serious than anyone had first thought. Indeed, the aged nun had been confined to an out-of-the-way cell, with just Elizabeth and the abbess herself to attend her. There were whispers of fever, of delirium, and even hints of plague. Elizabeth was closemouthed and harried. She rarely slept through the night, and Meg practically had to force her sister to eat.

Elizabeth grew more fretful, and more fragile, by the hour, hurrying to and from that far-off room. Finally, on the third day following the triumphant return of Enoch, she abandoned all pretense of sharing the small chamber she and Meg and Gabriella had lived in since their arrival at St. Swithin's some seven years back.

Meg contrived to get her sister apart, though only after repeated and strenuous efforts, and finally cornered her in the dooryard of the buttery, where the girl waited impatiently for a nun to ladle goat's milk from a crock and into a ewer. When Elizabeth turned to leave, clasping the vessel in both hands, obviously bent on hurrying back to the sickroom, Meg stepped into her path.

Elizabeth seemed startled. Her skin was transparent as a babe's, and blue veins were faintly visible at the base of her throat. She took a hasty step back. "Don't touch me, Meg," she said, in a voice as old as eternity itself. "And pray, do not come any nearer."

Meg folded her arms. "What terrible secret are you keeping, Elizabeth?" *Dear God,* she thought, *don't let the rumors be true. Don't let there be plague at St. Swithin's.*

"Be away, Meg," Elizabeth said, speaking firmly this time, and started to edge past her sister. "Flee, whilst you still can. Take Lord Sedgewick with you and *get away.*"

So it *was* plague that had struck down poor Dame Claudia. The reality, quite another thing from the mere suspicion she'd entertained earlier, struck Meg as painfully as a volley of frozen snowballs. Why had she not guessed, afore now? The secrecy, the prompt, stringently enforced isolation of the ailing nun, when normally she would have had a stream of visitors, saying prayers, proffering the last hardy wildflowers of the year, reading aloud from Holy Scripture . . .

"Mother of God," she murmured, making the sign of the cross. Bile surged into the back of her throat, searing as it passed, and cold fear seized her very soul. "You're certain there's no mistake?"

Elizabeth flushed, and the effect was alarming, in so pale a complexion. "Be still," she commanded, with more spirit than Meg had ever seen her show before. "We are not absolutely certain, Mother Mary Benedict and I. The plague usually brings a quick death, however—uncomfortable—it might be. Dame Claudia has lingered past the expected time."

"And you have been attending her, all this while." Meg was dizzy with horror; she wanted to lay hands to Elizabeth, drag her away.

Elizabeth did not make a reply. None was necessary.

"Come," Meg pleaded. "We shall flee now, today—you and I and Gresham—"

"It is too late," Elizabeth said quietly. "And besides, I would not leave Dame Claudia to perish alone. The abbess has other duties, and cannot keep a proper vigil, but I can. And I *will,* Meg, so save your precious breath and leave this place at once."

Meg's fury was made of grief and fear; she struggled in it like a mermaid hopelessly tangled in a fisherman's net. She tried to grasp Elizabeth's arm and, once again, Elizabeth evaded her.

"God's breath, Sister, come away!" Meg cried.

Elizabeth simply shook her head.

"Margaret." The voice was Dame Mary Benedict's; she stood at a distance of several yards. "Heed your sister's words. Take Enoch, and the gold in this pouch, and put St. Swithin's behind you without delay."

The pouch landed at Meg's feet with a solid, chinking sound. The tune might have been merry at any other time; now it was a dirge. Not just for Dame Claudia, but mayhap for Elizabeth, too. And for so many others they had come to care about.

Meg could not move, could not speak. If she did, she might begin screaming, ne'er to cease.

Elizabeth and Mother Mary Benedict took advantage of the moment and hurried away, together. Elizabeth looked back, her eyes full of pleading. *Go*, she urged soundlessly.

Meg watched, still stricken, as they went from her sight, that beloved pair, and then, when she had begun to breathe again, stooped to retrieve the small bag of gold. She found Gresham in the otherwise empty stables, currying Enoch, with whom he had evidently established some sort of prickly alliance. Like his missing brother, Zacheus, Enoch was an unworthy creature with no apparent redemptive qualities.

"Jupiter and Zeus, what is it?" Gresham gasped, upon taking in Meg's expression and surely dismal countenance.

She held out the weighty pouch, and faltered several times before she managed a coherent reply. "Plague," she said at last. "It would seem that Dame Claudia has been taken with plague, and Elizabeth is her nurse. My own Elizabeth—" Meg swayed slightly then, and Gresham caught her swiftly by the upper arms, supporting her in his grip until she could go on. "Mother Mary Benedict wants us to leave, you and me, taking Enoch and—and this gold."

"What of the others?" Gresham asked, in a baffled whisper. "The nuns, the schoolgirls and boarders?"

"I do not know," Meg said numbly. "Mayhap they've

been kept far enough from the sickroom to avoid conta-
gion. As for Elizabeth and Mother Mary Benedict themselves—"

Gresham put the gold back into Meg's hands and
folded her fingers round it. "Gather your things," he said,
"and make haste at it. As soon as the sun sets, we will
leave."

She stared at him. "But Elizabeth is here—"

"Aye, and cannot come away," Gresham reasoned gently. "We do her no good by staying, Lady Meg, but much
can be achieved by going. Have you forgotten the search
for Gabriella?"

Meg shook her head, biting down hard on her lower
lip in an effort to stay a passion of weeping. "Nay. I am
torn, my lord, as though caught in a thicket. Leave, and
mayhap save one sister. Stay, and save another."

"Even you," Gresham said quietly, "cannot save Elizabeth, if the plague has got her. We must trust to the Holy
Mother and all the saints and angels and do what is before us to do."

Glumly, her throat so thickened that, once again, she
couldn't speak, Meg nodded. She tucked the pouch into
the pocket of her cloak and turned away.

In the familiar cell, with its three empty cots to remind
her of other times, of nights spent giggling in the darkness, spinning all manner of tales, plotting great and marvelous schemes, Meg knew a side of solitude that she had
never encountered before.

She had few possessions—a prayer book, a second
gown and kirtle, the quill pen and vial of ink. Thereby, it
took but little time to tie them up in a bundle.

Having done so, Meg simply sat on the edge of her
cot, as unmoving as one in a trance, her few things,

bound in a wimple Gabriella had left behind, resting on her lap.

She did not go to supper, and only when the vespers bells sounded did she stir from her grim enchantment, rise to her feet and, after one last look about her, walk out of the small cocoon that had kept them all safe—her and Elizabeth and Gabriella—for so long.

She found Gresham waiting, as planned, by the postern gate. He had got a cloak from somewhere, with a hood that threw shadows across his face, and Enoch, though unsaddled, had been fitted with a halter.

Meg looked back once, her heart pounding in her throat, then hurried forward over the rough, uneven ground, and allowed Gresham to lift her onto the animal's back. He swung deftly up behind her, reached around her to take the reins, and she named herself wayward, for even in her state of silent panic, the feel of Gresham's embrace lent a peculiar comfort.

The gate stood open before them. Freedom, as Meg had always yearned for it.

It was the circumstances she had not bargained for.

"Courage, my lady," Gresham said in a soft voice, brushing close by her ear. "Fix your thoughts upon your hopes, not your fears, and look forward, not back."

Meg nodded, and in that instant some great event took place within the boundaries of her soul, a joyful, cataclysmic occurrence of such mystery and significance as to confound her utterly. While she was yet afraid, and sorrowing, Meg was also vastly altered, a far different creature than she'd been just moments before.

She looked back at Gresham, to see if he'd felt a change as well, but twilight had settled over the land, a purple mist shot through with black, and she could not make out his expression, only the patrician cast of his features.

Meg remembered that he was a stranger, this man who had transformed her into someone else, probably without knowing he'd done so, and would surely change her further. Yet with all he'd wrought, he was not only a puzzle to her, but to himself.

A chill spilled down Meg's spine, like a trickle of well water, and words Mother Mary Benedict had often said to her came back, as such words will, when they most nettle. *Have a care what petitions you put to heaven, Margaret Redclift. God hears every one, and He oft grants a foolish wish, that a lesson may be learnt.*

"Surely we cannot sleep in a tree!" Meg protested, when, deep in a wood and far from the abbey, Gresham drew up the mule beneath an aged oak and made his pronouncement. They had been riding for hours, and the sun had long since gone.

"Alas, my lady," Gresham replied. "We can and we shall." He got down and lifted Meg after him. "There isn't an inn for miles around and I wouldn't risk taking a room in a public house even if there were."

"But what of supper?" Meg inquired. A stream whispered somewhere nearby, amongst scraggly, leafless trees that seemed to claw at the sky; Gresham set off toward the water, leading a snuffling Enoch behind him.

"There are sweet potatoes in my bag," Gresham called back. "Have some."

Sweet potatoes? Somehow, Meg had envisioned the life of adventure as something different from sleeping in trees, like the African apes she'd heard tales about, and supping on raw tubers. She'd imagined Gypsy camps, brimming with music and firelight . . .

He returned some minutes later, her practical knight, again leading the mule. After hobbling Enoch at the base of the tree, Gresham handed Meg up to the first large branch, only some fifteen hands above the ground.

"Climb as high as you can," he said. "I'll be just behind you, with the bundles. Tomorrow, my lady, we buy a sword."

"Can we not have a fire?" Meg complained, though she did as Gresham bade her, albeit awkwardly, and climbed. It was Gabriella who inclined toward such feats, not Meg. "It is cold."

"No," Gresham answered patiently, prodding her higher when she would have nested on a likely-looking branch, "we cannot have a fire. Not unless you wish to bestow the makings of our humble supper—along with the gold, the mule, my neck and your virtue—upon the nearest band of cutthroats."

"You're afraid?" Meg demanded, mayhap taunting him just a little, dragging herself upward and ever upward through the brittle, naked branches. The height was making her head swim as it was—would the man never be satisfied that she had gone far enough?

"No, my lady, I am not afraid," Gresham replied, unperturbed. "Only practical."

At last he allowed her to settle in the curve where a giant limb attached itself to the tree's trunk. Far below, Enoch foraged in the leaves, a sharp carpet on the surface and a soft, rotting one beneath. An owl called somewhere, and the moon rose against a star-spilled sky, eerily majestic and almost close enough to touch. "What sort of adventurer are you?" Meg jibed.

She was not trying to be contentious, but merely attempting—without much success, as it happened—to distract herself from the danger Elizabeth was in, back at St. Swithin's, and she guessed that Gresham knew it.

"The sort who wants to live long enough to find out who he is," he answered mildly, rooting through his bundle for the promised potatoes and a small, sharp knife, probably stolen from the abbey's kitchen. He cut the potatoes into neat sticks, gave Meg her share, and chewed thoughtfully upon his own. "Mayhap I have a comely wife," he mused, and because he had thrust back his hood, Meg saw the laughter hiding in his eyes. "I hope she's fat, with a merry nature, and no teeth."

"No teeth?"

Gresham chuckled. "Never mind," he said, and took another potato stick.

"Why should she be fat, then?"

"To keep me warm, of a winter's night."

Meg blushed heartily, for she had heard the widows speak of their husbands often enough and she understood the reference. She was still perplexed, however, that a man so finely made should say he wanted a toothless wife, even in jest.

"I guess I wouldn't do, then," she ventured to remark, with a little sniff.

Gresham's eyes danced. "Nay, my lady," he agreed. "You haven't the merry nature."

Meg suffered an incomprehensible yen to be fat and toothless, but it passed quickly. "You are a mystery," she said, without admiration.

Gresham chuckled and fed her a bit of potato. "Eat," he said.

Meg obeyed, though not enthusiastically. "I never

thought I should miss Dame Alice's interminable dried pea porridge," she said. "But I do."

"I vow," Gresham said, trying to sound serious but plainly teasing, "if it weren't for the plague, I should take you back and dump you at the gate."

"Why?" Meg asked, offended. Not daring to pursue the thought of the plague too far into reason, for she might find Elizabeth at its end, wasted and dying. Or already gone.

"Because you are no fit traveler," he replied, chewing. "You have done nothing but complain ever since we stopped to take our rest. I've a good mind, in fact, to climb down and pass the night with the mule—he's more congenial than you, I'll warrant."

"He has teeth," Meg said.

At this, Gresham gave a low shout of laughter, and Meg was more confused than ever.

Much later, and after considerable shifting about, she dozed, leaning back against Gresham's chest, wrapped with him in his cloak, as well as her own, held tight in his arms. He rested his chin lightly on the top of her head and listened to the snaps and murmurs and calls of the night.

In the privacy of his mind, he repeated what he knew of himself—his name—over and over, like some unholy litany, or the words of a spell, hoping to woo other memories up out of the dark mire.

Nothing came to him and, not for the first time, Gresham wondered if he wasn't deliberately holding his past at bay, on some level. Were there things he didn't want—couldn't bear—to remember?

Mayhap the sheriff was right to hunt him; he could be a murderer, a thief. God knew, he was no stranger to vio-

lence and death. He'd seen enough blood in his dreams
to know that.

He might well be married, for he was in his mid-thirties
by all calculations, and therefore of an age to be long settled in matrimony. Was he the husband of a woman who
watched for his return, who prayed and burned candles
for the salvation of his soul? Or—and this was not unlikely,
either—one who cursed him, and even wished him dead?

Worse still, there might be children. And mayhap he
loved their mother, this wife he could not recall, with all
the means of his heart and soul. If that were so, and he
should be awakened to the fact, he would find himself in
the hopeless predicament of caring deeply for two women.

The presence of the plague at St. Swithin's had forced
him to undertake this journey with Meg, and now he
wondered if fate had played a part in the drama.

He had not allowed himself, until that moment, when
he was too weary to resist the flood of impressions, to
consider too closely the longings that Meg Redclift
roused in him. He rested his head against the rough bark
of the tree in which they'd taken refuge, letting it all wash
over him—the throaty way Meg laughed. The light in her
eyes, a light bright enough to lead a wanderer home over
dark roads. The scent of her, faintly spicy, but fresh, too,
like the purest water, bubbling from some secret spring.

Gresham closed his eyes against the onslaught, as he
might to the lancing of an infected wound, but the pain of
the prospect of having to walk away from this woman still
made him flinch inside. He felt himself slipping, losing
ground emotionally, mayhap even falling in love, though
surely it was too soon for that. He yearned to bed this
fiery woman, and if he had to take her to wife to do that,
he was willing.

In the circumstances, both approaches were forbidden by every definition of integrity, and yet he did not know how long he could go on wanting her the way he did, with naught done to ease him. He would have found broken bones easier to bear than this terrible, ceaseless, wonderful need.

Meg stirred, made a soft sound in her sleep, and Gresham felt himself harden as she wriggled against him, fitful in her shallow, restless slumber. Beneath the insides of his forearms, her small, firm breasts pressed, the hidden nipples leaving brands on his flesh, despite the layers of cloth between.

Gresham tilted his head back and groaned, trying to confine the sound to his throat. Meg was safe this night— his suffering be damned—but what about the next night, and the night after that? They could not go on sleeping in trees forever—there were bound to be haylofts, where the cold itself would force them together, and inns, where no lady dared take a room by herself.

"What is that?" Meg asked, yawning and a little petulant.

The question startled him so that he nearly fell out of the tree, taking her with him. "What is what?" he demanded. Though he knew precisely what she was inquiring about, God help him. He was as hard as an ax head, and he sorely wished that Meg might be transformed, if only for an hour's time, from a lady of noble birth to a tavern wench.

"That," she said, and wriggled against him.

He gasped. An old agony, fierce and sweet, jolted through him. "I believe you know full well," he managed, somewhat surly in his chagrin. "For all your purported innocence."

She looked up at him with eyes mischievous and sparkling a moment before, but now solemn, and he nearly tumbled into their shadowy emerald depths. "Will you hold me very tightly?" she whispered. "I am afraid." She uttered these last words as if making a confession of dire sin. "Gabriella and Elizabeth—they're all I have. I don't know what I'll do—what I'll be—without them."

He tightened his embrace, careful not to crush her, and let his lips pass lightly across her temple. There was nothing to say, so he simply listened.

She went on haltingly. "Gabriella and I look nothing alike," she sniffled, "but we are twins, and sometimes I truly think we have just one soul between us. That's— that's how I know something must have gone wrong after she left St. Swithin's to marry Sir Avendall—I felt it. And Elizabeth—she's the baby—we've always looked after her, Gabriella and I, and now that's impossible—"

He stroked her back. Listened.

She laid her forehead against his shoulder, and a sob rose from within her, quivering along her backbone before coming out in a burst.

He kissed the top of her head, and waited.

Dame Claudia expired quietly, somewhere in the depths of the night, beatific even in the profundity of her illness. That it was the plague that had taken her, Elizabeth could not doubt, for all the disparities between her symptoms and what was known of that most feared malady.

She prayed over the tiny, fragile woman, closed the staring eyes, and straightened the blankets. Then, too exhausted to weep, Elizabeth went to the door and tapped at it, to awaken the postulant keeping watch in the narrow corridor beyond.

"Fetch the abbess," Elizabeth commanded, through the thick timber panel, leaning against it for a few moments in unutterable weariness. "Hurry, but rouse no one else."

The postulant called back a soft assent and then there was no more sound.

Elizabeth pushed away from the door, forced herself to pace, to move about. Not to fold to the floor in a blathering heap of terror and dismay.

Presently, the abbess called to her from the passage, and she raised the bar on the door to admit Mother Mary Benedict.

The abbess moved to the old nun's bedside to gaze down upon that serene and waxen face. Dame Claudia looked as blissful as if the angels she had long expected had truly come to take her home; though she had suffered mightily, she had somehow transcended that, even during the worst hours of the struggle.

"When did she pass over?" Mother Mary Benedict asked.

"Just a few minutes ago. I sent for you straightaway." Elizabeth longed to sit down, for her knees had turned soft with fatigue, but she dared not, lest she find it impossible to rise again.

Mother Mary Benedict smoothed the blanket's edge with a tender gesture. "Dame Claudia came to this abbey when she was but seven years old. Her mother brought her—a great lady she was, with a title and lands of her own, or so went the tale—and said the lass would give her no peace for wanting to join us here. I came a year later—I was six, recently orphaned, and most unwilling, and Dame Claudia—only eight, remember—immediately befriended me. It was she who showed me the kindness and mercy of Christ. She who helped me to know that I wanted to be His bride, and His alone."

Elizabeth said nothing; no answer was needed or wanted.

"It is not for you, child," the abbess said, meeting Elizabeth's blurred gaze. "The life we know here, I mean."

Elizabeth raised her chin. Unlike Meg and Gabriella, she had no wish to go abroad, beyond the abbey walls, even now that the plague had found them, here in this place she loved. Still, she ached for the company of her sisters and sometimes thought she would go mad, worrying about them. "How can you be so certain that I am not fitted to take the veil?"

"There are signs, my dear, and I have had many, many years to learn to read them. Now, go, I pray you, and sleep. Leave Dame Claudia and me alone to say our farewells."

"But I have slept here these past nights," she protested, indicating the other cot with a gesture.

"No longer. Return to your room."

Elizabeth inclined her head in acquiescence and started toward the door.

"Elizabeth?"

She stopped, turned to look at Mother Mary Benedict, who suddenly seemed older, smaller, and somewhat less certain of herself and her convictions.

"Aye?"

"There will be others who follow our friend Dame Claudia along this path."

Elizabeth glanced at the small form lying covered upon the cot. The smell of death was suddenly pervasive, like an evil incense in the room, fairly choking her, clinging to her garments and her hair. "Aye," she said again, and went out.

By morning, another nun had fallen ill, and two children were brought from the village, wrapped in scanty rags that passed for blankets, burning with fever and crying out, when they could, in pitiful, strangling wails. Their tongues were swollen, and bruiselike patches marked their skin—the discoloration Dame Claudia had, mayhap because of her piety, been spared.

The abbey was further segregated, the sick from the well. Those who would serve from those who would hide.

Some of the nuns and one or two of the inmates came forward to offer their help, while others, the unwanted mothers and daughters, sisters and aunts, of the gentry, fled into the countryside. Even Mother Mary Benedict, that consummate diplomat, could not persuade them to weigh the perils without against those within, and stay.

Fools, Elizabeth thought, with an unusual lack of compassion. They would spread the plague if they had it already, or manage to come down with it if they didn't. Some of them, if they were fortunate, would find their way back, most likely in litters and the carts of charitable crofters.

She would not allow herself to think of Meg, to imagine these same frightful symptoms in her sister. As for Gabriella, well, God willing, she was far from this place, and better off for the distance, no matter what else she may be forced to endure.

By the abbess's order, the refectory became a hospital and the cots, carried there from the patients' own cells, multiplied until one could barely pass between them.

After a while, Elizabeth left off measuring time, or even attempting to discern day from night. She simply kept moving among the sick and dying, giving them spoonfuls of water, bathing their fevered heads, promising them with a brazen lack of theological certitude that they needn't fear death. The Virgin would be waiting to receive them, she said, in robes of such a blue that it hurt the eyes to see it. Her hair was shaped from strands of sunshine, she told them, and the summer sky had been fashioned to match her eyes. Her nature was mercy, her voice was music. A wave of her hand brought flowers popping out of the ground, in all the colors of the rainbow, and still others that belonged only to heaven.

After a while, they began to clutch at Elizabeth as she passed, mistaking her for the Holy Mother, imploring her to intercede for them.

She assured them all that Heaven was theirs. Even Tud Treeby, the village reprobate, who went wandering every year when harvesttime came, and only returned when the grain was in and the ale flowed freely in celebration. Who beat his wife and cheated anyone who had commerce with him.

And there were others, too. Be their sins large or small, heinous or petty, Elizabeth granted absolution to them all. If there were consequences for this presumption, she would take them.

Some of the stricken recovered, and went away, but for every one that left St. Swithin's, three more passed him at the gate, coming in. The blacksmith made a roaring and horrible fire, behind the farthest outbuilding, and fed it, night and day, with the bodies of the lost. The stench of the smoke crept into every nook and crevice of the abbey, and followed Elizabeth even into sleep, and she was certain that this place was Hell.

She fully expected to perish, and only hoped it would not happen too soon, before her work was through. On the other hand, what peace, what sweet oblivion death would bring.

Provided, of course, that she was wrong in her theory

that happiness was heaven, and suffering was hell, and both were realms of earth.

After that first night, traveling was easier, for Meg, at least.

She didn't mind eating tubers and roots—they might have had rabbits, but Gresham wouldn't allow it, even if he'd been willing to light a fire, saying he'd seen too many of the poor creatures scattered across the ground dead, with blood oozing from their ears and snouts. According to him, that was reason enough to believe they carried the plague, and Meg made no argument.

Not about that, at least.

They acquired a sword, in a village called Dilburn, along with blankets, a round of cheese, new wine, and some brown bread to sustain them.

At night, as Gresham had predicted, they slept huddled together, shivering, in haylofts and caves and the barns of inns. Meg would have given five years of her life for a simple fire, but he would have none of that, either. Fires attracted attention, and attention could be disastrous.

A full week had passed when they came, at last, upon an isolated crofter's hut, standing empty in the gathering, icy thickness of twilight.

5

The hut was long abandoned; when Meg stepped over the threshold, she heard the hasty, rustling flight of rats, and there was evidence that an owl or some other large bird had once nested in the soot-blackened rafters. For all of that, the weather was exceeding cold that evening, the sky was burdened with snow, and there was a fire pit in the center of the floor, beckoning, promising utter luxury.

Meg looked at it with a longing she could not disguise. She regretted sobbing in Gresham's arms that first night after they'd fled the abbey, and had been trying, ever since, to prove herself able and competent.

Gresham, for his part, seemed restive, like a hermit expecting guests. He said little, but brought their bundles inside, and kept going to the single window, which was high and narrow, to look out at the gathering twilight. He might have been expecting someone, so watchful was he.

Finally, he drew the newly purchased sword from its scabbard and laid it upon the only piece of furniture in the hut, a small, low table of worm-eaten wood, so rickety that Meg suspected a hearty cough would topple it.

"I'll be back soon," Gresham said, indicating the gleaming sword with a nod of his head. "If you have trouble, shout with all the lung you can summon and swing that blade back and forth before you like a blue-faced Celt."

Meg looked at the weapon and swallowed. She had tried it out once before, whilst Gresham was away in the woods on some business or other, and found she could barely lift the thing, even using both hands. She made a silent vow to practice, for by rights the burden of their defense should not fall upon Sedgewick alone. He was not, after all, her husband, her father, or her brother. Indeed, they had been cast together by happenstance.

"Aye," she said, pretending to bravery again. "But do hurry."

He left, after favoring her with a brief, preoccupied smile and returned presently, bearing an armload of dried twigs and fallen branches from the floor of the forest of oaks and birches and yews that surrounded them, leaving space only for the dwelling and a small field. His shoulders and hair were sprinkled with great, sparkling flakes of snow.

Meg made no attempt to hide her jubilation at the sight of the wood. She had hardly dared to hope, for Sedgewick had been adamant throughout the journey that no flames should be kindled. "A fire!" she crowed, like a child given a present. For a truth, she was cold almost beyond her ability to bear it.

Gresham gave her a wry look as he tossed the wood down beside the fire pit and squatted to arrange the smallest among the ashes, taking a tinderbox from the one pocket in his jerkin and settling in to the task of striking a spark. "I'd rather not, but there's a storm coming and I fear we'll freeze to death without it."

The chill, which bit deep into the flesh, even within those stone walls, made clouds of their breaths and reminded Meg of nights past, when they'd lain together, out of necessity, sharing the warmth of their bodies. She dreamed of another, more intimate sort of joining, one she understood but little, though she knew it was not fitting for a lady to lie with a man not her husband.

Gresham had kept a careful distance, even when they were curled together at night, but she knew he wanted her, and with every passing day, her own curiosity, and her own desire, mounted like a debt at high interest. How long, she wondered, could two people travel together, under such circumstances, and not succumb?

"There are rats here," she said, in a confidential whisper.

"Complaining again?" Gresham asked, with a teasing note in his voice, as a spark took hold, at last, and ignited the smallest twigs to a faltering blaze. He bent low, and blew on the flames, to encourage them, and they sprang to life, flickering gloriously.

"No," Meg answered, trembling, and it was quite true. She had only been trying to make conversation, break the silence. Change the dangerous direction her thoughts had taken. "But surely rats are unclean."

Even the subject of rats did not suffice to distract her from the width of Gresham's shoulders, the power of his arms and legs, the nape of his long neck. Meg grew over-warm, long before the fire was blazing properly, and she was agitated, rather than comforted. She wanted to be held, but in this place, in this state of mind, she did not dare make her wishes known.

"Aye," Gresham agreed, rising to his feet and tucking

the tinderbox away, gazing at Meg across the flames that danced and crackled cheerfully between them. "They are that. But the fire will keep them at bay, methinks."

Meg glanced at the door, because she had to look away, and saw, through the gaping cracks, that the weighted clouds had opened, and the snow was coming down hard. "We may not be able to travel on the morrow," she commented, and then bent to take hold of a branch, and stir the fire.

Gresham sighed at the prospect. Apparently, he never tired of trudging through wood and meadow on the back of that wretched mule, but secretly, all her aspirations to adventure notwithstanding, Meg was already growing weary of the sojourner's life. She was dirty as a peasant, and every muscle ached, and she felt as though she would never get warm. She could have slept, she was certain, for days on end and then, upon rising, eaten the entire contents of the abbey's winter-stocked pantries.

"If we must bide awhile," Gresham said, resigned, "we will. We shall see what the morning brings." He untied one of the bundles, got out the wine flask, and what was left of the cheese and bread, and bade Meg eat. While she did so, standing, he went outside again, only to return almost immediately with the mule.

"You don't mean to keep that creature in here," she challenged, even though it was plain that he did.

"We can't very well let him freeze, can we?" Gresham countered. "Besides, the smoke is enough of an indication of our whereabouts. A discontented mule might bring every scoundrel in the shire down on our heads."

Meg was nonplussed, although she had no choice but to acquiesce, and she knew it. Certainly, crofters and some of the villagers shared their homes with their animals, sheep and cows and even oxen, were they fortunate enough to own them, but she had been gently raised. It was bad enough that she could not wash, or eat sitting down, because of the rats.

Enoch gave a long and disgruntled nicker, as if to protest his poor reception, then settled in to sleep, his huge head lowered, his eyes closed. His flanks quivered, and he switched his tail. As long, Meg thought, as he doesn't lift it.

"Shall we truly pass through London-town on our way to Cornwall?" she asked, as she dusted her hands together, her portions of bread and cheese finished. She was restored, and eager for new adventures.

"Yes," Gresham answered, with a long and weary sigh, and took up the flask to drink. If not for that strong wine, Meg had to confess, they would surely have succumbed to the cold long since. "I have no real recollection of the place—only feelings. But 'tis not a carnival we're going to, Meg. There are brigands aplenty there, and probably pestilence."

Inwardly, Meg sagged a little, and unexpected tears sprang to her eyes. She did not want Gresham to see her weakness, and the private trepidations she worked so hard to hide. How tired and fragile she felt, when reminded of the dangers of a city such as London, how worried for Elizabeth, for Gabriella, for herself.

Adventuring, in reality, was quite different than she had reckoned it would be. How wretched to find, in this lonely place, that it was hearth and home she craved, and not this harsh and difficult life at all.

It surprised Meg greatly when Gresham brought her round again, and drew her into his arms, because she had not heard his approach. He cupped a finger under her chin and raised her face, and their eyes met.

"You'll feel better in the morning, Meg," he promised, and his voice sounded gruff. His mouth was very near to hers, sweetly scented by the wine, and his breath was warm, and set her lips tingling.

She put her arms round his neck, but it wasn't wantonness that made her do it. She needed to be close to him, needed that more than shelter, more than food—more, even, than clean clothes and a bath.

"Hold me," she said, as she had that first night, when they'd taken to the limbs of a tree, like birds.

He gave a low groan, turned his head aside, as if in struggle, and then turned back again, and crushed her mouth under his own. He tasted of that same wine, and of passion, only barely restrained, and when by instinct she pressed against him, plunging her fingers deep into his hair, he broke away. Grasping her wrists, he glared at her. She sensed, somehow, that he was angry with himself, not with her.

"You know not what you do, my lady," he whispered. "I pray you, do not test me so recklessly again, for I am ready enough to have you as it is." Flushed along the edges of his jaw, he took one of her hands and held it to his lips, his breath traveling warm over her knuckles. "I am, I think, a gentleman, Lady Redclift, but I am not a saint."

It was both a challenge and a warning. Meg was still recovering from the thrill that had shot through her system when he kissed her, and it was not the wine, she knew, that made her so unsteady.

"No," she breathed, "you are surely no saint."

Slowly, Gresham lowered her hand from his lips, but he still held her wrist, loosely, between his thumb and forefinger. A muscle bunched in his cheek, as though he'd bitten down on something hard. He measured out his next words slowly, as if they surprised him even as they left his lips. "When we get to London, I will hand you over to the king. He will see that you are brought safely to Cornwall, though not before spring, I'll wager."

She gazed up at him, wide-eyed. She did not wish to be "handed over" to the king or anyone else. She wanted to find Gabriella, and she wanted Gresham to accompany her until that end was accomplished. Once she and her twin were reunited, she would deal with the question of her growing feelings for him.

"You are acquainted with the king?" she asked.

He heaved a great sigh, and she saw a torment of confusion in his eyes. Finally, he shook his head. "I don't know," he ground out. He turned away, in a fury of frustration. "God's eyeballs, sometimes I think I can't bear this—at times, I come so close to remembering. Images form in my mind, like ghosts, but before I can grasp them, they're gone."

She wanted to lay her hands upon his great swordsman's shoulders, to lend what innocent comfort she could, but she knew that might only make matters worse. So she simply stood there, unmoving, saying nothing.

He faced her again, weary now, exasperated, even desolate. "Meg," he said, "suppose there is a woman? Suppose I am wed—"

"Then you are wed," she said, and nearly wept.

"I remember—someone," he confessed.

"A woman," she said.

He nodded. "If I've exchanged vows, then I must honor them."

She waited. She would not have expected anything else, not from this man. She knew little about him, certainly even less than he knew about himself, but she had been aware from the first that he was the sort to abide by his promises. A part of her, one she was not acquainted with, wished he were different.

He crouched beside the fire, stirring the flames with a stick of the wood he'd gathered earlier. "Lie down, Meg," he urged gruffly, without looking at her. "Get some sleep. If the snow stops by morning, we'll travel on, and it will be hard going, for the mule and for us."

She unrolled the damp, musty blankets, as instructed, and spread them out on the floor. It made her skin crawl to think of lying down on a level with the mice and rats and any spiders that might have survived the coming of winter, but since she lacked Enoch's ability to sleep standing up, there seemed to be little choice.

When that task was done, and the bed was prepared, Meg found a cracked wooden bowl and wiped it clean with her kirtle. "Here, then," she said. "This will do nicely."

"What?" Gresham asked, his brow furrowed. He'd been pointedly ignoring her whilst she laid out their bed, though she suspected he'd stolen a glimpse or two from under his lashes.

Meg went toward the door, passing a snoring mule on the way, and made no answer.

"Meg." Gresham had followed her outside, into the rising storm. There was a post in the yard, and Meg swept its white and glistening crown of snow into the bowl, gasping as she was buffeted by the wind, so searingly cold that it stung her skin even through her clothes. When she had contrived to fill the bowl, she came back in, and set the receptacle beside the fire.

Gresham looked the part of some fierce Norse war-lord, brows prickled with snowflakes, as he thrust the door shut again behind them. When he turned, she was standing with the folds of her kirtle grasped in both hands while she pondered removing it entirely. She was wearing a chemise as well, but he probably didn't know that.

"God's lungs, woman, are you mad?" he demanded. He kept his tone low, Meg supposed, only to avoid awakening the mule.

She peered into the bowl, lazing in its bed of ashes at the edge of the fire pit, and saw that the snow inside it was melting nicely. She would not have hot water for her ablutions, but at least it need not be frigid. "No," she answered. "I am quite sane. But I shall surely turn lunatic if I do not scour away some of this dirt. I am in the habit, sir, of bathing with unhealthy regularity."

Gresham opened his mouth, closed it again.

Meg tore off a piece of her chemise, which had worn thin anyway, to use for a washing cloth. There was no soap, unfortunately, but she would just have to make do. Difficult conditions demanded sacrifices of all sorts; no point in wishing and whining.

"You'll want," she prompted him cheerfully, "to turn away. Lest you besmirch that famous honor of yours by looking upon a naked woman." She had no intention of stripping off her clothes in the presence of a man, and could not guess what demon had caused her to speak so boldly, but the words were out and there was no calling them back.

Gresham stared at her, astonished. Furious. And quite unable, she saw, with a certain delicious satisfaction, to look away. "Are you *trying* to tempt me?" he demanded.

She smiled, enjoying a sense of power unlike anything she'd ever felt before. "Of course not. You may be married, and I want nothing to do with you if you are. However, I am tired, I am cold, and I am very, very dirty, and if I must lie down with rats, I will at least be clean."

Gresham's jaw dropped. He closed his mouth, then busied himself with the fire again, though it did not need tending. The back of his neck was red.

Dipping the bit of cloth into the cold water, Meg began to bathe herself, which was an awkward proposition, considering that she remained fully clothed the whole time. Oh, for the relative privacy of her cell at the abbey.

"Have you finished?" Gresham snapped, at some length, when she opened the door to toss the water out into the snow.

She struggled to close the heavy door, and leaned against it, a bit breathless from the effort. Gresham, watching her from the middle of the room, was flushed, and the flames of the fire seemed to catch and blaze in his eyes. The hut was very cold, but Meg was no longer aware of that, for Gresham's gaze warmed her, as surely as burning wood.

"I have," she said smugly. "My bath was most refreshing. Mayhap you will have one, as well."

He glowered at her, then at the empty bowl in her hands. A few moments later, he snatched it out of her hands and tossed it into the shadows. That done, he gave Meg his back again, and made himself busy, checking the hobbles that would, hopefully, keep Enoch from trampling them to death as they slept.

She lay down and stared up at the rafters in the ceiling, doing her best not to think of rats and other beasties, both large and small. "Suppose his tail catches fire?" she speculated, referring, of course, to the mule.

"We'll hear about it soon enough if it does," Gresham grumbled. "Go to sleep."

"Mayhap I do not wish to sleep," she retorted pettishly. "Pray do not give me orders."

Gresham stared at her for a while, in ominous silence, and she simply stared back, until at last he snatched up the bowl and went outside once more. When he returned, some time later, shivering and cursing under his breath, he began the same ritual Meg had undertaken, removing his boots, his leggings and trunks and jerkin with quick, angry motions. He thought, no doubt because she lay so still and silent, that she was sleeping, and, God forgive her, she did nothing to correct this faulty impression.

Through her lashes, she watched him, unflinching, with a sort of idle interest that nevertheless caused her heart to race, fleet as a she-wolf bounding across hard snow. Made of flame and of shadow, form more than flesh, Gresham took up the cloth Meg had used, and the bowl of snow, now melted, and washed himself clean. Naked and magnificent, he built up the fire, raising a shower of smoke and sparks and looking, Meg thought, as a savage Celt might have done, long ago, in the time only scholars and storytellers could describe.

She strained for a glimpse of his manhood and was quite relieved, as well as disappointed, that it was hidden from her view, for the hut was more dark than light. She affected a soft snore and wriggled between the coarse covers, at once dreading the moment when Gresham joined her in the blankets and anticipating it.

"You little fraud," he growled, with good-natured weariness, wrenching on his jerkin. "I should have known you weren't asleep."

She smiled sadly, and watched as he added more wood to the fire, then got into the makeshift bed with her. She thought of her sisters, of Elizabeth, still at the abbey, where there was plague, and of Gabriella. Tears of sorrow and loneliness burned in her eyes, and she turned her head, for she would not have Gresham see them.

"Meg," he said gruffly.

She sniffled. "Yes?"

"Are you crying?"

"No," she lied.

He didn't believe her. Took her chin in his hand and turned her head, so that he could look into her face. "You're safe with me," he told her. "You must know that by now."

She wasn't entirely sure she wanted safety, not when it came to this man. "I do think of other things—and other people—besides you, my lord," she murmured.

His teeth flashed white in a wolf's grin. "Aye," he said, and it was plain that he did not entirely believe her, the arrogant knave.

"Are you bent on giving me to the king when we reach London-town?" she asked, and the tone of her voice made his smile fade. "If so, I should rather go directly to Cornwall instead, to look for Gabriella at Avendall Hall."

He frowned. "Avendall," he mused. Tasting the name and, it would seem, finding it sour.

"Are you remembering something?" she asked, sitting up. When she'd mentioned Sir Avendall's name on previous occasions, during their long discussions upon the road, he'd shown no signs of recognition.

Gresham lay on his side, elbow planted in the dank bedding, his head resting in his hand. "The name is mildly familiar, that's all," he said. "Mayhap I am grasping at straws."

They were silent for a long while, each following their own thoughts.

"Yes," he decided, at some length. "We will go to London first. I am known there—for good or ill. I'm sure of that much, anyway."

Although Meg had ever yearned to see London-town for herself, she had many misgivings now. If Gresham abandoned her there, as he frankly intended to do, why, even with the favor of Edward III—and she had no earthly reason to expect such a boon—a long time might pass before she found her way to Cornwall and her beloved Gabriella. Surely kings had other things on their minds.

"Oh," she said.

He took her hand, beneath the blankets, and held it, his fingers interlaced with hers. "I make you this promise, Meg," he said quietly. "Even if I have a wife, and a dozen children, I will see that you and your sister are brought together."

"What," she whispered, "if you *don't* have a wife and a dozen children?"

She felt his smile in the darkness, warm as the fading fire, and his hand tightened around hers.

"Then," he answered, "I shall proceed to court you."

Gresham lay in the dark, listening to the special stillness that meant a thick covering of snow, a sleeping Meg cradled in his arms. He was furious with himself for feeling the things he did, and yet he supposed he'd known, mayhap from the moment he'd first opened his eyes in that potting shed on the abbey grounds, and seen her hovering over him, that he was lost. If he was married, he would not leave his wife—almost certainly, he loved this woman who might or might not exist—but simply get on with his life, with half his heart in Meg Redclift's keeping until the day he died. If, on the other hand, he was not bound by some earlier promise, he could rightly explore whatever it was that drew him and Meg to each other.

In the meantime, he pondered the question that was uppermost in his mind. What sort of man claimed the name of Gresham Sedgewick?

One who knew how to fight, surely, how to survive on little or nothing, how to lose himself in the pleasures of a woman's body and, alas, to deny himself those pleasures. One who remembered warfare too well, and with a measure of affection that shamed him. One who had felt naked as a newly hatched robin until he'd bought an innkeeper's sword. The relief of first holding the hilt in his hand, of running his thumb along the sharp edge of the blade, was with him still.

Why did he remember swordplay, but naught of wife and babes, hearth and home? Mayhap it was because he had none. Still, that didn't rule out the possibility that he was an outlaw of some sort—the sheriff had come to St. Swithin's, after all, seeking him out. Better to remain befogged, he thought, than to learn that he was trapped in the skin of a man he could neither like nor respect.

He closed his eyes and tried to sleep. At length, he succeeded.

The hut was brutally cold when Meg awakened, with the first light, and Gresham had already gone off somewhere. Mercifully, he had led Enoch outside, too, though she could hear the beast nickering conversationally somewhere just beyond the flimsy door.

Meg pulled the blankets around her in a tight cocoon

and listened. After a time, she sat up, pushed her hair back with both hands, and peered into the fire pit. There was a nice little blaze going, and that gave her the courage to arise and go to the door, there to look out through one of the broad cracks.

The earth wore an ermine wrap, deep and graceful and lush, and the silence had a dazzle all its own. Enoch was in the dooryard, nibbling happily at a pile of stale-looking hay, found heaven knew where, but there was no sign of Gresham.

Meg began to fear that he had been captured by the sheriff's men after all, or simply forgotten who he was, and gone wandering off. Wherever he was, he had taken the sword with him.

She got her bowl and filled it with fresh snow, which she melted and even managed to warm slightly by the stalwart little fire, and washed as best she could. She hurried, lest Gresham return and catch her.

He appeared after an hour, with the neatly butchered hindquarter of what must have been a sheep slung across his shoulders, and promptly arranged it over the fire, using sticks for a spit.

Meg did not ask where he'd gotten such a feast, or what he'd risked in the effort. She was starved, the bread and cheese were nearly gone, and she knew, by the visible weight of the snow, that they would not be leaving the hut that day. Hampered by virtually impassable roads and fields, they might become the prey of wild animals, if not sheriff's men and bandits.

She took some small solace from the logical conclusion that these last dared not travel abroad, either.

The mutton took an eternity to cook, and the smoky, savory smell of it was a torment but, finally, after several hours, Gresham sliced off portions of the meat with his knife, and they ate with good appetite.

In the early afternoon, the snow began to come down again, and the wind was high, keening round the walls of the hut, rattling the smoke door in the ceiling. Gresham brought Enoch back inside, but this time the mule was not so docile as before, but fitful, stamping his feet and rolling his eyes. Finally, he brayed fit to split Meg's eardrums and kicked at the wall of the hut with his powerful hind legs until she feared he would splinter it, exposing them to the elements.

Gresham spoke with brisk authority, and the animal settled down a little, though he still snorted and tossed his head.

"What ails that creature?" Meg asked, uneasy.

Gresham, who had been lying beside her on the blankets, dozing, until Enoch's tantrum, was already at the window. He had recovered his sword from its place on the small table as he passed.

"Wolves," he said, very quietly. "He probably caught their scent."

Meg's heart stopped, started again. She got to her feet and went to stand beside Gresham, gazing out through the shifting curtain of snow.

Four of the animals, slavering and ruffled, had arranged themselves in front of the hut, only a few feet from the door. Meg could hear them panting, see the stark, inconsolable hunger in their eyes.

"Will they try to get to us?" she asked, in a whisper.

"That depends," Gresham replied, "on when they last ate. It's the smell of mutton that drew them, I imagine."

"We could throw it out to them, what's left."

Gresham shook his head. "Oh, no. Once they'd devoured every scrap of that, they'd surely conclude that there was more food where that came from."

He might have spoken in prophecy, for it was then that the largest of the wolves, a long, slat-ribbed beast with a matted pelt, suddenly sprang forward and struck the rickety door.

6

Miraculously, the door held under the wolf's first resonant onslaught, but Enoch went into a frenzy. Whilst Gresham stood ready with his sword, bracing the wood panel against its frame with one shoulder, Meg hurried to the mule.

She had never been so frightened, and yet she had somehow become two persons—the inward one huddled and trembling, capable of no more than a mindless bleat, the outer, clear-thinking and calm. It was this second Meg, fortunately, who took Enoch's halter firmly in hand—the animal was quite capable of breaking down a wall in his panic, and thus exposing them all to the wolf pack—and spoke to him in firm, quiet words.

His long ears twitched, and he bawled once or twice, but he left off kicking, for the moment at least, and even appeared to listen.

"What is happening out there?" Meg asked of Gresham, in the same soothing tone she'd been using before, lest the mule go wild again.

"They're regrouping," Gresham answered, and gave a bitter, almost admiring chuckle. "Three of them are in counsel. I can't see the other."

Meg shivered, held Enoch, who had begun to fidget once more. There was only the one window, and that was too small to admit even a desperate wolf. The hut seemed smoky, the acrid smell of it burning the eyes, scratching at the throat.

There was an odd, skittering sound on the roof, and Enoch tossed his head and dug in his heels, braying fit to make the relics of a saint rouse and assemble themselves into a living person.

Meg struggled with the mule and the task took all her strength; she was aware of Gresham, every moment, tense against the door, braced for another attack. Eyes raised to Enoch, a looming creature, she necessarily saw the ceiling, too. Saw the wolf, peering down through the open hatch contrived to let out the smoke of the fire.

A scream wedged itself into Meg's throat, too large to pass, and she would not let it by in any case, knowing too well, even in her terror, that a cry from her now was sure to send the mule into a bone-breaking, wall-shattering frenzy.

"Gresham," she said, in a voice she did not wholly recognize as her own, and indicated the ceiling with a flick of her eyes.

He turned, saw the third wolf just as it plunged through the chasm, heedless, in its starvation, of the smoldering fire below. Emboldened, mayhap, by the wretched alternatives.

The animal landed in the embers with a wild scrabbling of limbs, oversetting the cooked sheep's carcass and, but for a momentary yelp and the singeing of its matted fur, seemed undaunted. Meg felt a brief appreciation for the beast and was sorry that, if she and Gresham were to live, it must surely die.

Maddened by a desperation Meg could not begin to comprehend, the wolf crouched beside the toppled spit, guarding the mutton. Teeth bared in a soul-chilling growl, the monster assessed its enemies with glittering yellow eyes and Meg trembled at the sight, even as she used all her will and might to hold the mule.

"Do not move," Gresham said, slowly and clearly, and with a calm almost as ominous, in its own right, as the presence of the wolf. Both Enoch and Meg were stunned into a brief and fragile silence, brittle as the thin covering of ice on a puddle.

The beast flung back its outsize head and emitted a howl as plaintive as the wail of a damned soul, and Meg shivered again, conscious of the other wolves, the mule who would surely panic at any second, and Gresham.

"Mother of God," Meg whispered. It was all she had at hand for a prayer; Elizabeth would have been more eloquent.

Two more wolves struck the door, and the separate impacts of their bodies against the worn wood echoed inside the hut like claps of thunder. Enoch gave a great, heaving shudder, and Meg felt him draw breath to spring in every direction except inward.

"Get on his back," Gresham said. "Now."

Meg was still hesitating mentally when she realized, a heartbeat after Gresham's quiet command, that she had obeyed.

"Don't try to hold him," Gresham went on, as though he were telling her how to tie a particular knot, or explaining a problem of ciphering. "Bend low to his neck and whatever happens, hold on."

Enoch was tossing his head now, beginning to dance and kick in earnest.

The wolf by the fire pit, soot-furred, growled again, and went back to his meal. Beyond the wall of wood and loosely-mortared stone, the others called to it, as if in longing and frustration, and then they came at the door again, en masse. That time, with their combined weight, they were successful, and the whole of the hut seemed to reverberate with the crash.

Meg screamed as the door came down on top of Gresham and the wolves rushed over it, and him, with a wicked grace, and ducked her head as Enoch made a dash for the opening, ears back, heels flying. She heard the mule's hooves clatter over the fallen panel and clung to his neck as he shot arrowlike into the yard, where he immediately foundered, struggling wildly in an ocean of snow.

The sounds from inside the hut were horrible to hear, but Meg's imaginings were far worse. She gave Enoch a smart whack to one side of the head to stop his cater-wauling, bounded off his back, and slogged back.

The wolves, she saw in a brief glimpse round Gresham, had surrounded the sheep's carcass, as they might a fresh kill in the wild, and turned their attention on the man standing upright just over the threshold, sword in hand, body tensed with a will to fight as viciously as the animals would.

Still scrambling through the deep snow, Meg watched in horror as one of the wolves sprang at Gresham, a feral, writhing snarl of fur and fury. She screamed, fair strangling on the shape of her cry, and Gresham faltered slightly at the sound, and moved as though to turn, but then he wielded the blade and the animal fell, still growling, at his feet. With a quick downward thrust of the sword's point, both hands on the hilt, he killed the beast.

The others looked at Gresham, then their fallen comrade, and stood their ground. Their breaths made clouds around their heads, and the low, unceasing sound rising from their gaunt chests caused Meg's very soul to quail.

At her back, Enoch continued to bray and flail, but Meg did not turn from the scene before her. Her entire attention, all the energy of her being, was focused on Gresham. She ached for a weapon to aid in his defense—a stick, a stone, anything that would have served to strike a sturdy blow, but she was powerless.

"Let them have the wretched meat!" she cried, in a hoarse whisper, when she could speak. She wanted to be away from that place, she and Gresham and the mule. Well away, and safe. The impossibility of that did naught to lessen the wanting.

Gresham actually laughed, and his answer was breathless. He ran his free hand across his mouth, but did not turn about or look back at her. "Do you fancy that it's the mutton I'm defending? Without this hut to shelter us, my lady, we shall both be dead afore nightfall. The supper of these hounds of hell, if we don't freeze first."

"Are you hurt?" Meg asked, noting at last the torn and bloodied state of Gresham's clothes and recalling that Enoch had trampled him beneath the fallen door. If the man had no broken bones, it would be a miracle.

"It hardly matters at this point," he answered. "I will say that I have neither the time nor the inclination to chat, engaging though I find your conversation to be."

Chagrined and, even in that coil, a bit indignant, Meg swallowed her next question and glanced back at Enoch.

He'd finally given up the struggle and thrown back his head to emit a deafening, bleating bray.

Meg ignored him and cast about for that weapon she'd wanted, finally uncovering a sizable stone near one corner of the hut. In the process, she noticed the sloping roof of some sort of shed, affixed to one wall of the structure and, no doubt, the means by which the boldest of the wolves had gotten onto the roof.

She made her way back with the stone and stood ready for battle.

Gresham spared her the briefest of glances as the impasse between him and the remaining wolves went on, eerier in its way than the bloody encounter that had preceded it.

"Pray use that," Gresham jested mildly, "to bash your hysterical mule over the head. The racket gives me an aching head."

"And 'tis more likely to draw further trouble than a rescue, I fear," Meg remarked ruefully, thinking of other predators, both human and animal.

"You are learning," Gresham said. " 'Twould better serve, my Meg, if you set yourself to the task of calming that charmless beast before I run my sword through his heart."

Meg's eyes widened. "You would do such a thing?" She had seen him slay the wolf, of course, but that had been quite different. A measure taken in heat and necessity, not the cool light of reason. Did he *enjoy* killing, this man she suspected she had begun, mayhap foolishly, to care for?

A smile quirked at the corner of his mouth and was gone. "No," he said sadly. " 'Twas merely a figure of speech, Meg. Now—go and make peace with that brute—we've grief enough, without him bringing another pack to our door. Alas, these mangy thieves before us have probably already raised the signal, with their howling, however inhospitable they will be to any new-comers."

Meg needed no further convincing. She turned and made her difficult way back to Enoch, caught hold of his halter, and, having no other plan at the ready, began to sing to him. It was a soft, silly ditty, one she and Gabriella had made up, long ago, to comfort a homesick Elizabeth when she cried in the night.

The stalemate dragged on, Gresham refusing to move from the doorway, the wolves guarding the roasted meat. The sky darkened, fresh snow began to fall, swirling, and the wind picked up. Enoch listened, snuffling pitiably, to Meg's tremulous, shivering tune.

She had no cloak, for that was inside. Her kirtle was wet through and her feet were numb; even if they sur-vived the wolves' visit, she and Gresham and poor terrified Enoch, there was every likelihood that one or all of them would take a chill and perish from the resultant illness.

Gresham must have come to the same conclusion and nearly the same moment for, without a word of warning to Meg, he suddenly lunged forward, out of her sight, bellowing a continuous, harrowing battle cry.

Meg let her forehead rest against Enoch's frosty, quiv-ering neck, and wept even as she continued to sing. The lyrics had changed from a lullaby to a prayer, however, of the most earnest sort.

The noise from inside the hut was a dreadful mael-strom of snarls and shouts, but the silence that came later—long minutes later—was far worse.

Meg dashed her tears away and sniffled, her heart in her throat, then called out Gresham's name.

There was no answer, but he appeared in the doorway,

bloodied and exhausted, leaning against its framework and struggling visibly for breath.

Meg gave a cry of jubilation and started toward him, but he held up a hand to stay her. She stood, puzzled and fearful, in the snow, halfway between the mule and the hut, and waited.

He disappeared into the hut, returning as quickly as he'd gone, dragging a dead wolf by the scruff of its neck. One by one, staggering a little, he hauled the broken, blood-washed creatures out into the cold, fading light and made graves for them in the snow, presumably to mask their scents from other animals. Only when all four had been brought out and buried did Gresham gesture for Meg to go inside.

She obeyed, too grateful that he was alive to balk, though as always it galled her a little, to be told what to do.

Gresham fetched the mule, raised the door back into place, its top only leaning against the lintel, and therefore providing only the illusion of protection, and approached the dying fire. He stirred it back to life, adding bits of wood brought in earlier, and then collapsed beside it.

Meg was, for a few moments, rendered immobile by the sight of him, fallen in exhaustion, covered in the blood of wolves and, she feared, his own as well. Gresham was the strongest of men, he had proven that this day, but he'd spent nearly every resource he possessed in the conflict just past.

Meg went to him only when she was sure she wouldn't fling herself upon him, sobbing, and ran her hands and her gaze over him, looking for injuries.

He'd been bitten in the calf of his right leg and on his left forearm, and the knowledge filled Meg with a new horror. She had heard of the madness and death that oft overtook a human being, after such wounds were sustained.

Using deep breaths and reason, she calmed herself. Gresham had done all he could to protect them both, and even poor Enoch. The rest was up to her.

Moving slowly, methodically, Meg rose, retrieved the mutton from the floor and, using Gresham's knife, cut away the places the wolves had torn with their teeth. While she did not relish the thought of eating what was left, she knew there was no choice. In order to survive, she and Gresham must certainly have sustenance.

That task completed, she set the meat on the table the sword had occupied, and found the wooden bowl she and Gresham had both used for bathing. In the commotion, it had gone rolling back into its corner.

Meg carried it outside, carefully dislodging the leaning door, and filled it with snow. She set this by the fire to warm and went about removing Gresham's clothes in cautious, peeling motions, fearing at every moment that she would uncover some new and more terrible wound.

Gresham was not unconscious, and yet neither was he truly awake. He watched Meg with half-closed eyes as she ministered to him, and made no sound, either of protest or of encouragement. She had, in fact, a disturbing sense that he did not even know who she was.

That alone was cause to bring sobs swelling, unshed, into her throat, but she merely continued her work, stripping him to his trunks, cleaning the tears and punctures in his flesh as best she could, and binding them with what remained of her chemise. She covered him in the dirty blankets, gave him wine from the flask and sat smoothing his hair, yellow and soft as the down of a hatchling it was, until he was deep in slumber.

The problem of the door remained, and Meg pondered it solemnly as she wiped the bloodied sword clean with what was left of the snow water and laid it ready to Gresham's hand. Such a weapon would be of little value in her own grasp, but its presence might provide Gresham with some solace, should he awaken suddenly, and in confusion.

There were no tools, no fittings for the repair of the door, and Meg knew that, even before she made a thorough search of the hovel. The trapdoor in the ceiling, through which the wolf had come, was still wide open, of necessity, for the smoke itself was deadly, when confined.

Still, she thought, gazing upward, head tilted back, hands on hips, the thing must have hinges of some sort. Not iron ones, probably, for this had clearly been a poor household and such things were dear and hard to find, but sturdy strips of leather might do for her purposes.

Meg gathered up her cloak and wrapped it tightly round her. Then, after a few soothing words and a pat or two for Enoch, in the recklessly optimistic hope of keeping him quiet, she moved the door aside just far enough to slip through and went out.

The world was utterly quiet, but for the occasional snap of an ice-coated twig, somewhere in the encroaching wood beyond the buried field, and what little sunlight that remained would soon be gone.

Meg shivered, giving a wide berth to the blood-marked snow graves of the wolves, and rounded the hut to the little shed she'd seen earlier. Knowing Gresham would already have searched it, she stole a look inside anyway, and was met by cobwebs and a few scraps of dry wood, but nothing else.

She resolved to come back for the wood before nightfall, closed her eyes for a moment to gather her courage, and climbed up onto the shed's slanting roof, praying she would not fall through the half-rotted shingling before she could assess the damage to the trapdoor and possibly prevent another attack like the one that had taken place earlier. The wolf's footprints were still faintly visible in the deepening snow, and she shuddered, remembering that moment when the beast had plunged through the opening, so consumed with hunger that even the fire could not stay it.

Carefully, her fingers burning with cold, Meg made her way onto the main roof, crawling forward, slipping twice and getting nearly to the eaves before she managed to catch hold. Her hands bled and her knees were scraped and her heart hammered painfully at the thought of falling, but she persisted, and finally gained the crest of the roof, where the smoke door was.

The fittings proved to be fashioned of iron, and time had loosened them from the crumbling shingles. They would be useful, reaffixed to the door of the hut. She pulled them loose with a couple of good tugs, and peered down through the hole.

Gresham lay sleeping next to the slow fire, and Enoch had wandered over to the roast mutton, where it rested upon the little table, to sniff at it with indelicate interest.

Meg made a snowball and lobbed it through the gap, striking the errant mule between the ears. "Don't you dare lay your tongue to that food, you beast!"

The creature whinnied in surprise and stepped back, his hooves making a cloppety-clop sound on the hard-packed floor.

Meg considered the slant of the slippery roof and the distance between the smoke hole and the nearest support beam in the ceiling. She heard a howl and, looking back over one shoulder, spotted a lone wolf watching her from the edge of the woods. If she tried to climb down and make her way to the door, the creature would be on her in a matter of moments, tearing out her throat. She made the decision, dropped the iron hinges through—still clinging to bits of the trapdoor, they were—and then turned onto her belly and let her legs down into the room below, then her hips. Finally, she was hanging by her stinging fingers, but her toes brushed the sooty beam and found purchase.

With the greatest of care, Meg eased downward until she sat upon the broad timber, one limb on either side, wet with snow and everywhere blackened with years of residue from the fire below.

Gresham turned onto his back, opened his eyes briefly, then opened them again, wide. He raised himself onto his elbows, squinting. "What the—?"

"It's only me," Meg said reassuringly, calculating the distance between the beam and the floor. She'd left that factor out of her previous reckonings. The single wolf she had spotted seconds before provided all the motivation she needed, however.

Gresham, evidently reassured, promptly lapsed back into a sound sleep.

Meg cast an eye on Enoch, recently snowballed for snuffling supper.

"Come here," she commanded, in an irritated whisper.

The mule stood fast, looking up at her, and snorted once, probably in spite.

"Here, Enoch," Meg coaxed, pointing to the place below her. "Nice mule. Come here." She meant to land on his back, but, not surprisingly, he wasn't inclined to co-operate.

Finally, she measured the length of her body against the approximate distance between the beam and the floor, eased herself downward until she was once again hanging by her hands, closed her eyes tightly, and let go.

She struck the floor with a jarring thump, but remained upright, and felt such triumph in her achievement that she was mildly intoxicated by it. Caring nothing for her blackened hands, thighs and bottom, her wet clothes and icy feet, she used Gresham's knife to prize the nails from the hinges she'd won at such cost and, using one of the stones from round the fire pit for a mallet, affixed the fittings to the ancient door and then to its frame.

The pounding did not disturb Gresham overmuch; he grumbled something and rolled onto his stomach, arms outflung on the blankets, hands clutching the cloth.

The hovel darkened, and outside, Meg heard the howls of other wolves, though distantly now. She shuddered and tried Gresham's sword again, only to find that she could barely lift it in both hands, let alone wield it with enough force to stave off an enemy. Nonetheless, she would keep it near, for she had no way of covering the smoke hole in the roof.

Because she was hungry—she would not have touched it otherwise—Meg ate of the now-cold mutton, wiped her scraped, sooty and greasy fingers on her kirtle with a grimace, and lay down beside Gresham upon the blankets. With the back of one hand, she tested his forehead for fever, found his flesh cool, and allowed herself to sleep at last.

She awakened much later to a stab of pleasure so intense that it displaced all other senses and emotions. Gresham had raised her gown and kirtle almost to her shoulders, and he was nibbling at her breast.

She put her hand in his hair, half-asleep still, but mindful of the sore place at the back of his head, and murmured softly, encouragingly, senselessly.

He drew on her hungrily for a while, then in a slow and sleepy way, and Meg marveled that, after all that had occurred in recent hours, despite all the problems and perils they faced, it took no more than this to give them both comfort.

"Beautiful," Gresham whispered raggedly, and laid his head upon Meg's belly, as though it were a pillow. "So beautiful."

Meg wound a finger in a tendril of his hair, content to lie thus forever, without anything further passing between them, and smiled to herself. If Gresham thought her beautiful, he could not have noticed the smears of soot that covered most of her body.

He kissed her stomach, then rested again, with a sigh and a murmured, "Monique."

It was several moments before Meg realized that Gresham had spoken a woman's name.

She blinked back hot, humiliated tears, made partly of relief.

He was remembering, then.

And there was—she had feared it all along—someone special to remember.

Monique.

Gresham opened his eyes, like a seaman coming to in the shoals, following a shipwreck. He was conscious of the pain first, then of Meg lying beside him, and then he remembered the wolves. He sat bolt upright.

"Good God," he rasped. "Are you all right?"

Meg didn't answer; he leaned over her, searched her

eyes, and saw that there were tears pooling in her lashes. Her face, flushed and soot-spotted, revealed a proud, heartbreaking effort not to weep.

"Meg?" Gresham said, smoothing a lock of tangled brown hair away off her cheek. She looked, he thought, as though she'd been caught in a chimney.

"You called me Monique," she said.

The name was familiar in a way that twisted something deep in Gresham's gut. "When?" he asked. Stupid question, that, and beside the point. But there it was, out of his mouth, trembling between them in the chilly air.

"Last night."

Last night. He was horrified to think what he might have done, out of his head, remembering some other woman. "God's breath, tell me I didn't—?"

Meg smiled with more sorrow than mirth, shook her head. "No, Gresham," she said miserably. "You—we didn't do that. Not exactly."

"What do you mean, 'not exactly'? God in heaven, Meg, if I've hurt you—"

"No," she said quickly. "No—it was harmless. Sweet. You wanted—you wanted my breast—"

Gresham heaved an enormous sigh. When had he not wanted that? He doubted there had ever been such a time. And Monique. Who the devil was she? Was she the wife he hoped he didn't have, didn't love? If so, why did his heart feel so heavy at the sound of her name, and so empty?

He tried to summon an image to his mind, and for once, something came, and with unsettling readiness. A dark-haired woman, nearly as tall as he was, with beautiful, angry eyes. Slate gray, those eyes, full of passion and

fury and the sure knowledge of him that could only come
with close and intimate association.

"My God," he breathed.

"You remember her, don't you?" Meg asked, very quietly. He'd rested his forehead on her abdomen, and she
made no attempt to push him away.

He felt, in his recollection, the crack of a feminine
hand—Monique's hand, surely—striking his face. She
had cursed him, in French, and then slapped him again.
Yet in the next instant, she had untied the laces of his
trunks and . . .

"Aye," he said, the word muffled by the blankets that
covered Meg. "I remember."

"Is she your wife, then?"

Gresham looked up, moved to lie beside Meg, his face
even with hers. "I don't know," he replied, in all honesty.
"I hope not."

She would have turned her head, but he stopped her
with a gentle hand.

Meg bit her lower lip, surely planning words that
would of necessity sting, though not out of malice. "You
must love her, this woman."

"Marriages are rarely made on the basis of such romantic sentiments, Meg," he told her gently. "They are
more often matters of property and alliance."

"But love often comes later. Mother Mary Benedict
has said so." She paused. "Oh, God," she cried softly, in
raw and utter despair. "Oh, God."

He closed his eyes for a moment, wounded by the
sound of her sorrow. "Don't," he pleaded.

"What name shall I bear when this is over? Shall I be
called mistress, or whore?"

Gresham was in a truer anguish than any he had

known since regaining consciousness in the potting shed at St. Swithin's. "You are no whore," he breathed. "And if it turns out that you can never be my wife, neither will you be my mistress."

A tear trickled down over Meg's left cheek, disappearing into the folds of the blanket. "No," she agreed bitterly. "I will be nothing at all."

"Shhh," he said. "Never that."

"If you love this Monique, and that love comes back to you, what will happen to me then? No other man will want me for a wife—they'll all assume I've been compromised by you—and I have no lands, no gold—"

"I will not put you from me, Meg. Not ever."

She believed he was telling the truth as he knew it, he could see that in her eyes, but she was skeptical. She said nothing, but simply lay there beside him in that cold hovel, covered in goose bumps and soot, and he was ashamed that he had brought her to such a place. At the same time, he knew there was little else he could have done, save abandoning her to the plague at St. Swithin's.

It was then, in that most tender and poignant of moments, that the mule chose to lighten the situation by holding forth with a ripping and noxious wind.

Meg laughed, while Gresham cursed and bounded to his feet with his jerkin pressed to his face, in a vain effort to mask the stench.

He went to the door, dragged it open, and shooed Enoch toward it, while Meg laughed all the harder, her mirth mingled with sobs.

The dazzling light of a snowy morning flooded into the hut, along with a fresh and welcome chill.

Gresham's attention was caught by the rusted metal

hinges fastened to the woodwork. "How did you manage this?" he asked, and then went through the whole interior of the hut, waving his shirt like a flag in an effort to dissipate the eye-watering smell.

Meg sat up on the blankets, delicately plugging her nose with a thumb and forefinger. "There," she said, in the resultant tone, "is a tale that wants telling."

7

$\mathcal{M}$eg and Gresham could stay no longer in that hut, if only because of Enoch's objectionable digestive system, but it happened that the world had somehow warmed itself a little, and there were channels amid the drifts of snow that were passable.

Haste must be made, however, for though the sky was a polished blue, and the sun cast countless blinding glimmers of light over the uneven mantle of white covering the ground, the weather could change with little or no warning.

Duly, the blankets were neatly rolled, the bundles tied. Gresham strapped on his sword belt and bound their possessions to the back of the saddle with a bit of slim cord brought along for the purpose. Meg led Enoch alongside a sizable stone and mounted, and Gresham vaulted up behind her, having made no complaint in regard to the injuries he'd sustained battling the wolf pack.

Meg did not look back at the hut where she had learned so much about her own courage, resourcefulness, and strength; instead, she took a lesson from Lot's

wife and fixed her gaze upon the future which, most as-
suredly, would hold sorrows and pleasures of its own.

They were silent travelers at first, she and Gresham,
thinking their own thoughts. Meg, newly confident, now
that she'd been tested and tried, was less fearful than she
might have been, but for her own experiences. Even so,
as she looked forward to the great parti-colored, gambol-
ing feast that was London-town, she could not help feeling some trepidation, and no small degree of impatience
at the delay. Her greatest concern was still finding
Gabriella—she would have no peace until she'd read a
letter written in her twin's own hand or, better still,
looked into her eyes. Then, and only then, when she
knew that all was well with Gabriella, could she concen-
trate on building a future of her own.

Mayhap she and Gresham would find, in their search for
his past, the woman he called Monique, as well. Suppose
she presided, this creature of mystery, over Gresham's own
household, reared his gold-haired children, even now, as
Meg lost more and more of her heart to him with every
passing moment?

Sedgewick was a man who kept his vows; he'd said as
much, and she believed him. Although he would wish
Meg well, upon his reunion with his wife, and might even
take pains to see that she would not be left destitute, she
knew there would be no real place for her, in his life, or in
his heart. Some men might have attempted to make her
their mistress, and indeed, according to those residents
of St. Swithin's who had reason to know whereof they
spoke, the lot of a courtesan was often more comfortable
than that of a true wife. Wives were expected to bear children, look after servants and fields and horses, while mistresses had only to watch and wait for their man, please

him when he was with them, and enjoy the trinkets and baubles he brought.

Not only scoundrels and rakes, but good and honorable men kept courtesans, even sired babes by them, and these women were usually accorded a degree of respect wherever they went, at least to their faces. What went on behind their backs was another matter, but easily ignored.

In any case, Gresham had never offered Meg such a consideration, and she would have been too proud to accept if he had.

Inwardly, she sighed. There was another possibility, too—Gresham might not merely *have* a wife, but cherish and adore her. Mayhap he felt great passion for this unknown woman, this Monique, mayhap they laughed together at jests no one else would understand, and shared their deepest secrets and sorrows.

The idea of Gresham entering into that kind of communion, with another woman, was incomprehensibly painful to Meg. She inclined her inner ear toward the small, insistent echo, piping in a far corner of her spirit, insisting that there was no other for Gresham but she, Meg Redclift.

Meg brought herself out of her reverie with a jerk; became physically aware of Gresham, riding behind her, his arms around her waist, his thighs aligned with hers. She felt overheated, despite the bitter cold, and dizzy, as though she might topple right off the mule, should he let her go. She fretted that she would not be able to resist him, even for the sake of all that was right, if he ever tried, truly tried, to lure her into his bed. He roused incomprehensible hungers within her, and with such ease that she sometimes wondered if he even guessed at the power he had over her.

Why, she asked, of herself and of fate, had men the

right to take their pleasure where they wished, while women must wait to be chosen, to be taken up or put aside as desired, like a cup of wine or a sweetmeat plucked from a tray?

Gresham surprised Meg, moved her hair aside and kissed the side of her neck, and the shiver of heat that went through her at even that simple contact did nothing to improve her darkening mood. The sweet shock of it echoed through her bones.

"I would ask what you are thinking, to bridle so at my touch," Gresham said quietly, his breath warm as it passed her ear, and wreaking a fresh and singular havoc upon her senses. "But, alas, I think I already know." He paused, sighed again. "She is but a scrap of memory, is Monique, and I feel naught when I think of her, Meg. No yearning. No anger. Nothing. Doesn't that indicate that we were probably never more than lovers?"

It was as the stab of a dagger to Meg, to hear Gresham admit to intimate recollections of Monique, even so indirectly, though she would have known he was lying if he'd denied it. Gresham was no monk; he was worldly, and a soldier, well traveled, with noble blood flowing in his veins, and he had surely bedded countless women. Indeed, his love of soldiering might prove a greater threat than any female rival.

"It indicates nothing," she replied, with a little sniff meant to convey disinterest in the subject, even boredom. Neither aspect bore any resemblance to the truth of the matter, which was that she was wholly, hopelessly besotted.

He chuckled, and his breath moved in her hair like a summer breeze. She felt the solid strength of him in every line and curve of her body, and now it seemed that her nerves were sizzling beneath the cool surface of her skin. "Do you know how fetching you are?" he asked. "Mayhap you are not the innocent you seem. It could be that you torment me on purpose."

"You are quite mistaken, my lord," she replied stiffly. "Should I decide to torment you, you will have no need to wonder what I'm about. You will *know.*"

He laughed again. Then, remarkably, he tasted her earlobe, ever so lightly, as though it were a most delicate confection, one to be savored. His arms still rested loosely around her, his hands holding Enoch's reins, but she felt as though she were tucked inside his embrace, and she liked being there. She liked the sense of belonging, false though it was.

"Sometimes," he confessed, "I wish I were a scoundrel."

"Mayhap you are," Meg pointed out. The touch of his tongue on the edge of her ear had sent a hot, illicit sensation quavering through her veins. "A scoundrel, I mean."

"Perhaps," he agreed, in a tone of amused reflection. Then he changed the subject. "You are very beautiful, you know, and exceedingly tempting."

She felt light-headed, as though her blood had fermented into strong wine, exotically spiced. She bit down on her lower lip, hard, glad that he could not see her face, which must have been pink, and struggled to retain her dignity. "Pray, do not trifle with me," she said, and was mortified to hear the threat of tears underlying her words. "It would be cruel."

"I'm sorry," he said, and the hoarse gentleness of his tone was nearly her undoing. "You have the face, body, and manners of a woman grown and seasoned. I forget, now and then, that you are but a lass."

She twisted in the saddle to look up at him with narrowed eyes. "I am *not* a child," she told him, oddly stung.

"No," he answered, smiling sadly, "no, you are definitely not a child." They traveled in silence for some time, and then he spoke again. "Methinks we want an inn this night, my lady, and baths in hot water. A board sagging with food, and new clothes as well, if we can find a tailor. We have the gold and to spare, thanks to the abbess."

She could not help being cheered by the prospect of such creature comforts and the relative safety of sturdy walls and a roof. She raised her chin, straightened her shoulders, and sniffled. "Yes," she agreed, significantly restored by the mere thought of sleeping in a bed, bathing, eating all she wanted. She paused. "How far is London-town?"

"I suspect the innkeeper will be able to tell us that," Gresham replied, unperturbed, apparently, by the fact that they were wandering in a wolf-infested wilderness with no idea of where they were.

"How shall we find an inn?" she asked, to distract herself.

Gresham lifted her chin on a warm palm. "Look there, Mistress Meg—see that smoke in the distance, beyond the tops of those birch trees? It's from a fair-sized village, methinks. And look, there's a spire, too."

"Aye," Meg said, seeing the rustic wooden steeple through the bare branches. She wondered who they would meet there, what they would find, how they would be changed by their discoveries. Certainly, she was not wise in the ways of the world—she'd had neither the time nor the opportunity to become jaded—but she knew that even the smallest experience could have a profound and permanent effect on a person.

Had Gabriella passed through this very village, she deliberated, on her way to Cornwall? If she had, then there were people who would remember her, and might know how she fared.

Meg stretched her legs, curled her toes in an effort to relieve some of the numbness brought on by riding in the cold. The heat in her blood had settled heavily into the deepest part of her pelvis, aching there.

"Where there is a spire," Gresham mused aloud, "there is a church, and where there is a church, there is surely a priest." His arms still rested lightly around her middle, and she felt breathless, as though she'd run the whole distance from St. Swithin's, instead of riding a mule.

"Why do you want a priest?" she asked. It hurt her neck, looking back at him, but she stole a single, hasty glance nevertheless.

"Mayhap," he replied, with a quirk at the corner of his mouth, "I wish to make my confession."

"And what would you confess, pray tell?" she asked, trying to sound casual, though in truth she was more than passing curious.

He was silent for a long while, perhaps considering her question, perhaps simply enjoying her discomfort. "You know the answer to that, I think," he said.

"I do not," she argued. "If I did, I should not ask you."

He chuckled at that. "Is it so hard to guess?"

She stiffened as a dreadful thought occurred to her. "It might be," she mused aloud, with rising alarm, "that you know precisely who you are, and you are playing some game with me."

He heaved a great sigh; she not only heard it, she felt it through the rigid muscles of her back, pressed, of necessity, against his chest. "Meg," he said, long-suffering and reasonable, "if I were inclined to do you some mischief, wouldn't I have done so by now?"

She could think of no response.

"What," he jibed, grinning, "is this silence? From Meg Redclift—she of the hasty speech and quicksilver opinions?"

Meg stubbornly held her peace, though an indignant and somewhat guilty flush climbed her neck on hundreds of tiny, prickly feet.

He laughed outright. "I vow, if I declared that you had the sense not to play with fire, stubborn as you are, you would hurl yourself into the flames to prove me wrong."

She bit her lip. "What," she wanted to know, *had* to know, "do you mean to confess? When you see the priest, I mean?"

She felt his smile touch the secret, shadowy side of her heart, warm as the first glimmer of morning light. "Mayhap it will shock you, my lady," he said. "Are you sure you want to hear my terrible sin?"

Her heart beat a little faster. "Yes," she dared.

"All right, then," he conceded, with an elaborate show of reluctance. "I must seek absolution because I want a woman I cannot rightly claim."

His words sent a thrill shivering through her. Again, she was rendered speechless.

He smoothed her trailing hair with a light pass of one hand. "St. Paul was right," he said, with a smile in his voice, "it truly is better to marry than to burn . . ."

"Not," Meg said, with a boldness she hadn't suspected she was capable of, for all her natural brass, "if you already have a wife."

"Mayhap I am widowed," he observed.

To Meg's enormous relief, a village dog bounded out of the bushes just then, yipping a cheerful welcome, and the mule shied, braying. She held on tight to the pommel of the saddle, while Gresham busied himself bringing Enoch under control, and there was no opportunity for further discussion.

The community, though small, consisted of nearly a dozen tiny houses, with smoke curling from their chimneys. Two crooked pathways served as streets, muddy and so narrow that Meg could have stretched out her arms and touched the weathered timber structures on either side. Curious children appeared in doorways, while their mothers came to stand behind them. One elderly man, leading a spotted cow, stopped to stare as Meg and Gresham rode toward the small church in the center of town.

The priest, a dwarf with dark, tonsured hair and classically handsome features, came out to greet them. He was a young man, and dignified, for all his small stature, and Meg liked him even before he smiled.

"Welcome, travelers," he said. "I am Father Mark."

Gresham swung down from the mule's back, leaving Meg mounted, and approached the priest. "Father," he acknowledged, and put out his hand. "Sedgewick is my name. Gresham Sedgewick. And this is Meg Redclift."

Father Mark's interest was piqued by this information, as well as the unexpected appearance of two strangers in his village, Meg could see that, though she had no way of telling whether he'd recognized her name, or Gresham's, or both. He made the semblance of a bow, and his eyes, though still friendly, were watchful. "You are come from London-town?" he asked, indicating, with a gesture and a step to one side, that they ought to precede him into the church.

"We're on our way there," Gresham said, coming back to help Meg down off Enoch's back. He did not mention that they'd left St. Swithin's, only a few days before, or that there had been plague. Even the charity of a priest had limits, she supposed.

A gathering of slat-ribbed dogs and ragged children had formed at the edges of the churchyard, and the latter stared at Meg and Gresham as though they had never seen such creatures before.

Father Mark smiled, clapped his hands together, scattering the motley group like chickens. He chuckled fondly and shook his head. "Poor little mites. Not much happens in Millfield, especially in winter."

They entered a small, dark sanctuary, where a few oil lamps flickered on a rustic altar. There were three rows of benches, arranged on either side of a narrow aisle, and the stone walls barely kept out the cold. The priest led them into a cell of a room, off to the side, where a paltry wood fire burned on a raised and open hearth.

"Sit down and warm yourselves," Father Mark urged, indicating another bench, drawn up close to the fire. "There is a little bread, but I fear—"

Gresham waited until Meg had taken a seat, careful of splinters, and put out her hands to the warmth of the blaze, then he drew a gold coin from the pocket of his jerkin and held it out to the priest.

Father Mark stared at the unsolicited contribution in amazement, murmuring his thanks. " 'Twill feed the whole village till spring," he marveled. "God is good, sir, and so, methinks, are you."

Gresham sighed at this, but offered no comment. He sat down beside Meg, watched as Father Mark tucked the coin into the pocket of his shabby robes, patted it once with the flat of his hand, as if to assure himself that he had not imagined this largesse, then beamed and tossed several chunks of wood onto the fire.

"What brings you here?" the priest asked. "Besides our earnest and unceasing prayers for just such aid as you've given?"

"We had hoped to find an inn," Gresham said.

"There is one farther along the way," Father Mark told them. "Let me fetch you some of that bread I mentioned, and mayhap a bit of wine?"

Meg was hungry, but she wasn't about to accept precious food from obviously limited stores, nor wine, however much she would have welcomed the warm restoration of such an indulgence, and she knew Gresham felt the same way.

"We will eat when we reach the inn," he said. "It's the fire we need now, and your good company."

The priest smiled. "What news do you bring? How does the king fare in France?"

Gresham looked a little forlorn. He was unable to answer either question, of course, having no memory. "Father—"

The priest drew up a small stool and sat facing them across the flames. He rubbed his hands together to warm them and waited. "What is it?" he urged, when Gresham didn't go on.

Gresham thrust a hand through his hair. "Have you been here long?"

Father Mark looked confused. "Five years," he said. "Before I came to Millfield, I served at St. Joseph's, near Warwick."

Gresham was silent for a few moments, then he spoke quickly, as if to get the awkward inquiry over with, out of the way. "Do you know me?" he asked. "When I gave my name, I would have sworn—" He let the sentence fall away unfinished, and stared into the fire as intently as if some important secret were hidden there.

The priest was looking at Meg. "Your surname is Redclift," he said. "Might you be a relation of Sir Redclift, my lady?"

"He was my father," Meg said quietly. An able knight, and one of the king's favorites, Redclift was apparently well known, and well remembered. She did not elaborate, for in truth she knew very little about the man, except that she had feared his hasty temper.

Father Mark nodded, assimilating her words, and studied her a little longer before turning his attention to Gresham. "Of course I have heard of you, Lord Sedgewick. Everyone has."

Gresham started to speak, then fell silent again.

"Why do you ask such a question?" the priest persisted gently, watching Gresham.

"I was struck a blow to the head," he admitted. "There is much I do not remember."

"Such injuries are rarely lasting," Father Mark said, with admirable confidence. "You are a knight, my lord. A king's man of some legend on the battlefield, I've been told."

Gresham swallowed, knotted his hands together where they dangled between his knees. "Have I a wife?" he asked.

Father Mark glanced at Meg, then smiled again. He was obviously bewildered, but determined to believe the best of his guests. "That I cannot say," he admitted, "though there was some talk of a French woman, mayhap a wife, mayhap a mistress." He paused, looked at Meg, cleared his throat, and went on. "One tale is that she set fire to your bed curtains and nearly roasted you alive when you scorned her, but you know what tales soldiers tell. They can gossip like old women, if they're in their cups."

Meg stared at Gresham, at once fascinated and horrified by the picture the priest had painted of Gresham bolting out of a flaming bed, mayhap with his nightclothes blazing. Provided he wore nightclothes, of course.

Hope stirred in her heart, like a tiny bird trying to flutter its way out from under a pile of cold ashes. "Jupiter's teeth," she exclaimed, in a whisper.

Gresham flung her an annoyed glance. "Monique," he recalled, in the tone of one undergoing a disturbing revelation, his eyes and the set of his mouth grim.

The priest merely shrugged. "If her name was mentioned, I've forgotten it."

"Were you a soldier yourself?" Meg asked Father Mark, having forgotten his diminutive stature. Standing beside the average warhorse, the priest's head would have reached only a little past the stirrup.

He shook his head, smiling at her gaffe, and at her subsequent embarrassment. "No," he replied, with gentle good humor, "but as I mentioned earlier, I served at St. Joseph's once upon a time. There is a hospital there, and many wounded men found their way to our gates."

"What else do you know about me?" Gresham pressed, none too patiently.

Father Mark sighed. "You are an unparalleled swordsman, and a friend to Morgan Chalstrey, Lord Edgefield, a companion and confidant of the Black Prince."

Gresham got up from the bench, paced. Again, he shoved a hand through his rumpled hair. "Morgan Chalstrey," he repeated. "Edgefield. I know these names, and yet—" He hesitated again. "I do not. Mayhap I might find this Chalstrey in London. If he is my friend, then he will tell me all I need to know."

"His holdings are in Cornwall," said the priest. "But he might be in London, attending the king. Or in France with the prince."

Gresham's expression was bleak. "Aye," he agreed, and he looked as if he were remembering things better forgotten.

Without comment, Father Mark got up from his seat by the fire, fetched a blanket from a battered trunk in the shadows at the edge of the room, and laid it gently around Meg's shoulders. She had not realized, until that moment, that she was shivering.

"Stay," the priest urged, in time. "Pass the night here, and sup with me."

Although the cell was certainly a humble place, Meg would have preferred to remain, rather than venture out into the cold again, but Gresham had other plans.

"We can reach the inn before nightfall," he said, "if we do not tarry."

Father Mark seemed to know that Gresham's mind would not be changed, and perhaps he was even a little relieved, given the straits he and the villagers were in. He ventured to put a question of his own, speaking mildly. "You and Lady Redclift," he began, looking from one of his guests to the other in benign concern, "are related? Cousins, perhaps?"

Meg flushed and averted her gaze for a moment.

Gresham smiled broadly. "I am the lady's guardian," he announced. "Her bodyguard."

The priest rubbed his chin thoughtfully. "Hmmm," he said, and pondered them both in silence for what seemed like an eternity.

Gresham reached out and pulled Meg to her feet, not abruptly, but with firm motions. The blanket slipped from around her shoulders and spilled onto the hard stone floor. "Thank you, Father, for your hospitality," Gresham said, a mite too heartily. "Best we be gone, while the daylight lasts."

Meg had no time to protest; within the instant, Gresham was all but dragging her outside, hoisting her up onto Enoch's uninviting back. A crisp wind nipped at her through her clothes, and made her pine for the priest's fire.

Gresham mounted, said their good-byes, and spurred the mule toward the snowy trail they had followed into the village.

"Why couldn't we have stayed?" Meg fussed. Her stomach grumbled, and there were goose bumps rising all over her body.

"I thought you wanted a bath," Gresham said, "and sumptuous fare for your supper. Pheasant, perhaps, or rabbit. That poor priest could have offered nothing more than a straw pallet and a bit of stale bread at best, and he would have had to sacrifice to do that, even with the gold I gave him. That, you may be sure, will go to feed the members of his parish."

Meg sighed. "Charity," she remarked, "can be very tiresome."

Gresham laughed. "Aye," he agreed. "That it can."

They came upon the charred, snow-covered ruins of the inn just as the sun was beginning to dip below the tops of the trees. Wolves called to each other in the distance, and the wind was picking up. It was too late to turn back toward the village and take refuge with the priest after all.

An old woman came trundling out of the woods, carrying a squirming piglet under one arm. "Gone," she said, no doubt referring to the inn that had once graced the clearing.

Meg wanted to break down and weep with fatigue, frustration, and hunger, and she found herself wondering how long it would take to roast a very small pig.

The old woman gazed up at the sky, assessing the gray-bellied clouds. "Snow coming," she said. She looked Gresham over, then the mule, then Meg. "Better come with me, the lot of you, or you'll freeze for sure," she decided. Then she slogged off through the crusted snow, still grasping her pig, and Gresham rode after her without further ado.

Within a few minutes, they came to a sizable farmhouse, fashioned of heavy timber and brick, with a sturdy thatched roof. It seemed a prosperous place, though there was nothing fancy about it, and Meg was filled with gratitude and relief. She and Gresham and the mule would not be forced to pass a cold and hungry night in the open after all.

"Go inside and warm yourself, my lady," the woman instructed, her manner both kindly and brusque. "Your man and I will see to the mule and little Bacon, here." She made a fond face at the piglet. "You'll want to build up the fire first thing, of course."

Gresham smiled as he lifted Meg down from Enoch's back, and she murmured her thanks to the farmwife and hurried inside. The house boasted a large main room, and Meg soon had a lively fire blazing on the hearth at one end, thanks to a good supply of dry wood and coals banked earlier in the day.

Rubbing her hands together, Meg looked around. There were stairs, each step a block of oak cut neatly in half, leading to an upper floor. Though she saw no sign of another person, Meg felt certain the woman must have a husband, for surely someone of her advanced age could not run such an enterprise alone. Furthermore, she wouldn't be safe, living alone in an isolated place.

Meg stood with her back to the fire, idly musing, and waited.

Presently, Gresham and the farmer's wife returned, chatting as if they were old friends.

"Let me show you where you're to sleep," the woman said to Meg, smiling broadly, and led the way up the stairs. "Name's Bessie."

Meg was too tired to ask any questions, though she knew she would have plenty when she'd recovered her strength a little. She simply followed Bessie, as she'd been instructed, and soon found herself on the threshold of a spacious bedchamber.

Soon, Bessie had a fire going there, too, the smoke curling up the small brick chimney above the open hearth. Frost curled on the glass windows in glorious patterns, and the chill began to recede almost immediately.

Gresham brought a tub, which he filled with many buckets of steaming water from belowstairs, and Meg nearly broke down and wept with delight and gratitude.

"Bessie thinks we're man and wife," Gresham confided, pausing on the threshold of the room with the final two buckets of water. "I told her we exchanged vows in secret. We're hiding from your uncle, who thinks I've besmirched the family honor and wants to have me hanged. Unless you'd like to sleep in the shed with Enoch and the pig, it will behoove you to go along with the tale."

Meg glanced at the featherbed in the corner, piled high with woolen blankets, and then looked longingly at the waiting bath, next to the hearth. Bessie had given her a chunk of soap and the loan of a warm sleeping gown, and she could smell some kind of fowl—chicken, perhaps—or pheasant, roasting in the kitchen. To leave all this for a shed, and the company of a mule and a pig, would require a far more sturdy character than Meg possessed. She bit down on her lower lip and then nodded her acquiescence.

"Fine," she whispered. "It does strike me, Sedgewick, that you are an uncommonly good liar!"

Gresham grinned mischievously, stepped into the hall, and, without a word of reply, closed the door smartly behind him. Meg promptly stripped off her kirtle and chemise and climbed into the water. It was bliss, sitting down and sinking to her chin in all that warmth.

She soaked awhile, then washed thoroughly, and climbed out of the tub to stand before the hearth, drying herself with a cloth reserved for the purpose. She wondered sleepily if she and Gresham hadn't stumbled into an enchantment of some sort; surely that was the only explanation for the luxuries she was enjoying.

She had just pulled the borrowed gown on over her head when a rap sounded at the door and Gresham came in, unbidden.

She might have challenged him for his effrontery, if he hadn't been holding a trencher filled with hot food. She gave a little cry, near to swooning with anticipation, as her eyes fell upon heaps of boiled turnips, succulent fowl, and a chunk of coarse brown bread. Gresham smiled and handed her the food.

She sat down on the edge of the featherbed and began to eat greedily, with little thought for manners. He watched her from a nearby chair, his expression solemn and somehow tender.

"What luck," she exclaimed, when her hunger had subsided a little, licking her fingers with an exuberance that would have won her a stern reprimand from Mother Mary Benedict, back at the abbey, not to mention extra chores for at least a week. The abbess put great store in what she called "the simple graces." "Who would have guessed that a woman would come along, out of nowhere, carrying a pig, and offer us beds in a place like this?"

"Bed," Gresham corrected. "She offered us *one bed.* We're married, remember?"

Meg pondered that. "You could sleep on the floor," she suggested. She'd eaten every scrap of food on the trencher, and she was still thinking of roast pork. Although she and Gresham had been sharing blankets since leaving the abbey, it seemed wrong here, in a fine, warm house, under a sturdy roof.

He gave her a wry look. "Not on your life, my lady," he said. "I am as fond of creature comforts as you are."

Meg narrowed her eyes at him. "Well, then, you'll have to keep to your own side. There will be no nonsense, Gresham Sedgewick, whatever you told that dear woman. Just you remember that."

Gresham grinned, stood, and executed an offhand bow. "Whatever you say, Lady Redclift."

Downstairs, Bessie sang a bawdy tavern song at the top of her lungs.

"Does she live here all alone?" Meg whispered, mercifully distracted.

Gresham took the trencher out of her hands and set it aside on the floor. His gaze was intent, even mildly troubled. "She has a son. Their bull ran away, and he's out looking for it. She was just coming back from spending most of the day on a neighbor's farm when we met her.

She delivered a babe there—a lass they mean to call Middy, she tells me, 'stuck crosswise' for most of last night—and the new father gave her the pig out of appreciation."

Meg was wide-eyed, and so tired she could barely straighten her spine. She looked down at the bed she was sitting upon and yawned. "I should think he *would* appreciate what she did," she said. " 'Stuck crosswise'? What does that mean?"

"I should think it meant pain," Gresham replied, and grimaced politely. Then he went out again, and Meg toppled over like a tree felled with a sharp ax.

When Sedgewick finally joined her, she had been asleep for hours, and barely stirred as he stretched out with a weary sigh.

8

Gresham was troubled, all that long night, despite the fortuitous comforts of Bessie's house, plagued with tossings and turnings and fitful, fragmented dreams that pitched him upward into wakefulness time and again, but always stayed just out of reach, like figures lurking in a fog. Meg, exhausted by adventure and hard travel, huddled against him, warm and pliant, wholly abandoned to the blissful slumber of the innocent. Though she was so often reckless and impetuous, Gresham knew Meg's spirit for a noble one, as pure and honorable as that of any martyred saint. Having her there beside him that way—so sweet, so soft—was surely payment for every sin he had ever committed, be it grievous or petty. He ached to touch her—really touch her—but he dared not begin, knowing what the end would be.

The dawn was icy and gray, blanketed in that dense, expectant silence that a new fall of snow brings. Meg stirred beside Gresham and he, already taut with desires entirely unfitted to a man who laid claim to honor, felt a mingling of dismay and reverence as he listened to the small sounds she made, stretching, waking by sumptuous degrees.

"Shall we take our leave today, my lord?" she murmured sleepily.

Gresham longed to put his arms around Meg, to guard her from all harm, but he knew that would only weaken both of them. "No," he said, with some regret, for he was anxious to solve the mystery of his own past, and plagued by a sense of formless urgency into the bargain. He allowed himself the slight but still dangerous indulgence of kissing her lightly on the forehead. "More snow has fallen. We could not get far, in such weather."

She started to get out of bed, and then immediately burrowed under the covers again, huddling close. Subjecting Gresham, knowingly or unknowingly, to the tortures of the justly damned. "God's knees," she exclaimed, "it's cold!"

Gresham laughed. "Pray, my lady wayward, do not take up the swearing of oaths. I have enough to answer for, where you are concerned, without being blamed for teaching you such talk." Without waiting for her answer, he scrambled valiantly out of the bed they shared and went to stir the embers in the hearth, and add small bits of dry wood supplied by the ever-generous Bessie. When the blaze was snapping cheerfully, he returned, with gratitude, to the bed, and Meg scooted over to admit him.

By all the saints in heaven, he thought, *and all the demons in hell, I will not yield, and use this woman.*

She had been silent all the while he was building up the fire; now, she spoke in a soft, uncertain voice. "Do you think me wayward?" she asked. "Truly?"

Gresham kissed her lightly on the mouth. "I think you beautiful," he said. "And brave."

Meg sighed contentedly, but he could tell she was not going to let the topic drop. "But I *am* somewhat headstrong, aren't I?"

"Aye," he answered, resigned. He would have preferred to lie, but it did not seem prudent to add to a growing account of sins, known and unknown, many of which were probably unforgivable. "A bit."

"Sometimes," she persisted, in a confidential and worried whisper, "I fear I am—wanton."

Gresham raised his head to look down into her troubled green eyes. "Wanton?" he repeated. For a fleeting and totally reprehensible moment, he thought she was going to tell him she'd lain with other men, actually given herself to someone, anyone, else, and he felt like tearing the house down around their ears, a raging bull, charging and goring with its horns, Samson gone mad.

"Am I?" she asked, and her lower lip trembled slightly. "Wanton, I mean?" Because Gresham knew the uncommon extent of her valor—he had fought beside seasoned soldiers who didn't have half the courage Meg had shown just facing down those wolves—he was all the more moved by her obvious misgivings. "Gresham, sometimes I have such—such thoughts, such *feelings*—"

He caught her chin in one hand and held her firmly, lest she look away. He wanted to laugh, with relief, with affection—hell, with simple jubilation—because whoever he was, whatever he was, he was in that time and that place, with that woman, and that alone was cause for celebration, but he wouldn't have trodden upon her sensibilities that way. For all her spirit, Meg was delicate, even fragile, in ways he was only beginning to understand. "That is as it should be, Meg," he told her. "You are young." His voice caught, and he searched her face. "Ripe."

She stretched, uttering a crooning little sigh, and stirred in Gresham an anguish so sweet and so violent that he nearly cried out. "Ripe?" she asked, and she looked confused.

So innocent, he thought. *Or so bloody clever.*

He wanted to kiss the small furrow between her brows, but he was on perilous ground as it was. "Grown up," he said, by way of explanation, and the words rasped in his throat, a rusty sound.

"I should think that would be obvious," she remarked, and now he suspected she was being coy. The little minx. She couldn't possibly have any idea, raised in a convent, what she was trifling with, or how she was tempting him. "That I'm a woman, I mean."

"It's more than that," he managed, moved in ways he couldn't define, not just physically, but in every other way as well, "and you know it."

"You think me ripe for bed-sport," she said, with a note of mild triumph in her voice.

Dear God, yes, he thought helplessly. Miserably. "What do you know of bed-sport?" he countered, looking stern.

She sighed, a small exhalation, filled with pretty regret. "In truth, my lord, little or nothing. Do you think I would be good at it?"

Let me die.

"Yes," he allowed, when he could trust himself to shape even so simple a word as that one.

She arched an eyebrow, puzzled. Hopeful. "How do you know?"

He chuckled. "Oh, I just do," he said. "There's a lot I

don't remember, but that is something that comes naturally."

She favored him with a smile, a slightly audacious one, in fact, though there was a suspicious, watery glimmer at the corners of her eyes. "I think you are probably expert in the ways of women," she said.

He did not deny it, for while his mind was a blank, where past exploits were concerned, his body remembered, with a visceral intensity, other snowy mornings, in other beds. His muscles recalled the form and movement of battles, and of long journeys over land and sea. When he took a sword in hand, it was as if his blood ran through the metal, and made the blade part of him, flesh of his flesh, and riding took no more thought than breathing. Would that so much else did not elude him.

Still holding Meg's chin, Gresham ran the pad of his thumb lightly across her lower lip. Outside the thick walls, creatures complained to each other—wolves and owls in the woods, Enoch and the pig in the shed. "I swear to you again, my lady, that I will keep you safe, whether I have a wife or not."

She stared up at him. "It is hard to think of it," she said, her voice small. "Your having a wife, I mean. I admit I do not favor the idea."

"Nor do I," he replied gravely.

Her eyes seemed especially bright. "What will happen to us?"

He tried to sound certain. Optimistic. "You will find your sister and, in due time, a good husband to look after you. You will be boundlessly happy all your long, long life, and bear many children who will 'rise up and call you blessed.' And I will return to whatever I left behind. And we will both be fine, Meg."

Meg blinked away the tears just beginning to pool along her lashes and made him a sweet smile. "Let us speak no more of parting, whether for a happy reason or not," she said. "You have been good to me, and dealt with me honorably, even when I might have wished—"

He groaned, started to shake his head in protest of what he knew she was about to say, and she pressed an index finger to his lips.

"Hush," she said. "I will tell you, Gresham Sedgewick, what's on my mind. It matters naught whether you wish to hear it." She traced the circumference of his mouth with the tip of that same finger, as if learning its contours, tucking them away in her memory. Fire blazed through him, followed by a searing chill.

He waited, gazing down at her face, learning it like a passage of exquisite and complicated verse.

"If I could have chosen a man to take as my husband," she said carefully, "I would have wanted you, Gresham Sedgewick. As little as I know of you, it is enough and more."

He bit the inside of one cheek to keep from saying something foolish, making some reckless promise he would not be able to keep.

She went on, slowly, gently. "Were I the sort of woman to be a mistress, and you the sort of man to keep one, I would gladly give myself to you."

He was undone; he let his forehead fall to rest beside her head, pressing his face into the pillow. "Oh, God, Meg—don't—"

She stroked his hair, let her fingertips trail down the nape of his neck, along the full length of his spine. A courtesan, skilled in the art of plying a man's senses, could not have stirred him as deeply as she did; he felt himself harden painfully and realized that, because of their close proximity, she had felt it, too. Her eyes went wide.

"Can we not steal one moment from time?" she asked, in a whisper. "Just one precious interlude, to keep secret in our hearts, ever after?"

He kissed her then, could not stay himself from doing it, pressed his mouth to hers, though not in an enticing way, but devoutly. He was a worshiper, paying chaste homage to a goddess. He found that his own eyes burned oddly as he looked down into hers. "No, Meg," he said. "The price would be too high."

She gazed up at him for a long while, and finally gave a despairing little nod, less of agreement, he thought, than unwilling concession. He got out of bed and was soon gone, nearly stumbling in his haste to escape what he wanted most in all the world.

The snow was deep and, in the way of so many deadly things, dazzlingly beautiful. Cold sunlight glittered upon the crusted surface, like a spill of jewels, and Meg, standing at Bessie's single downstairs window, was greatly stirred by the mysterious grandeur of the sight. Not for the first time in her life, she marveled to find herself in such a place as earth, and rejoiced, for in such moments her very breath and the steady beat of her heart seemed glory enough to appease even the greediest mortal.

Behind her, a fire blazed on the hearth, and precious oil burned in the lamps. Bessie sat spinning by the fire, her gaze going anxiously to the door at every small sound. She was fretting about her son, Tom, too long absent on his search for the lost bull. Gresham had saddled Enoch and gone out to search for any trace of the man or the beast, though the countryside was virtually impassable.

The weather was bitterly cold, but clear, and the snow was pristine. Meg hugged herself as she gazed out at it, and prayed silently that Gresham and Tom would both return safely. And soon.

"He's all I've got, you know," Bessie said, referring, of course, to Tom. "A big boy, he is. Why, he could lift a full grown sow over a stile, if there was a need of it." She made a soft clucking sound and shook her head. "Never married, my Tom. He'd have made a fine husband."

Meg had swept the floor industriously before taking up her post at the window; now, she put the broom away and went to sit upon a bench near Bessie and her spinning. "Why didn't he? Marry, I mean?"

Bessie's sturdy shoulders moved in a shrug. "Shy," she said. "Not like his cousin, Tangwyn. Prideful, is Tangwyn, and full of himself. Always snuffling up to his betters and wanting more than what he's got."

Meg paused. The name struck a disturbing note somewhere inside her, though she was sure she had never heard it before. She looked around at the simple, sturdy house, built to withstand the passing seasons and to shelter those who took refuge within it. "I can see why Tom would want to stay right here," she said. "It's a fine place."

Bessie studied her speculatively. "Mayhap you'd like to stay, my girl. Marry Tom."

Meg blushed. Gresham had told Bessie he and Meg were man and wife. Apparently, the old woman was not so easily fooled as he had thought. She knew she should protest that she already had a husband, but she wasn't a good liar, nor did she have the will to attempt it.

"How did you know?" she asked, very softly.

"The truth about you and Lord Sedgewick, you mean?" Bessie smiled, and stopped her spinning. "He took his sweet time going up those stairs last night, weary though he was. A man with a right to your bed would not have tarried at all, my dear."

Meg looked down, and her blush deepened. "He does not want me," she confided, ashamed. "Mayhap I am lacking—"

Bessie chortled, scoffing affectionately. "No, lass," she interrupted. "His eyes follow you, and I can see his heart shining in them. It is honor that stays Sedgewick from having you, not choice." She paused, sighed. "Alas, honor can be a hard master. Especially with a man like that."

Bessie's remarks at once uplifted and deflated Meg's spirits. No matter what Gresham might feel for her, he would not bend to it, and even if he came to love her, he would always love honor more. "You are perceptive," she said.

"And sensible," Bessie said, with gentle certainty. "Stay here and be wed to my Tom. He's a steady man, with a sweet nature—not the sort to raise a hand to a woman, nor to roam."

Meg thought of all the discarded women at St. Swithin's—and in places like it all over England, no doubt—who would praise God and all His angels and saints for a chance at such a life, and was chagrined. She had never met Bessie's Tom, but even if he were the handsomest of men, the wittiest and the most engaging, she still would not have married him, if only because he wasn't Gresham Sedgewick. She had been spoiled, she feared, for all others. "I'm sure Tom is wonderful," she said quietly, "but . . ." her voice fell away, and she could only shake her head.

"But your heart has run ahead of you, and left you to chase it," Bessie finished for her, her tone and manner so infinitely kind that Meg truly wished, at least for a few moments, that she *could* stay in this sturdy, well-supplied house, and live out her days as a farmwife.

Meg could only nod.

Hours later, with the sun already spilling gold and crimson over the western horizon, Gresham returned, tired, cold and alone, except for the recalcitrant Enoch. He had seen no sign of either Tom or the bull, he said.

Bessie was obviously worried, but she tried to put a brave face on the situation. She roasted venison, brought from her storeroom, and they all enjoyed a hearty supper. New snow was falling when Enoch, shut away in the shed, alerted them to the new arrivals with an earsplitting bray.

Gresham got up from the table before Bessie, being younger and fleeter, and made for the window. The old woman was right behind him, her face alight with hope.

"Damnation," Gresham muttered, plainly displeased, when he saw who was approaching, and the exclamation heightened Meg's curiosity by several notches.

Bessie peered past his broad shoulder, and Meg, watchful as she helped herself to a second wedge of cheese, saw the older woman's whole countenance slip into a sort of benign resignation. "Alas," she said, and drew open the door.

The man who stepped over the threshold was one Meg had met before; he was the same mummer she'd met at the fair. He'd promised to take her letter to Gabriella when he journeyed to Cornwall.

His resemblance to Gresham was quite startling, as before, but when the dim light from the oil lamps found his face, she saw that the likeness was only superficial. This man, clad in the poor garb of a wanderer, had lived a life much at variance with Gresham's, and it showed in the coarse texture of his skin and the keen, assenting glint in his eyes.

"Tangwyn," Bessie said, in desultory greeting. "Come in out of the cold."

He leaned down, kissed the older woman on the cheek. His gaze had locked with Gresham's, and it was not a friendly exchange. Meg could readily discern that, though neither man spoke to the other at that moment. Gresham's arms were folded across his chest, his blue eyes narrowed.

"The others are in the shed," said the man called Tangwyn. "I would not impose upon your hospitality to beg them shelter beneath your roof, good aunt, but since you are kin to my sainted mother, I thought you might take me in for a night or two." His glance left Gresham, at last, to flicker over Meg, lingering in places where it shouldn't have. "I see I am not the first to seek refuge from an unkind and early winter."

Bessie did not smile. "Go and stand by the fire," she said wearily. "I will fetch a plate for you."

"No introductions?" Tangwyn asked, wheedling. He tore his gaze from Meg to look at Gresham again.

"Gresham Sedgewick," Gresham said, without putting out his hand. "And my lady wife."

Meg had not had an opportunity to tell Gresham that the marriage ruse was lost on Bessie, and now she was glad. She misliked this Tangwyn, misliked, particularly, the way he looked at her. She nodded and made no correction to Gresham's claim, and took note that Bessie did not disabuse her nephew of the notion, either.

"Have we met before?" Tangwyn asked, watching Gresham and settling himself beside the fire, as bidden, awaiting the food Bessie had promised.

"Mayhap," Gresham allowed, and Meg could see that he was trying to grasp some elusive and troubling memory. "There is something familiar about you."

"Is there?" Tangwyn inquired easily. "I was thinking the same thing, as it happens."

Hostility fairly crackled between the pair, like unseen lightning, for all their carefully measured politeness, one to the other.

Bessie, meanwhile, was frowning, now at Tangwyn, now at Gresham. "You've the same blood in your veins, the two of you," she murmured. "I'd swear an oath to it. But how can that be?"

Tangwyn, accepting his supper with a little nod of thanks, was the first to reply. "We may have a common relative—somewhere," he said. He had to see that the supposition nettled Gresham, so obvious was that fact, and it seemed that the mummer took pleasure in the knowledge that he'd gotten under the other man's skin. "Was your father a soldier, Lord Sedgewick?"

Gresham's reply was a stubborn grunt. His arms were still folded, and he had taken up a proprietary stance nearer the table, where Meg sat, ignoring what remained of her meal.

"My mother—God rest her—was something of a strumpet," Tangwyn went on, either forgetting, or not caring, that the woman he slandered had been Bessie's relation, too. Taking into account her own feelings for Gabriella and Elizabeth, Meg secretly marveled that Bessie didn't clout the knave over the head for speaking so in her presence. "She liked soldiers. Found them lively company. Mayhap your father was among them."

Gresham said nothing, but Meg saw the muscles in his jawline clamp down with dangerous force, and she knew, as well as if she'd been inside that power body with him, that his fingers ached to close round the hilt of his sword.

"Nonsense," Bessie put in crisply, surely sensing the bristling energy in the room and striving to pour oil on troubled waters, "your father was a simple pig farmer, and you well know it. And your mother, by the way, was a good woman. *I* was the one who favored soldiers."

A startled silence descended over the room with Bessie's last statement—mayhap she had intended just that.

"What of your poor companions in the shed?" she went on, in due time. "No doubt they're hungry, and in need of blankets."

"Never mind them," Tangwyn said, temporarily thwarted, and none too pleased by the fact. "A couple of women, a boy. Harmless sorts."

"Ah, yes," Bessie said, sighing. "Harmless, indeed. Tell them to come in, and spread their bedrolls, if they have them, near the hearth. Mustn't leave them starving in the cold."

Tangwyn, warm and busily occupied with the task of filling his own belly, gave a distracted nod. "Where is Tom?" he asked.

For a moment, Meg thought Bessie was going to break down and weep, the worry stood so stark, so naked, in her face. In the space of a heartbeat, though still not quickly enough to deceive the very watchful Tangwyn, Meg concluded, Bessie summoned up a smile. "He's about his business," she said, and ran her eyes over Tangwyn's long frame once, assessing. "He's an industrious man, my Tom."

Tangwyn reddened slightly; he'd registered the jibe, then, as had both Gresham and Meg. "Always the noble one, our Tom," he said, after a pause. "Still too shy to ask for the hand of a cross-eyed milkmaid?"

Meg thought Bessie was going to take the broom to Tangwyn just then, so fierce was the fury in her eyes, but, to her disappointment, it didn't happen. A good scuffle would have been diverting, of a cold winter night. Alas, Bessie did not need a broom for a weapon, she had her tongue.

"The boy you mentioned," she said. "Is he a favorite of yours?"

Tangwyn went crimson at this, and Meg could see that he wanted to offer a scathing response, or even leap to his feet and do her some fierce violence, but he must have sensed that Gresham was ready to pounce on him at the slightest excuse, and he was wise enough to restrain himself. He made no verbal answer, but simply finished his supper, and when he'd eaten his fill, he rose, went out, and brought in his straggly little troupe, biding, until then, in the shed.

There were two women in the group, sharp-eyed and cautious, but it was the lad who interested Gresham and Meg. He was the same boy they'd encountered at the fair at Upper Gorse, in possession of Enoch, the abbey's missing mule. Seeing them, he nearly bolted.

"Come in," Gresham said, in a warning tone, and his smile was cold as a steel blade, and just as sharp at the edges. He got the lad by the scruff, and sat him down hard on a bench. "I would have a word with you," he told the boy. Meg had a few questions for him herself, for he'd spoken of Gabriella at the fair, referring to her as "Chalstrey's whore." She wanted to know who Chalstrey was, for a start, and why her sister was with him, and not her intended husband, Avendall.

"There's time enough for talk," Tangwyn interceded smoothly. "Pray, do not worry poor Blodwyn, for he is slow, and wouldn't know a truth if it bit him. Besides, on a night such as this one, we can surely make a *pretense* of friendship, can we not?"

Gresham leveled a look at the mummer that was more than an answer to his jovial question. Then he turned his attention back to Blodwyn, and the look in his eyes was as sharp as the blade he'd been honing. "You and I know each other," he said, in a deceptively easy tone. "Tell me who I am."

Blodwyn flung a pleading look at Tangwyn, and swallowed visibly. "Lord Sedgewick, sir. You're a knight. A servant of the king. That's all I know—truly it is!"

The fingers of Gresham's right hand flexed, then tightened around the handle of the blade. "You are a liar," he said flatly.

The boy opened his mouth, closed it again, clamped his jawline down hard. "Mayhap you would not like what he has to tell you," said the mummer.

Gresham pressed the tip of the blade into the hollow at the base of Blodwyn's throat, never breaking the skin, but causing beads of perspiration to break out across the boy's upper lip all the same. "Speak," he commanded.

Meg would have sworn she saw a dire warning in the look that passed from Tangwyn to the lad. The boy shook his head. His lips were a tight line.

Meg stepped forward. "My sister, Gabriella Redclift—"

The boy's eyes were hot with defiance, and Meg knew in that instant that he wasn't going to tell her or Gresham anything of substance, no matter what. Gresham had obviously come to the same conclusion, and his countenance was grim.

As the evening lengthened, Blodwyn kept a careful distance from Gresham, and watched him as though he might suddenly sprout horns, cloven hooves, and a tail with an arrowhead point. He ate, said nothing at all, and then curled up in a corner like a dog to rest, though Meg sensed that he wasn't sleeping.

Tangwyn sat before the fire, like a monk in meditation, and the two women, having eaten, produced a board and small, brightly colored stones from one of their bundles, and began to play some sort of game, speaking softly in a language Meg had never heard before. She was sure they were fortune-tellers.

Presently, Gresham went back to honing the blade of his knife against a whetstone, while Bessie returned to her spinning, and Meg cleared the table and washed the simple wooden plates and knives.

The scene might have appeared tranquil to an on-looker, except for Gresham's knife sharpening, Meg thought, turning from the basin to survey the odd little gathering, but her own emotions were churning with the need to know Gabriella's fate, and some less obvious element as well. Surely the others felt it, a thrumming tremor in the atmosphere, though only Blodwyn and Gresham showed any overt sign of doing so.

She looked at Gresham, saw the steel of his blade glint in the firelight. He caught Meg's gaze, and held it, and, as clearly as if he'd spoken aloud, directed her to leave the room, go upstairs. She shook her head in refusal—hope-less as it seemed, she was awaiting another chance to question Blodwyn about her sister—and saw his jaw harden and his eyes glitter with something more urgent than mere irritation.

Tangwyn rose with some ceremony from his crouched position on the hearth and stretched his limbs, giving a long, lusty groan as he did so.

Gresham set the knife on the table beside him, but made no other move.

As if Tangwyn's rising had been a signal, the others in his small troupe scrambled to their feet. Tangwyn stood midway between Gresham, who had risen without haste from the bench, ready for whatever was coming. Bessie stopped her spinning, but said nothing, and Meg eased closer to her, gripped the old woman's stout, work-worn hand in her own.

"Alas," said Tangwyn, spreading his hands and pulling a face in a parody of regret, "we must demand what gold and goods you may have." His gaze flicked assessingly to Meg, then swung back to Gresham, whom he probably saw as the only real challenge in the room, Tom being away. "You, my lord, can surely guess which treasure I would have from you." He paused. "After I've slit your throat, that is. I could have killed you once before, but you were insensate, and I wanted you to know it was I who brought about your end."

Gresham's expression was impassive, and somehow more terrifying than the bold threat Tangwyn had just issued. That he was quite capable of killing another person, this man she was starting to love, with little or no compunction, was plain to Meg.

"Take what you want of food and coin," Bessie said, rising to her feet. "But by God's best leggings, you will take naught else."

Gresham stood watching Tangwyn with that same chilling calm he had exhibited all along. Somehow, Meg marveled to herself, he had known that this was in the offing, and he was ready for it. "Have what your good kinswoman will give you," he told the mummer, without inflection, "but if you touch anything—or anyone—of mine, I will sever your arms from their sockets."

The boy lunged at him then, in a flurry of what looked like desperation to Meg, and Gresham subdued him easily, hooking one arm around his neck and holding him, struggling, against his side. Then, with a swift motion of one hand, he sent the lad sprawling to the floor, unconscious.

Meg gasped, and the two women, their board and pieces forgotten, looked at her with expressions reminiscent of the hungry wolves she'd encountered before. They seemed to move as one creature, in tandem, and she was discouraged, if not really surprised, to see that they each boasted a small knife, upraised and ready.

She shivered, then grabbed the broom and faced them, as fierce, in her own way, as they were.

Tangwyn chuckled at this. "Ah, she has spirit, as well as a comely face and appealing form. A woman like your lady wife, Lord Sedgewick, would bring fine prices at the fairs and markets. Aye, men would pay dearly for a few minutes in her tent."

Gresham made a low sound in his throat, like a growl, and Meg felt a shiver dance up and down her spine. Did they not see the danger, the mummer and his women? Were they too foolish, too greedy, to notice that they had awakened a ravening lion, unleashed a storm worthy of the Old Testament?

The two women came at Meg, and she wielded the broomstick handily, like a knight with a pole. Blodwyn remained on the floor, limp and still, while Bessie waded into the fray with a kettle. Gresham walked right through the tangle of angry females, like Moses crossing the Red Sea, and knocked the blade from Tangwyn's hand with one motion of his arm. Meg, busy with her own battle, saw no more of the encounter. One of her attackers slashed her forearm, drawing blood, and she rammed the woman in the hollow of the throat with the end of the broom handle, an act which, to her amazement, felled the pair. Before they could do more than raise themselves onto their elbows, Bessie was there with the fireplace poker, striking an intimidating pose.

Gresham, meanwhile, had got Tangwyn by the back of the head, and smashed his face hard against one of the timbers supporting the roof.

A slow trickle of blood trailed from one nostril and when Gresham released him, the mummer moved as if to wipe his hand upon his jerkin. Instead, with frightening swiftness and skill, he produced a second knife from inside his sleeve; it was small, but it looked sharp enough to cleave a single hair into two perfect halves.

Meg's heart fair stopped at the sight, but Gresham seemed pleased. Even relieved. There was something truly ferocious in his face, a passion for blood-sport.

"Stop," Bessie said quietly. Blodwyn moaned on the floor, starting to come around, and the others were still reclining as well, their gazes fixed on the poker still grasped firmly in the older woman's hand.

Tangwyn, still bleeding, stood gasping for his breath, knife in hand. Meg knew, by the look in his eyes alone, that he would gladly cut out Gresham's liver if given even half a chance.

"Take another step," Gresham drawled, his gaze unwavering. "I would relish tearing you apart."

Tangwyn hesitated, then let his hand drop to his side. The knife clattered to the floor, and Bessie hastened to snatch it up, dropping it into a pocket of her kirtle.

The mummer shook his head. "You don't want to do that, my lord," he countered, watching Gresham with an unnerving gleam of anticipation in his eyes. "You see, I know where your son is—and you do not."

Meg was thunderstruck, and Gresham was clearly shaken, though he did an admirable job of hiding the fact.

"What are you talking about?" he demanded. He got Tangwyn by the front of his jerkin and slammed him backward against the nearest wall. Tangwyn protested with a raw, gurgling cry. Meg heard both laughter and desperation in the sound.

"Gresham, stop," she said, not for the mummer's sake, but for Sedgewick's.

"Answer me," Gresham growled, ignoring her. There might have been no one in the world, save him and Tangwyn.

" 'Tis true, then," Tangwyn sputtered, apparently anxious, at this late date, to spare himself and his crafty head by any means possible, even cooperation. "You don't recollect the brat, nor the woman who whelped him—and lay with me when you were away playing soldier."

Gresham's hold on the mummer's jerkin did not slacken. The cold blaze in his eyes was unchanged as well. "You are a liar," he breathed. "There was no woman, no child."

Meg crept closer, holding her breath, grasping the broom handle in fingers slickened with sweat. At the edge of her vision, she saw the women getting to their feet, and Blodwyn, the lad.

She moved behind Gresham then, to guard his back, the broom raised high to show that she would use it if they advanced.

The players, none too brave without their leader to urge them on, hesitated. An oppressive silence settled over the room, heavy, like a ship sinking into the sand at the bottom of some fathomless and distant sea.

"Stay back," Meg warned the trio. Bessie, winded, had sunk into her chair at the spinning wheel, the poker still within easy reach.

Gresham's entire consciousness was trained on Tangwyn; Meg could feel the almost preternatural force of it. "Explain," Gresham said, with deceptive mildness, "or I vow I'll kill you by inches."

"The boy—" Tangwyn gasped, wiping his nose, "—is called Kieran—"

"Where is he?"

"He's—he's fostering at one of Lancaster's holdings—"

"His mother."

"Dead. God's teeth, Sedgewick, Monique perished in childbirth, trying to bear you a second babe. She died with the infant, cursing you to the everlasting fires of hell. Mayhap it is no wonder you don't remember—you'd been away soldiering with Chalstrey and the Black Prince, having yourself a merry time, for better than six months when it happened."

Meg's knees nearly failed her; she stiffened them just in time to keep from collapsing into a nerveless heap on Bessie's floor.

"What—" Gresham began, in a tone so confused and bleak that it broke Meg's heart to hear it, "what was your part in all this?"

The mummer's gaze was steady, full of hatred and challenge and a sort of frenzied cowardice. "I was the one who consoled her when you were away," he said. "She called me by your name when we made love."

Another silence followed, pulsing in the room like a drumbeat. Meg stepped a little to one side, her eyes burning with tears of sympathy for poor Monique, for the lost babe, for Gresham.

"Where is the boy?" Gresham said, and when the mummer hesitated, he took him by the front of his jerkin and pressed his own knife into the throbbing hollow at the man's throat. *"Where,"* he repeated, *"is the boy?"*

The flesh of Tangwyn's face was a ghastly gray white color, mottled with patches of blood pink. There could be no doubting his hatred for Gresham; it was complete, utter, and undisguised. He spat.

Gresham drew blood with the point of the knife. "Where?"

"Windsor," Tangwyn said at last. "Did I not say he was in Lancaster's care? He serves as a squire there and wants nothing so much as to be a man and, thus, a knight." He smiled as he watched the truth of his words saturate Gresham's beleaguered mind. "There is much you do not know, Sedgewick," he said. "Mayhap the best revenge will be watching you discover it all. There are exquisite horrors awaiting you. Reason enough, methinks, to let you live a little longer."

Gresham looked, to Meg, like a man who had been flogged from all sides. He was being consumed by suffering. Gresham's skin was waxen, like a dead man's. He glared at Meg, swayed slightly, and then sat down heavily on the bench behind him. The knife he'd held to Tangwyn's throat fell to the floor with a musical clatter.

"Get out," Bessie told the mummer. "Take these dogs you call friends with you, and never—*ever*—present yourself at my doorway again."

Meg held her breath, then watched in silence as they all left, vanishing into the night—Tangwyn, the women, the boy. Her arm had stopped bleeding, but she became aware of the stinging pain.

"Bolt the door," Gresham said. "Meg, let me see that cut."

"It's nothing," she protested, turning to Bessie. "Is there wine? Or ale?"

"Aye," Bessie replied, and hastened away, leaving Meg and Gresham alone in that too-quiet room.

Gresham immediately began to shiver, as though struck by a draft. His teeth chattered; his lips were blue.

Meg spoke mildly, though not meekly. "Come and stand close by the fire, my lord," she said. She saw, now that she was calmer, that he had been cut in the tussle with Tangwyn, mayhap even stabbed. "Perhaps you can ignore the marks of the mummer's blade, but a chill takes hold from the inside."

Gresham got up, with difficulty, and Meg was careful not to touch him as he moved across the room to the hearth and dropped wordlessly to his knees. There, he stared at the flickering blaze as if he longed to fling himself into it.

Meg added sticks of dried wood but did not draw too near Gresham. It wasn't that she feared him—she had known, even at the height of his rage, that he would never do her harm. No, it was the rawness of his emotions that made her hold back; he was like a man flayed until every nerve was exposed. To touch him would be to break his rigid control.

Bessie brought wine in a ewer; Meg handed it to Gresham without speaking, watched as he drank deeply. After a long interval, and a great deal of wine, Gresham seemed less distraught. Still, he would not look at her.

"We will find your son," she whispered. "We will go to Windsor and fetch him."

He made a strange, brief sound, far down in his throat

and bent double for a moment, like a man who had been run through with a sword. "Leave me," he rasped.

"I'm not going away," Meg told him. "As long as you stay here, on this hearth, so shall I."

"A son," he said. "I have a son."

"Do you remember him?" She spoke so quietly, with so little emotion, that it might have been another woman talking, a stranger.

Gresham's face, reflecting the flames, was a study in bemused agony, and none the less beautiful for it. He might have been an angel, gazing into the heart of hell. "No," he said hoarsely. "Or, at least, I can't make an image come to my mind. At the same time, I know the mummer spoke true. There was a woman, and a babe."

Meg waited a beat before responding. "But surely this is good news, my lord? Does not every man want an heir?" Her own father certainly had, and he'd made no secret of his disappointment in getting only daughters.

Gresham thrust a hand through his hair. "Aye," he said softly, "but what sort of man abandons his child, his wife?"

"You were a soldier, a knight, and soldiers must go away to war."

Gresham shook his head, and when at last he looked Meg full in the face, she ached for the bewilderment and the sorrow she saw in him, and the tentative, wondering joy. "A son," he reflected, once more.

9

"Do you suppose they've taken the mule away with them," Bessie fretted, still shaken, when Tangwyn and his troupe had been gone for the best part of an hour, "or my sweet little Bacon?" The cut on Meg's arm, her personal keepsake of the tussle with the mummer's women, had been washed and bandaged, and though it stung a little, she knew the wound was not a serious one. The worst of the experience was the way it caused her to miss Elizabeth, who would have treated it with an herb poultice and much sisterly concern.

Gresham, still dazed by the revelation that he had a living son, now biding at Windsor, recovered quickly. "I'll see to the animals," he said, donning his cloak to step out into the wintry darkness of a near moonless night. Meg was indeed grateful for his slight disorientation; without it, he would surely have gone chasing after Tangwyn and the others, bent on reaching the castle, and the boy Kieran, before him.

"I'm coming with you," Meg said quickly, thinking the

mummer might still be nearby, lying in wait, expecting Gresham to strike out on the journey immediately.

Gresham smiled, in a rather sad way, as if amused by her obvious conviction that she could offer any sort of protection, and she was nettled, for as it happened, she *had* acquitted herself well in the scuffle. "You ought to stay here, with Bessie, and let that gash heal properly," he said, watching with resignation as she steadfastly ignored him, pulling on a wrap of her own. "Not that you ever do what you ought."

"Have a care, the pair of you," Bessie warned, shaking a finger as she stepped into the good-natured fray. "There's naught that's decent about him, that Tangwyn. Think of it—setting out to rob his own kinfolk that way. Why, we was all he had, Tom and me, and when my lad hears what's come to pass this night, he'll thrash the knave for sure."

Meg and Gresham exchanged glances, and Meg knew Gresham was thinking what she was, that Tom might well be lying dead somewhere in the forest, past hearing the tale of treachery, let alone giving the culprit a thrashing. A multitude of evils could have befallen Tom in the time he'd been away, and with every hour that he tarried, the likelihood of his return was lessened.

The light of one of Bessie's oil lanterns revealed that Enoch and the piglet were safe in the shed, as were the old cow, Sweet-blossom, and several disgruntled laying hens, who evidently shared the modest quarters. While Gresham fed the mule from the ample store of hay laid up, no doubt, by the vanished Tom, Meg searched the straw for eggs and found several, small and brown. She tucked them carefully into the pocket of her cloak, already looking forward to breakfast, and praised the chickens for their endeavors.

"You'll be setting out for Windsor in the morning," she ventured, when Gresham did not volunteer the fact.

"Yes," Gresham said.

"Has it occurred to you that that's precisely what Tangwyn wants you to do?" she asked calmly. "Surely you can see that this might be some sort of trap."

Gresham leaned on the handle of the pitchfork. "I have no doubt that we'll meet again, the mummer and I," he said. "Plainly, there is much that is unsettled between us."

"You believe what he said, then," she pressed quietly. "That she perished, with the second child?"

He nodded. "I still have no image of Monique in my mind, nor of the boy, but, yes, it's true. I'm sure of that much, at least."

Meg drew a measured breath, let it out slowly, feeling as if she were about to pitch forward and tumble head over heel down some steep incline. "And you think to leave me behind, with Bessie?"

He chuckled, then sighed philosophically. "It would be best," he said, "but of course you will balk at the idea. If I went off without you, you'd set out on your own in a trice, bent on reaching your sister by whatever means came to hand, and probably wind up as wolf fodder in some field."

"I'm glad you see reason," Meg said, and he laughed and shook his head, marveling. Her thoughts took a new turn. "Perhaps there will be word of Gabriella at Windsor—surely travelers from all over England pass that way, with tales to carry."

He merely nodded, put up the pitchfork, and bent to lift each of the mule's hooves in turn, checking for stones. If the animal came up lame between there and Windsor, it would be the beginning of grief and the end of a great many other things, for they would surely be stranded.

"Is he in danger?" she dared to ask, at some length. "Your son, I mean?"

"I'll wager he's safe enough at Windsor, if he's fostered with Lancaster's brood." He looked most weary and distracted. Plainly, his thoughts had gone ahead, to the castle, or back, seeking some trace memory of his son, and of the woman who had borne the boy.

Meg, who had dreaded learning that Gresham was indeed wed to another, could take no joy in the fact that he was instead a widower. She felt a deep and genuine sorrow for the lost Monique and the infant who had perished with her, strangers though they were, and the knowledge of the boy Kieran's existence surprised her not at all. It would have been a rare thing indeed if a man like Gresham Sedgewick reached the age of majority without siring at least one child, within the bounds of marriage or without.

What concerned Meg now was the subtle but poignant awareness that this discovery about his past had opened a well of sorrow in Gresham, one long hidden away in the very depths of his spirit. She wondered if he hadn't been holding his past at bay, at least partly on purpose, because there was pain in it.

"What will you do," she asked, as they walked through the blue-shadowed snow toward Bessie's house, satisfied that all was well with the livestock, "when you encounter the mummer again?"

"I will kill him, of course," Gresham answered flatly, and without hesitation.

Meg said nothing to that, though the words sent a shiver tripping down her spine, for they came so easily, and rang with such conviction. They entered the house, setting the oil lantern aside on a table, and found Bessie waiting anxiously for word of the animals.

Meg hastened to assure the woman that the creatures were fine, and Bessie toddled off to bed, murmuring a litany of her trials and troubles as she went. Meg turned her attention to Gresham the moment the woman had disappeared into the little room at the far end of the house.

He was gazing into the fire, its light playing across his features. Memory was the soil in which the mind was rooted, it seemed to Meg, and for Gresham the connection had been severed, mayhap permanently. What was that like? Surely he must feel, at times, as if he didn't really exist at all.

Meg felt grateful for her own predicament, hurtful as it was. Better to brood, as she did, in the secret regions of her heart, over the perils Elizabeth faced, in a plague-ridden convent, and the mystery of Gabriella's long silence. At least she could link names and faces to her fears, instead of battling ghosts, as Gresham did.

Biting her lower lip to keep from offering sympathies she sensed would be unwelcome, Meg offered up a silent prayer that the Holy Virgin would guard and guide her sisters, and Gresham, too.

She bid him a soft good night—he did not respond, nor even seem to hear her—and went upstairs. There, she gazed briefly out the narrow, thick-paned window, wondering where Tangwyn and his band of thieving players were passing the remains of that cold night, and where Bessie's Tom had got to. Was Gabriella looking out some other window, even at that moment, thinking of her sisters? Was Elizabeth well, or had the plague taken her?

Restless, but very tired, she kicked off her slippers and shed all her clothes, but for the thin linen shift that served as an undergarment, washed, and went to the hearth to build a small fire and take the chill off the room. She'd set aside the tinderbox, and was kneeling, with her hands held out to the blaze, when the door of the chamber creaked open and Gresham appeared.

A moment before, Meg would have rejoiced, but she saw such melancholy in his countenance that she herself was nearly overcome by it.

Gresham's eyes burned as he gazed at her; it seemed, just then, that he did not recognize her. She knew, though, by the hunger etched deep into every line of him that the light of the fire shone through the scant shift and revealed each curve and plane and shadow of her body.

"I'm going mad," he said, in a ragged whisper.

Meg simply held out her arms to him. She was innocent, in the purest sense of the word, but she knew in that moment that she loved Gresham Sedgewick, whoever and whatever he was, with an ardor that was elemental and age old. He was not her husband, and he would probably never return her tender sentiments, but somehow, for that night at least, it didn't matter.

He closed the door behind him, and lowered the latch, but came no nearer. He said her name.

She stood very still. Waited.

Neither of them spoke for a long, long time. Then, "Send me away," he rasped. His eyes, his stance, made a very different entreaty.

"Never," Meg responded, softly but with all the force of her considerable will.

Gresham thrust an unsteady hand through already rumpled hair. "There is no wife waiting, no vow to be broken."

"No," she said, very gently. She wanted him, God help

her. Needed him. Fool that she was, she ached to give
herself to this man who was more a stranger to himself
than to her, and damn the consequences.

A great, despairing sigh erupted from somewhere
deep inside Gresham. "I would have you, Meg Redclift,"
he told her.

"My desire," she said, with brazen shyness, "is as great
as yours, my lord."

He leaned back against the door, mayhap mistrusting
his legs to hold him upright, and that was when Meg approached him. She plunged the spread fingers of both
hands into his burnished-gold hair, rose onto her toes,
bold as a strumpet, and pressed her mouth to his.

Gresham groaned aloud and moved as if to put her
away from him, but when, following some primitive instinct, she teased his lips apart with the tip of her tongue
and then made a gentle invasion, he returned the kiss in
kind, and with desperation.

Another woman might have been frightened by the
sheer force of Gresham's response, by the barely contained strength in the hardened muscles of his arms and
chest, belly and thighs, but Meg was indeed his equal, in
matters of desire if not in physical might. She knew
naught of lovemaking, but she was a most eager pupil,
ready to be taught.

While their mouths and tongues made fierce and tender warfare, Meg slid her hands down over Gresham's
shoulders, his sides, his hips, exploring. She swallowed
his moan of response and then clasped her buttocks in his
hands and pressed herself hard against him, as much in
warning, she thought, as need.

Some moments had passed when, with a sound that
was half gasp, half moan, he pushed her away. Then, tak-

ing a brief hold on her shoulders, he held her away from him, just far enough to search her face.

"Meg, you need only say it—say no—"

"But I will not," Meg heard herself whisper. "Nay, I *cannot.*"

He lifted her into his arms then, carried her to the featherbed, so innocently shared the night before, and laid her down. His shadow, cast by the firelight, moved over her; she felt the weight of it, the substance, like a caress.

"God forgive me," he rasped, and then he was beside her, gathering her into his arms, kissing her again. She was immediately lost—but nay, she thought. She had been lost since first she saw him, lying bloodied and unheeding in the stubbly garden patch at St. Swithin's.

Gently, reverently, and at the same time, with a fire that threatened to consume her entirely, Gresham Sedgewick introduced Meg to the singular pleasures of the flesh.

He kissed her until she was fair drunk on the touch of his lips and his tongue, stroked her, through the thin chemise, until she tossed fitfully on the mattress ticking, loving the ferocious tension rising within her, and at the same time craving its fulfillment.

Moving at his own pace, Gresham stripped away the single gossamer garment between them. At some point, he'd shed his own clothing, too, though Meg could not have said when or how he'd managed that feat, for she was wholly absorbed in sensation, and in wanting.

He tasted the tips of her breasts, nipped at them lightly, first this one, and then that, all the while stroking her belly, her hips, her ribs, her thighs. She made a low, continuous whimpering sound as he prepared her, with exquisite thoroughness, for the inevitable conquering.

When he parted her legs, and bent his head to partake of her, in the same way he had partaken of her breasts, Meg cried out in surprised ecstasy and entangled her fingers in his hair. The thought that Bessie might hear flitted through her mind, and was gone. Her hips flew upward, seeking more of Gresham, inexplicably more, as he slowly, methodically, drove her toward madness.

It was as though the sun itself were taking shape inside her, blazing more and more brightly, burning hotter and hotter, until it finally burst, flinging light into every part of her body and spirit.

She could not have imagined any greater pleasure, but when Gresham actually entered her body, minutes later, Meg was transported and forever transformed. The change was not simply physical, but all-encompassing, a thing of spirit and of mind, of earth and heaven, of all eternity and a single heartbeat.

The cataclysm possessed them both, and ended by casting them first to the heights, where they clung to each other, souls melded, and then releasing them slowly, slowly, from its grasp, until they both slept, exhausted.

When Meg awakened, with the first pink and lavender light of dawn, Gresham, God be thanked, still lay in the very depths of slumber, wholly and blissfully spent from the sweet rigors of the night.

Voices from downstairs caused Gresham to stir, but not awaken, and Meg scrambled into her clothes, certain that Tom must have returned at last. Had Tangwyn and the mummers come back, Bessie would not be speaking in moderate tones.

At the top of the steps, Meg froze, unable to retreat or even cry out a warning to Gresham.

Prigg, the sheriff, stood below. He considered Meg

with a pensive expression, and she knew he was trying to place her. He rarely visited St. Swithin's, after all, and she had seldom been to Upper Gorse, let alone beyond. Still, she had seen him that morning at the gate, when he'd demanded Gresham's surrender, and he had seen her, standing beside the abbess.

He was not entirely bereft of perception, and he took visible note of Meg's hesitation on the upper landing. No doubt he had seen the color rise in her cheeks as well, and even taken note of her brief, foolish temptation to flee.

Prigg, taking his breakfast alone at Bessie's table, did not rise from the bench upon Meg's entrance, nor did he lay down the wooden spoon grasped in his right hand. The flesh of his face and fingers, Meg saw, was riddled with raw chilblains.

"Good morning," he said, not unkindly.

Meg glanced at Bessie, who was watching her curiously. "He came about my Tom," the older woman said. "Seems he and the bull are both safe, tucked up at an inn near Chipping. Be home when the weather clears."

"That's wonderful," Meg said, meaning it, but still debating whether to join Bessie and the sheriff, or bolt to warn Gresham. She wondered what Bessie had already told the man about her visitors, and feared by the look in Prigg's eyes that it was too much.

"I cannot tarry long," the sheriff said, with some regret, glancing about him at Bessie's warm house. That there was an ample store of food, he knew, of course, since he was already partaking of it. "Business to do, even in this God-awful weather."

He turned his attention back to Meg, idly. Thoughtfully. "Indeed, I've more on my mind than bringing the happy news about Tom and the bull," he admitted. "I'm told there was a ruckus here last night."

It was a moment before Meg realized that Prigg was talking about the visit from Tangwyn and his troupe, not the pleasure she'd taken in Gresham's bed.

"Aye," she said, and started, at last, down the steps. She raised her voice a notch or two, hoping Gresham would hear, and be alerted to the sheriff's presence, but she feared he was dead to the world.

Prigg glanced at Bessie, who fussed, pouring him more ale from the ewer she'd probably drawn just for him. " 'Twas the lady's kith and kin, I'm told."

Just then, as luck would have it, Gresham emerged, hastily dressed but still more asleep than awake, by the look of him, from the room Meg had just left.

The sheriff got slowly to his feet. "I don't believe I've had the pleasure of your acquaintance, sir," he said, and Meg knew then that nothing save the king's own testimony would convince Prigg that Gresham was not the man he'd been looking for.

"Gresham Sedgewick," came the cool, measured answer. "And you are—?"

"John Prigg," he said, rising from the bench and laying a hand to the handle of his sword. "The sheriff." Clearly, he didn't believe Gresham.

"No need to fret about this one," Bessie said, indicating Sedgewick with a gesture, having suddenly realized, it would seem, what was actually happening. "He's but a poor traveler—"

"He'd want you to say that, methinks," the sheriff speculated, glaring at Gresham. "Might even threaten you, aforehand, just in case I should come round asking about him."

The man was not only persistent, Meg thought, he was

stupid. A disastrous combination. Her heart thumped against her breastbone. She could not move, either to retreat or advance, but simply stood there on the landing, every nerve crackling, her breath aching as it entered and left her lungs.

Gresham walked around Meg and down the stairs, without even his sword, to face the man. "Bessie's telling the truth," he said quietly, and with an obvious lack of hope that he'd be believed.

"We'll just see," said the sheriff. "There are those at Windsor who will know your name and face, I'll wager."

Meg crept closer. "The abbey near Upper Gorse—St. Swithin's—have you any word of those within?" she heard herself ask.

Prigg's bristly brown-gray brows drew together for a moment as he pondered not the question itself, it seemed to Meg, but her motives for asking it. The man was apparently suspicious of everything and everyone.

"There is plague at St. Swithin's," he said, momentarily subdued, and crossed himself. "I fear many have perished."

Meg blinked back scalding tears of frustration and sorrow. She laid a hand to her throat, unable to utter a response. *Elizabeth. Dear God, Elizabeth!*

"Come you from that place, demoiselle?" Prigg said, though he knew she did, of course. He was clearly not the sort to forget a face, once he'd had even a glimpse.

Meg did not see how a lie would serve; the sheriff would not believe a denial. "Aye," she said. "I lived there until I set out to join my sister." In going to search for the one, had she lost the other? Surely, if she'd stayed, she could have found a way to protect Elizabeth—

Gresham, sensing her turmoil, put an arm around her shoulders and held her against him for just a moment. As artless as the contact was, Meg felt the echoes of last night's lovemaking trembling through her, along with a great many other things, and she could not help looking up into his face. *Hold your tongue,* the blue eyes warned.

"Sit down, my lady," the sheriff said, with a charity Meg would not have attributed to him, and gestured toward the table. "I am an untutored man, 'tis true, but not so lacking in graces as to leave a lady standing whilst I take my food. Have you family at St. Swithin's?"

Meg, seeing no alternative, proceeded to the place indicated and took a seat. Immediately, Bessie set a serving of porridge before her. "Aye," she said. "A sister. Elizabeth."

"No doubt she's fine," the sheriff offered gruffly, and that was when Meg knew he was merely dedicated to his work, not cruel. His gaze lingered on Gresham's face all the while, and his hand was still on the hilt of his sword.

At a nod from Gresham, Meg forced herself to eat, even though every mouthful tasted like bile. All her powers of self-control were required, just to keep lifting that spoon to her mouth. She felt torn in two—a part of her wanted to bolt for St. Swithin's, and Elizabeth, but another part would not, could not, leave Gresham's side.

"You have the wrong man," Gresham told the sheriff, in a mild tone of voice. He had not lost the sunny aspect he brought from the warm bed where he'd taught Meg pleasure; indeed, he seemed almost amused by the situation in which they now found themselves. "Even as we tarry here, your true prey most surely makes haste to reach Windsor, having made certain that I will follow. He'll lighten a few purses there, I suspect, even as he consorts with his betters."

"A dodge," replied the sheriff, and though his tone was dismissive, his eyes were watchful. "Do you think me a fool?" He strolled idly across the chamber to stand facing his captive. " 'Tis not so far to Windsor, in any event. I shall take you there, and see if your story has credence. If you're proved a liar, and I'll wager you will be, you'll be handed over for trial and hanging. The royal bailiff can do naught but receive you gladly, for your perfidy is known in all of England, sir, and you are assured a great and merry welcome."

Unbelievably, Gresham smiled. "Methinks I am indeed known at Windsor, my lord sheriff," he said easily. "I am most curious to learn what I am known *for,* however."

The sheriff assumed an air of mocking cordiality. "No need to wait," he said. "I can enlighten you now—you bear the names of thief and liar, woman-beater and drunkard. Mayhap you are even called killer, but in the end that won't matter. Your sins are ample for hanging, and I wonder that this good woman has had to suffer your presence." Here, Prigg paused, gazing not at Meg, but at Bessie, in noble consternation. "Never fear, good dame. You are safe now."

Bessie reddened with frustration. "But—"

"Not another word," Prigg interrupted. "My mind is made up."

"Fool!" Meg blurted. "The mummer tried to rob us all last night, and even now, while you stand here bedeviling an innocent man, Tangwyn and his band travel farther and farther away!"

The sheriff inclined his head to Meg. "You will pardon me, my lady, if I put little or no credence in your word? Methinks you are no friend to truth, where this man is concerned."

"Meg," Gresham warned, grasping her arm when she started to speak, and though his tone was sharp, the look in his eyes was something quite different, an expression of tenderness and sad amusement. "I can afford no more help from you, my lady. If you would please me, then stay here with Bessie until I come back for you. I promise it will be soon."

Meg's face felt hot and ice cold, by turns, and her head swam. "Can you not see that the sheriff cherishes some private grievance toward you, and will not rest until he sees you mount the scaffold? How can you be certain he will not hang you himself, from the naked branch of some tree, between here and Windsor?"

Now it was Prigg who flushed, but Meg paid him no more attention than it took to notice his discomfort.

"See?" she flared. "I have guessed aright! The scoundrel means to murder you, Gresham, at the first opportunity— why, 'tis likely you will never see Windsor, let alone find justice there!"

Gresham gazed blandly into Prigg's face, one brow raised in silent inquiry. His ease of manner both puzzled and enraged Meg; did he not comprehend what was happening? Mayhap his mind had come unhinged.

"Those words be slanderous!" the sheriff boomed, hurling his response toward Meg in a thunderous volley of breath and spittle. "Heed your man's wise petition, pray, and mind your tongue!"

Gresham heaved a martyr's sigh. "She will never do that," he said, with piteous resignation. "I bid you to leave her here, my lord sheriff, lest she drive you to some sin you cannot now imagine, with her mischief and her prattle."

Meg whirled on Gresham. "No!" she cried. "I would not be parted from you, whatever you say. We have things to do. If I must commit some crime to remain at your side, I will!"

The sheriff decided the matter. "I want this devious little vixen where I can see her," he said. "No doubt, being your woman, she is also your accomplice, and will want a trial of her own." He went to the door, opened it, and summoned one of his men the way he would a dog or a horse. "Accompany the lady to her chambers," he commanded, "that she might gather such possessions as she has, and mind you do not touch her in any untoward way. Mistake me not: by my saint, I will sever the offending hand from the wrist if you fail to heed me."

The sheriff's man, shivering from the cold, seemed desperate to obey. Meg glared at Gresham in injured defiance as she swept past him to fetch her belongings, and he glared back, unrepentant. If he'd had his druthers, he would most certainly have left her behind.

"You might do better to stay, my lady," Bessie prattled kindly, following Meg and her appointed escort. Apparently, she had missed the sheriff's decision to place Meg under arrest as well as Gresham. "They'll clear all this up soon enough, once they get to Windsor. Besides, the weather is uncommon bitter, and the way ahead is long and hard."

Meg stopped on the steps and took both Bessie's work-worn hands into her own. "I cannot," she said simply. "But I will never forget all your kindnesses. May the Holy Mother and all the saints bless you."

Presently, they stood in the bedchamber, where Meg and Gresham had enjoyed both tenderness and passion, and an overwhelming sadness overtook Meg as she looked around, remembering. Chances were, she would not see that small, safe, cozy room again. Mayhap, if fate were no more charitable than it had been that morning, she would nevermore laugh with Gresham, or lie sated in his arms, or lend him comfort in the singular ways of woman.

She blinked back a fury of tears, collected her few things, and Gresham's, and tied them together in one bundle.

The sheriff's man stood just inside the door all the while, apparently unable to meet either Meg's gaze or Bessie's. The old woman's lips moved as she prayed in silence and made the sign of the cross with one practiced hand.

The gesture was so familiar and so graceful that it nearly proved Meg's undoing. She would not surrender the bundle to the guard, though he reached out for it, and pushed past him to lead the way back downstairs.

Within minutes, she was mounted on Enoch's broad back, shivering despite the cloak wrapped tightly around her.

Gresham, now bound at the wrists, was allowed to ride a gelding, apparently brought along for the purpose, but the sheriff held the reins in his own hand.

The snow was hard crusted and glaring with the light of an icy sun when they rode away, Meg and Gresham, the sheriff and his four grim-faced men.

Mayhap, Meg reflected fancifully, they would raise an insurrection, these half-starved, half-frozen wretches, and she and Gresham might escape in the confusion.

Spurring Enoch to keep pace with Gresham's gelding, she cast a sidelong look at the man who had so handily relieved her of her virtue the night before, and received in return a glance so poisonous that it raised warm color in her cheeks. Like everyone else in the party, Gresham was already blue with cold, but the barely banked fires of his temper must have provided an illusion of warmth, for he did not tremble or chatter his teeth. Plainly, he was outraged that she had refused his initial urgings to stay with Bessie, and incurred the sheriff's ire in the process, making herself a prisoner as well.

Meg kept her chin high and her shoulders straight, but by then her bold truculence had thinned to mere bluster. "I have had enough of your moods," she said, with ill grace.

"I assure you, my lady," Gresham drawled, "this is more than a 'mood.' Had you kept your lovely mouth shut, matters would be considerably less complicated right now. I have a mind to take you over my knee for this day's mischief!"

Meg lengthened her spine still further. "As I have had my fill of moods, my lord," she answered, "so it is with your threats."

"Well, then," Gresham hissed, "let this be taken for a promise. I will not rest until I've raised blisters on your backside!"

"You wouldn't *dare!*"

"Wouldn't I?" His blue eyes snapped with conviction.

Meg was grateful for the righteous indignation she felt just then, for it warmed her a little. She only hoped that the flat of Gresham's hand wouldn't warm her further, in a most humiliating place and fashion. "You are a fool, as well as a braggart," she whispered. "Were it not so, you would have overcome the sheriff and fled before you could be bound and carted off to—"

Gresham regarded her silently for a long time, and she thought she saw a smile lurking in his eyes. "To precisely where I wanted to go in the first place," he said. Then he drew a deep breath, let it out in a long, philosophical sigh.

"The guilty take to their heels," he said, at last, in a calm and reasonable tone. "The innocent put their trust in honor, and in justice."

Meg gave him a look. "A pretty speech, my lord," she replied, "but have you not noticed that the guilty are free, whilst we face a criminal's fate?"

10

❧

Snow fell all the day, with blinding fury, stinging Meg's face and hands, biting through her cloak and kirtle with teeth that chewed her flesh numb. When at midafternoon they came upon a village, Meg took heart; surely they could rest awhile, if not pass the night.

She and Gresham had not exchanged many words, mainly because it was difficult to make oneself heard over the fiendish and incessant howl of the wind. Now, Meg turned toward him, expecting to see in him the same profound relief she felt.

Instead, his eyes were narrowed, and his expression grim. The sheriff raised a hand to halt the small party, apparently sharing Gresham's obvious misgivings.

Prigg gave over the reins of Gresham's gelding to one of his men and reined in his own horse, now grown skittish and fitful. Meg had no doubt that the animals suffered as bitterly from the cold as did their masters, mayhap more so, for the burdens they bore. She patted Enoch on the neck, frowning as the sheriff and one member of his company slogged through the deep snow toward the little cluster of huts.

She realized then what had troubled the sheriff and Gresham; there was no sound, no movement. No barking of dogs, no curious children peering at them from the sides of the path, no smoke curling above the thatched roofs.

The place was utterly, ominously still.

Gresham leaned toward Meg to speak, and though he did not raise his voice, neither did he try to keep the others from hearing. "None of your recklessness, my lady. Much is amiss here."

A fierce quickening sensation struck Meg in the pit of the stomach; she stood in her stirrups to peer through the ever thickening snow. "Where," she murmured, expecting no reply, "are the people?"

"Where indeed?" Gresham said, fidgeting in his bonds. He had been working at them for some time, but of course Meg had ignored the process as best she could, lest the sheriff's attention be drawn.

Prigg and his chosen companion disappeared, still mounted, into the heart of the small village.

Only moments later, they came out again, spurring their exhausted horses to haste.

"Plague!" bellowed the sheriff's man. "Saints and angels, there be plague in this place, and corpses all about!"

Meg felt her gorge rise. Enoch, taking his lead from the nervous horses, began to nicker and fret, and the three men left to guard Gresham looked as though they would bolt and scatter in all directions, with no thought, one for the other.

"We must burn the huts," the sheriff said, upon reaching the anxious knot of people and horses in the middle of the field, "and the bodies with them. Else others will surely stumble upon the place, and fall sick."

The men began babbling and shaking their heads, uttering a torrent of protests and excuses, but Gresham nudged the gelding's sides with the heels of his boots, urging it forward, its reins trailing in the snow. Meg followed, though belatedly, for Enoch balked at venturing any closer to the silent village.

"Untie my hands," Gresham said to the sheriff, "and I will help you look after the dead."

"No!" Meg cried, having gained his side at last. "The plague can be caught in such wise—you must not lay hands to the remains, nor even go near them—nay, the very air they breathed is poison!"

The look Gresham fixed upon her panicked face was one of complete calm, and because of that, it was almost reassuring. She realized that she trusted him, even in the face of a pestilence more horrible than any fate she could imagine, including death itself. "Be still, Meg. The sheriff is right—the place cannot rightly be left as it is."

The guards were wheeling their horses round, abandoning the sheriff, Gresham and Meg, and even the fierce, shouted commands of their leader would not bring them back. They feared nothing so much as the Black Death, and not without reason.

Gresham had at last loosened his bonds enough to free himself; he tossed the leather thong into the snow and rotated his shoulders, then set to rubbing the life back into his wrists, one and then the other. The sheriff made no move to contain him again.

"Take your woman and go, while you can," Prigg said, with a sort of dejected resignation. "By my saint, when I catch up with those cowards, I'll flog the flesh off them all, one by one."

"I have no doubt that you will," Gresham said evenly. His expression was almost, but not quite, cordial. "Let us make a camp in the woods there, where my lady might be safely sheltered, and then we will do what we can, you and I, to lay the dead to rest."

Meg could smell the decay now, the putrid stench that had long since reached Enoch and the horses and stirred them to near frenzy. She bent to one side and retched gracelessly into the snow.

The sheriff led the way into a copse of birch and alder trees, at some distance from the village, his breath and that of his horse trailing white behind him.

Gresham reached out and took hold of Enoch's halter, as though he thought Meg would flee, like the sheriff's men had done, and she was so insulted by the gesture that she nearly slapped him with the reins.

He smiled at the flash of temper in her eyes. "Nay, my lady," he said, with a nod toward the disappearing guards. "I do not think you such a one as those gutless knaves. I would but keep this mule from tossing you headlong into the snow and making for the next shire."

It was true that Enoch was behaving in a fractious manner, as though he would take to his heels if given the chance and thus escape the clear proximity of death. "Very well, then," Meg said, in haughty agreement, just as if she'd been offered a choice. Then, grudgingly, she added, "Thank you."

Gresham's laugh was muffled by the unremitting snow.

Inside the trees, the ground was almost bare, though wet and mirelike beneath a layer of sodden leaves. Gresham and the sheriff dismounted, and Gresham reached up to help Meg down from the mule's back.

While Gresham tethered the animals to a fallen log, the sheriff busied himself searching for the makings of a fire. Finding nothing, he cast his gaze toward the village, now almost hidden behind a swirling veil of snowflakes.

"Surely the scourge cannot live even in flames," he said, and started resolutely toward the cluster of huts, where there were surely stockpiles of wood. Gresham immediately followed, and Meg hesitated only a moment before setting out after him.

He spun on her, and the look on his face stopped her in the prints of her soft leather boots. "Stay here," he commanded, "or, by God and His angels, I will tie you to one of these trees like a martyr for the stake!"

Meg bit her lip, for while impulse bid her argue, prudence offered other counsel: Gresham was in deadly earnest, he would not permit her to accompany him, even if he had to make good on his threat.

"Make haste, then," she said, unwillingly, "and have a care where you step and what you touch."

Gresham came back and kissed her lightly, quickly, upon the mouth. It was not a farewell, that kiss, but a reassurance. An unspoken promise that other, better days would follow.

It was a hard thing to believe, just then.

"Mind the horses," he told her, as he walked away, "and fetch my sword from the sheriff's scabbard. I'll be wanting it."

Meg watched Gresham and the sheriff vanish into the naked trees and the spinning flakes of white, into the stink of pestilence, and held back her weeping until she could no longer see them.

Then, crying silently, she went about comforting the horses, and Enoch, and somehow managed to unbuckle the scabbard that held Gresham's confiscated sword. It fell to the ground, narrowly missing Meg's toes, and its hilt struck a stone with a resounding clank.

Meg grasped the weapon in both hands and marveled at its weight. As she had discovered long since, when she and Gresham had taken shelter in another hut, she could barely lift the blade, let alone use it in her own defense.

Only a few minutes had gone by when Gresham and the sheriff appeared again, their arms full of seasoned wood. They made a fire—the warmth was blessed, and the smoke masked some of the smothering, noxious smell—and Meg sat forlornly upon a large stone beside the blaze, staring into the flames.

Gresham crouched beside her and took her hand. "You understand, don't you?" he asked, with a gentleness that thickened Meg's throat. "That we cannot leave them as they are?"

Meg nodded. It would make no difference to the dead, whether they lay atop the ground or beneath it, but unwary travelers might wander in, and mayhap animals could spread the pestilence as well.

She clung to Gresham's forearm, though, when he would have withdrawn and risen to his feet.

"What if you fall ill?" she asked, in a small voice.

He kissed her wind-chilled knuckles. "I will not," he assured her.

"But—"

Gresham pulled free, though very gently, and stood. "Wait here," he said and, after retrieving his sword and belt and strapping them on, slipped away, into the first shadows of twilight.

❖ ❖ ❖

"Such horrors would surely haunt even the devil's sleep," the sheriff muttered, as he and Gresham entered the village once again. Prigg carried a burning brand from the fire and, like Gresham, had drawn the front of his tunic up over his mouth and nose in an effort to block the stench.

"I do not think the devil sleeps," Gresham answered. Bodies lay everywhere, inside the huts and out, in all stages of decay, partially clothed and naked, large and small, babes and ancients. Some were covered in dried blood, and worse, while others were unmarked, as if they had perished from sympathy, or from sorrow.

Inside one of the huts, Prigg put the burning brand to a pile of twigs waiting in a fire pit, laid for a supper that would never be cooked, and a cheerful blaze leaped, crackling, to life.

Working quickly, for it would soon be dark and the stink was vile almost beyond bearing, they found precious stores of hay in several sheds and carried most of it out in armloads, scattering it over the dead in thick piles. To this they added every stick of firewood and every piece of crude furniture in the village.

When they were sure the pyre would burn with a heat sufficient to consume, they made torches of brooms and thrust their flaming ends into the straw. Despite the damp, and the steady fall of snow, the hellish blaze caught, and spread, as ravenous as the plague itself.

Gresham found more brooms, and these too were set alight, and hurled atop the thatched roofs and through the gaping doorways. Crimson flames shot up all around them, and it was as though the end of the world, so long anticipated, had come at last.

They fed the hideous fire everything they could find and fled only when the heat became too intense to bear, both of them covered in soot and coughing fit to tear out their lungs. Bits of flaming thatch rained from the sky, and Prigg stumbled once, and fell to his knees, foundering in the deep snow.

Gresham caught him by the back of his jerkin, hauled him to his feet, and hurled him into motion again.

Meg was waiting at the edge of the trees, arms folded, bathed in the crimson light of deepest hell. When she saw Gresham, she hurtled toward him, and flung herself into his arms, calling him every sort of fool even as she held him close with frantic strength.

It was full dark by then, but the burning village glowed like a great torch, and the flames did not die down until dawn came sneaking, gold and purple, out of the eastern skies. None of the three of them thought of food the whole night through, nor did they sleep, but kept vigils of their own.

Once or twice, as the long hours passed, Gresham thought he heard the cries of the unshriven dead; mayhap, he would reflect later, he had slept after all, and the horrors had followed him even into his dreams. The sights and smells, sounds and textures of that night took root in his broken memory, amid the ruins and fragments of that other life, the lost one peopled by ghosts and shadows and always, always just beyond his reach.

It seemed, in that cold and sorrowful hour, that forgetfulness was not without its certain mercies.

Meg took the corner of her cloak, wet with snow, and tried to wipe the grime from Gresham's face, but the task proved impossible. He wore the soot like another layer of skin, and his hair stuck out in blackened spikes, made worse for the constant raking of his filthy fingers.

He laughed, though there was no humor in the sound, and caught her wrists in his hands. "Hold, woman—can you not see there is no hope of making me clean?"

Gresham's words and the way he'd spoken them fair stopped Meg's heart, stalwart though it was, betwixt one beat and the next. He'd sounded like a leper, warning off one who would draw nigh, and thus be blighted.

"I would see what you have seen," she said, and stepped away from Gresham, skirting his grasp when he guessed her intentions and went to stop her. "What pictures are in your head shall be in mine as well," she called back, already breathless.

The snow had not abated throughout the night, but it was powdery stuff, and melted here and there under the sun's cold light, leaving straggly paths between the white, peeling trunks of the birch trees.

"Let her go," Prigg interceded. "She has a right."

She heard Gresham's growled "no!" behind her, but quickened her pace, hiking up her kirtle to keep from stumbling on the uneven ground.

Gresham was soon beside her. "Meg," he hissed, "there were babes—old women—children—"

"Aye," she said, almost running now. "And if they can die, I can look upon them, and not turn away—"

"Why?" Gresham demanded, though he made no move to stop her. Mayhap he knew she would not be waylaid.

Tears tickled Meg's chapped face; she wiped them away with the back of one hand. "Because of Elizabeth!" she half screamed, half sobbed. *"Because of Elizabeth!"*

"My God, Meg, don't do this to yourself—you'll never forget—"

She had entered the charred remains of the village; the fallen roofs of the huts were still smoldering.

Meg crossed herself and went on, until she came to the great pyre, and the black and twisted bodies that lay upon it, covered now in a fine dusting of new snow.

It was as Gresham had said—they were all here, children, old people, babes. Wives and husbands. The weak and the strong, the saints and the sinners; the plague, like Almighty God, was no respecter of persons.

Meg might have slipped to her knees, but for Gresham's quick grasp. He put an arm around her waist and kept her upright.

"Come away," he said gently. "You have seen. You have acknowledged them."

Meg nodded, turning her head into his shoulder, and allowed him to lead her away, back to the camp in the trees.

She had seen. She would always see, waking or sleeping, even if she lived to a great age.

"Elizabeth," she whispered, in anguish, and Gresham swept her up into his arms then, holding her close against his chest. His breath brushed across her temple, warm and soft.

"Surely she is safe," he whispered, "if only because you want it so much."

Meg closed her eyes, but the images of the dead, smoldering beneath their thin cloaks of snow, were as vivid as if she were yet gazing upon the actual scene. "It matters not what I want," she whispered. "Nor what any mortal wants. Surely they made prayers, and God did not hear—"

They had reached the trees, where the two horses waited, along with Enoch.

Without speaking again, Gresham lifted Meg onto his own saddle and swung up behind her. The sheriff handed him Enoch's reins.

"What now?" Gresham asked gravely, intent upon the other man's face.

Prigg heaved a vast and weary sigh. He looked gaunt to Meg, as though he could lie down in the melting snow and die, without the aid of plague or fire. "I owe you a debt," he said, after a silence, "and yet I am sworn to keep the law. It is I who would ask 'what now'."

"We are bound for Windsor, whether I be freeman or prisoner," Gresham said. "Give me your word that no trouble will come to my lady here, and I will surrender to you there."

Meg stiffened, even in the stupor of horror that had held her in thrall since she'd gone into the village and looked upon the work of the Black Death. "Surely you have the wit, my lord sheriff, to see that this *cannot* be the man you seek, that he cannot have done thievery or murder, for he has naught of those flaws in him?"

Gresham simply tightened his arm around her, but she knew the gesture to be a bid for silence, and she obeyed. She had no strength to spare, just then, for rebellion.

"Mayhap at Windsor," he told the sheriff, "we shall both uncover the necessary truths."

Prigg made no attempt to hide his bewilderment as he regarded Gresham for a long moment. Then he mounted his own horse, and turned its head toward the grandest of the king's palaces.

The journey would demand the better part of a fortnight, and at its end lay a multitude of possibilities, both sorrowful and splendid. Behind was the past—not just the little village, but the abbey of St. Swithin's, and Elizabeth, and most of Meg's memories of herself and her sisters. Lost, mayhap forever, in smoke and plague and mystery.

Meg burrowed close against Gresham, and he wrapped her in his cloak, guiding the gelding with one hand, encircling her with the other arm. She allowed herself the illusion of safety, there within his embrace, but her mind was numb, her flesh chilled beyond feeling—mercies, both.

At the end of the day's ride, they came to another village, this one alive and busy; the plague had not yet visited there. Gresham and Prigg kept the curious at bay, for they could not know what ill humors clung to them from that place of pestilence. A young priest, his robes hardly more than rags, insisted that they take their rest within the stone walls of the church, where at least the night winds would not reach them.

The three travelers accepted the invitation gratefully, and made their beds within the nave. The priest brought a meal of cold roast fowl and boiled turnips to the door, along with a flask of good wine, and gave them a tallow candle to see by.

The floor of the church was hard and cold, yet Meg slept peacefully there, with food in her stomach and Gresham's arms about her. The simple kindness of the priest had done much to offset the horrors of the day just past, for Meg was young and strong, and when she awakened to an icy morn, she was much restored.

She laughed at the sight of Gresham, sitting up beside her, still streaked in soot and plain dirt, made muddy by the hours of riding through snow. There was no sign of the sheriff; mayhap he had come to his senses during the night, realizing at last that Gresham was no criminal, and gone to seek his true quarry, Tangwyn the mummer, instead.

Gresham leaned against a nearby wall, arms folded, one knee drawn up. Clearly, he had been watching her sleep, and he flashed a devastating grin and arched one eyebrow in response to her mirth.

"I must needs make a worse appearance even than I feared," he remarked, and it was apparent from his voice as well as his manner that his confidence had not suffered in the slightest.

"Aye," Meg agreed, with a merry twinkle, sitting up and shivering inside her cloak. For all that she had looked upon death of the cruelest sort, or mayhap *because* of that, she was keenly aware of the richness of life, and wont to celebrate what was good. "But your charms are such that your need of a bath, dire though it may be, does little to detract." She paused, looked toward the church's single frost-patterned window with cheerful impatience. "Mule feathers, but I'm hungry, and my bladder is like to burst. Cold as it is, there are surely fleas amongst these rushes, and I could hear rats skittering about in the night. Where is the sheriff?"

Gresham laughed. "Such a jumble of words, my lady— it gives me fright that I follow them with such ease. Prigg has gone to consult with the priest, at a safe distance, of course, with regards to food. Aye, it is cold, there are certainly fleas, as well as rats, and I'm afraid I can do naught about your bladder."

Meg scrambled awkwardly to her feet, half entangled in the cloak, her limbs still slow and clumsy from sleep. "Come with me," she said. "Mayhap there are wolves on the midden, or scoundrels who would do me injury."

He rolled his eyes, but stood, with no sign of stiffness. "Surely even wolves and scoundrels, my lady, could find better places to bide on so cold a morn."

"I need you to hold your cloak wide, and make a curtain for me," Meg said, braced for opposition and mildly indignant.

Gresham sighed. "Ah, chivalry," he said, and put a hand to his heart. "Its demands are many and inglorious."

When they returned, the sheriff was back, with hen's eggs and a bit of yellow cheese. The men cracked the eggs and ate them uncooked, but Meg would have starved first. She got most of the cheese, and was content with it, and grateful.

Even though the sheriff had paid for their breakfast in good coin, such foodstuffs were precious, especially in winter, and rare. Selling them had been an act of generosity, as well as commerce.

When they made to depart, the priest came again, and blessed them, and flung up a little pouch that jingled when Gresham caught it.

"Plague bells," the priest said, with his usual good cheer. "Ring them when someone approaches, and call out, 'Plague! Plague!' "

Meg shuddered, but Gresham made much of the gift, and emptied the pouch into his palm. Three small silver bells lay there, gleaming in the icy light of the sun.

He handed one to Meg and one to the sheriff, and tucked a third into the pocket of his jerkin.

"A better gift, methinks," he said quietly, "than swords and maces."

"Aye," the sheriff agreed, though Meg was mystified.

Nonetheless, she appreciated the thought, and the priest had been most compassionate from the first, as had the villagers, offering shelter and food as they had. In many places, they would have been turned away, even driven off by the hurling of sticks and stones, because of their admitted contact with the plague.

Meg, riding Enoch once again, smiled her thanks as

Gresham and the sheriff turned their geldings away from the village and set out. She made haste to catch up to them.

"What do we want with plague bells?" she muttered to herself, frowning with distaste as she studied the small object clasped in her hand.

It was later that day that they came within sight of a band of horsemen upon the king's road. The riders were ragged, and their mounts slat-ribbed, but every man was armed with a sword.

"Bandits?" Meg asked of Gresham, and swallowed in dread. There must have been a score of them, milling and murmuring among themselves, their eyes mean and watchful, their hands upon the hilts of their blades. The sheriff and Gresham were both trained to fight, but there were too many enemies.

"Aye," Gresham answered. "Ring the bell."

"Plague!" the sheriff called, jingling in earnest.

"Plague!" echoed Gresham.

Meg made her bell peal wildly. "Plague!" she cried.

The outlaws parted to either side of the road, scared and suspicious both at once. Gresham leaned forward in his saddle, filthy as a beggar he was, and all the more convincing for the fact, coughing fit to heave out his insides.

"Plague—" he burbled, and the thieves, convinced, spun their scrawny horses around and fled at top speed.

"You might have been a mummer," Meg said admiringly, when Gresham ceased his performance and sat upright in the saddle once more.

"My thought, exactly," the sheriff agreed, but with a look of wry speculation.

Gresham made a bow, as best he could from the back of a horse, and then turned a look of mock injury upon the sheriff. "Will naught but the testimony of three angels and a saint convince you that I am an honest man?"

"Are you?" Prigg asked. "When last we spoke of the matter, you had no memory of your past. Mayhap things are coming back to you?"

A fleeting look of desolation crossed Gresham's soot-smudged face, but he was quick to summon up his former grin, full of mischief. If Meg could see behind the mask, to the sorrow and confusion he made to hide, it seemed that the sheriff could not, for he relaxed visibly.

"I remember everything," Gresham said, performing again. "I was a sultan, with a hundred wives, who danced for me day and night, and made music, and fed me with figs rolled in sugar." He paused and gave Meg a sidelong look, assuming a pensive countenance. "You, of course, are my favorite."

Meg's cheeks were warm, and she felt a particular ache that was no longer a riddle to her—nor very likely to be assuaged in the near future, given the circumstances. She lowered her eyes, lest Gresham—or, worse, the sheriff—should take note of her discomfort.

It was soon evident that she had not fooled Gresham; he continued to tease her, at least intermittently, throughout the day, making up silly songs and lengthy stories about his exploits as a sultan in a far-off land.

When, in the middle of the afternoon, with the sky turning gray and heavy with new snow, they came upon an inn, Meg had so given herself over to fancy that she dared to dream of a bath, a real bed and a meal, served at a real table and still warm from the cook's fire.

11

❦

In the coming days, Meg marveled that she had ever aspired to an adventurous life; she and Gresham and the sheriff traveled diligently, through ever-deepening snow, bitter winds, and lonely, barren countryside. They avoided towns and villages, taking a night's refuge, when they could, in a barn or a cave or an abandoned hut. When there was no better shelter to be had, Gresham made a lean-to of broken branches, while Meg and Prigg built a fire.

At last, when nearly a fortnight had passed, the great castle called Windsor came into view, a sprawling edifice of stone, bustling with the comings and goings of a lively community, smoke from cooking fires and hearths curling against a pearl-gray sky.

Meg looked upon it with yearning. Oh, to be warm, well fed, able to scour herself clean, and put on fresh clothing.

"What of the plague?" she asked, looking at Gresham, who had drawn the gelding to a halt beside Enoch, and was leaning thoughtfully upon the pommel as he surveyed the scene. "Mayhap we will infect the others—"

It was the sheriff who answered. "Methinks we would be ailing or dead by now, were the plague in any of us."

Meg waited for Gresham to venture an opinion. He sighed, and Meg thought the glance he tossed in her direction was somewhat rueful.

"He's right," Gresham said. "We have taken care to keep ourselves apart, but there is no longer any need of that. Just the same, it will be best to burn the garments we've been wearing all this while."

Meg shuddered, as she had not done while speaking of the plague, and neither did the reaction have anything to do with the cold. "I should burn these wretched clothes anyway, my lord, if for no other reason than that I can bear them no longer."

Gresham smiled at that. "Aye," he agreed. "I am sore weary of my own hose and jerkin."

They started down a slight hillside, riding single file, the sheriff in the lead, Meg after him, and then Gresham. Despite her anticipation of the simple creature comforts that awaited them, Meg was distinctly wary, too.

Here, the sheriff would bring Gresham before the king, accused of all manner of crimes. Here, Gresham's past, so long a mystery, might be made clear. Here lived Gresham's son, who might or might not remember his sire with fondness. Here, the mummer waited, still to be dealt with.

Meg set her will against the despair that would have encompassed her spirit all about; for the time being, she meant to think only of the obvious consolations, and of Gabriella. Perhaps there would be news of her here, news, even, of plague-ridden St. Swithin's.

The three riders were seen and hailed long before they reached the wooden bridge spanning the moat, and guards rode out to meet them, ready, Meg knew, to make them welcome or drive them away.

Prigg was known at Windsor; that was plain from the gruff and familiar reception he received. Meg was thoroughly scrutinized, but for Gresham there were broad grins, bobbing heads, and eager "my lord" this and "my lord" that.

Gresham's expression was one of troubled pleasantry. It was obvious that the guards knew him well and regarded him highly, and equally clear that he could find no traces of these men in memory. Had they been alone, Meg might have laid a hand to his shoulder or forearm, in an effort to reassure him, lend what slight comfort she could. The sheriff wore a look of mingled relief and resignation. Gresham had been his prisoner for many days, albeit a willing and extremely helpful one, and now it was evident that a great deal of time, effort, and physical discomfort had gone for naught. Even an ox-headed man like Prigg, Meg thought, with no sense of triumph, must now accept that he had been mistaken in his suspicions.

The hooves of their mounts made a hollow clatter on the ancient wood of the bridge as they passed over, the towering gates swinging open before them.

Inside the walls, much attention awaited the newcomers—inevitably, the busy residents of the castle were curious, they with their burdens of firewood, their buckets spilling water, bags of grain and cornmeal, squawking chickens and squealing pigs. Meg stared back at these men and women proudly, holding her head high.

A man strode out of the guardhouse, his broad face reddened by the cold and, after greeting the sheriff with a nod, beamed at Gresham. "At last you are found, my lord. I dare say, Lord Chalstrey was much troubled by your mysterious leave-taking."

Meg watched Gresham out of the corner of her eye, and saw the mention of Chalstrey strike him with an impact that seemed to bewilder, rather than enlighten him. "Chalstrey," she heard him murmur, and he gave the name the tone of a question.

"Lord Edgefield knows you, does he?" the sheriff asked, in a world-weary tone, turning slowly in his saddle to regard his erstwhile captive.

"Knows him?" boomed the soldier who had come out to meet them. "Why, they were fostered together, my lord Sedgewick and my lord Edgefield—Morgan Chalstrey's his right name—and have ever been the best of friends." He turned his attention back to Gresham, and for the first time uncertainty flickered in his eyes. "Is that not so, my lord?"

"Aye," Gresham said quietly. "It is so. Pray—is he here, that I might put a finish to his concerns?"

The soldier smiled again, heartened, but shook his head. "We have not seen him, my lord. He sent a messenger from Cornwall to inquire for you, and we could tell him naught of your whereabouts or your welfare."

Gresham swung down from his horse, and Meg longed to follow suit, though she did not move. She was sore weary of riding; her limbs, bloodless and numb, wanted stretching, and her heart ached for many reasons.

"My lady," Gresham said, standing easily before the captain of the guard, reins in hand, "is in need of food and a fire. Mayhap there is a fit welcome for her here?"

The captain flushed slightly, pleased. "Aye, my lord— she is welcome, as are you." He gestured, and one of the mounted soldiers rode forward, being careful not to look directly at Meg while he awaited his orders. Instructed to house "Lady Sedgewick" in suitable accommodations, the man leaned over and took Enoch's halter in hand.

"Come, my lady," he said. "There are proper quarters nearby, and servants to attend you."

Meg had never been addressed as "Lady Sedgewick" and the title settled comfortably upon her, and caused her to smile, though it did not rightfully belong to her, despite her hunger, her exhaustion, her dismal state of grooming. At the same time, she had not expected to be parted from Gresham—indeed, she had not been separated from him in many days—and she was unsettled.

Gresham reassured her with a smile. "Peace, Meg," he said, before she could speak. "I will come to you soon."

Because neither the captain of the guards nor the sheriff raised a word of opposition to Gresham's quiet pronouncement, Meg allowed herself and Enoch to be led away, through the crowded courtyard. She kept her shoulders straight, her chin high, as she left Gresham behind, and did not once look back, though the price of her restraint was very great.

The aforementioned quarters turned out to be a stone house, of considerable size, tucked away in the oak trees behind the castle proper. Meg was immediately taken with the place; it reminded her of her own home, Redclift Hall, though it was, of course, in much better repair.

Her escort helped her down from Enoch's back and untied her bundle, as well, that she might keep her belongings close to hand. The front door opened and a servant girl stood upon the threshold, clad in a coarse robe, her hair properly hidden, unlike Meg's wild mane, beneath a wimple.

"Pray, make a fitting welcome for my lady Sedgewick,"

the soldier ordered, though not unkindly. "Her lord will join her here soon."

The girl greeted Meg with a bob of her head and half pulled her inside, out of the cold, then across a rush-covered floor to a slow-burning fire. Meg shivered suddenly, breaking out in goose bumps, and hugged herself, yearning for a roaring blaze and wondering—should she not correct the misconception that she was Sedgewick's wife?

The servant took Meg's bundle from her with a practiced grace. "I'll make a better fire in the bedchamber, my lady," she said, with surprising perception, "and bring hot water if you would have it."

"Oh, aye," Meg cried, and nearly wept, so poignant was her gratitude. She decided that the truth should be dealt out with discernment, and in no appreciable hurry. "Such would please me very greatly—thank you."

The response was a hint of a smile and another deferential nod. "Pray, take your comfort here, lady, while I make your bath and bed ready. I shall send to the kitchens for foodstuff as well."

With that, the girl took her leave, and Meg huddled close to the puny fire in the main hall, overjoyed by the prospects of sustenance, cleanliness, and heat. Though she had not once complained, during the many days and nights she had spent upon the road with Gresham and the sheriff, the privations she had endured seemed unbearable now, in the face of such luxury and succor as Windsor Castle had to offer.

Alone, she assessed her surroundings. The hall was so large and so ill lighted that Meg could not see the walls, but only dense shadows, spilling down from the rafters. There was little furniture; a rough table with a long bench on either side, a pair of straight-backed wooden chairs facing the hearth.

She sank into one of these, stretching her chilled feet toward the struggling fire. Her boots, fashioned of thin leather, were wet through, and yet she dared not remove them before traversing the rushes, for nasty things oft littered the floors of even the most prominent households.

Presently, the girl returned to say the fire on the bedchamber hearth burned hearty, and Meg should come and warm herself before it. As they crossed the hall and mounted broad steps hewn of timber, the servant confided, at Meg's bidding, that her name was Allena, and her man tended the king's pigs.

The bedchamber proved a pleasant surprise, for it was lined with windows, and filled with such light as so wintry a day could spare. A brisk fire snapped upon the hearth, gnawing greedily at the large pieces of seasoned wood laid crosswise over the kindling. Within the glow of the blaze stood a small table and two chairs, promising many cozy and cheerful meals.

A great bed stood opposite the windows, piled high with pillows and fur coverings, with heavy draperies to pull against the cold.

Best of all, there was a large bathing tub, affixed to the floor in a corner of the room, lined with brightly painted tiles.

" 'Twas a prize taken in the First Crusade," Allena said, following Meg, who was already beside the long, square object—a work of art, it was—peering down into its inviting depths. Bending, Allena grasped a small brass plate, revealing a hole in the bottom. "The water runs out, through a pipe, when you want it no more."

Meg crossed herself hastily, in wonder as much as reverence.

"I'll have it filled while you take your supper, milady," Allena offered, with a knowing smile.

" 'Tis a miracle," Meg marveled, kneeling beside the tub now, and running her hands along its wide, colorful edge. "I cannot think why every house in England does not have one of these!"

Allena sighed. "Most folk are fearful of too much washing. A body can take a chill, 'tis said, and after that comes plague."

"Mule feathers," Meg scoffed, rising to her feet once again. "Methinks it is dirt that makes disease, and poor food. What harm could come from a simple bath?" She did not pause, for she expected no reply. "Why, my sisters and I scrubbed ourselves from head to foot whenever we could, while we lived at St. Swithin's."

Sadness squeezed Meg's heart, for she had taken herself by surprise, in mentioning her twin, and Elizabeth, and the abbey that had been their true home for so long.

She had made no progress at all toward finding Gabriella, for all her much-doing, and poor Elizabeth might already be among the dead, her delicate body blackened and swollen by the plague. She blinked fast and hard for a few moments, then spoke again, too loudly. "Pray, Allena, make haste, for I do think hot water will do more to restore me than any other remedy."

"As you wish, my lady," Allena said, and went out.

The moment she was alone, Meg climbed into the vast, empty tub, clothes and all, and stretched her legs out to their full length. Even lying down flat, with her head on the bottom, she could not touch the other end of the bath with her toes.

She was soothed, anticipating a wealth of steaming water and soap, and heard the door creak open on its hinges just then. Blushing, Meg sat up, expecting to see Allena, back with a tray of bread and cheese or a ewer of wine, but it was Gresham who stood just inside the room, a mischievous grin upon his face.

"Were it not for my presence," he said, "you might think you'd wandered into paradise."

"Is it not a wonder?" Meg expounded, referring to the bathing tub, though her voice was thick with the lingering rawness of missing her sisters. "Look—it is longer than you are, my lord. It is bigger than a horse trough, bigger even than the fountain at St. Swithin's!"

Gresham laughed and crossed the room to sit upon the tub's edge, and his eyes twinkled as he gazed down at Meg. "Aye, my lady delicious, it is indeed a phenomenon fit to astound a wizard. No doubt you will like the thing better still when it is filled with water."

Meg knew she was being teased, but she cared not. "Do you think, my lord, that your household—wherever it is—has one of these?"

Gresham brushed her cheek with the backs of the fingers of his right hand. "I know not, my lady. If there is none, I promise I will have one made, as my gift to you."

Meg scrambled to her knees in the bottom of the great vat and put both arms around Gresham's neck. "You can be a most agreeable companion, when you try," she said, and kissed him lightly on the mouth.

"Ummm," he replied. "I should like to be more than a companion, methinks." He might have deepened their contact, so charged was the air around them, if the door hadn't sprung open behind him.

"My lord, my lady—I am sorry—" Allena blurted, an unwilling intruder, plainly mortified.

Gresham sighed and shoved splayed fingers through his matted hair. "All is well, lass," he said, turning to face the servant, who struggled to balance a heavy tray. "Pray, do not flee, especially since you've brought food."

Allena set her burden on a small table, standing quite near the fire, and ran both hands down the front of her kirtle in a gesture of nervous compliance. Her color was high, and she would not meet Meg's eyes, nor Gresham's.

"I have sent to the kitchens for water," she said. "Mayhap when you've had your meal and rested awhile, it will be ready."

"Thank you," Meg told her, climbing out of the tub to stand beside Gresham. She was ravenously hungry—there had been no breakfast and no midday meal for them all the day, for the sheriff and Gresham had found the hunting poor in the frozen woods and broad plain over which they'd traveled.

Allena nodded, turned on one heel, and fled, closing the heavy door behind her with a thump.

"She was frightened of you," Meg observed, with mischievous levity, going to the table and taking up a large piece of yellow cheese. "Mayhap you are a famous scoundrel."

Gresham helped himself to a chunk of brown bread and poured wine from a ewer into a single pewter chalice, meant to be shared. "Mayhap something worse," he said gravely.

Meg stared at him, ashamed. In thinking of Gabriella and Elizabeth, and in her subsequent excitement over the splendid bathtub, she had completely forgotten that Gresham had been recognized by the guards and their captain.

"Have you told them—those men who greeted us, I mean—that you don't remember what happened before you came to St. Swithin's?"

He shook his head and stared down into the chalice for a long moment, before taking a sip, swallowing. Meg made no barrier to his gaze; he saw through her, as though she were a vapor, not a person. "Nay," he said. "But I've no doubt that Prigg will tell the tale."

"Sit down," Meg said gently. "We are beside a fire, and beneath a roof. We can take our bread and wine in comfort."

Gresham met her eyes, and she was solid again. He saw her, and smiled. "Aye," he said, and nodded toward the chair nearest Meg. "You are right, my lady."

When she just stood there, he nodded again.

"Pray, lady, seat yourself. I cannot sit while you stand."

Meg fell into her chair and took a bite from the slab of cheese forgotten, until then, in her hand. "Have you been before the king?"

Gresham shook his head. "Nay. Edward is down with a chill, and receiving no one besides his mistress, Alice Perrers."

"You know his mistress?" Meg asked, intrigued. If he recalled that, then mayhap other things would come to him, by and by.

Gresham sighed. "No," he said, tearing his bread thoughtfully between his fingers, like a distracted priest about to offer communion. "But it means naught, my calling her by name. I know the king's name, too, and those of his favorite horses and all his children." He gestured toward the wall of leaded windows. "I can tell you what the trees are called, and the animals of the wood. I can identify plants and stones and even stars in the heavens. And yet I have no recollection of my own son, nor the woman who bore him, nor this man Chalstrey, who must indeed be my finest friend." He paused, looked at her in anguish. "Tell me, Meg—how can this be?"

Meg could no longer remain seated; she rose and went to stand behind Gresham, resting one hand lightly upon his shoulder. "It is this way with the very old sometimes," she told him. "I've seen it at St. Swithin's. Some of the most ancient nuns remember their childhood in the most amazing detail, and yet they cannot say if they've taken their breakfast." Seeing that this was no comfort, she touched his face. "Is there no one here who can tell you about your life? The boy Kieran, mayhap?"

Gresham covered Meg's hand with his own, squeezed lightly. "I shall not leave Windsor," he said, "without learning all I need to know, but that is not the same as re-membering, is it?"

She kissed the top of his head, in need of washing though it was. "Will you see the boy?"

He nodded. "Aye," he replied wearily, "but do not ask me when." Still holding her hand, he guided her back to her own chair without rising from his own. "I am not ready to seek him out just yet."

They ate in companionable silence after that, and warmed themselves with wine and the festive heat of the fire. Beyond the windows, the snow, having ceased for some time, began to waft past in great, fat flakes.

A turn of the hourglass had passed, by Meg's best reck-oning, when she heard servants mounting the stairs, a horde of them by the sound they made. She rushed to admit them, knowing they brought water, and so they did—covered cauldrons of the stuff, with steam escaping from beneath the lids. The wimples of the women and the jerkins of the men were dusted with snow, and hands and noses glowed red with cold.

Meg counted more than a dozen water bearers, and Allena came behind them, bearing soap and clothes for scrubbing and for drying. The glorious tub was filled nearly to overflowing, and Allena led the small army out again, without ever looking directly at Meg or at Gresham.

With a shriek of pure joy, Meg tore off her much-soiled surcoat and kirtle and flung them both onto the fire, followed immediately by her grimy chemise. As she kicked off her boots, she saw the discarded garments catch fire and then melt to strands of glowing crimson. All were unsalvageable, she'd worn them so long.

Naked, utterly without inhibition, Meg dashed across the room to the tub and climbed in.

Gresham laughed aloud at her lusty sigh.

"You would do better to join me," Meg said loftily, before sinking to her chin in water so lovely, so stinging hot, that it reddened her skin like a fever, "than to stand by, yammering like a jackal. You shall not share *my* bed, Lord Sedgewick, in such a state as you find yourself now."

With a sound of mock horror, made low in his throat, Gresham shed his own garments, and threw them into the fire, after Meg's things. In a thrice, he had closed the space between them, and joined her in the bath.

Forgetting their private sorrows, forgetting that they were not truly man and wife, as most at Windsor believed, they stole a glimmering slice of time, and used it as they would. They scrubbed each other clean, splashing exuberantly, like children playing in a pond on a hot summer's day, and left the bath only when it had grown cold, and murky, and they were shivering. Meg took time to draw the plug, and the water gurgled away through the pipe leading down into the floor.

They went, water-slickened skin shimmering, to dry themselves before the fire, entirely forgetting the cloths provided for the purpose. There was a comb on the mantel—surely Allena had left it apurpose—and Gresham used it to pull the tangles and snarls from Meg's hair.

She could not have said when the lovemaking began, or even when it ended; Gresham turned her in his arms and kissed her, she remembered that much. And it seemed, for a while, as though the fire had escaped the hearth to consume them both with flames, not of pain, but of pleasure.

Hours had crept by, and the light had gone, when Meg came back to herself, and realized she was curled up with Gresham in the center of the bed, beneath a pile of fur coverings, her body deeply soothed as well as washed, her hair nearly dry.

She started to rise, shocked that the day had passed into night without her seeing, only to be pulled back down into the soft, feather-filled mattress. Gresham, lying on his side, slid one hand under her rump and laid the other lightly upon her breast, there to make certain mischief.

"Cease," Meg said, and swatted at him, but it was to no avail, for he continued to fondle her. She made no further effort to escape.

A noise in the corridor caused Meg to tense, but Gresham simply raised his head from beneath the covers and shouted, "Be gone!"

"Gresham," Meg scolded, as he threw a fur wrap over them both, shutting out even the paltry light of the fire. "That may be our supper."

He kissed her—it was plain enough where his hunger

lay—but whoever was at the door took to rattling the latch.

Gresham stuck his head out again. "Did you not hear me?" he bellowed. "I said *be gone!*"

The door opened with a crash, hurled inward upon its hinges, and Meg, buried under the bedclothes, could not see what was happening. Gresham, for his part, growled an oath and made to scramble off the mattress, but before he could free himself from various entanglements, something struck the headboard above their heads with an ominous *thwack*.

Meg rolled her eyes upward to see a dagger splashed in firelight quivering in the wood, and might have screamed, had she been able to gather enough breath. Gresham bounded off the bed, naked as a babe in the birthing chamber and fair roaring with fury.

"What insolence is this?"

"Die, knave!" came an answering roar, though from a much smaller and younger lion, by the high, broken sound of it. "Die and burn in hell!"

"Fling another dagger," Gresham answered, "and by my saint I'll thrash you within reach of God and glory!"

"Another dagger?" Meg glanced again at the one embedded in the headboard, then hauled herself up and squinted into the gloom. Except for the light of a dying fire, they might have been sealed into a tomb, so dark and cold was that chamber.

After a few moments, her eyes adjusted, and Meg saw Gresham, then a tall young man—nay, a boy, really—standing just inside the doorway. The fair hair, the fury, and the deadly aim told her all she needed to know; this was Kieran, Gresham's son. Kieran's pale face and hands gleamed like alabaster amid the heavy shadows that filled the room.

Meg felt the lad's gaze find her, saw his small hand tighten upon the hilt of the second dagger. She knew, with horrified clarity, that if he hurled the blade again, whether toward her or his father, he would not miss. Indeed, he had not missed before, in puncturing the headboard, but had struck precisely the target he wanted.

The first knife had been an announcement, a warning, a gesture of defiance. But it had not been a mistake.

"Is this your whore?" the boy asked. His eyes glinted, capturing stray light, as did his shining hair.

"This," Gresham said evenly, "is Lady Redclift."

Kieran spat, though the knife remained at his side, dangling from his fingers. Ready to be clasped again, and thrown, within the length of a heartbeat.

"Why did you bring the wench here?"

Gresham's voice was smooth, even cordial. He did not move, and yet Meg sensed a storm of motion inside him. "Lay aside the blade, and I'll tell you everything you want to know," he answered. "Provided you mind your tongue, that is."

Kieran spat again. "Why should I trust the word of a dog like you?" he demanded.

"No reason at all," Gresham said. "Except that I'm your father."

"You are a nameless cur!"

"What does that make you?"

Meg drew in a sharp breath, for she saw—could not have missed—Kieran's fingers convulsing round the handle of the knife. Just when she thought he would surely hurl the weapon, not at his father, but at her, he released his hold, and the dagger clattered to the floor.

Gresham did not cross the room to collect the discarded blade, but instead opened the pack containing his spare garments, and hastily dressed himself, except for boots. He made no move to take up his sword, nor did he retrieve the dagger still stuck in the wood above Meg's head.

Kieran stood fast, throughout that uncertain interlude, and despite her fear and annoyance, Meg felt a certain grim respect for the boy. Just about anyone else she could think of would have fled by then, rather than waiting, still as a statue, while his father, the enemy, made ready to deal with him.

"Make a light," the boy said coldly, and with utter contempt, and Meg could not be sure who he was addressing, herself or Gresham. "I would look upon this creature in your bed. The whole of Windsor says she's your wife."

Meg began inching her way toward the side of the bed, but when she reached it, she remembered that she was wearing nothing at all. Certainly not the state in which to greet a visitor, hostile or otherwise, but she could take an illusory comfort in having distanced herself from the blade in the headboard. It did not occur to her, until much later, that she might have taken hold of that knife herself, and thus been armed against an unpredictable foe.

"You will not inspect the lady," Gresham said moderately. "She is not, after all, a mare to be sold at market."

Kieran took a step or two nearer the foot of the bed, and Meg could see that his eyes were narrowed, more from curiosity, she thought, than ill temper. She did not believe for a moment that he had decided to take a more charitable view of her.

"I will have my chance to see her clearly," Kieran replied, with a shrug. "You cannot think I meant to kill the lady—or you. Had I intended to do murder, you would both be dead."

Meg felt a chill, warm though the bed was, but fear had long since given way in her, replaced by a desire to get hold of the beautiful boy's ears and give them a good twist.

"It takes no skill to finish a helpless female," Gresham said, in an offhand voice. "Nor a man lying naked in his bed. That is coward's work."

Meg glared at the phrase "helpless female," though if Gresham saw, he gave no sign of it.

"I am too young to face you on the battlefield, or in the lists," Kieran said, with obvious regret and a smooth rancor too virulent by half for one of his tender age. "It is a pity that you will not live until I am a man, and thus able to slay you honorably with my own hands. Alas, that pleasure must fall to someone else."

Gresham's teeth flashed in the firelight. "Ah, yes, the mummer," he said. "Well, I hope, for your sake, that you are not overfond of the churl."

12

❧

Gresham stood facing his son, there in that darkened bedchamber, battling wildly conflicting desires. He could barely restrain himself from reaching out to throttle the pup and, yet, at the very same moment in time, he ached to embrace the boy. To swear that all would henceforth be well, that he, Gresham, would make it so.

He had no memory of this angry child, but neither could he deny him. Kieran was Gresham's image, in miniature, his reflection. It was as though he had actually *been* this person at one time, so well did he comprehend the fury, the defiance, the obdurate pride.

"Sit down," Gresham croaked, and gestured toward one of the chairs at the table before the dying fire.

Kieran, slender and agile in a jerkin and hose and soft leather boots, made no move to comply. Indeed, he stiffened slightly.

"Will you make me a sermon on the conduct fitted to a son?" Kieran responded, in a silken snarl. "If so, save your breath—Father."

Gresham took up a post behind one of the chairs, closing his fingers round the top rail on its back. "Why did you come here, if you have no wish to talk?" he asked quietly. "If not to murder the lady or myself?"

Kieran swallowed visibly, cast a fleeting, sidelong glance toward Meg, who was still trapped in the bed, unclothed and, rare as it was, rendered speechless.

"Mayhap I have a question to put to you, my lord," he told Gresham, after a long and very stiff silence, putting a slight but wholly disdainful emphasis on the salutation.

Gresham merely waited.

Kieran indicated Meg with an inclination of his head. "You are willing, then, that she—this wench—should be privy to whatever I may have to say?"

"Lady Redclift—who is not a wench, by the way, and I will thank you to remember that and save me the trouble of boxing your ears if you use the term even once more—may hear your wretched secret, such as it may be. I have shared all I know of myself—which is, admittedly, little enough—with Meg."

Gresham sensed a certain quickening in Kieran, although the boy revealed nothing outwardly.

"Are you claiming now that you don't remember me?" the man child demanded. "What foolery is this?"

" 'Tis no foolery," Meg put in defensively, from the bed, before Gresham could shape an answer. "My lord was struck over the head with a stone—by a nun if the tale is true—and remembers naught of his life before."

Gresham closed his eyes.

" 'By a nun'?" Kieran drawled, plainly delighted.

"Have you no words of your own," Gresham snapped, irritated beyond common reason, "that you must keep parroting those of others?"

The boy smirked. "By a nun," he repeated, with pleasure. "Tangwyn will make simple work of you, if you cannot even defend yourself against a maid of Christ."

Gresham flung a look at Meg, meant to daunt her into silence, and then turned his attention back to Kieran. "I shall be delighted to prove you wrong," he said, sighing, and rubbed his eyes with a thumb and forefinger. "Now—explain yourself. What glorious mission inspired you to disturb the privacy of my bedchamber at such an hour?"

Kieran hesitated only a moment. "Very well," he said. "I want to know this: why did you leave my mother to die bearing your babe? Why did you leave me?"

It was the question Gresham had expected, the one he had feared, and yet it pierced his vitals like the point of a lance, sharpened and dipped in poison. "I do not know," he replied, on a ragged breath.

Kieran paled; Gresham saw the color drain from his son's face even in that poor light. "You are a liar, as well as a drunkard and a knave."

Gresham sighed. Mayhap he was all of those things, mayhap he was none; he could not be sure either way. "Tell me what I am," he said, with misery and with pride, and indicated the chair on the opposite side of the table. "I will listen."

He waited a wing's beat, the wary child, then took a seat and folded his slender hands on the tabletop before him. Kieran's dignity was undiminished by this capitulation, and there was no sign of surrender in his manner; Gresham looked upon him, and was glad that he had sired this lad, however insolent and troublesome.

No doubt, he, Gresham, had been much the same, in his time.

He sat down opposite his son, reached for the wine

ewer and the chalice, now empty, poured, and thrust the cup across the table, still littered with crumbs of cheese and bread, to Kieran.

Kieran was unhurried; he took his father's measure yet once more, then raised the chalice in both hands, and drank deeply.

"I had but four years when you took me from my mother, and brought me here, to be fostered with Lancaster's brats. In time, she sickened, for grief I am told, and perished bearing your child."

Gresham tried to summon the woman's image from his deeper mind, but naught came to him; Meg filled every part of him, his brain, his heart, his spirit. She pulsed in the very marrow of his bones, and fed his lungs, and left no room for anyone else. Now, although she was silent, still cosseted in their bed, he was almost more conscious of her presence than his own.

"I do not suppose an apology will suffice," he said, taking the chalice by its heavy pewter stem, pulling the wine toward him—and pushing it away, untouched, when he heard his son's voice reverberate in his head. *Drunkard . . .*

"Nay," Kieran replied. "Your remorse means naught to me. Go ahead and drink. I have heard you have a head for the stuff—aye, that you can drink for days on end and still keep to your feet."

Gresham folded his arms. "Your case seems mostly made on hearsay," he remarked. "You have already confessed that I have been a stranger to you for most of your life."

Kieran too folded his arms, mirroring his gesture, though Gresham believed the motion to be unconscious. The child hated him vehemently, and seemed too occupied with keeping a hold on his slippery temper to engage in so subtle and perfect a mockery.

"You know, then, for all your ignorance, that I am two and ten."

"Aye," Gresham allowed. "I might have guessed that by your size. Your friend, the mummer bandit, told me one or two things about you, as well, some days ago. He means to kill me, at least in part as a favor to you."

"I shall be most grateful," Kieran said. There was just the slightest tremor in his voice now; he was far from flinging himself into Gresham's arms in joyous reunion, but he cared. He'd shown that by coming here, even with a dagger in hand.

"Have you been unhappy with Lancaster's bastards?" Gresham asked, careful to let none of his own riotous emotions show. As he knew the names of trees and shires and the king's horses, so he also knew of John of Gaunt's children, got on Katherine Swynford. "Are you mistreated? You look well enough—sturdy and big for your age, with no bruises showing. Your clothes are good, you seem to have all your teeth and you are well spoken, for all your impudent rantings—I'll warrant you can read and write. Pray, do you sleep in the rushes, with the hounds? Are you flogged, fed on table scraps?"

Kieran's jaw tightened; he relaxed the muscles there with a perceptible effort. "I am not misused," he confessed, but grudgingly. "You are an unaccountable favorite of the king—His Majesty's powers of discernment are not what they once were—and as your son I have enjoyed a certain privilege in the royal households."

"Then what is your complaint—besides the ill use of your sainted mother?" Gresham was purposely taunting the boy now, trying to push him into revealing more and thus enlightening him on the subject of his own past. "You called me a liar, a drunkard, and a knave, if I recall correctly. What exactly did I do to win those names?"

Quickly, but not quickly enough, Kieran reached for the chalice, and might have flung its contents into Gresham's face, except that Gresham saw the intention in the boy's eyes, and closed his hand hard around the smaller one, forestalling the motion.

"A waste of good wine," Gresham said. "Tell me why you hate me. For bearing you away from your mother? Would you have preferred to remain with her, wailing and clinging to her skirts?"

Kieran was on his feet with breath-stopping speed, his hand still trapped within Gresham's, where he clasped the stem of the chalice.

"I wanted to be with you! I might have been your squire when you went with Chalstrey to France—"

"Sit down," Gresham said moderately. "You were too young, even for a squire."

The boy stood stubbornly for a long moment, then sank furiously onto the chair seat again, having little other choice. When Gresham freed his hand, Kieran withdrew it as if from a fire, but he had evidently given up the idea of hurling wine into his father's face.

"I hate you. I *despise* you. I should have killed you and the—you and your lady strumpet, when I had the chance!"

Gresham ignored the outburst, turning the chalice slowly round and round upon its base. "You could not have gone to France," he said. "A battlefield is no place for a mewling, bed-wetting boy."

Kieran's face contorted with rage, but he brought it under control with unsettling swiftness. "I am the best squire in the realm," he said, and although he almost whispered the words, the flash of his eyes gave the lie to any appearance of timidity.

"You are immodest, as well as brash," Gresham said.

Meg had got out of bed at last, wrapped in shadow and a sheet, and she made irritated sounds as she dressed herself. Neither Gresham nor Kieran looked in her direction; they were staring at each other in silence, Gresham's regard pensive, Kieran's stony and unyielding.

Gresham wished mightily that Meg had stayed put, though he knew she wouldn't welcome a suggestion that she go back to bed. At this juncture, her presence could only make matters worse, for Gresham had no intention of sitting by while the boy insulted her. He would thrash Kieran if he dared belittle Meg in any way, and that would probably preclude all chance of familial reconciliation, for that night and always.

Deliciously appealing in a robe of dark gold, her rich brown hair trailing down her back in a cascade of fire-shot curls, Meg came and stood beside the table, her hands on her hips.

Even then, with his son sitting across from him, yearning to cut his throat, Gresham felt a sweet stirring at her proximity.

"Tell me about your mother. Monique—wasn't that her name?"

The question bludgeoned Gresham, and made Kieran smile, albeit sadly.

"She was beautiful. Far more beautiful than you, milady."

Gresham leaned forward; Meg laid a hand to his shoulder and restrained him by some feminine magic that was past understanding.

"That is not difficult to credit," Meg replied moderately, and if she was stung by the boy's answer, she gave no evidence of it. "You must have loved her very much."

"I did," Kieran said, with a lethal softness, "unlike my father." He was made of Turkish brass, this lad, but he was no fool. He knew how to get under an adversary's skin, though he was but two and ten. "He has had many mistresses. The troubadours sing songs of them still, and—" here, he paused, turning his guileless blue eyes upon Gresham, "of my lord father."

"Songs," Meg said.

"Aye," Kieran answered helpfully. "Mayhap I might sing one for you—"

"Do not dare," Gresham interceded, forcing the words between his teeth.

Kieran wet his lips, and bent his head for a moment, as though cowed, but his eyes were soft with malice when he looked at Gresham again. "But my lord—they tell of your great prowess as a knight and as a—"

"Enough." Gresham gave the word barely any breath, but it seemed to peal within that warm, darkened room all the same.

"As a lover," Meg finished, regarding Kieran coolly.

"You would know," Kieran said, and his tone and manner were so angelic that a few seconds passed before Gresham really took in the remark. When he did, he got to his feet with such haste that he overset his chair and made to round the table and get the boy by the scruff.

Meg set herself in his path, however, and Kieran, proving himself capable of some prudence, however belated, sprang from his chair and ran for the door as though pursued by the devil.

"It will do no good to thrash him," Meg insisted, holding on when Gresham made to set her aside. "Neither these hurts nor any others can be mended by violent means, my lord. Let the boy go."

Gresham breathed deeply and, after a little while, had found his wits again, and got a hold on them, however tenuous. "He is a demon!" he rasped. "A monster, spawned in hell!"

To his amazement, Meg laughed. "Aye," she agreed. "Methinks you were much like him, once upon a time. You had best make a friend of your Kieran before he is a man, my lord, for he would make a formidable enemy."

Gresham thrust one hand through his hair. "He wants a thrashing—"

Meg sobered, gazing toward the open portal as though she could still see Kieran there. "No, my lord. He wants a father."

Gresham stepped away from her to shut and bar the portal. Then he retrieved Kieran's daggers, first the one on the floor, then the one protruding from the headboard.

He turned the second knife, the one that had struck only inches above Meg's head and his own, against his palm, and saw that his own initials were etched deep into the base of the blade.

Where had the boy gotten such a weapon? Had he, Gresham, left it behind, as some sort of deadly remembrance?

"Come, my lord," Meg said soothingly, "let us return to our bed."

"Why, Meg?" He laid the knives upon the table with a clatter. "Why does nothing come back to me, even now? Will I never remember?"

She slid her arms round his neck, stood on tiptoe to kiss him with quickness and with fire. "On the morrow, surely, you will be told all that you wish to know—may-hap more, if we are to judge by Kieran's remarks."

"Aye," he muttered, and glanced toward the door, now prudently fastened against unknown enemies. Against his son. He gave a heavy sigh and pressed his forehead against Meg's. "Aye."

She kissed him once more, and led him back to their bed, and he did not know sorrow again until he slept. And dreamed of a dark-haired woman, sobbing wretchedly and calling out to him as he rode away from her, his back rigid, his heart cold and dead within him.

She had been great with child, this woman of his nightmare, and he knew that she had been his wife, that she was Kieran's mother, that he would meet with Morgan Chalstrey, the Duke of Edgefield, at Portsmouth, there to take ship for France.

It was, Gresham knew, the day of parting Kieran had described to him, except for one small detail. He carried no four-year-old child in his arms, to be taken to Lancaster's household for fostering.

Meg awakened full of energy the following morning, and was neither surprised nor daunted to find herself alone in the vast bedchamber, but for Allena, who stood at the hearth, stirring up sparks from the fire with an iron poker.

"I pray you've brought me food," Meg said, snatching up her gold woolen gown, which had been flung across the foot of the bed the night before, and struggling into it before tossing back the covers. "I am fair starving to death!"

Allena smiled serenely, and Meg wondered if she was happy with her maid's duties and her husband, the pig tender. "Aye, milady, there is fruit and bread, and good wine, there on the table. Your lord has already taken his breakfast and gone, though; he bids you wait here until he returns to fetch you later in the morning."

Meg grumbled a little; she was not good at biding, though for love of Gresham, she would try.

She sat on the bedside to pull on her boots, then cross the room. She took a chair, crossed herself and murmured a prayer of gratitude, and began to eat.

"Is the king in residence?" she asked, when she'd taken the painful edge off her hunger, and could nibble delicately instead of thrusting food into her mouth like a beggar.

Allena had busied herself tidying the well-tossed covers upon the bed. "Aye, milady," she replied. "He is yet ill, and grows fitful, because he cannot ride or hunt." She lowered her voice. "My sister Mary works in the laundry, and she says His Majesty's shouts can be heard even there, when he's in a temper. Yester-eve, Mary says, he threw his wine at his mistress and stained her best gown!"

Meg knew little about the king, except that he had been a great soldier in his prime, and that he was much loved and admired by his subjects, unlike his father and predecessor, Edward II. She crossed herself again, and shuddered, for there were those at the abbey who said *he*, poor wretch, had died very horribly indeed.

"I suppose if you're a king, you can throw things at people when it strikes your fancy," she said, more to make conversation than because she'd ever taken the time to make an opinion on the matter. She hoped she would get a glimpse of His Majesty while they were at Windsor, but in truth that was the least of her worries.

She was most concerned about Gresham, of course.

Tangwyn the mummer, for all his threats, was a felon, after all, and might not dare to make an appearance within the castle walls. If he did choose to make good on his threat against Gresham, the sheriff would know immediately that this was the man he sought, and place him under arrest.

No, it was Kieran who presented the greatest danger now, and not because of his propensity for hurling daggers. Kieran, the beautiful, hateful, frightfully intelligent boy, who knew much more of Gresham's past than he had revealed, and possessed a power to wound his father as no one else on earth could have done.

"Milady?" Allena inquired worriedly, bringing Meg out of her miserable reflections and back to the cold, sunny morning. "You look sore peaked, Lady Sedgewick—has the bath brought on a fever?"

Meg smiled. "I am well, Allena," she said, and taking the serving woman's roughened hand in her own, she pressed it to her forehead, for proof. "See? There is no sickness in me." She laughed. "Alas, the bath was my salvation, not my doom. I would take one every day if it were possible."

Allena looked amazed, even horrified. "*Every day,* milady?" She crossed herself, eyes wide, cheeks aflame. "Why, your skin might—might come apart, like a cloth will, from too much washing—"

"Mule feathers," Meg said happily, wondering how soon she could decently prevail upon Allena and her legion of fellow servants to heat and bear water for another luxurious soaking. "My lord has promised me such a tub for my own, one day, and I shall use it as often as I wish."

Some of Allena's horror gave way to admiration. "You are very brave, milady," she said. "But do you not know your husband's house, and all that's in it?"

Meg shook her head, and for no good reason, her high spirits faltered a little, and she felt her smile stumble upon her lips. "I've never been there." She sighed, reached for a lie. "We've only been wed a few weeks and my lord—my lord was injured. There is much he cannot recall."

Allena's eyes widened again. "He cannot remember where he lives, milady?"

Meg started to protest, then sighed and shook her head. "I do not think so," she confessed, in a hushed voice. "What do you know of Lord Sedgewick, Allena? You have seen him before, haven't you?"

The servant hesitated, surely weighing risks, and then blurted out, "Aye, milady. He is an important man—a friend to Lancaster, and the Black Prince, and to Chalstrey, the Duke of Edgefield. Indeed, even the king calls him friend—"

"Yes? Has he a family, Allena?"

Allena was trembling; Meg took her hand and squeezed it in an attempt to reassure the other woman. "A father, I think—yes, he's called Lord Sedgewick, too, of course—" Allena flushed painfully. "An earl, he is, your lord husband's father, I mean."

Meg was overjoyed; she could hardly wait to carry this news to Gresham. Surely it would comfort him, to learn that he had a parent somewhere . . .

Then she thought of her own late sire, and of Kieran, and her joy was dampened. "Where? Where is Lord Sedgewick the elder—here?"

"No, milady—he keeps to his estate—I think it is near London—I can tell you naught—"

"But you can," Meg insisted, for Allena's eyes had betrayed her. She knew more, mayhap much more, than she was willing to say.

"My lord and his father—the earl—are estranged, milady. It had to do with a woman—the lad Kieran's dead mother—"

Meg had long since forgotten her food. She stood facing Allena, holding both the other woman's hands in her own. There was no need to ask how a servant could know such things; she remembered Kieran, taunting his father the night before with references to songs the troubadours sang. Tales, strung upon strands of merry music, like beads on thread.

Everyone knew the truth, except Meg, and Gresham himself.

"Tell me," Meg said softly.

Allena's lower lip quivered. " 'Tis said that the earl disinherited his son," she went on softly, reluctantly.

"Why?"

"He—" Allena swallowed, started again. "He took a woman to wife, and then he left her, and denied her child. She followed after him in the rain, when he would ride away to fight, and still he would not speak to her. She was—was swollen with his babe, and yet he had no compassion for her. He f-finally told one of his men to take her back home, where she belonged, and her wet through by then, and broken in spirit. She perished afore the new day, milady, of sorrow and fever. The babe went with her."

Meg's eyes stung with tears she would not shed, but only because the tale was a vivid one, and melancholy. She believed it not, for she knew Gresham, knew his soul and his substance, if not his history. He could never have done such as the troubadours claimed.

"These tales are oft more akin to lies than truth, Allena," Meg said gently.

"Aye," Allena agreed, but she still looked unhappy.

Meg made a smile, for Allena's sake as well as her own. "No more sad tales," she decreed. "Tell me—where should I seek the lad, Kieran?"

"But, milady, you were to bide—"

"I am not a bird in a cage," Meg interrupted, with some impatience, "to sit upon a perch and wait until I am called upon to chirp. Where, please, is Kieran?"

Allena sighed. "He is a squire, milady, and might be in the stables, tending his master's horse, in the armory, or even in the lists—"

"The lists," Meg muttered, alarmed and annoyed, and started toward the door. Kieran was but a boy, and had no business frequenting such dangerous places, squire or none. She would find him, and fetch him away to a safe place, before he hurt himself.

"Milady, you wouldn't go to the—to the lists—?" Allena pleaded, hurrying after her. "Kieran is used to such places, but you—you might be run down by a horse—"

Meg went out into the corridor and then started down the stairs, holding her kirtle up so she wouldn't take a tumble. "I am not an idiot, Allena," she said briskly. "I will not step in front of any horse."

Allena grew more frantic still. "Please, milady, they are rough men, these knights—"

"And I shall have no truck with them," Meg answered, hastening across the rushes in the main hall now. "It is young Kieran I seek, and none other."

Hurrying along beside her, Allena murmured what sounded like a prayer. "I will send for him, milady—"

Meg had reached the front door. She hauled it open and stepped out into a cold day, and for a moment her eyes were dazzled by the sunlight, glaring upon the crusted snow. Finding the knights' training ground, and thus the lists, would not be difficult; the clank and clamor resonated in the crisp air, as did their curses and the fretful cries of their horses.

Brutes, Meg thought, and strode without hesitation toward the sound.

Allena scrambled along at her side. "There are swords," she warned breathlessly, twisting her hands together. "And lances. Crossbows. And those great enormous horses, milady, with hooves the size of trenchers!"

Meg stopped just long enough to fix the servant, the nearest thing she'd had to a friend since leaving the abbey, except for Bessie, with a scolding glower. "If you are so afraid, Allena," she said, "I must advise you not to follow!"

She set out again.

"But my lord bid me keep you in my sight—"

Meg walked faster. "Bid you watch me, did he?" she said. "Well, he should have known better, and after this, you will, too."

"Aye, milady," Allena said meekly, but she kept up. "Do you think he will have me flogged?"

"If he did," Meg replied, as the crashes and shouts grew louder, "I should cause him to regret it sorely."

Soldiers and servants made way, their faces gone slack with amazement, as Meg marched onward. Mayhap she should have covered her hair, she thought, instead of letting it fall unbound down her back like a harlot's, but there was no point in regretting the oversight now. Everyone had seen her, and the damage was done.

She rounded a stone building and the field was before her, splotched with rags of dirty snow and promising to turn to mud at the first thaw.

Knights, some in armor and some in mere tunics and hose, fought diligently, wielding swords and, as Allena had warned, lances. A real battle, Meg thought disgustedly, could not have been much different, except there would have been more blood.

She stood briefly on the sidelines, arms akimbo, eyes squinted against the bright winter sun, while she scanned the fools' skirmish for Kieran.

He was in the center of the melee, soiled and bloodied and beaming with pleasure, and Meg felt a moment's foolish pride before good sense took over.

She marched right through the fighting, between swordsmen, between men on horses, slamming each other with poles. Reaching Kieran, she took him hard by one ear and started off the field. "Are you *trying* to get yourself killed?"

13

꧁

Kieran glared at Meg, red to the roots of his pale golden hair, his dirty hands knotted at his sides. For a moment, it actually seemed as though he would come at her in a blazing fury, flailing his fists, but if ever that was his intention, he managed to restrain himself.

"How dare you?" Kieran hissed, exuding such hatred that, had he not been essentially a child, for all his size, Meg might actually have been frightened. They had reached the edge of the field, and comparative safety, but Meg's heart was still thundering in her ears, and her mind was teeming with visions of blood and gore.

She set her hands on her hips and breathed deeply in an effort to restore her composure a little. As difficult as this boy was, as contemptuous and disrespectful, she had come to care for him. He was, whatever his feelings on the matter, Gresham's son. "You are—too young—" she gasped.

The blue, blue eyes flamed. "I am *a squire!*" the boy spat.

He was so like his father in that moment that Meg

nearly laughed, but her better instincts warned against it. Instead, she leaned forward, so that her nose was less than an inch from the boy's, and replied, "You are *a child!*"

A crowd had gathered nearby, and some of the men— rough sorts, just as Allena had warned—were grinning and calling to Kieran, mocking him. Bestirring him to even greater anger.

"Mind the lady, little lord," cried one.

"She's come to wipe your nose," taunted another.

"You'd better have a care—she may take a switch to you!" said someone else.

"She can take a switch to me whenever she likes," offered still another, and brought a stinging blush to Meg's cheeks.

At this, there was much merriment and jostling about, and Meg had her fill of the ruffians and their interference. Breaking away from Allena, who tried valiantly to hold her back, she strode over to them, leaving Kieran looking as though he would ignite like a dry haystack under a hot summer sun.

"I will thank you to stay out of this matter, since it is none of your affair!" Meg told the scruffy assembly, arms akimbo. Her face throbbed with heat, and she knew her eyes must be blazing. "Young Lord Sedgewick is my husband's son and I would speak to him in private!"

She heard Kieran groan in what sounded like utter despair, but if he knew the truth, he did not disabuse the others of the belief that Meg and Gresham were not, in fact, married. She wondered about that—it would have been a perfect opportunity to retaliate.

Leaving some of the knights gaping and others making obvious efforts not to smile, she turned back to Kieran.

Only then, gazing into his smudged face, did she realize the magnitude of her mistake. Alas, Meg had been raised in the company of women, and because of that, she knew precious little about the ways of men, and still less of boys.

Now, too late, she understood that, by wishing to save Kieran from injury, she had instead held him up to ridicule. If ever there had been a chance of peace between them, she had most likely spoiled it.

"I have shamed you," she said softly. "I am sorry."

Kieran glowered at her for a long interval, and then spat, narrowly missing the hem of her gown. Obviously, a simple apology, however heartfelt, would not suffice.

"Go back to your bedchamber," he bit out, but quietly, fair strangling on the words. His eyes, now a frosty shade of cornflower blue, took in her person, her crumpled gown and unbound hair with contempt. "No doubt my lord father awaits you there, to get another heir on you!"

Meg retreated a step, feeling as though she'd been slapped, then her temper rose and she started forward again, only to feel a hand catch her by the arm and stop her progress.

Gresham stood beside her. His grasp, though painless, was like a manacle.

"That will be enough," he said calmly, "from both of you."

Kieran flung his head back, to spit again, no doubt, but Gresham had released Meg and taken his son hard by the chin before he could execute the plan.

"I said," Gresham reiterated, sweeping the watching knights up in one scathing glance before dropping his eyes to Kieran's face, *"that will be enough."* He lowered his voice, so that only his son and Meg might hear. "If you think you've been mortified already, lad, simply spew forth a mouthful of spittle—you will discover then the true nature of humiliation. By God's nightshirt, I will take the hide off your rear end, here and now, with all Windsor looking on."

Kieran considered, and then swallowed.

"It is my fault, my lord," Meg began, anxious to make amends for her impulsive indiscretion. "If only I had waited—"

"Silence," Gresham interrupted, without sparing her so much as a look. "I have not decided your precise fate, except to conclude that it must needs be more private than Kieran's."

Meg bit back the defiant response that leaped to her tongue. She was outraged, and rightly so, but in that particular time and place she had no more recourse than Kieran did.

Gresham released Kieran with a slight flinging motion that threw the boy off balance, though he quickly caught himself. A fact which brought the merest hint of a smile to his father's lips.

"What took place here?" the man asked.

"She," breathed the boy, pointing at Meg with one grubby finger, "came onto the field and, taking me by the ear, dragged me off like a—like a babe, gone wandering in the road!"

Meg looked down at her feet. "I feared for your life," she whispered, at once chagrined and truculent. While it was certainly true that she'd made an abominable bungle of the situation by stepping in without thinking first, her intentions had been unimpeachable. She had sought to protect a child from lasting injury, perhaps even death.

"The boy has been raised amongst fighting men and

their weapons," Gresham said reasonably. His gaze, avoiding Meg, seemed fastened to Kieran, who was a little more composed than before, although he still seemed poised to spring. "He wishes, it would appear, to make a soldier of himself."

"I told you last night that was what I wanted," Kieran snapped, and Meg caught a hopeful note in his voice, barely discernible for all that impudence, but there to be heard nonetheless.

Gresham sighed like one crushed, yet resigned, beneath a great weight. "You are too ill tempered to make a knight," he said, with sorrow and another, smaller sigh. "There is no place in any army for such a peevish nature as yours. You would either be flogged to death by your own captains or, being too aggrieved by a multitude of supposed injustices to pay proper attention, killed in battle."

"I am not peevish!"

Gresham smiled in a way that made even Meg want to strike him; she could only imagine the cost of the uncommon abstinence Kieran showed.

"Go back to your games of war," Gresham said, with the faintest emphasis on the word 'games,' and then, before turning to walk away, and as an apparent afterthought, he reached out and tousled the boy's hair.

Kieran's restraint, made of flimsy stuff in the first place, fell apart. He launched himself onto Gresham's back like a stone from a catapult, much to the entertainment of the onlookers. Meg now recollected, however, that they had ceased teasing Kieran upon Sedgewick's arrival.

The boy had got a stranglehold on Gresham, and it was plain that he was strong, slight though he was. Gresham gave a great bellow—at first Meg thought the

236 LAEL ST. JAMES

sound was made of rage—but she soon recognized it as
something else altogether.

Laughter.

With an easy motion, Gresham flipped Kieran over one
muscular shoulder, and the boy landed on his back at his
father's feet with such force that the breath left his lungs
in an audible rush. He lay there, Kieran did, suffocating
like a fish on a stream bank, for what seemed an eternity
to Meg, then hoisted himself onto his elbows, clearly prepared to make a second charge, however inadvisable.

Before the boy could rise further, Gresham grinned,
shook his head, and laid the sole of one foot in the center
of Kieran's heaving chest, and cast him down again.

"You have the disposition of a tomcat caught in a thorn
patch," Gresham said. "Learn to govern your wits, and
you *might* make a soldier."

Kieran was breathing rapidly and hard. "When Tangwyn gets here—"

Gresham withdrew his foot. "The mummer has arrived, but I don't think he'll be of much use to you. He's
been taken prisoner, at the sheriff's suggestion, on
charges of thievery. Among other things."

Color suffused Kieran's perfectly formed face, then
subsided again, like some bright tide. "You are a liar!"

"Go to the dungeons and see for yourself," Gresham
answered. And, with that, he got Meg by the arm and
squired her away.

He did not speak again, or release his hold, until they
were alone in the bedchamber they had shared so conge-
nially the night before.

"What possessed you?" Gresham demanded, though
he seemed distracted now, rather than angry. Standing
beside the table, he took up a piece of bread left from

Meg's breakfast and bit into it. "Those men out there will bait that boy from now till the sounding of Gabriel's trumpet—he'll not know a moment's peace, and God knows where he will dredge up the dignity to face them again."

Meg was not so reckless as before, nor so hasty. And of course she was sorry for Kieran's predicament, though not yet ready to confess to the fact to Gresham.

She found a scarf and tied it round her hair, wimplelike, as she should have done before leaving the house. "I merely wanted to ask Kieran about the songs," she said. "The ones the troubadours sing about you. I thought to learn something of your past from the words." She paused, bit her lip. "And it was not *I*, you must concede, who threw the poor lad onto the ground and then trod upon him. No doubt *that* will inspire some comment among his peers."

"He was fortunate I did not do more," Gresham said flatly. "Still, it is one matter to take your comeuppance from a sire, be that sire despised or beloved, even before witnesses. It is indeed another to suffer in public at the hands of a woman." He stared through the misted windows as he spoke, and there was a subtle altering of his countenance; he was subdued, and seemed to see things that were invisible to Meg. "You should have left the boy alone. He is like a badger with a stick through its paw, sharp toothed, wild with his pain, and much inclined to bite."

Meg took a breath and then attempted to wrest the subject onto another, more encouraging course. "Is it true that Tangwyn is at Windsor, and in the dungeons?"

Gresham met her gaze at last. "Aye."

"I cannot believe he was so foolish as to come here, for all his threats and conceits!"

"The mummer depends heavily on his alliance with

Kieran—who will be, after all, the next Earl of Sedgewick, once my esteemed and noble father takes up his heavenly crown. Humble squire though he is, Kieran will have command of lands and gold one day soon, and all the influence that goes with them."

Meg caught her breath. "Your father? You mean—you remember him?"

Gresham's eyes were bleak, and much of the color had seeped from his flesh, leaving him waxen and gaunt, as he had been that morning so recently, and yet so long ago, when Meg and Elizabeth had found him lying senseless in the abbey's squash patch.

"No," he said. "I remember naught, as before. But I passed much of the morning in the king's company, and he, being bored of his indisposition, and thus quarrelsome, saw cause to enlighten me in more detail than I ever desired.

"I am the only son of the Earl of Sedgewick, and we are estranged, my father and I. Indeed, it is more than that: I am disinherited. The title, when my sire perishes—he is of great age, according to the king—will settle upon Kieran, and even if the boy doesn't know that yet, which is unlikely, Tangwyn—consoler, it would seem, of my scorned bride—surely does."

It was true then, at least that much of what Allena had said. Gresham had been cast out of his home, in disgrace. Meg braced herself to hear the rest.

"Sit down—please," Gresham said, with a gesture.

Now, Meg thought in despair, he would tell her about the woman. About Kieran's mother.

She sat, hands folded in her lap, backbone aligned, and held her tongue.

"In my father's place," Gresham said, after a lengthy pause, during which he did not sit, but took up a post behind the chair opposite, gripping its back with such force that his knuckles shone like ivory through his flesh, "I, too, would have banished such a son. I have named Kieran monster and demon, but as God lives in the hearts of saints and virgins, Meg, the little knave is my better by a hundred, nay, a thousandfold!"

He fell silent, momentarily, and it seemed that all life stopped with his voice, but Meg did not prod him to go on. Neither did she attempt to smooth his way; he would finish when he was ready, when he was able. He would find peace in his own time and way.

In his present state, however, there were no words to coax Gresham out of the black sorrow that had so plainly engulfed him.

"Kieran's mother—Monique—was pretty and devoted, according to the king's account, even pious. My father arranged our marriage—like all such unions, ours was an alliance of property and influence, rather than love—and I refused to attend the ceremony, though there was naught I could do to prevent it from taking place. A proxy bridegroom was sent in my stead, the vows were made, the documents signed and witnessed.

"I finally went to her, though unwillingly, got her with child, and spent the best part of the following year drinking and whoring. My father sent a warning: comport myself in a fashion befitting a future earl, or surrender all claim not only to my inheritance, but even to my name.

"I defied the earl and, joining with my friend and foster brother, Morgan Chalstrey—Edgefield—and his army, went off to fight in France. I left the woman, Meg, just as cruelly as Kieran said I did, though not before I put another babe in her belly. She perished, with the child, and still—" He paused, drew a breath that sounded painful to Meg, like the harsh rattle of some fever of the lungs, and let it out slowly. "It was Tangwyn, it seems, who brought my son to Lancaster for fostering, though Kieran remembers it differently. Not surprising, I suppose, considering that the boy was yet so small, and the mummer and I bear a certain unfortunate resemblance, one to the other."

There was wine left from breakfast; Meg filled the chalice and pushed it toward Gresham without a word. He hesitated, then took the cup, with a trembling hand, and drained it in a few swallows.

"Mayhap it is a mercy," Gresham said presently, his voice hoarse, "that I have lost myself."

Meg spoke for the first time since Gresham had begun telling her what he had learned of his past. "No," she said. "No."

Still another silence descended, this one thicker than the last, and weighty, fit to crush them both.

Gresham shoved a hand through his hair, which was already in fetching disarray, and went to stand at the windows, far away from Meg, with his back turned to her.

"It will snow again this night," he said. "The sky is gray at its edges."

Meg offered no comment on the weather. "You are not the man the king described to you, Gresham. That man would not have risked plague to give the dead a proper burial. He would not have traveled willingly with the sheriff as a prisoner, in order to prove his innocence, nor loved the young son who speaks of naught but his penchant to murder him. Most of all, that man would not have loved me so tenderly as you have done."

Gresham turned to face Meg at last, his eyes glittering. "You are too charitable by half, my lady," he said bitterly, "and you deceive yourself. You have been witness to my temper—it is the match of Kieran's. I have made that boy, that little fiend, from the worst parts of myself."

She got up and crossed slowly to stand before him, setting one hand upon his forearm. The muscles beneath the sleeve of his tunic, beneath his flesh and the light touch of her fingers and palm, were like iron.

"Are you God, to make people either good or evil?" she asked quietly, insistently. "Besides, Kieran is not bad. He has been lost from his father these many years, but now he is found. He acts as he does because, after all the years of dreaming, hoping, that you would come back, he is afraid you will find him wanting, and turn away."

Gresham smiled sadly and brushed the outline of Meg's cheek with the backs of his curved fingers. "You are a fey and fanciful creature," he said. "Would that you were right about my son, but I fear that your bent toward kindness misguides you. Have you not looked into his eyes and seen the hatred there, heard the vile utterances of his tongue?" With a sudden and impatient motion of the same hand, he indicated the enormous bed. "Were you not lying there, with me, when the Beautiful Child hurled a dagger at our heads?"

"He never intended to strike either of us with the blade, and you know it well, my lord. Kieran is given to spectacle, that is all."

"Mayhap he will be a mummer, then, like his good friend Tangwyn, whom he holds in such high regard, and practice robbery and murder as an avocation!"

Meg smiled benevolently, for she knew that Gresham did not mean what he said, any more than Kieran had. Like his son—and virtually everyone else in the world, herself included, Gresham was wounded, damaged, in part by his own choices, commissions and omissions, but also by the stabs and buffets of unaccountable fortune.

"There is no profit in such ravings, my lord," she pointed out sweetly. "You mourn your past, because you cannot remember it, but we are all robbed by time, are we not? For all that I recollect much, my yesterdays are as truly spent as your own, and our tomorrows could be as easily stolen—there is naught but now, today, to trade upon. What will you buy with this moment? More sorrow and bitterness and hatred? Or will you purchase some sweeter portion—forgiveness, mayhap? Hope, or patience? Surely these are good bargains—"

Gresham turned his head slightly and tasted her lips with his own. His eyes smiled as he put a mere breath of distance between them.

"But for your affinity for bed-sport, my lady love, I might think you were a guardian angel, sent to guide me aright." He tugged at the wimple, hastily and belatedly donned upon her return from the fray, so that Meg's newly washed hair was revealed. "Kiss me sweetly, pray, and then stay here, as you were bidden, while I go to the dungeons and speak with Tangwyn."

Meg pulled out of Gresham's embrace, confused and a little injured. "You would leave me behind *again*—like a hound that is too old to keep pace or the jerkin you wore yesterday?"

Gresham reached for her, but when she withdrew further, he sighed and let his hands fall to his sides. "That is naught but waspish prattle, and you well know it," he said, and the very calmness, the very quietness of his voice made a sore irritation for Meg. "The dungeons are filthy and dank and generally unfit to look upon."

"I have looked upon the plague. The king's prison can

hardly be worse than that." She snatched the wimple out of his hand, covered her hair anew, and tied the veil's linen ends at her nape with a neatness the dames at St. Swithin's had despaired of imparting to her. "I would see this Tangwyn again, and discern for myself what manner of threat he presents."

"Let me save you the trouble: he is quite helpless, as of now," Gresham said tautly, and Meg noted that the edge of his jaw was pale and rather more sharply defined than usual. "Still, I feel there are other things he wants me to know, for whatever reasons."

Meg gazed up at him. "The boy, Blodwyn, spoke of Gabriella, and of Chalstrey, that night at Bessie's house. He might have said something to Tangwyn."

Gresham held her shoulders, his thumbs caressing her. She could see in his eyes that he did not expect the mummer to be forthcoming, even if he did have knowledge of Gabriella. "Very well," he agreed reluctantly. "I don't suppose there is any hope of dissuading you."

"None at all," she replied quietly. "I would see the man with my own eyes, as he tells his tales, so that I might take a true measure of his words. A secondhand account is not enough."

Gresham started to speak again, then stopped himself. Finally, he turned and stalked toward the door, and Meg hastened after him, though she kept a diplomatic distance and did not plague him with further opinions. There were ways he could have made her stay behind in that chamber—right or wrong, his word was law where she was concerned, at least in their present surroundings, where everyone believed they were man and wife—and he had not employed any of the means at his disposal, probably because she had made an apt case for her position.

All the same, it would not do to push, so Meg held her peace and assumed an air of sweet docility. A close observer might have noted, however, that she kept pace with Gresham, instead of moving in his wake like flotsam on the tide, and her head was quite erect, within the enfolding shadows of the cloak's hood.

Indeed, Meg's tractable demeanor was entirely an illusion, in no wise physical, a bit of magic shaped within the innermost regions of her heart and cast upon passersby like light through the globe of a lamp.

The dungeon, hidden away beneath the oldest part of the castle, was, as Gresham had warned, a dark place, evil smelling and unutterably cold. There were chains affixed to the stone walls, rusted and ominous, blessedly empty. The musty straw spread over the floor had not been changed in recent times, and it was vile stuff, rife with all manner of detritus. Here and there, a startling furrow appeared, made by the skittering passage of a rat.

The stench was not overwhelming, but in its own way as horrific as the stink of the plague itself, for this was a place of fear and hopelessness, and those things, when blended with the baser odors of humanity, made a distinctive and peculiar miasma.

Tangwyn sat alone in a cell, his back to the outer wall, his head down.

He looked up eagerly at the sound of someone approaching, but when he saw who his visitors were, he thrust a hand through hair that must have been vermin infested, and went back to contemplating the worn toes of his boots.

"Why have you brought the lady to such a place?" he asked. Meg could not ascertain, from his tone and aspect, whether or not he was mocking them.

"I have not done so willingly," Gresham answered, and would not look at Meg. He stepped up to the bars, and grasped them in both hands, almost as though he himself were the prisoner, yearning for liberty, instead of the mummer.

In a flash of realization, bright as a spill of sunlight upon clear water, Meg knew that Gresham did indeed understand captivity; he was separated from all the years of his life by the unknown barrier in his mind, as surely as Tangwyn was parted from the world of sky and earth and untainted air.

Tangwyn raised his head and met Gresham's gaze and, despite everything, Meg felt a rise of sympathy for the man. His plight was of his own making, for a certainty, yet it was hard to see another human being in such misery.

"Have you come to gloat?"

Gresham made a sound too brusque and bitter to be mirth, although it came disguised as laughter. "No," he answered. "I am not above taking pleasure in your circumstances, but there are less foul places in which to celebrate."

The mummer's gaze slid to Meg, assessing her, and she burned with indignation, though she would not stoop to protest. Gresham had tried to discourage her from coming to the dungeon; her pride made it impossible to complain.

"Aye," said Tangwyn, drawing the word out, and smiled. "I wonder that you ever leave your bedchamber."

Meg's stomach tightened painfully, but she did not speak.

Neither did Gresham, though Meg could not discern whether it was rage that kept him silent, or disdain. Although they were not touching, she felt the hard tension in Gresham's muscles, and the mysterious burning in his bones.

Tangwyn laughed. "You must forgive a poor mummer's rude manners, my lord, my lady."

"Must we?" Gresham asked. The tone of his voice made Meg shudder as nothing else had done since they'd descended into the gloom and chill and damp of the king's displeasure, the hidden scurrying and the smell.

"Tell me," Meg blurted, "if you know anything about my sister!"

Tangwyn's gaze was locked with Gresham's. He was going to ignore her, and there wasn't a blessed thing she could do about it.

The mummer rose with the fluid grace of a performer and came through the fetid straw to stand facing Gresham, through the bars. "You hate me as much as one man can hate another," he said, "but you do not know the whole reason." He smiled. "What a consolation that is, Sedgewick, to know how such mysteries must torment you."

In the merest portion of an instant, Gresham had grabbed hold of Tangwyn, reaching through the heavy bars, wrenching the other man against the pillars of iron with such force that blood spouted from his nose, seeped between his lips, outlined his perfect teeth in etchings of crimson.

Meg gasped, but before she could say a word—she had no idea, ever after, whether she would have lauded Gresham's action or objected to the violence of his action—someone grabbed her and threw her aside, sending her tumbling onto the floor.

Kieran flew over her like a young falcon taking wing to hunt and, even then, in those first startled moments, she knew the attack had never been meant for her; she was in the way, that was all, an obstacle standing between him and the true object of all his ire: Gresham.

Gresham swore and grappled with his son, and Meg was reminded of his struggle with the wolves, so fierce was the engagement. Kieran made no sound at first, but he moved with the same terrible, ferocious grace as an animal would have done, twisting and writhing, lusting for blood.

After a struggle, which both Tangwyn and Meg watched in silence, Gresham wrenched the boy around and against him, Kieran's back to his chest. Still, the child flailed and squirmed, and it was then, and only then, that he gave a cry that was part sob, part snarl.

"Damn you!" Kieran sobbed, held fast by his father's arms yet as far from surrender as east is from west. "Damn you to hell! *You* should have died, in my mother's stead! *You* should be naught but a pile of moldering bones, drying in some tomb, not her . . . *not her!*"

Tangwyn, still gripping the bars of his prison, slid slowly downward to kneel in the straw. Meg had managed to gain her feet, but stood unsteadily, one hand extended toward Gresham, though even she did not know whether the gesture was one of conciliation or revulsion.

Gresham, heedless of everyone but his son, said nothing, but neither did he release his hold. Meg saw that his face was wet, as wet as the boy's, and the muscles in his neck corded with effort, with emotion, but he made not the smallest sound.

"Stop," Tangwyn begged hoarsely, without looking up. "In God's name, Kieran, be done with this. I can bear it no longer."

Kieran dragged in several deep, desolate breaths, his strong young body trembled once, twice; Meg thought he might swoon, for his pain was rooted in his soul, and his fury was as vast as a clear and star-laden sky. Plainly, all that he felt was destroying him, yet he could neither contain his passions, nor let them go, for they flowed in his veins like blood and sustained him like air.

Gresham spoke at last, breathlessly, and with neither kindness nor cruelty. "Bid your friend farewell, Kieran," he said evenly, "for on the morrow, you will be gone from here."

14

❧

Gresham tossed Kieran into the stinking straw outside Tangwyn's cell door and stood over him with his hands resting upon his hips. Meg, who might have argued against Gresham's arbitrary decision to put Windsor Castle and all its singular comforts behind them at any other time—after all, she had learned little or nothing of Gabriella, despite questioning everyone who would stand still—chose to keep her own counsel and let her private opinions on the matter remain precisely so—private. The mummer, too, was silent, and had not risen from his knees.

"I will not leave this place with you," Kieran told Gresham, with quiet and utter contempt. There was, in his defiant fortitude, much of his father's temperament, and Meg took a certain delight in that, despite the seriousness of the situation.

She looked at the boy pityingly, for she knew, if he did not, that he was wasting his breath and his passion. The decree had been issued, and when Gresham spoke thus, it was a certainty that nothing short of his own death would turn him from the course he had set for all of them.

Gresham bent from the waist, grasped the boy by the front of his green woolen jerkin, and hauled him to his feet. Without a word of response to Kieran's challenge, he thrust the boy, stumbling, toward the dungeon's doorway, an arc of light looming far off in the darkness, and turned to the mummer.

Tangwyn remained on his knees like a supplicant, head bowed. Meg was not deceived by his meek countenance, and neither, she knew, was Gresham. Within the mummer's chest beat the heart of a ravening wolf, whatever guise of manner he might assume for present purposes. She hadn't forgotten the encounter at Bessie's farmhouse that night; indeed, she had a small cut on her forearm, likely to scar, to remember it by.

"Much remains to be settled between us," Gresham said mildly, looking down upon the fair head of his enemy. "There will undoubtedly be another place, another time, another chance. You know, I trust, where to seek me?"

The mummer looked up and, even in that fetid gloom, Meg clearly saw the hot light of hatred in his eyes. "Aye," he said. "I know. And I will come to you."

Gresham nodded. "In some better world, mayhap," he said. "It is my understanding that Prigg has persuaded the king to hang you with the next batch of irksome criminals."

Tangwyn laughed, a raw, scraping chuckle, and shook his head. "Nay, my lord," he taunted. "You see, our good king is addled these days. Once or twice, he's even mistaken me for you."

Gresham said nothing to that, but simply glared at the mummer.

"Tangwyn will live to kill you, Sedgewick!" Kieran

rasped, a shadow wraith calling to them from the foot of the dungeon steps. "He will escape this place to cut your throat, and watch your blood soak into the dirt like that of a slaughtered ox!"

Gresham sighed. "Precious child," he said. He might have been speaking to himself, or to some unseen spirit, for he did not look at Meg or Tangwyn or the boy pulsing like a storm at the end of the passageway. Reaching out, though, he found Meg's arm without faltering, took a light hold, and started from the dungeon, leaving her to follow.

She paused, instead, gazing at the mummer. "The letter I gave you for Gabriella?" she asked, very softly. "That day at the fair?"

Tangwyn shrugged. "Alas, it seems to have fallen from my pocket somewhere along the way," he said, with mock ruefulness. "Mayhap it will still find its way to Cornwall, though, by some other means."

This latest defeat in her long and frustrating efforts to reach Gabriella, in some way, served only to redouble her determination. "Aye," she replied, as cheerfully as if he'd said he'd placed the missive in her sister's own hand, " 'tis true that the right has a way of prevailing, when all is said and done."

He narrowed those eyes, so like Gresham's and yet so different, but made no answer. Meg turned and hurried after the others.

At the doorway, Meg glanced back once and saw, to her consternation, that Tangwyn was smiling, his teeth gleaming, beastlike, in the darkness. Ahead, the boy waited, trembling with fury and, Meg suspected, the secret hope that, for all his, Kieran's, railings, his father would not fail him by giving in. Would not let go, but hold on tightly, all his rage and rancor notwithstanding, and keep him safe from every threat of harm.

How lonely this child must have been, Meg thought, and how frightened. She, too, had been abandoned by both mother and father, though in quite a different way, but she had ever been able to depend upon Gabriella and Elizabeth, upon their love and their laughter and their faith. Kieran had been entirely alone but, she guessed, for the occasional, good-natured and poisonous visit from Tangwyn.

And what else could the boy have taken away from these contacts, but for venom, hatred, a penchant for the blood of the man who had sired him and subsequently left him behind?

It was the most natural of ends that he loathed this father he little knew. Kieran's was a viper's soul, full of bitterness and gall, and he had a propensity for violence that might never be stemmed. Only the very foolish would make little of his power to avenge his grievances, simply because he was a youth.

Meg despaired of reaching him, for it was only too plain that he had also nursed a mistrust of any woman save his mother, from earliest awareness. Most especially, most treacherously, he had clearly brought all this ire to focus on Meg herself.

Catching up with Kieran in the blessedly sweet air beyond the guarded entrance to the king's dungeon, Gresham let go of Meg's arm, took the lad by the back of his jerkin and steered him toward the quarters he and Meg had occupied since their arrival at Windsor. It was a long way, made through crowds of people, but Gresham did not acknowledge any one of them with a word or a look, nor did he slow his pace at any time, even in the thickness of their midst.

He merely expected them to make way, and they did precisely that.

The boy, too, was silent, though Meg could not guess whether from prudence, disdain, or simple astonishment. He had been raised roughly, that was for certain, for it was the lot of a squire to be treated so, in the hope that he would learn Christian humility, obedience, and patience. Kieran had surely gone hungry, slept in the cold, had his nose bloodied and his ears boxed, and been called every vile name imaginable.

No doubt he expected a beating now, and all the saints and angels knew he'd done what he could to earn one, but Meg would have wagered almost anything that he was hoping for something quite different—tenderness, mayhap. And understanding.

On the threshold of their chamber, Gresham tossed Kieran toward the center of the room, sending him skittering through the rushes, and raising the scents of sage and rosemary and other herbs scattered through for the sake of freshness.

While Kieran scrambled to his feet, ever ready to fight even though he could not hope to win, Gresham produced a slender length of hemp. Then he got Kieran by the arm, set him none too gently in a chair, and proceeded to bind him there, with his hands caught behind him.

Meg, silent until the moment of realization, could no longer hold her tongue. "My lord, this is not fitting. He is but a boy, and it is wrong to hold him prisoner—"

The look Gresham flung in her direction was recalcitrant. "Do you fear I will beat him?" he asked, still busy at the task of tying Kieran to the chair. "I will not, though 'tis the grace of God that stays my hand, and not my better nature."

Kieran did not struggle, physically at least, but he wore an expression of sublime scorn that would have moved the most devoted of saints to mayhem. "He knows he can keep me here in no other way," the boy said coolly. "If I were free, I should take up a dagger and skewer his liver!"

Gresham tied the last knot and straightened with a martyr's sigh. "I grow weary of your boasts, lad. Must I gag you to put an end to your silly prattle?"

Kieran reddened at this, made as if to speak, and then restrained himself.

"I would have words with the king," Gresham said, addressing Meg now. "Do not free my darling son unless the house takes fire—and then only when the flames are licking at his toes. Let none of his speeches, however pretty, persuade you to undo his bonds, either—I suspect he can be charming when it serves him."

Meg did not like being in the position of jailer, but she would no more have set Kieran free than overturned a hive full of bees and poked at it with a brand from the fire. She bit her lip and nodded in silent compliance.

"If the fair and fragrant demon mocks you," Gresham said, already halfway back to the gaping door, "cut open the mattress and stuff his mouth full of feathers."

With that, Gresham sailed out, leaving a scowling Kieran and a very uncomfortable Meg behind.

"Do you do all that he tells you?" Kieran asked, with soft sweetness, when they'd both heard the distant sound of the outer door slamming shut.

"I do not," Meg answered, with dignity, taking off her wimple and laying it aside. "Are you hungry?"

"No," Kieran answered, "and even if I were, I would not take food from the hand of a jackal's mistress. You may have fooled the rest of Windsor, you and my father, but I know you're not really wed to each other. I heard you talking."

Meg arched an eyebrow. Kieran knew their marriage was a nonexistent one, hers and Gresham's, and yet he had not exposed the deception. Interesting. Mayhap he did not despise his sire as much as he claimed.

Although she did not feel she owed this churlish boy an explanation, she felt compelled to keep to the truth in their exchanges whenever she could, tempestuous as they were. "Sedgewick," she said moderately, "is not a jackal."

Kieran sneered a little. "There are surely other women besides you, methinks, who believe the same comely tales he tells."

Meg drew up the other chair, so that it faced Kieran's, and sank into it. "Spare yourself, and me," she said, with quiet irritation. "I am most weary of all your raving and carrying on. You will have something to eat or starve. The choice belongs to you."

Kieran simply glared at her, eyes narrowed, elegant nostrils flared. How beautiful his mother must have been, she thought, for as clearly as she saw Gresham in him, she also glimpsed the cast of another face, as fair or fairer.

She went to the door and called to Allena, who came, timidly, her gaze straying toward the imprisoned boy and then darting away. Meg smiled, to reassure the servant, then dispatched her to the kitchens to bring back whatever might be found there to assuage the appetite of an active lad.

"Where does Sedgewick think he is taking me?" Kieran demanded, when Meg returned to sit across from him again.

"He has not confided that," Meg replied, with a calmness bordering on disinterest. "Methinks, though, that he would make peace with his father, the earl."

"What part have I in such an occasion?"

"Probably none," Meg responded lightly. "If you weren't such an ass, Sedgewick might want to present you to his sire as a prospective heir." She pressed the tip of her right index finger to the tabletop, raised up a crumb of bread, and studied it as though it were the most profound of oracles. "As matters stand, you are fit for little more than gathering firewood, carrying slops, and tending to the horses."

Kieran lapsed into silence at this, and maintained it until Allena had come and gone, leaving behind a wooden bowl brimming with a fragrant and savory stew.

Meg took the accompanying spoon in hand and tasted the food. Then, after a few moments of consideration, she took a full bite.

"Very good," she commented.

Kieran's belly gurgled loudly.

"Would you like something to eat?" Meg asked.

"I would rather starve than be spoon-fed by my father's—"

"Oh, do be careful," Meg interrupted, waggling one finger in cordial warning. "You do not want to insult me. My lord will endure much, when he is the object of your taunts, but he will not suffer the like on my behalf."

Kieran swallowed, looked at the stew with a yearning he could not quite disguise. When, Meg wondered, had he eaten last? Surely, as a squire and the ward of Lancaster himself, the child was well provided for.

She took another hearty bite, chewing thoughtfully, dipping the spoon again. Kieran followed its progress back to her mouth.

"You don't deceive me, you know," Meg remarked presently. "You are hungry. You are afraid. And you do not want to see your friend, the mummer—or anyone else—murder your father."

Kieran bit his upper lip. His attention was fastened upon the stew, still steaming, smelling richly of meat and turnips and bright with great orange chunks of carrot. "I'm not afraid," he insisted.

"Liar," Meg said, in a conversational tone. She held the spoon to Kieran's mouth and, after a moment of manly resistance, he accepted the offering.

"Let me go," he entreated her sweetly, after swallowing. His eyes were wide now, soft and guileless, with lashes so long that even dear Elizabeth, who was utterly without vanity, would have envied them. "Now, before he comes back. If you do not, he will surely beat me."

"I think not," Meg countered, feeding him more stew. "Nay, my lord will only do that if you run away, and force him to give chase. He would catch you, of course. Then your punishment would be assured, and I should be subjected to a lengthy and very tiresome lecture on obedience and responsibility."

Kieran smiled beatifically, though Meg was neither naive nor stupid enough to trust him. "Are you obedient?" he asked.

"No," she answered. "Not usually."

"Then cut these bonds. Release me."

"Never."

"Why not?"

"Gresham was the one to bind you—he must needs be the one to set you free."

"You are afraid of him, then."

Meg smiled, shoveled in more stew. "Is that your best

effort? I must say, it is a very poor one. With me, Sedgewick is the gentlest of men—I do not fear him."

Kieran might have spat the food at her, but either he was too hungry or it didn't occur to him. Meg suspected it was the former case.

He chewed, swallowed, and gave Meg a long and measuring look that came nearer to swaying her than the round-eyed winsomeness he'd employed earlier ever could have done. "Are you afraid of me, then?" he asked. "You should be, if you're not."

She knew he spoke true. Though Kieran's was a noble soul, his passions were quick and fierce; he was the sort to act rashly, and feel remorse too late. "Really? Why?"

"I am as good with a dagger as any man, including my father."

Meg pondered that. "Aye," she said, in due time, and it was his nobility that she addressed, not his superficial nature. "But if you'd wanted to spear me—or your sire, for that matter—you'd have done so in the first place. You deliberately missed, and you have doubtless had other opportunities to do one or the other of us harm since. Methinks you are mostly wind." She put the spoon to his mouth again. "More?"

"Untie me, that I may eat like a man, instead of a drooling babe!"

Meg laughed. "No," she said. "When you behave as a man, I am sure you will be treated as one. In the meantime, eat or go hungry, speak or be silent, as you choose."

"Suppose I need to make water?"

"I would advise you to wait, lest you mortify yourself."

He sighed, spent a few fruitless moments struggling against his bonds, and reluctantly took another bite when Meg offered it, and then another. The bowl was almost empty when they heard a door open belowstairs, and she made haste to set the food aside, along with the spoon. Then, just as quickly, she wiped Kieran's mouth clean with a bit of cloth, not because she feared Gresham's wrath, but because she'd already caused the boy enough mortification, dragging him off the practice field by his ear.

Gresham entered, bringing with him a rush of cold air from the yawning hall below, and set a bundle made of tanned leather on the table with a resounding thunk.

"Your things, little lord Sedgewick," he said, sketching a slight bow. "We leave at dawn." With that, Gresham turned to Meg. "I've asked your servant woman for another tub full of water," he informed her merrily. Everything about him seemed exasperating, which, Meg had no doubt, was what he had intended. "Naturally, you won't want to bathe in the presence of a gawping youth, but I suffer no such compunction."

Meg drew a deep breath and let it out slowly. How, she wondered, had she got to this time and place? She'd set out to find Gabriella, that was all. That worthy goal seemed very far away at the moment, though she could not give it up. "Fine," she said.

"It is hoped," Kieran interjected, obstinate to the end, "that you will have a less odious smell after washing, my lord."

Gresham tousled the boy's hair, mayhap in retaliation for the observation. "I have been remiss, as a father and as a host," he said, beaming. "It is you who shall have the first dousing and scrubbing, as befits the heir of an earl. Leave us, Meg, that I may extend this courtesy without causing my dear son, sprung beauteous from my loins, to be seen naked by a lady."

For all his beauty, Kieran was indeed ripe and probably lousy, and a bath would not be untoward. On the other hand, he looked so horrified at the prospect—one might have thought drowning was imminent—that she could not bring herself to abandon him.

"I fear I cannot leave, my lord," she said, meeting Gresham's gaze. "But I shall take care, for the sake of decency, to turn my back."

"Excellent," boomed Gresham, who did not usually boom. His jocularity was, of course, all for the boy's benefit, and though there was nothing cruel in the sound, there was no mistaking its meaning. *I am the father, you are the child. The sooner you learn to obey, the easier your life will be.*

The water was brought, mayhap an hour later, and the tub was filled. The servants came and went, bustling and earnest, deaf to Kieran's loud and piteous pleas for rescue, and the door was, at last, barred behind them.

Meg set a chair before the hearth and winced inwardly as Gresham untied the boy, stripped him of every stitch, and forced him bodily into the wonderful tub.

"Throw his things into the fire," Gresham commanded, in the somewhat breathless voice of one who is struggling, all the while, against a worthy but already defeated foe. "They're crawling with vermin."

Meg obeyed, and the action brought on a fresh round of shrieks, oaths and splashes from the vicinity of the tub. There was a bubbling gulp, then silence.

Meg whirled. "You haven't—?"

Gresham, seated on the side of the bath and every bit as wet as if he'd taken a washing himself, drew his son's head up out of the water by the hair. "Drowned the little treasure? No," he said, with a grin, "though I confess I was and am yet sorely tempted."

Kieran bellowed a curse no boy his age should have known, and took another dunking for his trouble. Meg turned hastily away, squeezed her eyes shut, and heard a loud gurgling sound, followed by a spate of gasped curses.

Gresham laughed and conducted yet another rousing baptism, and when Kieran was wrenched to the surface again, his temper was spent. He endured the scouring his father subjected him to in murderous silence and, when next Meg dared to look in his direction, he was standing beside the tub, wrapped in a length of cloth and shivering.

Kieran still resembled a handsome falcon, but a ruffled one now, recently doused in a trough and quite without means of avenging itself.

"Go and stand by the fire," Gresham told him, sternly but not without kindness. Meg thought she heard a certain note of respect in his voice, and even pride in this hellion boy he'd made with a woman he did not remember.

Meg made room, and Kieran came to the hearth, staring into the flames, his golden hair fitted to his head in long, thick strands, like a fancy cap. At the table, Gresham went through the boy's belongings and brought out passably clean hose, a tunic and another jerkin.

"If I die of a fever," Kieran said, "it will be your fault."

Gresham shoved the garments into his son's hands. "In the event, I shall endeavor to feel some measure of remorse," he promised. "For the moment, I can summon naught but relief that you didn't force me to drown you."

"Stop," Meg said, frazzled. "You have baited each other long enough. Now, if only for a little while, let there be peace in this chamber."

Kieran glared at Gresham, and Gresham glared back, but some time passed before either of them spoke.

"Where," Kieran ventured, when his shivering had

ceased, "shall I pass the night, dear father? Curled up at your feet, like a hound?" He looked proud as a young Caesar, standing there bundled in his drying cloth.

"In yon chair," Gresham said, indicating the place where Kieran had sat, bound hand and foot, prior to his unwanted bath.

"You don't mean to tie me up again?"

Gresham stood near the windows, one foot resting atop the lid of an old wooden trunk. "Aye," he replied. "I mean to do exactly that. If I don't, you will either escape or murder me in my bed."

Meg heard the unmistakable sound of approaching servants, knew they were bringing food, mayhap even more water for the bath. She lowered her voice and spoke in haste. "Surely, my lord, there is another way— the boy will suffer, methinks, sitting in such wise—"

Gresham was about to reply when Kieran, blue eyes fierce, cut him off.

"I pray you, lady, do not attempt to get me mercy," he said sharply, bristling with regal dignity. "I seek no kindness from the likes of you."

It was then—just when Gresham strode across the room and took Kieran by the scruff again, like an ill-mannered pup—that the servants reached the door, and made their presence known. Meg, fearing catastrophe, hurried to admit them.

Allena and her company had brought a fine array of foods: bread, roasted meat, boiled turnips, cheese, and cowslip wine.

While the table was laid and the fire fed with dry, fragrant wood, Kieran and Gresham stood by, both of them ominously still. Kieran, who had begged the servants to save him during their last visit, kept a stately silence now.

Gresham, for his part, gave an appearance of black clouds and thunder, melded into the shape of a man, but barely contained and shot through with lightning.

Meg thanked Allena and the others and tried to hurry them away, but they would not go until the tub had been rinsed and drained and another chair was found and brought for the "young lord."

When at last they left, twilight had gathered at the windows, purple and gray, and there was no light except for the dancing, merry flickers cast by the fire.

"Get dressed," Gresham said to Kieran, and gave him, quite ungraciously, the garments he had taken from the boy's bundle after the bath.

Meg busied herself at the table—the food looked savory and she was hungry, having eaten naught but a few bites of Kieran's stew—and after a few moments, she heard the youth putting on his clothes.

He came to take his chair without being told, for rebellion is vigorous business and cannot be adequately sustained without nourishment, but met neither his father's gaze nor Meg's, and said nary a word throughout the meal.

The night, Meg reflected ruefully, would be a long one, and difficult. The new day would be no less challenging—they would take horse, the three of them, and set out on a new journey.

She cast a yearning glance toward the bath—many days might pass before she could avail herself of such a luxury again—but she could hardly take off her clothes and revel in hot water and soap with Kieran in the same chamber.

Meg turned further into herself, mashed her turnips with the flat side of a spoon and thought of Gabriella, and of Elizabeth, and she could barely stay herself from weeping. When she felt Gresham's gaze on her face, she looked up and found him watching her as he set his wine cup down.

"What is it?" he asked, with a tenderness that squeezed her heart. Did he care for her, she wondered, as she was coming to care for him?

"I sorrow for my sisters," she confessed.

Kieran, apparently oblivious, ate with controlled frenzy, poised as if to guard his food from scavengers, like a wolf with a fresh kill.

Gresham reached across the table and closed his hand over Meg's. "We will find Gabriella in Cornwall, me-thinks," he said. "Prigg has promised to stop at St. Swithin's when he returns home, and ask after Elizabeth. If there is news, he will send a messenger."

We will find Gabriella in Cornwall, methinks. . . .

Meg's heart leaped with hope at those words. "You've changed your mind, then, about leaving me in the king's hands? You will take me to Cornwall?"

"I will take us all to Cornwall," Gresham said. "You, me, and the lad."

Kieran might have been deaf for all the mind he paid them, but when he was replete, it became clear that he'd been listening. "I am squire to a knight called Hugh Pen-shackle," he said. "If you would take me away from Wind-sor, you must pay him amply."

"I am aware of the rules," Gresham assured him mildly.

"He is mean when he gets too much ale," Kieran went on. It was as though the surfeit of food had drugged him into some sort of temporary stupor; he seemed not only disinclined toward belligerence, but incapable of it. "I took my share of hidings from him, and more."

Meg was horrified, and opened her mouth to say so, but Gresham silenced her with a look.

"So I have been told," he said, without emotion.

"When I'm grown," Kieran elaborated, warming to the subject, forgetting, evidently, that he was chatting with people he claimed to despise, "I mean to find the lout, run him to ground, and loosen his teeth."

Gresham poured wine into the chalice that had served them all, as was the custom, and took a sip. Only when he had set the cup down again did he offer comment on Kieran's vow. "No need," he said.

Kieran's interest visibly quickened. He sat up a little straighter on the hard-backed chair and peered at Gresham in the thin light from the hearth. "You've spoken to him? To Penshackle, I mean?"

Gresham extended a hand, and Meg saw, as did Kieran, that his knuckles were cut. Indeed, until he'd forced Kieran into the bath, and gotten so wet, they'd probably been smeared with blood.

"He got some of your hide," Gresham said. "It seemed only fitting that he have some of mine as well."

Kieran squinted at the evidence that he had been avenged, then looked away, but it was too late. Something had been altered between father and son and, although Meg believed peace, and even civility, would be a long time in coming, she could not help being encouraged.

"Violence is no solution," she said, nonetheless. "Wise men employ reason, not their fists."

Both Kieran and Gresham gave her narrow—and nearly identical—looks.

"Penshackle," Kieran said presently, relenting a little, "does not understand reason. And I'm still going to find him, when I grow up, and give him a proper thrashing."

Meg, who was privately glad that Penshackle had been dealt with, felt compelled, nevertheless, to make a stand for chivalry. "He will be older then. Much older. You, on the other hand, will be young and strong. What sport is there in such a match?"

"I do not want sport," Kieran said flatly. "I want vengeance." His mellow mood, it would seem, had passed. He fixed his angelic eyes upon his father's face. "And I shall have it," he added coldly.

Gresham sighed. "You have it now," he said, "for I am heartily sick of you and your mouth, baby knight. If I hadn't gone to all the trouble of bathing you, I vow I would toss you into the dungeon with your beloved mummer until morning, that my lady and I might have a rest from you."

"By all means, carry out your threat. I should rather be with Tangwyn in hell than in the heart of heaven with you."

"That," Gresham replied, "is why I will keep you here. Imprisonment would make you entirely too happy. I suppose I shall have to gag you, though, if I want an hour's sleep."

Kieran looked as though he would spit, as he had done on several previous occasions, but in the end, either his courage failed him, or he took heed of his good sense, and restrained himself.

"Why has no one come to save me?" he asked, and although Meg knew the question was calculated to win sympathy, she still felt sorry for Kieran. After all, he was only a boy, and one who had been abandoned and abused in the bargain. "Penshackle is Lancaster's man, and I am fostered with the duke."

"You are my son," Gresham answered, and his voice carried neither a rebuke nor an offer of conciliation. "You will remain with me until I decide what to do with you."

"Does it trouble you not at all to know that I hate you?" Kieran sounded baffled, as well as stubborn, and his brow was creased with consternation. "That I would kill you, if you gave me the chance?"

"Have you finished eating?" Gresham inquired of his son, with such politeness that Meg was taken aback. It was as if the boy had not spoken.

"Aye," Kieran said, frowning, as baffled as Meg.

Gresham pushed back his chair and stood. "Then it is time," he said, "for the gag."

15

❧

The night had not been a restful one, and when the dawn came, it brought brutal cold and the threat of heavy snows. Meg sat stalwart upon a shivering, snorting Enoch in the icy gloom, and thought with longing of the warm chamber she had just left, of the featherbed mounded in covers and the wonderful, decadent bathtub, of the plentiful food and the fire. She would have kissed the devil's big toe before uttering a word of complaint, however, for she knew that hers was a singular destiny, entwined with Gresham's, and that the path that lay before them must be trod, whatever hardships and discomforts were entailed. She *would* learn the fates of both Gabriella and Elizabeth, and see both her sisters again, whatever she had to do to accomplish those ends.

She allowed herself a slight, rueful smile, perceptible to no one but herself. All her life, she had wanted adventure, and now her wish had been granted. In future, she would be more prudent, she thought, and desire suitable things: warmth and comfort, a home and children, peace and good health, and the man she loved for a husband.

Gresham, becloaked and mounted upon his handsome horse, made his way to her side. His gaze caressed her, and she saw understanding in it, and wry amusement. "I will make this up to you," he said, in a voice too quiet to reach beyond her ears.

"When you have cause to chastise yourself on my account, my lord," she answered, "I shall advise you of the fact."

He laughed and bent to leave a quick, wind-chilled kiss upon her mouth. "For all my sins," he said, "and I am sure they are many, the angels must have recorded some great deed under my name, that I should be blessed with one such as you."

Kieran, nearer than they had thought, made a rude regurgitory noise. He sat his own horse with an inborn ease, though his hands were neatly bound before him, beneath the folds of the heavy cloak Gresham had procured for his use.

"A sage comment from the fruit of my loins," Gresham said, with mocking sweetness. "How rich are the rewards of fatherhood."

The boy merely scowled; he had, after all, not much in the way of immediate recourse, though he need only to bide his time, await his chance at havoc. Even Gresham, Meg thought with unease, could not be vigilant every moment. It was inevitable that one day, one night, Kieran's chance would come.

"Put an end to your fretting, lady mine," Gresham instructed her, still close. "The pup snarls, 'tis true, but he still has his milk teeth, and can manage naught but harmless nips."

Meg remained doubtful on that score, but as this was neither the time nor the place for a debate on the matter, she held her tongue. The captain of the guard had come out of his burrow, shivering and wet nosed, smelling of ale and fusty woolens, to make a jovial protest to their leaving.

More snow coming, he warned, blustering. Bandits about, and wolves prowling the woods. Three days of hard travel before they could hope to reach Gresham's father's estate, suitably called Sedgewick. Why, even the sheriff, John Prigg, intrepid soul that he was, had decided to remain at Windsor until there was a break in the weather.

Gresham listened politely, for the captain's good esteem had a certain value, and might be needed at some future time. Then, because he was Gresham, because he had already set his mind on tracing this new path into his curious, shrouded past, he disregarded every word.

He bid the captain and his men farewell, the gates were drawn, and the small party rode through the opening, making a great and resonant clatter as they passed over the frozen timbers of the bridge.

Enoch, though always fractious, had taken a liking to Gresham's newly acquired gelding, a gift from a doting king, and kept pace, while Kieran trotted sullenly at his father's other side.

Meg dreaded the journey ahead for a private reason, quite apart from danger and discomfort. They would be in close quarters, she and Gresham, and in Kieran's company for the duration, which meant there would be no privacy and hence no lovemaking. Her body, so well schooled in pleasure since her flight from St. Swithin's, had not known her beloved's attentions in the night just past, and had become one bruised, burning ache for want of the release only he could give.

Not only did Meg suffer for the yearning she felt, but for the guilt her own hungers roused in her. Surely it was not meet for a woman to know such longings—were they not the exclusive province of men? Elizabeth would surely name it the devil's work, this penchant for wantonness.

How she longed to confide her feelings for Gresham Sedgewick to Gabriella, who would surely help her to make sense of them. Indeed, she would have given a good deal just to lay eyes on her twin, to hear her voice, expounding on any topic whatsoever. She would gladly have endured Elizabeth's long and pious speeches, too.

Alas, she was beginning to fear that she would never see either sister again, and that made her feel all the more desperate. She'd begun to dream of them in her fitful sleep—Gabriella, laughing with a dark-haired man, Elizabeth, lying ill at St. Swithin's—Meg blinked back hot tears, grateful that the hood of her cloak must surely cast her face into shadow, and grimly instructed herself to think happier thoughts. If only she could be with Gabriella and Elizabeth again, for five minutes, she vowed to herself, she would never utter a single complaint about anything, as long as she lived.

Meanwhile, the journey to Cornwall progressed, over fields of crusted snow, through woods in which Gresham kept his sword unsheathed. He was watchful and grim during those intervals, and refused to make conversation.

By midday, the sky was burdened with snow, and the wind sharp. They stopped, the trio of uneasy travelers, to take shelter in a crofter's barn, knowing that a roof, however humble, was no small blessing in such weather. The corresponding hovel—it was too plain a structure to be called a cottage or a house—huddled at a little distance, and resounded, in its very silence, with emptiness, like a bell without a clapper.

Meg studied the place warily, thinking of the village they had passed through on the way to Windsor, she and Gresham and the sheriff, Prigg, and found ravaged by plague. The images and smells of that place were imprinted, then and forever after, upon her soul; she hoped never to encounter them again, outside the realm of memory. Gresham dismounted, explored the inside of the barn, and came out to pronounce it habitable. He helped Meg down from Enoch's back and ushered her inside, into the dank shelter, rife with the scents of rotted hay and mildew, old manure and mice, then went back outside for his son. There were words exchanged, muttered and by their texture unfriendly, and then Kieran, still bound, fairly flew through the doorway, his nimble legs scrabbling for balance.

He looked back over one shoulder, shrieked a curse, and then spat into the moldering straw.

Meg sighed. Failing civility, it seemed to her that father and son might at least contrive to ignore each other.

"Be still, Kieran," she said. Half her mind was with Gresham, who had surely gone to investigate the hut, wondering, dreading, what he might find there. "I am weary and cold and much disinclined to hear your grievances."

Kieran sniffed. "Little good it would do me to seek mercy from you. You are his accomplice in this crime, after all."

Meg sighed again. "What crime?" she inquired reasonably. "Bearing you away from your wondrous life as squire to a surly and profoundly ignorant knight?"

Kieran was stubbornly silent.

"Pray, do not let your resentments blind you," Meg said, speaking more earnestly than she had intended. "My lord has brought you with him because you are his son, and not sensible enough to come willingly. He hopes, in time, to make some measure of peace with you. Indeed, he would show you the estate that will one day be yours, and see that you are fitted for an earldom. Where in all of that, please, is the misdeed that nettles you so much?"

"He hates me as much as I hate him."

Meg found an old chopping block and sat upon it. "Your judgment is faulty. Gresham knows well enough that you would not receive his love—a gibbering idiot could see that—and therefore he withholds it. Preferring, if you will forgive the reference, not to cast pearls before swine."

Even in the dimness of the barn, Meg saw Kieran's face redden, and behind him, through a window with dangling shutters, the first fat flakes of snow began to drift down at their leisure.

"What can you know—a mere woman, and a young one at that?"

Meg smoothed the folds of her cloak and smiled to herself. "I will not be stirred to wrath or pity, Kieran, no matter what you say, so do leave off trying. Indeed, if you cannot be mannerly, have the charity to be silent."

He took an uncertain step toward her, but there was nothing threatening in his stance. "It is a peculiar way to show love, half drowning me in a bath, binding my hands, making me sleep upright in a chair."

"He had good reasons for doing all those things, Kieran, and you know it well. I am no believer in violence, but indeed, were my lord to take you across his knee and thrash you until you were blistered, I should not blame him. You are, after all, quite impossible."

The set of Kieran's jaw was reminiscent of his sire's, when in like moods. "I mean to continue being impossible."

"Then things will go on just as they have been, indefinitely. Is that really what you want?"

"What I want, milady, is to cut his throat."

"I know. But there is a better person inside you, deeper down, who would never do anything so cowardly and dishonorable. It is that other Kieran who prevented you from killing one of us with your dagger, that first night. Let him come to the fore, let him guide you."

Kieran drew nigh, and sat down heavily, awkwardly in the straw at Meg's feet. She barely restrained herself from smoothing his glittering golden hair, as a mother might do, or a fond elder sister.

"I need to make water," he confided miserably. His lashes drooped like birds' wings upon his cheeks, and Meg felt a clenching sensation, far within, in some dark and secret fold of her heart. Had she had a knife at her disposal then, knowing better all the while, she would have freed him.

"Go and tell your father."

"And have him mock me?"

"He will not," Meg said.

Kieran struggled to his feet, glaring fiery arrows at Meg all the while, lest she offer him aid, and made his way out through the gaping doorway of the barn, into the dancing flakes of snow.

Presently, she heard him speak to Gresham in low, grudging tones, and receive a taciturn reply. They both joined her in the barn mayhap a quarter of an hour later, Kieran bound once again, with his hands behind him this time, and Gresham bearing an armload of wood.

From Sedgewick's manner, Meg knew he had found

nothing horrible in or around the hut, and she was greatly relieved. Still, he had evidently decided they would pass the night in the habitation of animals, rather than humans, and she wondered at that.

"There is a stream just beyond the hovel," Gresham said. "I will fill our flasks and, if I can find a kettle or a bucket suited to the purpose, I'll bring you enough water to wash in."

Meg could have kissed him for the kindness of his offer, although such a small amount of water would serve for only minimal ablutions, but of course she did not. Not with Kieran looking on.

She inclined her head slightly, in what might have passed for submission, as well as gratitude, if the observer had no knowledge of her true nature, and smiled. "You are kind, my lord."

"He is a dog," said Kieran.

"Better, methinks," retorted Meg good-naturedly, "than a badger, snarling in a hole."

Kieran opened his mouth, his blue eyes gleaming with pleasure in the reply he planned, but Gresham silenced him with a look that would have set a Viking back on his heels.

Meg was left to wonder, for all eternity, what animal she would have been compared with, in Kieran's opinion, at least. It was not a heavy burden to bear.

Gresham put the wood down near the open window and set himself to clearing a place for a fire. He worked methodically, bringing stones in from outside to make a circle for containing the blaze, using dry straw from the loft to kindle the flames.

"Why are we sleeping out here, with the horses, instead in the hut?" Kieran bestirred himself to ask. He

had been sitting on the ground, looking put-upon and pa-
thetic, by turns, but as neither aspect had done him any
good, he had apparently decided to behave himself for a
while.

"You are sleeping in the hut," Gresham told his son.
"Milady and I will take our rest here."

For a moment, Kieran looked alarmed, and Meg
knew, if Gresham did not, that the boy was afraid, terribly
afraid, of being alone in a strange, abandoned place,
though he would never admit as much.

An instant later, however, Kieran's expression had
changed to a smirk that made Meg, who had never struck
another person in her life, long to slap him.

She tried not to think about the sweet, unceasing ache,
and the hot jubilation Gresham's pronouncement had
stirred in her most private places.

"I see," said the boy, all insolence. "You mean to get
her under you."

Gresham moved so quickly that before Meg could intercede, he had crossed to Kieran, got him by the front
of his jerkin, and hauled him to his feet and then onto
his toes. Jawline like granite, the man thrust the boy
hard against a support beam, though not, Meg knew,
with as much force as Gresham would have liked to employ.

"One more word," Gresham drawled, half in warning
and half, it seemed to Meg, in invitation. "Just one,
Kieran, and I swear by all the old gods, I will beat you for
the churl you are."

Kieran did not open his mouth, did not breathe, as far
as Meg could discern, but his gaze was as defiant as ever.
Gresham released the boy with a thrusting motion that
almost made him fall.

For the next hour or so, a blessed if venomous silence prevailed.

Gresham led the way to the brook he'd mentioned earlier, with Meg's hand clasped firmly in his own. It was a vast relief to be out of Kieran's damning presence, even for a short time.

The world was white and pure, of a sudden, and silent but for the natural noises of the woods. The air was sharp in the nostrils and harsh in the lungs, but it bore no stink of stables or humanity or pestilence. One could almost forget that such horrors as plague existed at all.

Beside the stream was a shallow pool, frozen over. While Meg watched, Gresham broke the ice with the hilt of his dagger. Beneath were the plump, nearly still forms of fishes, oddly huddled and half asleep in their wintry stupor. With quick and merciful skill, Gresham speared three of them, one after the other, allowing no time for suffering. After cleaning them on the bank, his hands red with cold, he threaded a twig through their gills and inclined his head toward the barn.

"Pleasant as it is, this respite from my son's company, we had best get back. We make easy prey, you and I, just like these fishes."

Meg linked her arm through his. "He's frightened of spending the night alone in the hut," she said.

"Frightened?" Gresham scoffed. "Nothing scares that little weasel."

"I saw his face, Gresham. He's terrified."

"He has no reason to be. I'll be within shouting distance the whole night through, and he must know, brat though he is, that I would protect him. The fact that he lives to cut my throat notwithstanding."

"Kieran wants to know if you love him, Gresham. He

can't find that out by being good—almost everyone at least tolerates a good child. It's when he's reprehensible that he learns your true feelings toward him."

Gresham frowned. "I suppose I've made a poor showing, then. Knocking him off that post in the barn and the like."

Meg stepped away from Gresham, held her arms out, and twirled once, glorying in the snowfall, as she had done in childhood. "You are wrong there, my lord," she replied, with a happy laugh. "Kieran *wants* to be corrected—that way he can be certain that you care what he says and does. And it's obvious that you do."

Gresham looked at her in consternation, even as she came back to his side. "Why isn't he satisfied with that, then? One of these days, he's going to push me into thrashing him."

"He would prefer that to being ignored or left behind. I think Kieran fears that above all else. Your leaving him, I mean."

"Bloody hell," Gresham complained. "If the lad wants me to be a father to him, why does he spend his every waking hour trying to drive me mad?"

Meg entwined her fingers with Gresham's, squeezed. "I told you, Gresham. Because he has to find out if you'll stay, no matter what." She paused to put her own wishes resolutely aside, for the moment at least. "Please, my lord, do not make the boy sleep alone in the house. He will never confess to his fear, but it is there all the same, and it is more than a child's fancy."

Gresham looked aggrieved. "How then," he asked, "am I to make love to you?"

She let her head rest against his upper arm for a few moments, while they walked. "So Kieran was right," she teased. "You only wanted to 'get me under you.' "

He groaned. "It has been too long."

"Two nights, my lord," she said. The snow made a swirling fury around them, and she put herself in front of her beloved, and stood on tiptoe to kiss him. "I, too, have suffered, for mine is a wanton temperament."

Gresham laughed, dropped the fishes onto the cold, white ground, and took Meg's waist in his hands. "How you tempt me, my lady," he said, and bent his head to kiss her in return, playfully at first, and then with a man's earnestness.

Breathless, her will as weak as her knees, Meg pushed Gresham away, not because she did not want his caresses, but because she knew she would raise her skirts for him then and there if things went any further.

"Come with me, to the hut," he bade her, his voice low and husky, as her own would surely have been, were she able to utter a word. "Let me love you."

Meg nodded, but she was practical enough to bend down and recover the fishes from the snow. They would want their supper, later on.

The tiny hovel was a humble place, no better, in many ways, than the barn. There was a rope bed, with no ticking of feather or straw, and a fire pit in the center of the single room, long since gone cold. A clay jug stood upon the floor, dusty and draped in soggy cobwebs, but nothing else remained.

"Where do you suppose they've gone," Meg mused softly, sadly, "the people who lived here?"

Gresham took the brace of trout from her hand, set it beside the fire pit. Then he removed his own cloak, spread it over the bed, and came back to Meg to lift her into his arms. Only when he held her did he kiss her again, and only when he had done with her mouth did he answer her question.

"I don't know," he said. "I'm only glad they aren't around to see me take off your clothes, kiss you all over, and then bury myself in you."

Meg trembled, not with shyness, but with anticipation. "I fear I shall cry out."

Gresham chuckled as he laid her on the bed and knelt to push her skirts and chemise up and up, over her ankles, her knees, her thighs. "Cry out all you like, my lady. I assure you—no one will rush to your rescue."

He leaned down and kissed her knees, one and then the other, and the gesture was so erotic, and promised so much, that Meg moaned softly. "My lord," she whispered, "have me now, I pray you. With haste."

He kissed her white, firm thighs, while tracing the length of her shins, first one and then the other, with the lightest passes of his fingertips. "Nay, my lady. I would rather savor you, a nibble at a time."

Her fingers had found their way, unerring, into his soft golden hair. She could make no answer just then, but for a ragged little whimper—longing and protest it was, in equal measure.

Gresham bared the silken delta at the juncture of her thighs, caressing her with the backs of his fingers now, in strokes as gossamer as the flutter of a butterfly's wings, and the very gentleness of his touch set her afire. When his fingers slid inside her, and his thumb found the bud of flesh where her passion centered, and made slow, wet circles around it, Meg arched high off the bed and gave a hoarse gasp.

"Shhh," Gresham said, uncovering her belly, kissing her there, tracing pathways over her trembling flesh with the tip of his tongue, his hand continuing its work all the while, driving her to fever, to flight. "If you make noise now, what will be left to do when the world flies apart?"

Meg made a low, keening sound, deep in her throat. She wanted, *wanted*—the whole of her being was distilled to one desperate desire. "Please," she pleaded. "Oh, Gresham—please."

He tasted her belly again, but his fingers went on making their dangerous magic, now moving in and out, fast and faster, now just stroking her, deep inside. Deep, deep inside, where a nest of nerves pulsed just beneath the layer of smooth skin, as rhythmically as a drumbeat, as if to break through and explode in all directions, like the spindly gray petals of a dandelion's ghost, raised to a high and sudden wind.

"My lord," she murmured. "My lord—"

"Soon," he promised, and used his free hand to open her bodice, and lay her eager breasts bare for his perusal. He admired them for a time, pondered his choices, and fell at last to a nipple, using his tongue first, like a babe sampling a sweetmeat, then taking her full into his mouth and drawing hungrily. There was naught of the child in him then; he was full grown, uncompromisingly male, a man in every sense of the word.

Meg's knees fell wide of each other, and she writhed upon the spread cloak, the ropes creaking and swaying beneath her, like the rigging of a ship cast up and up on the crest of an ocean tide. The air grew thin, she could not breathe, she gasped and pleaded and then it came, it came, the blessed, torturous release, shaking her in its fiery teeth, wringing from her the last strangled wail, the last joyous sob, before it slowly subsided.

She lay sated, dazed with dreams, as Gresham undressed, lowered himself to her gently, and, after murmured words of love, of reassurance, of supreme tenderness, took her in a single hard, smooth stroke.

It was, for Meg, like rising out of a half sleep to embrace a bolt of lightning. Passion, satisfied only minutes before, rose ravening within her, greedy and wanton, causing her to claw at Gresham's back and shoulders and buttocks with her hands, to toss beneath him, to nip and nibble at his jaw, his neck, his shoulder—any part of him she could reach.

They whirled skyward in a storm of simultaneous release, clinging to each other, their mouths and bodies joined even as their souls were flung asunder, only to meet again, somewhere behind the moon, fuse into a single being formed of silver fire, and then to descend, ever so slowly, back to the grim and grimy realities of earth.

"You will be my true wife," Gresham said, when an interval had passed, and the beginnings of twilight had crept into that hut. "Whatever we find at Sedgewick, whatever we learn there, *I will not be parted from you.*"

Meg was at once exhilarated and chilled by the vow, for as much as she wanted to wed Gresham, and remain at his side always, the fact was that his future, and thus her own, was as mysterious as his past. Too, she would not be able to settle into the marriage, however much she wanted it, until she'd completed her personal quest—finding Gabriella, and learning Elizabeth's fate. "I must find my sisters," she reminded him. "I cannot truly rest without knowing for certain what has become of them."

He nodded, his expression grave. "I know that," he said.

She wound a finger in a lock of his hair, and hoped for a child, with just such hair, and eyes so blue that just to look into them made something pull, in the very center of her heart.

"Have you no memories of your father?" she asked quietly, when a few moments had passed. She knew the answer, had known it before she spoke—what Gresham remembered, he shared with her. And he had shared nothing since the sad, vivid dream he'd had of leaving Kieran's mother, of her following and pleading, and, sometime after he'd gone, perishing.

He sighed. "I fear I must accept—we must both accept—that my memory may never return. As far as I know, Meg, my life began the day I opened my eyes in the potting shed at St. Swithin's and saw you peering down at me." He lowered his head to nuzzle her neck. "In a way, it's fitting. That I had no life before you."

"But you did. You had a soldier's career, with your friend, Morgan Chalstrey. You have a father, the Earl of Sedgewick, and a son. Whether you remember or not, you owe those people something, especially Kieran."

Gresham let his forehead rest against her own; she felt his breath fan warm and sweet over her face. "Aye. Kieran. No doubt he has contrived to run off by now, making it necessary for me to find him and bring him back before he freezes to death or is devoured by wolves."

Meg laughed softly. "No doubt he set fire to the barn first, just to complicate matters."

He thrust himself away from her with a heavy sigh, made mostly of resignation, got to his feet, and began pulling on his clothes. Meg righted her own, and had not even the redemption of shame for her trouble. In the presence of this one man, she was not lady, but wench, and she hoped it would ever be so.

Gresham shook out his cloak and put it on again, after

draping Meg in hers. The blue of his eyes spawned a fresh ache in her heart as she clasped his mantle at the neck, her motions tender.

"Collect the fishes, my lady," he said. "Loving you is demanding exercise; we will be even more in need of our supper than before."

Color rose to Meg's cheeks at his words, but it was pleasure that caused her to blush, and not chagrin. "I would cheerfully miss my supper, my lord, if only I could lie with you again, right now."

Gresham laughed and swatted her lightly on the backside. "Get you to the cooking fire, temptress," he chided. "Once more would surely be the finish of me."

She touched him, boldly, at the front of his body, and felt his manhood stiff and powerful beneath his trunks, beneath the long hem of his tunic. "You speak false, my lord," she replied coyly. "You are ready, even now."

He directed her to the door and gave her another swat to set her on her way. "Aye," he said. "Ready I am. But unfortunately, I have other duties, and cannot dally here with you."

Meg pretended to pout and, carrying the fishes, marched off toward the shadowy hulk of the barn, barely visible now, through the snow and the early gathering darkness of a winter's eve.

"The barn," she observed unnecessarily, "still stands."

Gresham nodded, somewhat grimly. "But what other mischief has the boy made, while we were gone?"

Kieran had, as it happened, made no mischief at all. He sat near the fire, which was dwindling now, and Meg saw relief at their return spring into his eyes before he contrived to mask it with contempt.

His smile was brazen, mocking, and too knowing for a

youth, but Kieran had mapped the present boundaries of his sire's patience, and he was not so foolish as to venture a comment. It was enough, the look in his eyes, to let Meg know he understood exactly what had passed between her and Gresham, in the hovel, and she was torn between furious humiliation and a wild desire to pull his hair out by its silken roots.

She made herself busy, building up the fire, unrolling blankets for their beds, while Gresham found long sticks for roasting the fishes, and sharpened the points with his dagger. When it was time to eat, he cut the bonds at Kieran's wrists, and did not replace them when the meal was ended.

16

❧

The following day's travel was rigorous, but Kieran, though closemouthed and sullen, did nothing to cause his father to bind his hands again. He took care to pass his sly glances in Meg's direction when Gresham wasn't watching, and she refused to acknowledge the silent taunts. She was, she told herself, no fretful maiden, but a woman grown, with choices, limited as those choices sometimes seemed, and she need not allow this cub to nettle her.

They passed that night, Gresham and Meg and Kieran, in the crowded common room of an inn, lying together beneath a long trestle table. For the sake of chivalry, she supposed, Gresham slept on Meg's right side, and Kieran on the left. So suspect were their surroundings— although Gresham never admitted that there was reason for concern—that Kieran was restored of his knife.

It was with relief that they quit the inn at first light, collected their mounts from the stables, and rode on, toward Sedgewick. That day was bitingly cold, but the sky was clear and the sun shone bright upon the snow, causing it to glitter like the spilled plunder of some celestial pirate. Gresham was vigilant and thus silent, as always, and Kieran's blade remained in his possession, although there was no discernible change in his attitude toward his father, or Meg.

It was enough, for the moment, that the boy had not plunged his well-used dagger between her ribs, or Gresham's, while they slept.

They traveled until nightfall, and found themselves at the edge of London. Gresham took rooms in a house, after inquiring in a tavern, and it was a comfortable place, in comparison to previous lodgings. There was no bath to be had, but there were clean beds, water and soap, and palatable food.

Best of all, Kieran slept in an adjoining but wholly separate chamber, and Gresham made thorough love to Meg, catching her cries of pleasure in his mouth, where they blended with his own. It was a celebration, this joining of their bodies and souls, at once sacred and solemn, and it was a pledge, at least on Meg's part.

Lying beside Gresham, in the bed, Meg gazed up at the rafters, a bittersweet joy pooling in the deepest chambers of her heart. She wanted to spend the rest of her life, every moment of it, beside this man, but she knew fate would not be so kind. Gabriella was still unaccounted for, for all practical intents and purposes, and Elizabeth might be dead or dying. Whatever it took, she must know the whole of the truth about them, or she would never be able to forge any sort of life with Gresham.

"What are you thinking?" he asked, at considerable length. He was still breathing hard, and his voice was raspy.

"That you are a remarkable lover, my lord."

He chuckled. "What else?"

She sighed. "That my sisters and I are linked by more than flesh and blood. I dream about them nearly every night; it's as though there are unseen cords, binding the three of us to each other, no matter how far apart we are."

He put an arm around her, hauled her close, kissed the top of her head. Both of them knew, though neither said the words aloud, that their personal quests—his to settle the remaining mysteries about his past, hers to make sure Gabriella and Elizabeth were safe—might well take them in separate directions one day. And only too soon.

"Meg, the king—" Gresham began presently, and then faltered.

"Yes?" she dared to ask.

He rolled onto his side, searched her face, and then kissed her. After that, there was no time for conversation.

Meg half expected to find Kieran gone when she rapped at the door of his room that next bright morning, but he was there, sleepy and rumpled, with a smirk lurking in his otherwise guileless eyes. He got out of bed at her bidding, wearing his trunks and tunic and, she could not help noticing, the dagger he so prized.

They passed along London's outermost fringes that day, a disappointment to Meg, who would have liked to see something of the city she had heard about all her life. There was too much danger of the plague, Gresham said; the fewer people they encountered, the safer they would be.

It was early afternoon, and Meg's feet, dangling over Enoch's portly sides, were numb with cold, when the estate called Sedgewick came into view.

Meg's heart quickened at the sight, for it was a sprawling place, draped over hill and valley. It had sturdy walls, bell towers, and orchards, and near the main house, an impressive structure made of white stone, was a village, plainly prospering.

Gresham, having drawn his gelding to a halt beside her, reached out to touch her hand, and the gesture was cautionary, an unspoken reminder that there was no telling how they would be received. Kieran, for his part, was standing in his stirrups and squinting thoughtfully—there was no reading his thoughts now, for he could veil them when he chose—except to see that he was curious and mayhap even eager.

Meg herself felt drawn to Sedgewick, on a much deeper level than the natural wanting of warmth and shelter. It was almost as though this place had always been her home, calling to her in dreams and reveries, and she had found it at last. Were it not for Gabriella, and for Elizabeth, she knew even before she set foot over the threshold that she could have stayed forever. She was equally certain that fate had other plans for her and for Gresham.

She spurred the mule forward, and Gresham had little choice but to follow. Kieran, she saw, in a backward glance, rode beside his father, his expression utterly unreadable.

There was no moat at Sedgewick, but the holding was well guarded all the same. The towering gates glided open on oiled hinges, and soldiers clad in their lord's colors of black and gold came out to meet the arriving party.

Their leader, a red-haired man with a pitted complexion and intelligent gray eyes, looked at Gresham with frank surprise.

"My lord?" he muttered, as though he could not believe the evidence of his own senses.

Gresham sat still and proud upon his recently acquired gelding, and Meg ached for him, for it was plain by his expression that he recognized neither the captain

nor the castle itself. He simply inclined his head, ac-
knowledging the greeting.

The captain turned his gaze upon Kieran, and Meg
saw his small eyes widen in greater amazement. "And
this—this might be yourself, my lord, when you were off
at Cornwall, fostering with Chalstrey!"

Kieran listened intently, but except for shifting slightly
in his saddle, he made no other sound or motion.

Gresham spoke at last. "Aye," he said gravely. "This is
my son, Kieran—the future earl, should he prove fit to
bear the title—come to meet his grandfather."

The men behind the captain exchanged somber looks,
but none dared to speak. That was reserved for the captain, who had at last noticed Meg.

"And this fine lady?"

"This is Meg Redclift," Gresham said. "I hope to make
her my wife before we move on." Only then did he sound
like himself, and not some stranger, feeling his way
amongst people who might be friend or foe.

"The earl will be pleased by any sign that you might be
settling down at long last," the captain allowed. "Come,
I'll take you to him."

"Send word to him first," Gresham replied. "My father
is too old for such surprises." He set his gelding moving
again, riding beside the guard, letting Meg and Kieran
follow. The common soldiers fell in behind them, and
Meg, so at ease upon their initial arrival, had a peculiar
sensation of being placed under arrest.

The captain's laugh was at once joyous and raucous, the
laugh of a good-natured soldier with cause to love peace.
"Surprises? My lord the earl lives in the highest part of the
castle, and would have seen you approaching long before
we in the guard tower did." He was silent for a few mo-

ments, studying Gresham, feature by feature. "You may not remember us, my lord, but we remember you."

Gresham's jaw took on hard lines. The aging soldier could not know that he'd just uttered the consummate irony.

They rode through the gates and along a road lined by bare-limbed apple trees, and had just reached the edge of the village when a man shivering in the garments of a house servant came sprinting toward them. He made a curious and comic figure, with his long, thin legs, gangly arms, and lugubrious manner.

Meg saw, in a sidelong glance, that something had quickened in Gresham's countenance. He did not recognize the servant, but he knew that he should, and the effort both strained and vexed him.

"My lord," the man panted, red faced from running. "My lord, His Grace the earl would see you immediately, in his chambers—the lad and the lady, as well, of course, but later."

Gresham's mouth went hard—indeed, there was stiffness in every line of him—but he nodded his agreement. Plainly, his body remembered the visceral responses appropriate to a meeting with his estranged father, even if his waking mind did not.

The house servant trotted alongside Gresham's horse, breathless and shivering, looking neither friendly nor unwelcoming. "My lord would know who they are, please. The lady, I mean, and the boy."

Meg was mildly annoyed; she and Kieran might have been insensible objects, or not present at all, the way the earl's emissary spoke of them.

"I am accompanied by Lady Redclift," Gresham said evenly. Patiently. "And the lad is my son, Kieran."

The servant's eyes widened, just as the captain's had earlier. Smug in his knowledge, the old soldier said nothing, but simply rode a little ahead, leading the way into the great holding, clearing a path through the curious villagers, gathered to gape at the visitors, as he went.

Not many outsiders would have been admitted, Meg surmised, in these times of rampant plague. Mayhap the elderly earl had been waiting for his son's return, that the rift between them might be mended, once and for all.

She hoped the guest quarters had thick walls and plenty of firewood on the hearth, for she was weary and cold. She longed for hot, clean water and savory food that did not have to be examined for weevils and mold before it was eaten, like the poor fare they'd had along the road.

The doors of the white stone castle were fit for the entrance of a cathedral, and one stood open, just far enough to admit the travelers.

Gresham dismounted, lifted Meg down from Enoch's back, and squeezed both her hands in his own, as if in reassurance. She wondered what he was thinking, but the place was not private enough to ask, and of course there was no time for an exchange of confidences.

"Make milady comfortable," Gresham said to one of the servants, a plump, ruddy-faced woman who waited, apron twisted in her hands, in the yawning entry hall. "She will be cold and no doubt hungry. My son is probably ready for a meal himself."

"Aye, my lord," the woman said, with a quick bob, and gestured hastily to yet another servant, hovering a few yards away, in a great arched doorway. "Take the young lord to the kitchens," she hissed at the plain-faced girl. Then she turned a nervous smile upon Meg. "Won't you follow me, my lady? You may take your rest in my lord's own rooms—already the linens are being changed and fresh rushes laid upon the floor."

"Is there any fruit?" Meg asked hopefully. Now that the soldiers had gone, their captain with them, she felt like a guest again, rather than an honored prisoner. "I should like an apple, however withered."

Gresham overheard and chuckled as he headed up the stairs, following the manservant who would lead him to the father he did not remember. Kieran had already gone to the kitchens.

Meg sent her heart after Gresham, then turned her attention back to matters at hand. "Have you any mulled wine? My muscles do ache so."

The servant nodded. "Aye, milady. There's spices to add to it, too."

"Very well," said Meg, overwhelmingly grateful as she tarried a few moments beside a fireplace, where a great blaze crackled, flinging dancing shards of light over the rushes on the floor. "You have my thanks. Tell me, though—what sort of man is the earl?"

The woman crossed herself. "You'll be finding that out for yourself soon enough, methinks," she said quickly. Another swift sign of the Holy Cross, along with a raising of the eyes to the ceiling. "Just listen for the very timbers of the place to shake, once he and my lord Sedgewick are closed away in the same room. They're that alike."

Again, they were moving, mounting a staircase of worn stone.

"And Lady Sedgewick?" She'd never heard Gresham mention his family; not surprising, since he didn't remember them. She both looked forward to, and dreaded, meeting his mother. "What is she like?"

The serving woman looked back at Meg with tears standing in her eyes. "She was an angel. Went to her rest when milord was but a babe. That's where he got his good looks, young Sedgewick, from milady."

"Did you know her well?"

"I've seen her. Was but a babe myself, at the time she passed over. Me own mam, God rest her, was milady's maid."

"She was kind? Lady Sedgewick, I mean? You called her an angel—"

The servant sighed. "She was that," she said reverently. "Always kind. Smiling and singing, whatever task she was at. And how she loved that boy." A sad sigh. "The master was out of his mind when she died. That's when things started to go wrong betwixt father and son, if you ask me."

They had gained the first floor, and the servant trundled along a sun-splashed corridor. "No kinder woman was ever born than milady," she went on. "Such weeping when she perished as you've never heard the like of. In time, the young lord—Gresham—was sent away to foster at Edgefield, with the Chalstreys, far off in Cornwall. We all missed him something dreadful. The earl's word was law, of course. He'd made his decision—said he couldn't bear the sight of the boy, he was so like his mother—and there was no moving him, though some tried."

Meg felt a pang of sorrow, sorrow she knew Gresham would share, when and if he recalled his past. Had he grieved at leaving this place, the boy Gresham, or had he been relieved—glad to escape a grief-stricken and probably imperious father? And what of these people called Chalstrey—what marks had they left upon him, body and soul, for good or ill?

Tallie—she'd interjected her name at some point—
was still chattering when they reached the tall door at the
end of the passage. It stood open, and there was bustling
within, while the busy servants exchanged nervous speculations. *The young lord's come back, and after the earl
told him to stay away forever, too. There will be trouble
indeed. And did you see that woman with him? A girl,
more like, and a strumpet if ever I've seen one . . . You
ought to recognize one, Mary Jane . . . You be still, Tom
Tall, or I'll tell Cook what's become of the eggs she set
aside for the master's custard. . . .*

At Tallie's loud and glowering entrance, they all fell
silent, and on sight of Meg, following close behind, they
looked stricken. She smiled to let them know she had
taken no offense—not just yet, anyway.

"Back to work, the lot of you," Tallie thundered. "Except for you, Mary Jane Wheeler—you'll go direct to the
chapel and pray for a milder and more charitable
tongue—and you, Tom Tall. Cook will want a word with
you, concerning the master's custard."

Mary Jane and Tom Tall skulked out, their eyes lowered, while the four remaining servants, three women
and a youth close to Kieran's age, turned their energies to
sweeping out the hearth, spreading the new rushes, and
smoothing the linens on the enormous bed.

In a corner of the vast room, praise be, stood an old
copper bathtub, of the sort one stands upright inside,
with a set of wooden steps beside it. Meg inspected the
tub, then personally attempted to drag it closer to the
fireplace.

Tallie was horrified. "Cease, my lady," she pleaded,
but it was plain that she knew her dire advice would not
be heeded. "Benj here will do that for you. Benj, be

about it! Jessamyn, have you *still* not finished with that bed? Slow, that's what you are. Take yourself to the kitchens, and tell Cook we'll be wanting water in the young master's room, and plenty of it." She shook her head and made a clucking sound with her tongue. "I shan't bathe before spring, milady, you can be sure of that. Too cold by half. Why, a body could catch her death."

Meg suppressed a smile, for she could not help being touched by the woman's well-meant fussing. "I assure you, Tallie," she said, "that I am of a most stalwart constitution. You needn't fret for me."

Tallie merely shook her head again, as though she simply couldn't credit such recklessness. "Jessamyn, I thought I told you to leave the bed and go to the kitchens to ask for water."

The girl, no more then ten years old, scampered out. The others went, too, by their turns, until only Meg and Tallie remained in the chamber.

It was a sunny place, boasting that greatest of luxuries, thick glass windows, and the bed, with its piles of fluffy linens, was as white as a mound of the purest snow. Meg imagined lying upon it with Gresham and flushed, fearing that she had revealed too much.

Indeed, she had, for Tallie was smiling thoughtfully. "'Tis past time there were young ones in this place again," she observed. "You look the sort to bear a flock of children, and thrive on the doing of it. Mayhap you won't succumb to the bath after all."

"If I perish," Meg said, returning Tallie's smile, "it shall not be on account of bathing." She looked, wishing that Gabriella and Elizabeth were there to see and share in the comfortable surroundings. "Will he be welcome

here?" she heard herself ask. "The young Lord Sedgewick, I mean?"

Tallie, almost to the door by then, turned back, her expression solemn. "His lordship has prayed for this day, I
know that much, and his pleas have been answered. Now
we shall see whether it is God's wrath that has brought
the young master home, or His mercy." With these cryp-
tic words, Tallie took her leave.

That he had to be led to his father's room was not so
trying to Gresham as the fact that he did not know what
he would find when he got there. He had learned at
Windsor, from the king's own lips, that he and the aging,
infirm earl had severed all filial ties years ago. Still, he recalled nothing of the man who had disinherited him, and
sent him from his sight in frustration and fury.

If these things were true, and Gresham had only to
consider Kieran's hatred to know that they were, why was
the earl willing to receive him now? Why not turn him
away at the gate, as he had every right and reason to do?

The manservant, who had given his name as Haggin,
with some astonishment at being asked for it, approached
a set of double doors, ornately carved and three times the
height of a rearing horse, to scratch lightly at the wood.

"Enter!" commanded a gruff masculine voice.

Gresham glanced heavenward, full of dread, and,
when Haggin opened the door, stepped without hesitation across the threshold.

His father lay upon what looked like an acre of mattress, covered in green and white satin and velvet quilts
and wearing a blue silk nightcap with a long golden tassel.
His face, though weathered and gaunt, was still aristocratic, still imperious. His eyes, like Gresham's own, were

a searing blue, capable of searching the soul, uncovering secrets and leaving scars in the wake of his gaze.

Gresham thought he should have remembered such a man, but for him it was as though they were meeting for the first time. He came to stand at the foot of the earl's ludicrously sumptuous bed.

"You have come back."

The statement required no reply, being so obvious, yet Gresham made a response. "Aye," he said.

"Why?"

Gresham turned to look pointedly at Haggin. If there was to be an interview, it would be conducted in private, or not at all.

"Be gone with you," the earl told his faithful and plainly disappointed servant. "I would speak with my— with our visitor in private."

Haggin ducked his balding head and went out, closing the heavy door behind him with a grace that indicated years of practice.

"What do you want?" the earl demanded.

Gresham's hackles rose, and he told himself it was the old man's rudeness that caused his reaction, all the while knowing it was something else. Something more. If mere rudeness could injure him, after all, Kieran would already have done him in. "I was struck over the head by a—by a brigand," he said. Not for all the earl's lands and gold would Gresham have admitted that, according to reports, it had been a nun who had felled him, and a diminutive one at that. "I have forgotten all that happened to me before that. I came to ask you who I am."

"An easy question to answer," the earl replied. "You are a waster and a drunkard, a misuser of women, most probably a thief and without doubt a murderer into the

bargain. When I sent you from this house, I did not ex-
pect to lay eyes on you again. Ever."

Gresham took a moment to absorb his father's words.
Although he did not know the man, and thus could not
care for him, the accusations pelted him like balls of ice,
leaving bruises in places far beneath the flesh.

"Mayhap all you say is true," he responded, after a long
time. "I could not refute it, having no viable knowledge of
myself. Tell me what you know of me—not, pray, merely
what you surmise—and I will leave your sight forever."

The earl settled back against his pillows. "And you
mean to trade the boy for this information? You must
know I will not permit you to take him away—he is, after
all, the heir I have prayed for."

"Forgive me, my lord, but you are no match for the
likes of Kieran. You are an old man, and infirm. He is a
demon child."

A muscle quirked at one side of the earl's mouth, and
he made a dismissive gesture with one hand. "He might
yet be salvaged. What of the woman? She is quite beautiful, and very young. Have you wed her?"

"Not yet."

The earl smiled, but his jubilation was not the fatherly
sort. It raised prickles along the length of Gresham's
spine. "Is she with child?"

"She could be," Gresham admitted, and he felt considerable shame for succumbing to his desire for Meg, without benefit of clergy. In the end, he had simply needed
her too much.

"I see. Do you love her?"

He averted his gaze for a moment, heaved a long sigh.
"I do not know," he confessed, knowing that was not what
his father wanted to hear. Indeed, from what little

Gresham knew of their shared past, it would probably be about as welcome as a sharp jab to a sore spot. "She is a spirited woman, with no wrong in her, and merits only honor and kindness. Therefore, if you will vent your spleen, let me be the target, not her."

Sedgewick the elder raised an eyebrow. " 'Tis like you to answer a direct question indirectly," he mused. "Methinks you *do* love her, and you are reluctant to admit it." He sighed. "Well, in any event, the lady is in no danger of my temper. I glimpsed her from the window there, as you rode up. She is a lovely creature, and rides that mule like one born to the saddle. Mayhap, she could be called foolish, though, in her choice of men." The old man squinted, frowning hard. "Come closer—I would look upon you."

Gresham took a step nearer to the bedside, then another. He felt younger than Kieran in those moments, and far more vulnerable. "Have I changed, your lordship?"

"Probably not," the earl responded, "though I will confess that you've lost that look of boyish impudence that always made me want to box your ears."

"Did you? Box my ears, I mean?"

"Oh, aye, indeed I did. Thrashed you once or twice, too, for all the good it did either of us."

Gresham could not resist a barb. "Imagine how wretched I would have been if you had raised me yourself, instead of sending me off to the Chalstreys to be fostered."

"So you recall the Chalstreys, and your good friend, the young duke."

"Not at all. The king told me about them, and about you."

"He is a poor excuse for a king, our Edward. Always snuffling after that scheming mistress of his. But he was a grand man once, a soldier the likes of which this realm has not seen since Arthur, and will not see again, I fear."

"There are those who admire the Black Prince, and his brother, the Duke of Lancaster," Gresham pointed out mildly.

The earl made a soft, spewing sound of contempt. "Ruthless jackals, the pair of them. Treacherous knaves."

Gresham sighed. He was not fond of the Black Prince himself—the man loved killing too well—but he had served with Lancaster, and liked him.

The realization that he had brought these facts from the depths of his memory came a few moments after he'd spoken, and Gresham was stunned by it. Indeed, he remembered the duke, whose hair was fair, like his own. He was a man of humor, of dedication, of intelligence and, occasionally, of mercy.

Gresham groped for a chair, dragged it close, and sat down without waiting for the earl's invitation. He searched all he could of his mind, all that was not closed to him, but found no recollections of his son, his father, or Morgan Chalstrey, who was supposed to be his closest friend.

"Something come back to you, did it?" the earl asked.

"Something," Gresham admitted.

"Bring the boy. I want to see him."

Gresham had recovered enough to smile. "You will not like him," he answered.

"I did not like you," the earl answered reasonably. "Alas, methinks Chalstrey used you too gently. . . ."

"I remember naught of that," Gresham said coldly.

"You were a great disappointment to me."

"I can only imagine." He paused. "What was her name—my mother's, I mean? She is dead, isn't she?"

"Aye, God forgive her, she lies in yonder churchyard, under a decent monument. Her name was Arabella—I called her Bell. It is true, then? You really don't remember her, or me. Tell me, what *do* you recall?"

"Battles," Gresham answered forthrightly. "Blood and screaming. The Duke of Lancaster. And a woman— Kieran's mother, Monique, methinks." He knew his lost and apparently mistreated wife was a bone of contention between himself and his father, but there was no sense in sidestepping the subject.

"Naught else?" the old man prompted. There was a sly look about him, quickly gone.

Gresham shook his head.

"Tell me, then, about the woman, the mother of your son."

Gresham was at a loss. "She was—beautiful, I suppose," he said. The image taking shape in his mind was still impossibly vague, formed mostly of mirage and vapor.

The earl laughed, and the sound was derisive, bitter. "Indeed," he replied.

Gresham slumped in his chair, ran a hand over the length of his face. Had he been cruel to his wife, as well as callous? And if he had been, did he dare take Meg for his own? Would he find, when and if his memory returned, that he was ill-natured, with a propensity for meanness, like his father? Like his son?

"I'm told you caught her with another man. Little wonder that she was unchaste, with her husband home only long enough to get a babe on her and leave again."

Gresham's stomach rolled painfully. What kind of man was he?

The old man's blue eyes gleamed, but there was something stricken behind his mirth. Some grave wound.

Gresham was certain that, whatever that pain was, he himself had inflicted it. "I could overlook all that—I wasn't the best husband myself, though God knows I loved your mother more than my own soul. It's the lost years with the lad that I begrudge."

"He's here, now," Gresham said, spreading his hands as he rose back to his feet. "Your grandson. Raise him as you see fit."

"Ah. So you've brought him here just to abandon him. As you have abandoned so many others in your time."

Gresham felt as though he'd been struck in the midsection with a battering ram. "I do not remember living here," he said quietly, "but I am sure that, at least as a boy, I wished to remain. And you sent me away. I am well aware that I left Kieran and his mother, but when, old man, did I abandon you? The king himself told me that you sent me away, not just when I was a lad, but more recently, as well."

A dangerous silence throbbed between them. They were, Gresham thought, with both satisfaction and chagrin, very much alike, he and his sire.

"Fetch the boy," the earl barked. "I wish to look upon him."

Gresham merely nodded, suddenly feeling weary to the soul. There was a manservant hovering in the hall, and he dispatched him to find the lad and bring him to the old man's rooms. Then, moving in something of a daze, he descended one of a maze of rear stairways, struck by the fact that he knew the way, and made for the chapel.

The small, cavelike grotto was empty, although there were candles flickering on the altar and the scent of incense pervaded. The place was hardly warmer than the snow-crusted yard beyond its walls, but it was clean, and the bright colors in the stained glass windows glowed like jewels even in the gloom.

Gresham stood still in the center aisle, between the rough-hewn pews on either side, and thrust a hand through his hair. He felt like a quintain on the practice field, hung from a post, battered and torn, run through by a dozen lances. He was a man lost in darkness, but for the one glowing beacon that was Meg. Meg, who had objectives of her own to pursue, and who did not know what the king had demanded of him before they left Windsor.

Edward was not a man he could safely disobey.

He walked forward, slowly, and knelt in the shadow of the rough-hewn cross suspended above the altar. Shades of memory teased him, but none came near enough to be fully grasped.

He bowed his head. *You made me,* he prayed silently. *Tell me who—and what—I am.*

17

Receiving no discernible answer to his prayer, Gresham got to his feet and turned, only to find himself standing face-to-face with an aged, wiry priest.

"Milord," the holy man said, by way of a greeting, inclining his tonsured head slightly.

"Father—?"

"Francis," replied the priest.

"Should I remember you?"

Francis laughed. "Hardly," he said. "I have just come to Sedgewick from the north of England, barely seven months past." His kindly gaze probed deeply into Gresham and, it seemed, saw a great deal. "I could not help noticing that you were at prayer."

Gresham shoved a hand through his hair. "Aye," he said, "for all the good it's done."

The priest indicated one of the pews with a gesture of one hand. "Mayhap I can serve in some small way, if only by listening?"

Gresham was not a loquacious man, but he sat down,

nonetheless, and Father Francis took a seat on the next
pew. To his abject amazement, he heard himself telling
the priest about his son, Kieran, and about Meg, who had
found him lying in the garden patch at St. Swithin's, with
a wound to the back of his head. He poured it all out, his
many and torturous doubts, his need for Meg, his fears
that he would not be a good husband to her. And he made
still another confession, as well, revealing the secret he'd
kept since leaving the king's company at Windsor.

"I promised to take her to Cornwall, to find one of her
sisters," he said, gazing downward because he could not
look into the priest's eyes. "It is a vow I fear I cannot
keep, thanks to the king."

Francis sighed. "You are in a great deal of trouble," he
confirmed, and both men laughed, though ruefully.

"You'll pardon me, Father, if I do not find your assess-
ment especially comforting," Gresham said.

"You must tell her the truth. Now. Is it your plan to
leave the lady here, at Sedgewick, as well as the boy,
while you return to Windsor to await the king's orders? I
assure you, your father, for all his blustering, will be delighted if you do. He is a man starved for family."

"Is he not dying?"

"Of loneliness, perhaps," the priest said. "But the boy's
presence will rouse him, I suspect, as little else could. Do
you mean to marry the woman?"

"If she'll have me," Gresham replied. "Once I tell her
that the king has commanded me to come back—no
doubt he will send me to France, there to assist the Black
Prince—she may well change her mind. Mayhap I should
marry her first, and *then* give her the news that she will
not be going on to Cornwall until after my return."

Francis looked at him narrowly.

"All right," Gresham snapped, slapping his hands down on his thighs in irritated capitulation, "I'll tell her I'm leaving *before* I ask for her hand."

"Good," said Francis, smiling his approval. "I suggest you find Lady Redclift now, while you are resolved to do right."

Gresham nodded. "I didn't mean to deceive her, you know," he said, rising to leave, his mission before him. "It was just—"

Father Francis held up one hand to stem the tide. "Save your protestations for the lady," he said. "In the meanwhile, I shall make preparations for a wedding."

Gresham gave a rueful chuckle. "Perhaps you should have a funeral in reserve as well. Mine, of course."

The priest laughed and waved him out of the chapel.

He found Meg in the bedchamber that, according to Tallie, who escorted him there, had once been his nursery. She looked scrubbed and well fed, clad in a green gown of frayed but clean velvet. He knew, without asking, that the garment had been his mother's, brought from some trunk on the old earl's orders.

She rose, seeing him, the firelight dancing in her just-brushed hair, which trailed loose down her back. Gresham's fingers ached to lose themselves in those tresses, but this was not the moment for lovemaking. Mayhap, that blessed time would never come again, once he'd made his admission.

"Meg," he said.

She beamed at him, and dismissed the maid who had been attending her. "Did you meet with your father?"

He sighed. "Aye, and with the priest." He drew a deep breath, thrust it out of his lungs. "Meg," he went on, in a rush to get it all said, "I would make you my wife, if you'll have me." He saw the flash of delight in her eyes, held up a hand to waylay the ready acceptance shining there. "First, you must hear me out."

She frowned. "What is it?" she asked, holding one of his hands, her fingers interlaced loosely with his.

"There is something I haven't told you."

She stared up at him, worried, but not, it seemed, overly surprised. "Methinks there is a great deal you haven't told me," she allowed.

"Well—" He searched his mind, found nothing else that he'd withheld. "No. You know as much about me as I know about myself, if not more. But there is this one thing."

"Which is?" she prompted, when he got into the mire again.

"While we were at Windsor, the king told me that things are going badly in France. He ordered me to return to Windsor within two months, and bring a company of fighting men."

Her knees must have gone slack; she sank a little way, and Gresham caught her by the elbows, eased her into a chair near the fire.

"I know you were counting on going to Cornwall, finding Gabriella—"

"Bother Cornwall," she blurted, her beautiful green eyes brimming with sudden, furious tears, "I can get there on my own, Gresham Sedgewick, without you for a nursemaid."

He clamped his jaw against an impulse to warn her not to attempt such a foolish journey before his mission for the king—that would only spur her on—and crouched before her. "Then why the tears, milady?" he asked, with gruff gentleness. "Can it be that you will miss me, just a little?"

She dashed at one cheek with the back of her right hand and bristled. "You might have told me you were going away," she said.

"I didn't know how," he replied. It was no fitting excuse, that reply, and it did naught to vindicate him, but it was the plain and bitter truth. "The priest will marry us, now, this day, if you but say yes."

She bit her lower lip and gazed at him suspiciously. He knew she wanted to accept his proposal—her body had long since revealed her true feelings toward him, even if she hadn't spoken of them out loud—but she was balking. "Mayhap you will forget me," she ventured, "as you forgot Monique, and your son."

She had not meant to be cruel, he knew that, and yet her statement punctured him like the point of an icicle. "A thousand blows to the head could never cause me to forget you," he said, and he was sincere. Ironic, given the fact that Meg clearly did not believe him.

There was a silence.

"Suppose you never return?" she asked. He was clasping her fingers in his own, though he did not remember taking hold of her hands.

"All the more reason for you to be here," he said. "You may be carrying my child, even now. Has that not occurred to you? If we are wed, and something happens to me, the babe will be legitimate, and have a place here at Sedgewick. If we are not—"

Meg looked pained. "Then he or she will be a bastard," she finished.

He didn't speak, but simply waited, his gaze locked with hers.

"Very well," she said, in her own good time. "I will marry you."

"For the sake of decorum," he said wryly, "restrain your joy at the prospect."

"What if there is no babe?" she asked, glancing down once at her flat stomach.

He smiled. "I shall do my best to make certain there is," he replied.

Barely an hour later, a small assemblage gathered in the earl's bedchamber: Gresham and Meg, of course, and the priest. Kieran and a tearful Tallie, the maid. Vows were exchanged, and it was done.

Meg and Gresham were well and truly wed.

Of everyone attending the ceremony, the bridegroom thought, only his father seemed truly pleased. Kieran had answered the old man's summons promptly, it would seem, and the two had already formed some kind of private alliance. Had he had the time or inclination, Gresham might have marked that down in his mind as a point worthy of concern.

In the bedchamber, a roaring blaze awaited the bride and groom, and there were apricots, dried and rolled in sugar, arranged upon a pewter tray, next to a ewer of wine and a chalice. A maid was just turning back the bed-clothes, and she blushed and scampered out of the room as soon as they'd entered.

Meg stared at her husband, hardly believing her good luck, or the trouble she'd gotten herself into. What, she wondered, would become of them? Sudden tears scalded her eyes, nearly blinding her. "Damn you, Gresham Sedgewick," she blurted, and snuffled inelegantly.

He stared at her in bewilderment. "For what?" he demanded.

"For making me care about you," she answered, wip-

ing her cheeks furiously with the backs of both hands.
"For coming into my life in the first place, and then leaving me behind—" She all but strangled on her emotions,
in those moments, certain that something inside her
would break, simply shatter, if she came to love Gresham
more than she already did, and yet what she felt for this
man continued to unfold, to change, to grow, instant by
instant. She was powerless before the enormity of her
own love for him, sure to be washed away.

He grasped her wrist with a gentle firmness. "*Do* you
love me, Meg Redclift?"

She glared at him through a shimmering mist of sheer
sorrow and an almost frightening sense of joy. "Yes," she
confessed, after a lengthy struggle to keep the truth inside, where it could not be turned against her. "Yes."
Then, having sealed her fate, she waited.

He did not respond in words, but simply pulled her
into his arms, fair crushing her against him, and she cried
out in welcome and in fury as his lips came down on hers.

It was not the time for talk, for questions and quan-
daries, but for lovemaking. When, at some length, the
kiss ended, Meg took her husband's hand and led him toward the bed. He undressed her, kissing and caressing
each new part of her as it was unveiled, and then removed his own garments, with a hasty grace, leaving her
side only to bolt the bedchamber's heavy door.

He put Meg in mind of a golden panther as he approached her, perfect in form and grace, at once beautiful to look upon and very, very dangerous. The light of
the fire danced over his flesh, and Meg felt a primitive
surge of passion and wanting, watching him.

He paused, just a few steps from the bed, waiting, con-
suming her with his gaze.

Naked and proud, caught in a tangle of emotions, Meg held out her arms, and her husband came to her, fell to her, like a starving man at a banquet.

He made free with her breasts, suckling until she panted, and pleaded with him to make her fully his own. Instead of complying with her wishes, however, he knelt on the floor, arranged her hips at the edge of the bed, and parted her legs to master her, yet again, with his tongue.

She was sobbing in pleasure and need, her legs locked around his head, when the first storm of satisfaction overtook her; unrelenting, he cupped her buttocks in his hands and raised her higher off the bed, went after her more greedily, and wrung the last whimper of surrender, the last spasm of pleasure, from her already exhausted body.

She was still floating somewhere above the roof when he took her in earnest, and ignited her all over again, mounting her, riding her into an ecstasy that took them both apart, piece by piece.

"When will you go?" Meg asked, hours later, as they lay in the tangled bed. "To Windsor, I mean?"

He sighed, drew her back into his arms. "In a fortnight," he answered. "There are things I must settle with my father first. With Kieran and—" he paused, gave her a nibbling kiss, "with you." He smiled. "You are a stepmother," he marveled. "Amazing."

She snuggled against him, unwilling to let him go, but knowing she would have no choice. "I had expected making a family to take a bit more time," she said.

"Kieran will present a challenge," he told her warily.

She laughed. "Kieran is not so bad, Gresham. And he'll do well here at Sedgewick. Has he told you that he is to have ponies and swords and tutors from the Continent? He's been given his own bedchamber, and a flock of servants to look after him."

Gresham frowned. "He will be spoiled."

"Alas," she said, tracing the outline of his mouth, the mouth that had given her so much pleasure, with the tip of one finger, "he shall indeed be spoiled. But he will also learn, in time, that he is loved."

"A surfeit of ease makes a man weak, not strong."

"You fret too much, my lord. Kieran will grow to be a fine man, and he's more good than bad, for all his mischief, though I am certain he would prefer that we believed otherwise."

He kissed her. "How did you get so wise?"

She felt a pinch in the depths of her heart. "Oh, my lord, I am not wise. If I were, I should never have—" she stopped, turned her head to one side, wishing she'd held her tongue.

He clasped her chin in one hand, made her look at him again. "Never have what?" he insisted.

"Never have fallen in love," she whispered, and he did not press her to say more, but simply held her for a long time, his lips brushing softly, now and again, across her temple.

"Nothing," she said, much later, "has gone as I thought it would."

He was silent, but she knew he was listening by the way he held her.

Tears stung in Meg's eyes. "Even knowing you are leaving, it is a happy day for me." She stopped, sniffled. "Still, I cannot help thinking of my sisters, my lord—Gabriella, mayhap lost or ill or even gone. Elizabeth, in the midst of plague—possibly dead and buried. It shames

me, that I can know such joy, even while I grieve for
them."

"We will find Gabriella," Gresham vowed tenderly.
Then he chuckled. "Was that not why you took up with
me in the first place, Lady Sedgewick? So that I would
take you to find your twin?"

She turned far enough so that her forehead rested
against his shoulder, and her shoulders trembled in
Gresham's hands. "Yes," she said, and looked up at him
again, knowing her face was smudged and awash with
tears. Her mouth curved, of its own tremulous accord,
into a smile. "I have had enough and more of adventuring, my lord. I cannot think why minstrels and storytellers
make so much of it. But no matter how glad I am to be
your wife, I shall never truly be whole until I know what
became of Gabriella and—and poor, sweet Elizabeth."

Gresham laid his hands to either side of her face,
brushed away her tears with the sides of his thumbs. "When
I come back, in a year or so—" He stopped in midsentence.

The color drained from Meg's face, and she was utterly
still, like some small, cornered creature, not knowing
which way to run. "A *year?*" she whispered, horrified.

"Aye," he said, and she heard anguish in his voice. He
dared not flout the king's wishes by staying when he'd
been ordered to go, of course. Such disobedience
amounted to treason, and was punishable by death. "It
will pass quickly."

She gave a bitter, rueful little laugh. "Mayhap for you,
it will. For me, it will seem an eternity."

He smiled down at her. "Will you miss me as much as
that, Meg?"

She could not make herself answer with the truth—*as
much as I should miss my next breath, my lord, should I*

wait a year for it—so she simply glared at him, through tears of sad defiance. Suppose he returned a stranger, a man who loved soldiering above all else?

He kissed her, lightly, teasingly. "Come, Lady Sedgewick. Let us make good use of our wedding night and save our sorrows for another time."

Soon, they were once again caught up in the throes of their lovemaking, and the king was forgotten.

"She is breeding, methinks," said the Earl of Sedgewick fondly, the next morning, watching his daughter-in-law as she conferred with a bevy of servants in the Great Hall. "And still you would leave her."

Gresham, whose gaze had been following Meg as well, spared a glance for his father. For all his bristling speeches, the old man had rallied considerably, just since the wedding. He'd left his bedchamber—it was the first time in months, according to Tallie—and there was a little color in his face. His eyes glinted with the light of battle.

"I don't have a choice," Gresham answered belatedly, "and you know it. Edward will have me drawn and quartered if I don't do as he says."

Sedgewick the elder sighed. "Aye," he agreed, but reluctantly. "The boy will not be happy to see you leave, you know. For all that he spits in your eye every chance he gets."

Gresham tore his attention from Meg, though he knew it would wander back in short order. "He will be safe here."

"Yes," the earl agreed.

Meg broke away from the servants and came toward them, smiling. Gresham felt his heart turn over.

"She is so beautiful," he breathed.

"Aye," agreed his father. "She's a treasure, your Meg.

Mind you do right by her, or you'll have me to reckon with."

Gresham chuckled, went to Meg, took her hands in his own, kissed her. He was falling apart inside; in just two weeks, he would be leaving for Windsor, and then, very possibly, for France, beyond the Narrow Sea. The prospect of the journey alone, never mind the battles waiting to be fought, filled him with dread, but something else bothered him more—he would be leaving the woman who had changed his life. The woman who *was* his life.

She withdrew from his embrace, too soon, and went to stand beside the earl's chair. She bent and kissed the old man's cheek. "Good morning," she said.

Sedgewick patted her hand. "Good morning, my girl," he replied, with a warmth Gresham wouldn't have thought him capable of exhibiting.

"Where is Kieran?" she asked, looking from the earl's face to Gresham's.

"Up to some mischief, no doubt," Gresham said.

"Nonsense," huffed the earl, insulted on his grandson's behalf. "He's at the stables, looking over the horses. After all, they'll be his one day."

As if conjured by the mere mention of his name, Kieran himself entered the Great Hall just then, at the far end, flanked by two of the biggest hounds Gresham had ever seen. The dogs sprinted across the rushes, barking as they came, and Meg, far from being frightened, as many sensible women would have been, hurried forward to greet them, along with the boy.

Kieran's response was cool, but the hounds plainly adored Meg, and would not be distracted from her even when their young master tempted them with a bone taken from the pockets of his tunic.

The earl looked on, smiling. "She is worth any sacrifice, your Meg," he said. "Methinks those dogs have sense enough to know that, even if you don't."

"I will be back," Gresham said evenly, aching, long aforetime, with missing Meg.

"You had better keep that promise," the earl replied. "For if you do not, and I learn that you are alive, the king will have no chance to draw and quarter you. I will attend to that myself."

"Will you look after her? She's bound to make for Cornwall before I've been gone a day, and convince the boy to go along."

The earl looked at him sharply. "What is in Cornwall?"

"One of her sisters," Gresham replied, watching as Meg charmed not only the hounds, but the reluctant boy, Kieran, as well. "Her twin."

Sedgewick laughed. "Her twin? Do you mean to tell me there are two of her?"

Gresham smiled. "It's a daunting thought, isn't it?"

"Are they alike in appearance?"

He shrugged. "No," he answered. Then he smiled again. "But I'll wager their temperaments are two sides of the same coin."

"I'll send horsemen to Cornwall," the earl said presently. "They'll bring back word of my lady's sister, or not dare to come back at all. Mayhap that will satisfy her, and keep her here, where she belongs."

She joined them, followed by the boy and the adoring dogs.

"Mayhap *what* will satisfy me?" she asked.

Gresham folded his arms, too polite by far to answer such a question.

❊   ❊   ❊

That night, directly after supper, Gresham latched the door, lest a servant enter, and made love to Meg, as slowly, as thoroughly, as skillfully, as he had done the night before. Then, leaving her boneless in the center of the mattress, her body humming like a bowstring after expelling an arrow, he rose, washed at the basin, and dressed in woolen leggings, trunks, a heavy tunic, and leather boots.

"Where are you going?" Meg asked, raising herself onto one elbow and immediately collapsing again.

"I would speak to my father," he said.

Meg curled up on her side, reveling in the warm softness of the bed, the lingering scents of her husband and of their lovemaking. He was as beautiful as an archangel to her, for all his impossible faults and surprises. "About what?"

"Now that he's had time to tell me—repeatedly—what a disappointment I've been, I am hoping he'll tell me other things about myself. Something will surely stir a memory."

She sighed, gazing up at the ceiling.

"You think I'm wasting my time," he said.

"No," she replied gently. "Never that. We each have our own quests, you and I—yours is to find yourself, and mine is to make certain my sisters are safe."

She sensed his sudden stillness, did not have to look at him to know he'd frozen. "Meg—"

"I must find them," she said.

"My father will send men to search for them. He's already promised me that."

"Then I shall accompany them."

"No!"

She turned her head, gazed at him sadly, and with

love. "Do you think you, or anyone, can stop me?" she asked, without rancor.

"No," he replied, not so forcefully this time. "Please, Meg—"

"Do not ask for a promise I cannot make," she interrupted.

He fell silent, and left the room, and when he was gone, Meg allowed herself to weep at last, weep because her husband was going away to war and she might never see him again. Because she missed her sisters so sorely that, at times, she could barely catch her breath.

In time, she slept.

Gresham came back to bed, made love to her again, and rose with the sun. She rolled over, sated, and tumbled back into the warm, welcoming depths of sleep.

At midmorning, when Kieran came to call, Meg was resplendent in a heavy blue woolen gown. She had consumed a hearty breakfast and was making ready to seek out Gresham's father.

The boy was pale with fury, but no less beautiful for his anger.

"He is leaving—going to fight in France methinks—and he refuses to take me with him!"

Meg dismissed her maid, who was clearing away the crumbs and cups of breakfast, and indicated a chair.

Kieran ignored the offer and strode to the nearest window instead, keeping his back to the room. To Meg.

"He is *leaving*," he said again. Miserably.

"Aye." Meg did not approach. "I would go with him, too, if he'd let me."

"You are but a woman," Kieran said, with contempt. Not turning.

She might have countered that he was but a boy, but

she refrained. Kieran had lashed out at her, at least in this instance, from pain, not malice. "We must believe he will return," she said. Orchards would bloom, bear fruit, and shed their lives in that time. Fish would grow fat in the streams, and flowers would blanket the meadows and fields, and Gresham would not be there to see the spectacles. She drew a breath, folded her arms, spoke moderately. "Are you not glad to see him go? You have said, again and again, that you hate him."

Kieran's shoulders slumped slightly, and he lowered his head. "I am a squire. I could mind his horse, his armor."

"You hate him," Meg said again. Softly. Carefully. "Don't you?"

Kieran turned round, at last, to face her. His youthful face was contorted with emotions he could not quell and hide. "I am a squire, and one day, I will be a good knight. I could be a boon to him."

Meg would not let him wriggle free; she simply waited, arms folded, head tilted to one side.

Kieran, more stubborn still, glared at her and said nothing.

She laughed. "You have betrayed yourself by your silence, Kieran. You care more for your father than you will admit." Meg went to him, linked her arm through his. "Come—show me this grand chamber you've been given. And I should like a close look at the ponies, too."

The boy scowled, but did not wrench away from her, as he might have done on another day. "It's in the other wing, my chamber—close by my grandfather's rooms."

"Ah."

Along the way to Kieran's new abode, a considerable distance given the size of the castle, Meg discovered that it had been the earl who had first told Kieran that

Gresham would be going away. The boy had not slept, for making plans to accompany his father to Windsor and then the Continent, there to keep his armor polished, his swords and blades sharpened, his horses well fed, doctored and exercised. Then, just moments before joining Meg, Kieran had encountered Gresham in the corridor, and asked to take part in the venture.

Gresham had rejected the idea without hesitation and, probably, without any particular effort at grace.

Meg listened to the account, but did not sympathize. After all, Kieran was a child and, squire or none, he had no place in the midst of bloody battles, where he might be trampled, pierced by arrows, run through by swords, daggers and lances.

The chamber assigned to Kieran was indeed grand—with a fireplace big enough for him to stand inside it. The bed was massive, and the walls were covered with brilliantly colored tapestries, all of hunting scenes. The windows overlooked the rear gardens, the chapel and churchyard, the distant hills behind the castle walls.

"It is a wondrous room," Meg said.

"Better than yours," Kieran replied.

She hid a smile. "Even if you were old enough, you would still be too rude to go to war, Kieran. You would surely be killed by your own army long before the enemy got a chance at you."

The boy flushed. "Well, it is better," he muttered.

Meg simply shook her head and went to study the stack of carefully copied books teetering on an ancient, sturdy desk. Indeed, Kieran's room *was* better, for he had these splendid volumes—epic poetry, an account of the life of Arthur, Plato's *Republic*.

"Can you read, Kieran?" she asked, and watched the boy's response out of the corner of her eye.

His cheeks turned bright. "A soldier has no need. Such is the comfort of priests and women."

Meg bit her tongue as she often had with this child and, she suspected, often would, in the future. "Ignorance is never an advantage," she said. "May I borrow this—" she picked up the history of Arthur's reign, "—since you won't be wanting it?"

Kieran looked as if he would like to protest, but he couldn't, of course. He'd made such a point of scoffing. "What—what is it about, that book?"

She smiled inwardly, but outwardly, her expression was serious. "Oh, 'tis naught but battles, really, and tales of gallantry. King Arthur—you've heard of him, surely?—drove back the savage invaders for many years. Until he was betrayed, of course, by those he most trusted."

Had the volume been edible, Kieran would have snatched it from Meg's hands and gobbled it down whole, by the looks of him. "Take it," he said, but grudgingly.

"Mayhap I might read to you, now and then. After my lord has gone to war, I mean."

"You would do that? Why?"

"Because I shall miss your father so greatly that I will need such diversions."

"Does he know how to read?"

"Gresham? Of course." Meg did not know this for a certainty; she had never seen her husband take up a book or document, but he was well spoken, and the very motions of his body were poetic. Such a man could not be illiterate.

"My grandfather has many books. He said they would all be mine one day."

"Then I should think you had better learn to read in the meantime. It would be a shame to waste such treasure."

He studied her warily. "This Arthur. Tell me about him."

Meg smiled, sat down on a long bench, in a spill of wintry sunlight, and made room for Kieran beside her. Then, slowly, she opened the book.

18

❧

That starry, winter-white evening, the earl attended vespers in the village chapel, and Meg guessed by the whispers and stares of the villagers, servants, knights, and squires that it was a rare event for him to do so, akin to Christmas, mayhap even Easter.

A restive Kieran sat in the pew between Meg and his grandsire. Gresham, busy with horses and soldiers, hired at the king's expense to accompany him to Windsor, had declined to attend, but he'd promised to sup with them all, in the Great Hall, when the service was ended.

Meg, facing the prospect of Gresham's inevitable and fast-approaching departure, felt an uncommon need for prayer. Too, she found special solace in the familiar sounds and rituals, the brave, flickering candlelight and pungent incense; Gabriella and Elizabeth might have been very nearby, just at the edge of her vision, so many times had they sat together in just such a place, wishing they were elsewhere.

She smiled sadly to herself. *Would that we had been*

aware of our blessings, she thought, *and therefore, grateful.*

A sweet and nearly unbearable sorrow swelled within her heart, and her eyes burned with the effort to keep back tears. *Gabriella, twin of my soul as well as my body—are you safe in Cornwall, with your husband? Elizabeth, beautiful angel, featherless bird—do you still live, or are you in Heaven, watching over us all?*

Kieran must have noticed Meg's tears, already winning the battle against her formidable will, for he reached out, tentatively, to touch her hand. With that shy, simple gesture, a lasting bond was formed, strong enough to endure the trials ahead, and she knew that, no matter how many children she might bear in the years to come, she would love none more than this one nigh-to-impossible boy. It was as if he'd been born from her own heart, and not the body of another woman.

She wanted to embrace him, but of course she didn't dare. It was too soon for such demonstrations; she would not risk driving him away. Still, she met and held his gaze steadily. Over Kieran's head, the earl caught her eye, and winked.

She had had a short talk with her husband's father that afternoon, and found him amusing and intelligent, if insufferably stubborn, though she could not discern whether he would prove a help or a hindrance in dealing with her stepson. His relationship with Gresham had obviously been a difficult one.

Indeed, the earl was something of an enigma, to Meg's mind, at least. He had sent Gresham away, as a small child, and later disinherited him entirely. Still, Gresham's return had worked a miracle where the elderly man's health was concerned; bedridden for many months, according to the servants Meg had questioned, his lordship was now bright in countenance and spry of step. He was washed and groomed and wore a tunic and hose, and it was said that his appetite, long a worry to the household, was now restored.

Gresham insisted that it was Kieran who had brought about these marvels, but Meg was not convinced. Plainly, the earl was deeply fond of his grandson—they were alike in many ways, for good and for ill—but there was something in Lord Sedgewick's manner, in his eyes, when he spoke of Gresham, a certain glint that gave the lie to even his most inflammatory words.

Now, nudged by his grandsire, Kieran faced dutifully forward again, and bowed his golden head for the last of Father Francis's prayers. Meg, herself in a reverent mood, followed suit.

After vespers, the worshipers left the chapel in a sort of merry procession, skirting the inner door for the outer one, bearing lit candles in their wind-chapped hands. Pitch torches, held by servants, helped to light their way through the courtyard, orange flames smoking and sparking in the crisp winter air. Gresham appeared at Meg's side, materializing out of the darkness and linking his arm with hers. He favored her with a private smile, and they proceeded, with the others, into the castle and the Great Hall.

A fire roared in the massive hearth at one end of that vast chamber, and a long table had been laid with bounties of food before the hearth, and the earl took his rightful place at its head, indicating that Kieran should sit at his left, and Gresham at his right. Meg sat beside her husband, feeling festive, despite missing her sisters and, though he had not yet gone, Gresham. As she ate of boiled turnips and roasted fowl, of potatoes and bread,

Meg watched the interplay between the three Sedgewick men with affectionate interest.

The conversation at table was pleasant enough, although no perceptive person could have missed the undercurrent of conflicting and very volatile emotions. The earl spoke to Kieran about his ponies, and to Gresham about the fighting in France, and the soldiers he'd been training. Gresham said little, but listened intently, and occasionally flashed a smile in Meg's direction.

"Will you not change your mind and take me with you, milord?" Kieran's voice was eager and hopeful as, midway through the meal, he faced Gresham and pressed his case. "I would be no trouble, I swear it—"

Meg, who knew that the answer would be—indeed, should be—"no," felt sorry for the boy nonetheless, and was careful not to let her sympathy show.

"Nay," Gresham said, but he did not speak harshly, or with impatience. He set down his wine chalice and regarded his son as he might another soldier, an equal. "We've been over this ground before, lad. You are needed here. I depend upon you to look after Lady Meg and your grandfather." When Kieran would have interrupted, in a fit of protest, Gresham stayed him by holding up one hand. "One day," he went on, "you will be the Earl of Sedgewick, and wiser, methinks, in the ways of war."

Meg winced as bloody images came to mind, and watched as Kieran lowered his eyes. Firelight flickered over his features, pursued by shadow, and once again Meg was left to guess what he was thinking, what he felt. Nothing showed in his face.

"Your father speaks the truth, lad," the earl put in, after a few moments of heavy silence had passed. "You shall have more than enough to occupy you, young

Sedgewick, learning to run this estate and manage the fortune that accompanies it."

Kieran remained silent for a time. Meg saw the motion of his throat as he swallowed. "Aye, then," he said. "But suppose one day the king summons me to fight, just as he has summoned my father? I will know naught of soldiering."

"When and if that happens," the earl replied, more subdued, "the king shall find you ready."

Gresham pushed away his food and got up from the bench. Meg, having eaten her fill, rose too, said a polite good evening to the earl and then to Kieran, and left the table with her husband.

Inside their chambers, Gresham splashed water into a basin, stripped off his shirt, washed, and then dried his face and chest vigorously, his hair in delightful disarray.

Meg drew near to her husband, and smoothed his beautiful, damp hair with her hands. How would she bear it when he went away? she asked herself, for the hundredth time. And for the hundredth time, she knew no answer to give.

"Your memory is returning," she said.

He frowned. "Why do you say that?"

She smiled, stood on tiptoe to place a kiss, light as her breath, on his mouth. "You have been training men for battle these many days," she pointed out. "How did you know what needed to be taught, and how to go about teaching it?"

He let out a long breath. "Hmmm," he said, and she knew he was marking her words, testing the implications in his mind.

She changed the subject again, giving the first idea time to simmer in Gresham's brain. "Your father is a sweet and gentle man, beneath all that fuss and bluster."

"Oh, aye," Gresham mocked, grinning. "He has all the charm of a rabid hedgehog, my sire." He pulled her into his arms, kissed her forehead. "I suppose he's fond of Kieran, and he definitely has a soft spot in his heart for you, Lady Meg."

"I think he wants a chance to make up for the way he treated you," she ventured.

Gresham shook his head, though he looked more re-signed than angry. "I doubt that the old man regrets any-thing, where I'm concerned," he said. "He believed he was doing the right thing at the time, and I'll wager it would be handier for him to change the color of his eyes than his mind." He searched her face. "What about you, my lady wayward? Do you have regrets? Are you sorry for wedding yourself to me?"

She rested her head against his chest, felt his heart-beat in her own flesh, like an echo. "Nay, my lord, I could never regret that."

He took her chin in his fingers and made her look at him. "Not even if I found another child and brought it home for you to raise?" he teased.

"Mayhap," she responded, "if you presented another *wife,* I should be forced to make a new opinion of you. But I could make room in my heart for as many sons and daughters as you might have." She traced the line of his jaw with the tip of one finger. "Of course, I shall ex-pect you to sire all *future* children by me, and none other."

Gresham had been jesting before, but now his expres-sion was utterly serious. "From now until the end of my days, my lady wife, I swear to you, I shall never lie with any woman but you. On that, you have my most sacred word."

Meg raised both hands to his face, in a tender caress. "I need no more than your promise, my lord," she answered softly. "Come, bring me to your bed, that there may be another babe on the way when you return home. A daughter, mayhap, since you already have a fine son and heir."

He chuckled and bent his head to kiss her sweetly, softly, and then with growing passion. "A daughter it is," he replied presently, before bearing Meg off to their bed.

That night's lovemaking was made of fury and splendor, and the sky was turning lavender and pink at its edges when they finally slept.

Despite Gresham's impending departure or, mayhap because of it, the coming days and nights were celebrated, each single moment cherished for its own sake. Meg worked with a subdued Kieran in the library, marveling at how fast he progressed, learning his letters, and watched Gresham on the training ground whenever she could. He was a magnificent horseman, and wielded his sword as easily as if it were a part of his arm. He drove his soldiers unmercifully, and they grumbled under the load, but when they took the field of battle, in France or elsewhere, they would be ready to face any opponent.

For the time being, Meg put aside her concerns about Kieran, and the earl, and even managed to fret less over Gabriella and Elizabeth. Instead, she threw herself into loving her husband, not only physically, but mentally and spiritually as well. She learned the shape of his soul, and the special delights of his body. She surrendered to Gresham, lost her own being in his, and returned from those tender sojourns more completely and truly herself than before.

She learned that love meant something more than pretty words, something more than fiery passion. Something that would take a lifetime to learn and understand.

She was determined to trust in a kindly fate; he *would* come back, the Gresham she knew.

Inevitably, and much too soon, the day arrived when Gresham rose with the dawn, secreted himself away with his father for over an hour, and then spoke earnestly to his son. When that was done, he led Meg into the nave of the chapel to kiss her good-bye.

"There will not be a day, an hour, or a moment, when I do not think of you," he said, his eyes tender.

She looked up at him through tears, unable, for that instant at least, to speak.

He cupped her chin in his hand, brushed the pad of his thumb across her mouth, so well kissed in the night just past. "Wait for me," he said. "We will travel to Cornwall together, and then to St. Swithin's."

Still, she said nothing. She was not willing to make a promise she couldn't keep. With an exasperated sigh, a sound torn from him, Gresham bent and touched his mouth to hers just once more. Then, taking Meg's heart with him, he mounted his favorite horse and rode away from the castle with a company of some thirty well-trained and battle-ready men, plus six more drawn from the earl's own ranks. These last would journey to Portsmouth with him, if the king sent him to join the Black Prince, and then on to France, and serve as couriers, as needed.

The first of them, Gresham had promised, would return to Sedgewick within a few weeks' time, bearing whatever news there was to be borne. Others would follow, bringing other messages, until the last remaining man was sent to herald Gresham's homecoming.

Meg lived for that seemingly far-off day, breathed for it. Was determined to be brave in the interim, as brave as her soldier husband.

She stood with the earl and with Kieran, and watched while Gresham rode away, through the village and the great, leafless orchard, through the wide gateway and over the frozen road. Away and away, until he and the others were but specks of color and motion in the far distance.

Only then, long after Kieran had run off to the stables, red eyed and defiant, long after the earl had gone back to his books and his fire in the castle, muttering to himself as he went, did Meg meet the eyes of the priest, Francis, who waited patiently, at a little distance.

I am desolate, she thought. Now, truly, with Gresham out of her sight, she began to understand the cost of love. He had borne a part of her spirit away with him.

"Come inside, my lady, and make yourself warm," said Father Francis, extending a hand.

She nodded, reluctantly, and allowed him to lead her into the vast house, which seemed to echo, now, with Gresham's absence.

She was sitting at an upstairs window, perhaps an hour later, lost in thought and in heartbreak, when Kieran appeared, splendid in his sumptuous new cloak of black velvet, trimmed in gold.

The earl's colors. And now his own.

She smiled at him, with pride, and thought what a marvelous man he would make, once he'd grown to majority. "There is a meal waiting in the Great Hall, milady," he said. "Surely you are hungry."

For a certainty, the last thing Meg wanted at that moment was food, but she stood, and took the arm Kieran offered, allowing him to escort her down the stairs and into the hall, where he saw her seated, with no little ceremony, at the earl's table.

When the food—roast quail and numerous vegetables and tubers—had been served, sampled and then removed by servants speaking in muffled voices, Kieran turned so that he sat astraddle of the bench, facing Meg. It was as though he had put aside his childhood, at least for a little while, and become a man. The earl, pleading exhaustion, had already taken his leave.

"Shall I sing for you, milady?" he asked. "Would you find that soothing?"

Meg was touched. She wanted to lay her hand against Kieran's cheek, but the moment was fragile and she feared overstepping, and spoiling things. "You are a singer? Your talents are many, young Sedgewick."

He preened a little at the use of his title. "I learned from Tangwyn. I could have been a mummer, myself, you know. Had I not been fostered to Lancaster, I would have traveled with the troupe."

Meg suppressed a shudder at the mention of Tangwyn, but her curiosity proved ungovernable, as usual. "You knew the mummer when you were with your mother," she ventured.

The boy nodded, gazing into the fire, and she knew he was remembering Monique. He'd been small when he left her, and he would have a child's memories, faintly luminous ones, no doubt, not entirely accurate. "Aye—he was *Maman's* companion for a long time. I used to pretend he was my father."

Meg started to lay a hand on his arm, then thought better of the idea. "He was kind to you," she said. Everyone, she had learned, had a good side, even thieves and scoundrels such as the mummer.

"Aye," Kieran said, and smiled wistfully. "Things will be different between us now, though."

Meg waited.

Kieran sighed, shoved a hand through his hair in the same way she had so often seen his father do. "Mayhap I will never see him again."

"Mayhap," she agreed.

"My mother—"

Again, Meg waited, inwardly holding her breath.

"My mother was not a saint," he managed to say, on the second attempt. "She had a temper. I recall a night when she set a bed afire, with Sedgewick in it." He paused and looked away again, flushed. "I believe Tangwyn was more than a friend to her, as well. Perhaps that drove my father away."

Now, at last, Meg dared to touch her stepson's shoulder. "All that is past," she said gently. "Remember the good things."

He smiled, still gazing into the fire. "Yes," he said, and she knew he was doing precisely that.

"Were you happy at Windsor, with Lancaster's brood?" she asked, in good time, recalling the harsh life he'd led in that place, as a squire. No doubt the duke's own children were being subjected to a rigorous upbringing, as well, for they were in line for the throne, however unlikely their ascension.

Kieran shrugged. "I was not unhappy," he allowed. "Still, it is better here."

She gave in to a motherly impulse and placed a light kiss on his cheek. "Yes," she agreed, and got to her feet. "I am past weary," she confessed. "Will you sing for me another time?"

"Aye," he said, and rose, like a gentleman, to escort her to her chamber. "Another time."

Minutes later, alone in the room she and Gresham had

shared, Meg closed the door behind her and leaned against it for a moment. Then, bracing up, she straightened again, squared her shoulders and blinked very rapidly to keep back tears. She had promised Gresham, between frenzied bouts of lovemaking, that she would not weep on account of his going, but only when he returned, and then for joy.

"Godspeed, my lord," she whispered, and her heart took wing, carrying the words far away, over frozen roads and fields of snow, to her husband.

Kieran worked diligently at all his lessons in the days and weeks to come, with Meg and with his tutors, and minded his tongue, for the most part. There were a few shouting matches with his grandfather, behind closed doors, but with Meg he was respectful, though often distant. He threw himself into riding, sword practice, Latin and astronomy, and his French, of course, came easily, since he'd spent a portion of his childhood across the Narrow Sea.

Meg, for her part, was grateful for the occupation teaching Kieran to read provided; without it, and the time she spent each day with the earl, reading to him, writing the letters he dictated to her, going over household accounts and the like, she might well have gone mad for awaiting word of Gresham. Too, she chafed to be off to Cornwall, in search of Gabriella, though she was loathe to leave either Kieran or the earl. The men her father-in-law had sent to make inquiries might never return, and waiting for word, like waiting for her husband, was excruciating.

Resigned, she began making quiet arrangements for the journey, choosing a horse, a fine spotted mare, and riding whenever she could. She studied maps, in the earl's study, and carefully plotted the route to Cornwall.

Once there, she would find Avendall Hall, and Gabriella. She had already dispatched several messages to St. Swithin's, asking after Elizabeth, but so far, there had been no reply.

One morning, when Gresham had been gone a full month, and no word of his safe arrival had arrived, Meg arose from her too-empty bed and was instantly ill. Heat swept through her, followed by wretched nausea that sent her rushing to the basin, where she was sick over and over again. She was sure she had plague, and collapsed to her knees when the spate of vomiting was over, too dizzy to stand.

Tallie found her there, raised her tenderly by the shoulders, squired her back to bed. "Ah, milady," she said, with pleased sympathy, "methinks there is a babe growing in you. Bide there awhile, and you'll feel better."

Meg was thunderstruck with delight, with amazement, with a longing for Gresham so powerful that it nearly doubled her over. " 'Tis not the plague, then?"

The serving woman brought her a cup of water, and washed her face with a cool, damp cloth, chortling all the while. "No, milady," she answered, " 'tis surely a babe. The earl will be that pleased, and so will your husband, when he learns of it."

Tears pooled along Meg's lashes, against her will. To bear a child, Gresham's child, was a gift beyond any she could imagine, and yet she missed her husband, and her sisters, even more sorely, even more desperately, than ever before.

Tallie smoothed her hair gently away from her forehead, as though she were a little girl, not a woman, grown and breeding. "There, now," she said. " 'Twill all turn out as it should. Just you wait and see."

Meg had had her fill of waiting. If this morning's spate of sickness was any indication of what lay ahead, she'd better make for Cornwall at the first opportunity, while she still had the determination and the strength.

Huddled under the covers, shaken and sick, utterly determined, she began to lay the final, careful plans for her departure.

Edward surveyed the troops Gresham had brought to Windsor with undisguised pleasure. The king's health was fragile, but he was still a warrior, a fitting sire for sons like the Black Prince and the Duke of Lancaster. "Methinks you would be wasted, fighting the Gaul," he said.

Gresham, chilled by a winter wind, missing Meg in a way that made him regret having any memory at all, stood in the courtyard, his hands clasped behind his back, and said nothing.

"These are farmers' lads?" the king asked.

Gresham nodded. "Aye," he said. "I gathered them from the countryside around Sedgewick, fitted them with horses and swords, and taught them to fight."

"Can you bring me more like them?"

Time slowed by lurches. One heartbeat thundered past. Then another. Gresham finally caught his breath. "Aye," he said, again.

Edward rubbed his stubbly chin, inspecting the line of soldiers and horses once more. "Methinks you might be of greater use at Sedgewick, than on the battlefield," he said at last. "Return there at once, and send me more horses and men like these. I will provide the necessary gold."

Gresham could barely believe his ears. He was being

sent home to Sedgewick, to Meg, to his son and his father—the place, and the three people, who meant the
most to him. It was almost too much to credit.

Edward laughed at the expression on his face. "Be-
gone," he said, with a dismissive wave of one beringed
hand. "I'll look for another crop of soldiers, twice the
number here, in three months' time."

Gresham held back a shout of jubilation, and inclined
his head respectfully. "You will not be disappointed, Your
Highness," he vowed.

At dawn the next morning, he was riding hard for
Sedgewick, his saddlebags loaded with the king's gold,
his heart full. He still had no clear recollection of the
time before he'd run afoul of the nun and found his
way to St. Swithin's, but he didn't care. He was ready to
make new memories, and all of them revolved around
his lady, his Meg, and the life they would make together.

Kieran started when the earl's fist slammed down onto
the tabletop, making the ewers, bowls, plates and knives
jump, then fall back to the board with a clatter.

"Gone?" the old man bellowed. "Impossible!"

Kieran bit down hard on his lower lip. "Milady is not in
her rooms, milord," he said, "and that horse she favors—
the spotted mare—is gone from its stall."

"Is the woman mad?" the earl raged, though Kieran
knew it was fear, not anger, that raised his grandfather's
ire. " 'Tis still winter, and there are brigands of every sort
between here and Cornwall!"

Kieran wanted to weep, though of course he would die
before he gave into that impulse in front of the man
whose regard he valued above all but his father's. Some-

how, he reasoned, Meg's vanishing was his doing. He was sure of it. If anything happened to her, he would never forgive himself. "Aye," he said, for he could not disagree. The situation was dire, and Gresham was far away. The earl was old and, despite recent strides toward health, too unwell to travel.

He would have to find Meg and fetch her back on his own.

The earl got shakily to his feet. A vein bulged in his neck, and his eyes were glazed. "Fetch the guards," he commanded.

Kieran did not bother to argue, nor did he obey his grandsire's order. He went to the stables, collected his own mount, a lively bay gelding, and approached the gates just as a featherlight snow began to fall.

The guard smiled up at him. "Off on a hunt, milord?" he asked.

Kieran returned the smile. "Aye," he said. It wasn't actually a lie, he thought, as the gates were opened, so that he could pass into the great world beyond. He was hunting for Meg.

He paused outside the entrance, wheeling his horse around. "Did Lady Sedgewick pass this way earlier?" he inquired casually.

The older man shook his head, plainly confounded by the question. "Nay, milord," he said. "Surely she would not go out alone."

As he'd suspected, Meg had slipped out by another way, perhaps a postern gate, long unused and probably forgotten. If he hadn't been so frightened for her, Kieran might have laughed at her brazen ingenuity.

"Surely not," he agreed, in belated reply to the guard's remark, and then he turned his face toward Cornwall, and spurred the gelding into a trot. Behind him, the castle gates ground shut.

She was dressed as a man, in robes she had stolen from Father Francis's chest a few days before, while he was conducting a special Mass. With bare hands and naught but sandals on her feet, Meg was already freezing when she came to the first farmhouse, just at dusk. She supposed her discomfort was just punishment for breaking a commandment, especially when the victim of her latest crime was a servant of God.

The crofter's wife peered at her, in the gathering darkness, plainly suspicious of the traveler, priest or not. Meg disguised her voice when she spoke, and kept the hood of Father's robe covering her hair and most of her face, but the woman was still wary.

"Just a bit of food," she pleaded, "and a place to sleep—"

"You can pass the night in the barn," the crofter's wife relented, though grudgingly, and started to shut the door.

"A piece of bread—" Meg persisted, naming herself seven kinds of fool for forgetting the bag of food she'd filched from Cook's pantry that morning, before sneaking out of the rear gate. "Some hay for my horse?"

The woman opened the door again, studied the pretty mare with squinty eyes. "A horse, is it? Well, blessed if it isn't. Fine looking animal, too. Where would a priest get such a prize?"

Meg lifted her chin. "He is my own," she said. "I wasn't always a priest."

"No," said the woman, "I don't reckon you was." She heaved a sigh. "Very well, then. You and the horse, you can take your rest in the shed. Give the beast some hay—

mind it's not too much, for I've a cow to feed—and help yourself to some milk and an egg, if you find one about."

"Thank you," Meg said, with true gratitude, and unconsciously laid a hand to her belly, where the babe, her child and Gresham's, had taken hold. Mayhap she was a fool, undertaking such a journey alone, and in a delicate condition, but staying at Sedgewick would not have served, either. Even with all her pursuits, as lady of the household, she had had too much time to think there, too much time to worry and mourn. There was but one way to ease her mind where Gabriella was concerned, and that was to see her, face-to-face, and speak with her. Together, they could work out the problem of Elizabeth's well-being.

By the time Meg found her way to the crofter's little barn, a shack with great gaps in the walls, the snow was coming down so hard that she could barely see. She led the mare inside, tied her within reach of a manger and, with no little difficulty, removed the saddle. After giving the animal hay, and fetching a bucket of water from the well, Meg crawled under a pile of straw and tried to go to sleep.

She was too hungry, and a feather drifting down from the rafters reminded her of the egg the farmwife had offered. She got up, scrambled about in the hay, while the roosting hens squawked overhead, until she found what she'd been looking for.

Her stomach rolled as she held the speckled oval up for inspection. She would have to eat it raw, since there was no fire, and even if she somehow managed to swallow the slimy yoke and white of the egg, she knew it wouldn't stay down.

She squeezed her eyes shut and recalled the comforts of Bessie's house, where she and Gresham had taken shelter, and the plenty of the kitchens at Sedgewick.

Come the morn, she promised herself, she would find food, for the babe's sake as well as her own.

She burrowed into the hay again, pulled Father Francis's pitifully thin robes tightly around her, and closed her eyes. She was awakened, in full darkness, with a leap of fear. A hand rested on her shoulder.

She cried out and bolted upright, shedding straw as she came.

"Peace, my lady," scolded a familiar voice. "It is I, Kieran."

She laid a hand to her bosom, gasping with relief and ebbing terror. "What are you doing here?" she snapped, when she had the breath to speak.

"I might ask you the same question," her stepson replied. He had a blanket, and he wrapped her in it. "By the saints, what are you wearing?"

"The priest's spare robes," she confessed.

Kieran laughed. "No ordinary sin, stealing from a priest," he commented. "Are you hungry?"

"Yes!" she gasped.

He rummaged through a bag of some sort, brought out bread and cheese, and handed them to her. She ate ravenously, and her eyes adjusted to the darkness, revealing the shadow of a second horse.

"How did you find me?"

"I was a squire," he reminded her solemnly, "and I've hunted all my life. I suppose I learned one or two tricks in the process."

She hid a smile. "Oh, yes. Well."

"Now what?" he asked.

"Indeed," she replied. "Now what?"

"You're coming back to Sedgewick with me. The old man is out of his mind with worry."

"I'm going to Cornwall," she said, in calm tones. "Will you come with me?"

He studied her in silence for a long while, probably debating the matter in that lethal mind of his. "You are bound to go, with or without company," he observed. "Therefore, I do not see a choice in the matter. It seems to be decided."

She smiled. "You are perceptive," she said.

"And you, my lady mother," Kieran told her, "are impossible. Now, sleep. We will both need our rest, methinks."

19

❧

Gresham had an unsubtle sense that he was being followed, as he traversed the king's roads, bound for his father's estate, and for Meg, and he reasoned that the attraction was the gold he carried. He waited until nightfall to test the theory, reining the gelding off the path and into the trees and brush alongside, to wait.

The rider pursued cautiously, but, alas, not cautiously enough. Gresham had been gripping a bent branch in his left hand and, precisely as the man came abreast, he released his hold. The tree limb flashed out, with a faint whipping sound and a rustle of leaves, to connect smartly. With a cry, the rider tumbled backward, over the horse's rump, and sprang back up in almost the same motion, dagger in hand.

Gresham slid off the gelding's back, sword drawn, and sent the beast deeper into the woods with a jabbing motion of his elbow.

"Tangwyn," he said.

The mummer grinned, bowed. "You must have thought I'd been hanged by now," he said. The knife glinted in the light of a fledgling moon. "Alas, the king is not himself these days. Methinks he confuses the two of us, you and me, and when he happened to see me in the dungeons this morning, he ordered my release. And here I am."

"What," Gresham asked, with hard-won patience, for he was impatient to be away, to reach Meg, "do you want?"

"The gold, for one thing," Tangwyn replied.

"And you shall have it, mummer," was the reply, "when milk cows take wing. Get on with it. I have things to do."

Tangwyn ran his thumb expertly along the blade of his knife. "It isn't just the gold," he said quietly.

Gresham sighed. He was still thinking of Meg, the warmth of their bed, the welcoming softness of her body, the way his flesh seemed to burst with light when she touched him. "I thought not," he allowed. "My patience wears thin, mummer. Speak or use the knife—I care not which—but let us be done with each other, once and for all. What the devil do you want?"

"Interesting you should mention the devil," Tangwyn said, "since you, changeling, are almost certainly Lucifer's own get." He paused, drew a measured breath, and released it. "I want what is rightfully mine, Sedgewick—nothing more, nothing less. Your name. Your title. Your lands and fortune. Your wife and son."

Gresham did not relax his grasp on the hilt of his sword, or react in any way, but he was taken aback by the mummer's claim. Was the man merely greedy, or outright mad? He waited.

Tangwyn smiled bitterly. "I am, you see, the firstborn. Your father, the earl, is my father, as well. My mother—Bessie's dear sister—was his favorite, until your dam came along and turned his head. When that happened, the earl passed my mother and me off to the pig farmer, as if we were livestock. We'd served our purpose, apparently. I waited, but there was never another word from Sedgewick. He'd forgotten me."

Gresham felt his gorge rise, along with a denial that he knew was in vain. His own eyes told him that this man was blood of his blood, bone of his bone, flesh of his flesh. "If my father wishes to recognize you now," he said, "I have no objection. My wife and my son, however, are precisely that: mine, and they will remain so."

Tangwyn sighed. "Alas, you will be dead before the sun rises again, and your devoted sire will soon follow—after recognizing me before the world as his elder son. Kieran is already very fond of me, and in time, when she's through grieving for her first husband, lost so tragically on the road, while carrying the king's gold, your lady will turn to me for comfort."

The man was raving, out of his mind, and yet a chill spiraled the length of Gresham's spine all the same. Except for the part concerning Meg—he knew she would never succumb to the mummer's charms, under any circumstances—the mummer's plan might work. Kieran was certainly open to Tangwyn's influence, and the earl, still weak from years of indolence and self-pity, would probably buckle, if only out of guilt. Meg, when she proved a problem, would probably perish in some convenient mishap, leaving the erstwhile mummer free to remarry and carry on, virtually unquestioned, as the Earl of Sedgewick.

"Let it be decided here, then," Gresham said, at last. "Yonder is a clearing, and there is moon enough for swordplay. Whoever walks away from the fight will ride on to Sedgewick."

"I have no sword," Tangwyn said, with an easy shrug. "Knives?"

"Knives," Gresham agreed.

It was all very civilized. Neither would turn his back on the other, so the two combatants walked, side by side, through the woods to the little plot of land Gresham had glimpsed earlier, while upon higher ground.

"He'll not forgive you, if you win," Tangwyn said, when they faced each other, in the center of a circle in the pristine snow. Soon, the patch would be bloodied, the glittering diamonds of ice turned to ruby red.

Gresham drew his own dagger, held it ready. The mummer was referring to Kieran, of course, and regrettably, he was probably right. When Gresham brought the mummer home, for burial among other Sedgewicks, the fragile alliance he had been able to forge with the boy would be shattered forever. "Aye," he agreed, "but my son is my son, and you would not make a fit guardian for him. Nor can I let you kill my father, though I will admit there have been times when I was so tempted myself." It was true, he realized, as light first seeped, then flooded, his mind. A door had opened, for a reason he might not live to explore and understand, and through it walked his past—Morgan Chalstrey, his foster brother and closest friend. Gabriella, Meg's sister, and Chalstrey's prisoner. He'd wanted Gabriella, though he'd never let on, though he'd known Morgan was drawn to her, despite their circumstances, and she to him . . .

"It comes back, then," Tangwyn said, with some satisfaction.

"I was taking Blodwyn, the squire, and Dame Johanna, the nun, to St. Swithin's—"

Tangwyn waited, knife poised for battle, teeth flashing

in a grin. "She smashed you in the head with a rock and left you there by the stream bed, taking your horse. I happened along soon after. Fate, it was." He gave a long sigh. "I took you to the nunnery myself. Brotherly love, I guess. I wish now that I'd finished you then and there." He held up his free hand, the mummer did, and Gresham caught a glimpse of his own signet ring. In many quarters, that ring would be proof that Tangwyn was, indeed, Lord of Sedgewick. With its seal, soldiers could be rallied and sent on the march, crops and fields could be bought or sold, covenants of all sorts could be made. "It would save me the trouble of killing you now."

Gresham did not want to kill this madman, he was, after all, his half-brother, but he could see no viable alternative. Any reason Tangwyn might have possessed in the beginning had been eaten away by a lifetime of hardship, resentment, and sorrow. There was no going back now, no bridging the gap between them. "Have done with it, then," he urged. "This snow is cold, and my feet are freezing."

Tangwyn lunged at him then; he was sturdily built, and agile, and the blade connected, slicing Gresham's upper arm. He barely felt the wound, so crisp was the night wind, and so heady the battle lust that arose at the first challenge.

"First blood," Tangwyn said, with satisfaction. "Now, for last."

The fight took a furious, elemental turn then; Gresham and the mummer were like two wolves, facing off over a prize kill. Only one would partake. At some point, the knives were lost, thrown aside, and they fought with their hands, their knees and elbows, even their teeth. The snow turned ruddy with blood, and they rolled, a savage parody of lovers. Then, after time itself had wandered off the track, and ceased to matter, the end came.

Tangwyn was on the bottom, Gresham astraddle of his hips, when the mummer produced a blade and thrust it hard into Gresham's belly. Stunned, Gresham pulled the knife out of his gut with both hands and raised it over Tangwyn's throat.

The mummer laughed, awash in his own blood, and that of his brother. "Do it," he cried. "Let us *both* perish this night. 'Tis a fitting end!"

Gresham was frozen, numb for the moment to the inevitable pain in his middle, in a state of the purest shock. *Meg,* he thought desperately. *Meg.*

In the next instant, Tangwyn's crimson hands locked, slippery but still strong, around Gresham's. With the last of his strength, the mummer thrust Gresham's hands downward, forcing the knife through his own jugular vein. The bastard son literally died laughing, the sound a horrid gurgle that pursued Gresham into the frigid darkness waiting to swallow him whole.

Meg sat bolt upright in the straw of the crofter's shed and cried out, grasping at her middle with both hands.

Kieran was instantly awake. "What is it?" he rasped. "Is it the babe, coming too soon?"

Meg gasped, breathless with pain and a horror deeper than she'd ever known before. "I dreamed—"

"What?" Kieran prompted, chafing her hands between his. "What did you dream, lady?"

"It was so real—"

"Tell me."

Meg was already scrambling to her feet. "It's Gresham—your father—he lies stabbed somewhere, mayhap dying—"

Kieran stared at her, the whites of his eyes starkly visible in the gloom of that hay-and-manure redolent shed. "What witchery is this?"

Meg began to sob, to scramble for the mare's harness. "I don't know," she cried, fumbling in her efforts to make the animal ready for travel. "We must go back to Sedgewick—now—tonight—"

Wisely, Kieran did not argue. He simply got the horses ready, helped Meg to mount, and rode bravely out into the still and icy night.

It was midmorning, with a light snow falling down all around them, when Meg and Kieran finally came within sight of the earl's estate. Two guards rode out to meet them, their faces grim.

"It is the young lord," one of them said, without preamble. "He lies in the chapel, yonder, near to death."

Meg, now weary to the center of her bones, gave a cry of protest and sorrow, and spurred her weary mare forward. Even Kieran, riding hard, had trouble keeping up. The hooves of the mare, then the gelding, clattered noisily over the hard-frozen ground, then the cobbles of the small village inside the walls. Meg was off the horse and running toward the chapel door long before the animal came to a halt, and Kieran was right behind her.

Gresham lay on a pew, drawn up beneath the altar, like a sacrificial offering. He was bloodied, as Meg had first seen him, and she pushed past the priest and the old earl to kneel at his side, clutching his hand.

He turned his face to her, smiled. "Meg. Do I dream?"

Tears slipped down her cheeks. "No, milord, oh, no. I am truly here. And I carry your babe inside me. You must not leave me."

He stared blindly up at the invisible ceiling. " 'Tis a

pretty place," he said. "There, on the other side of the river."

Meg clasped his hand, lowered her forehead to his chest, felt his thready heartbeat through her own flesh. "Aye," she agreed, "but you mustn't go there. Not yet. We need you here."

He swallowed, looked past him to Kieran. "I—killed him—" he said.

The boy knelt opposite Meg. "Who?" he asked, and Meg saw that his face, too, was wet with sorrow.

"The—mummer." Gresham gave a raw, throaty chuckle. "Alas, he killed me, as well, it would seem."

"No!" Kieran shouted, and his grandsire stepped forward, laid strong hands on the lad's trembling shoulders.

Meg stroked Gresham's forehead. "I love you," she said urgently. "Go, if you will, but you will not find love as strong as mine, even beyond that river of yours. Do you hear me, Gresham Sedgewick? I am the beat of your heart. I am the breath in your lungs. I *will not let you die!*"

Again, he laughed. Then he closed his eyes and expelled a breath so deep that it must have emptied his entire body of air.

Meg grasped his shoulders, prepared to shake him awake, but the priest, Father Francis, gently prized her away, ready to give Last Rites. Almost as an afterthought, he laid the tips of his fingers to the side of Gresham's neck, and in the next moment, he started visibly.

"By all the saints," he rasped. "He still lives."

Meg was beside her husband again, elbowing the priest aside, grasping the stained front of Gresham's tunic in both hands. "Stay, Gresham. Stay with me, with your children, born and unborn. Stay with your sire—" She kept up a version of that litany until she literally collapsed, and the earl summoned a soldier to carry her to her chambers, where Tallie forced a potent sleeping draught down her throat.

She slept, against her will, and traveled in her dreams, first to St. Swithin's.

She saw Elizabeth there, kneeling beside another man, loose limbed and insensate, he was, just as Meg herself had knelt beside Gresham in the chapel. Elizabeth was praying, her dark hair falling free around her shoulders, her body thin, almost emaciated, beneath ragged robes.

She turned from her prayers, looked directly at Meg, and smiled. Warm reassurance swept through Meg, and she started toward her sister, only to be swept away by unseen winds, hurled through spinning stars and darkness. She landed hard in a patch of sweet grass, and opened her eyes to see Gabriella looking down at her, smiling.

"Goose," Gabriella said. "Did you think we could ever really be parted?"

Meg felt such an upsurge of emotion that she wondered if she was not dreaming, but truly with Gabriella, in some unknown realm of the mind and heart. "Are—are you dead?"

Gabriella laughed. "I've never been more alive," she said, and tugged Meg upright, to a sitting position. "We will be together soon."

"Where? How?"

"Soon," Gabriella repeated. And then, as quickly as that, she vanished.

Meg awakened with a cry, much as she had done when she had seen and felt Gresham's stabbing, in the depths of her slumber, and her heart was pounding. She laid a hand to her abdomen, as if to reassure herself that the tiny, precious babe was still with her. She thought of

Gabriella, and of Elizabeth, and knew that they were safe, and that she would see them again, one day, if not in this world, then the next. For the time being, that was consolation enough.

Finding herself in bed, she scrambled out and dressed hastily. Without bothering to light a torch, she dashed down the corridor to the stairs leading into the Great Hall.

At the bottom, she collided with the earl, who stayed her by grasping both her shoulders in strong hands.

"Halt," he said.

Meg struggled. "I would see my husband!"

"He is with the surgeon," the earl said gravely. "You may not go in to him now."

"The surgeon?" Meg all but screamed. "What are they doing to him?"

"Mending him, as best they can," said the elder Sedgewick wearily. There was a light of pride in his eyes, and love for the son he had been estranged from for so long. "To the chapel with you, if you would be useful. He needs our prayers now, Gresham does."

Meg hesitated, then nodded. She went to the chapel, knelt as she had done so many times at St. Swithin's, and folded her hands together as she had seen Elizabeth do, in her dream. Then she bowed her head.

She stayed, pleading with Heaven, until she could no longer kneel, but had to offer her petitions sprawled on the cold stone floor of the chapel. In time, Father Francis came, gathered her up in a bundle of blankets, and made her a bed on one of the pews, where she could keep her eye on the rough-hewn cross suspended above the altar. She slept and prayed and slept again, and it was the cold sunlight of a winter morning, shining on her face, that brought her around.

She blinked, remembered, bolted to her feet with her husband's name on her lips. She found him asleep in a bed set up especially for him, there before the fire in the Great Hall. Gently, she stretched out beside him on the mattress, in an instinctive effort to lend what solace, what strength, she could.

In time, he opened his eyes.

"Meg," he said.

Her heart leapt with joy, for she had feared, with cause, that she might never hear his voice again. "My lord," she whispered, and raised up to peer into his face.

He smiled. "My lady," he responded.

"I love you, Gresham."

"And I you, Lady Wayward," he answered.

"Will you recover?"

He considered the question with wry deliberation. "Aye," he said. "Methinks I shall, if you stay nearby."

"I will," she promised, with all the solemnity of a soul vow.

The road back was a long one for Gresham—he nearly succumbed to infection once, and to a spate of bleeding another time—but by the time Meg's belly began to swell with their babe, in the early spring, he was on his feet again.

"Tell me what happened," Meg asked, when they were back in their own bed together, the songs of crickets at the windows, their bodies sated with lovemaking. "That night when you were stabbed."

Gresham spoke slowly, even reluctantly. He explained about Tangwyn, and their gruesome encounter in the snowy clearing. He spoke of the king, who wanted him to stay at Sedgewick and train horses and soldiers for the battles in France. And finally, he told her what he knew about Gabriella, and about Morgan Chalstrey.

"He kidnapped her, to keep her from marrying Avendall," Gresham finished. "Methinks they were in love, the two of them. We'll make for Cornwall as soon as I'm well enough, I promise, and lay this matter to rest once and for all."

Meg nodded, huddled close to her husband's warm, scarred, and perfect body. She'd listened hungrily to his account, her eyes bright with tears of hope and wonder. "Aye," she said, "but Gabriella is all right. So is Elizabeth."

"How do you know?"

"The same way I knew you'd been hurt," she said.

He accepted that, for the time being at least, and they drifted off to sleep, their hearts matching each other, beat for beat.

Months later . . .

A horn sounded, and the guard in the gate tower shouted out his news. "Riders coming from the west, my lord!"

Gresham, who had been teaching Kieran to wield a sword, there in the courtyard, looked upward. "Colors!" he shouted. It was a demand for the identity of the approaching company, which might or might not be friendly.

" 'Tis Edgefield's livery!" the guard shouted back.

"Fetch your lady mother," Gresham told Kieran, who put up his sword and then bounded off to do his father's bidding. He'd been more pliable since the birth of his baby sister, Ariel Gabriella Elizabeth, just two weeks before, though Gresham suspected the spirit of cooperation was short-lived. Once the novelty of having a sibling wore off, the youngest of the Sedgewick men would wax stubborn again, for certain.

Meg was soon beside him, holding his arm. She'd apparently left their child, due to be christened the following Sunday, with her nurse, and her chestnut hair was unveiled.

The gates opened, and Morgan Chalstrey rode through, the lovely Gabriella smiling at his side. She was mounted on a white mule, not unlike the recalcitrant Enoch, and her fair hair gleamed in the sunlight. With them was a contingent of soldiers, nursemaids, and the like.

Meg gave a cry at the sight of her sister and bolted forward. Gabriella responded by dismounting nimbly and running across the courtyard, into her twin's embrace. The two women sobbed happily and clung to each other, and Gresham watched until his throat threatened to close with emotion, then looked up at his old friend.

"So," Chalstrey said, with a slight smile. "You are not dead, after all."

Gresham glanced at Meg, still in her sister's arms, and smiled as well. "No," he said. "I've more than survived. Which is not to say it was easy."

Chalstrey laughed and got down from his horse to shake Gresham's hand. "I have a lot to tell you," he said.

"And I you," Gresham replied, and they walked, side by side, into the Great Hall, leaving their wives to follow when the mood struck them.

With their children sleeping and their husbands engaged in a lengthy and sometimes spirited conversation of their own, Gabriella and Meg sat talking by the fire in the master bedchamber, chalices of mulled wine long since emptied.

"What of Elizabeth?" Meg asked, when each had given a detailed account of her adventures since their parting that long-ago day, at St. Swithin's.

Gabriella sighed. "Methinks she's having an adventure of her own, our little sister," she said, gazing into the blaze for a long time before meeting Meg's gaze. "I've seen her in my dreams."

Meg waited, not mentioning that she, too, had caught that one brief glimpse of Elizabeth.

"She was kneeling beside a man, and praying. She looked at me and smiled."

Meg's heart felt swollen, not only with love, but with a thousand other emotions. "We'll find her," she said.

"Aye," Gabriella agreed. "We shall find our Elizabeth."